Wild Magic

Wild Magic

By Alexandra Ivy

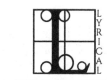

LYRICAL PRESS
Kensington Publishing Corp.
www.kensingtonbooks.com

LYRICAL PRESS are published by

Kensington Publishing Corp.
119 West 40th Street
New York, NY 10018

All Kensington titles, imprints, and distributed lines are available at special quantity discounts for bulk purchases for sales promotion, premiums, fund-raising, educational, or institutional use.

Special book excerpts or customized printings can also be created to fit specific needs. For details, write or phone the office of the Kensington Sales Manager: Kensington Publishing Corp., 119 West 40th Street, New York, NY 10018. Attn. Sales Department. Phone: 1-800-221-2647.

Lyrical Press Books and Lyrical Press eBooks logo Reg. U.S. Pat. & TM Off.

First Electronic Edition: January 2024
ISBN: 978-1-5161-1138-1 (ebook)

First Print Edition: January 2024
ISBN: 978-1-5161-1141-1

Printed in the United States of America

Chapter 1

Elias Mitchell was king of the world—at least in his own mind—as he watched the crowd churn and sway to the music thumping through the air from the shadows of his private balcony.

Neverland Nightclub was currently the place to see and be seen for the movers and shakers in Manhattan. It wasn't just the beauty of the smoked-glass walls that reflected the laser lights bouncing over the dance floor, or the floating spiral staircases that led to the upper floor that lured the cream of society through the front door. It was the exclusive privilege of being built in the center of a Gyre, which meant it was surrounded by a pool of magic. And it was also one of the few clubs that catered to both humans and demons.

Not that the humans realized they were sharing their space with creatures who possessed the blood of goblins and fairies.

It wasn't that mortals were stupid. No, wait. That wasn't true, he wryly acknowledged. They were utter idiots. But that wasn't why they didn't realize they were living side by side with demons.

Long ago, goblins and fairies wandered the earth, but over the centuries they developed the ability to disguise themselves. These days they could easily pass as mortals. It was only demons who could see the auras that surrounded their species. Red for goblin and green for the fey. The darker the aura, the stronger the old blood ran in their veins.

And Elias's aura was dark indeed.

It was a damned shame that they had to hide. But it was the only way to survive in a world being overrun by the rancid tide of humans.

Learn. Adapt. And take advantage whenever possible.

And speaking of taking advantage.

Elias slowly leaned forward, his attention captured by the stunning red-haired woman who strolled toward the bar that ran the length of the far wall. The flash from the overhead laser lights danced over her, emphasizing her stark beauty. It was a pity that she was tall. And that beneath the clinging material of her satin gown he could see lean muscles, not the soft curves he preferred.

Still, she was stunning enough to attract his jaded attention and best of all, there was no aura glowing around her.

She was a human.

After his last disastrous affair with a fairy, Elias had sworn off demons. Not only did they have the power to stop him from doing what he wanted with their bodies, but they had a nasty habit of blabbing about their relationships to anyone who would listen. His wife had threatened to do unspeakable things to his private parts the next time he cheated. The bitch.

Smiling in anticipation, Elias rose to his feet and headed down the spiral staircase. His wife was a snob. She never mixed with humans. Which meant there was no fear of her or her snooty friends being at this particular bar. And what she didn't know wouldn't hurt her, right?

He forged a path through the customers, lifting a hand to smooth back his dark hair. He wasn't worried about whether the woman would accept his invitation to visit his nearby lair. They always accepted. But he took pride in his appearance. He had enough ancient blood pumping through his veins to ensure his features were flawless and his sturdy body was without an ounce of fat.

At last reaching the bar, he shoved aside the men who'd gathered around the stranger like bees to honey. He ignored the muttered curses, moving in close to blatantly study the woman's elegant profile.

"Welcome to Neverland, babe. Your night is about to become unforgettable."

* * * *

Peri Sanguis clenched her teeth as the male's arm pressed against her boob. The urge to teach him a quick and painful lesson in personal space was nearly overwhelming. Unfortunately, tonight she was working and her prey had just scurried into her snare like a rabid rat.

Time to close the deal.

"I'm just here to enjoy the music and have a drink," she informed him, her smoldering glance promising she was willing to change her plans. With the proper persuasion.

On cue he motioned toward the bartender. "Let me assist you." His gaze never left her face as the uniformed man obediently appeared in front of them. "The lady will have..."

"Casamigos Blanco," Peri broke in before he could order her some cheap-ass drink.

Elias flinched as she named the top-shelf tequila, and Peri hid a smile. Her research had revealed that this male was not only a sleazebag, but he was a stingy sleazebag.

"An expensive lady." He allowed his gaze to boldly roam down the length of her body. "Are you worth the cost?"

Peri tossed her hair. She'd created a simple glamour spell before arriving at the club, tinting her hair with red highlights and concealing the scar that would have been revealed by the plunging neckline of her gown. She didn't think the male would recognize her, but she didn't want to take a chance.

"I've never had any complaints," she assured her companion.

"Good to know. I'm Elias."

"You can call me Diana." Peri always used the name of the Goddess of the Hunt when she was working. It felt appropriate.

"Diana." He murmured her name like a caress, running his finger down the bare skin of her arm.

Peri didn't pull away. Instead she leaned forward and absorbed the demon essence he leaked with reckless abandon. It bubbled through her like champagne before she reluctantly stored it in the bracelet she wore around one slender wrist. If the male hadn't been such a self-centered bastard he would have noticed the way the jade glowed in the darkness of the club.

Instead, his gaze was locked on her boobs.

Typical.

"I haven't seen you here before," he drawled.

"I'm passing through town."

"Passing through, eh?" There was a hint of satisfaction in his voice. If she wasn't a local, then there was obviously less chance of his wife discovering he was with another woman. "Business or pleasure?"

"That has yet to be decided."

He laughed. A sharp sound that grated against her ears. "I like your style, babe."

The bartender arrived with her drink and, lifting the chilled glass, she offered a toast.

"To absent friends." She swallowed it in one gulp. Smooth fire slid down her throat. "Yum." Holding Elias's gaze, she slowly licked her lips.

The red aura surrounding the male pulsed in anticipation. "I have more of that at my apartment."

"More what?"

"Whatever you desire."

She licked the rim of the empty glass. "And what do you assume I desire?"

His breath hissed through his gritted teeth. "Let's go to my apartment and I'll teach you."

Teach her? Gag. Peri set aside the glass. The innuendoes were obvious to anyone, but the contract she'd signed demanded a clear and concise declaration of intention.

"You want to have sex with me?" she asked.

"Oh yeah." He leaned close enough she could catch the musky scent of goblin beneath his expensive cologne. "In every position possible. And some that haven't been invented yet."

Double gag. Disguising her revulsion behind a smile, Peri reached up to brush her fingers down the side of his face. At the same time, she released the curse she'd created that afternoon.

A raw, addictive magic swirled through her, heating her blood and sending shivers of pleasure down her spine. It was always thrilling to call on her powers, but standing at the epicenter of the Gyre, it was... staggering. For a glorious moment she held the magic inside, savoring the epic buzz before releasing it through the tips of her fingers. She smiled as she watched the tendrils of the curse sink into his flesh.

Contract complete.

She went on her tiptoes to whisper in his ear. "Maybe we should ask your wife if she cares if you hook up with random women."

"What?" He jerked back. "Is that supposed to be funny?"

"It's mildly entertaining. At least to me." Peri wrinkled her nose. "Stella, however, doesn't look amused."

She pointed toward the dark-haired female sitting at the edge of the bar. Stella Mitchell was short and solid with a square face. Tonight she was wearing a designer dress that cost thousands with diamonds flashing on every stubby finger, but it was her deep red aura that revealed her true worth. In the demon hierarchy, she stood above her husband. Which was no doubt why he'd tried to hide his inability to keep his dick in his pants.

"Shit. You..." He whipped back toward Peri, the words dying on his lips as his gaze caught sight of the jade bracelet that continued to glow.

"Mage." The word came out as a curse.

"Yep."

"What did you do?"

"A simple curse."

His aura flared with fury. "What curse?"

"You want the gory details?" She waited for the jerky nod of his head. "Okay. First, you're going to endure a bout of explosive diarrhea that will last for around an hour. But that's only a prelude to the main event. At precisely midnight, your balls are going to swell up to the size of cantaloupes." It was Peri's turn to run her gaze down his stiff body, her smile mocking. "If you don't mind a suggestion, you might want to head home before the diarrhea hits. And make sure you have some ice packs ready for your balls. I'm told the pain is intense."

Elias made a choked sound. Was he struggling to breathe? Peri hoped so.

"How much?" he at last managed to wheeze.

"Excuse me?"

His face turned an interesting shade of purple. "How much to remove the curse, bitch?"

"Oh. Unfortunately—at least for you—your wife paid a very generous sum to make sure the curse remained in place for at least forty-eight hours." Peri reached into her push-up bra to pull out a gilt-edged business card. "Come into the office on Monday and we can negotiate a new contract."

The purple drained from Elias's face to leave it a strange shade of ash. "Why you—"

Peri braced herself as the demon prepared to lunge at her. She wasn't scared. She was far from helpless, especially with the magic of the Gyre pumping through her. But she preferred to avoid drawing attention. There were worse things than being beaten by an enraged goblin.

Thankfully, there was a blur of motion and suddenly a male was standing between them. He was well over six foot with copper hair that was pulled into a knot on top of his head. He was wearing a black T-shirt with gold lettering that spelled out Neverland and black jeans that fit with heart-stopping perfection. His face was impossibly beautiful and his dark gold eyes usually held a sinful promise of endless pleasure. At the moment, however, they were hard with warning as he glared at Elias.

Aston Wellman was the manager of Neverland and one of the most powerful fey creatures that Peri had ever encountered.

"Don't make matters worse for yourself, Mitchell." His voice was soft, but the threat carried easily over the thumping music. "Not unless you want to be banished."

The demon clenched his teeth, but wisely backed away. Carefully, he inched his way around Aston, but as he stepped past Peri he bent to the side to whisper in her ear.

"I won't forget this."

She blew him a kiss, not bothering to watch as he stormed out of the nightclub. Her interest was locked on the fairy, who leaned casually against the edge of the bar. His green aura shimmered so bright Peri found it impossible to believe that the gathered humans couldn't see it.

"Always a pleasure to see you in action, Peri," Aston murmured.

"Not much action. But the contract paid well."

Aston folded his arms over his chest, his muscles rippling beneath the tight T-shirt.

"I could pay more."

Peri's heart fluttered. Really, a woman would have to be dead not to be bedazzled by this exquisite male.

"I prefer my independence."

He studied her with a searing intensity. "Are you truly independent?"

She arched her brows. Was he referring to her two partners, Maya and Skye? Or the mysterious Benefactor who provided protection for them?

"For the most part." Her tone warned she wasn't going to discuss private mage business.

"I could triple whatever you're getting paid." A warm pulse of energy swirled around her, seeping into her skin. Her bracelet glowed as it absorbed the fey magic. "I could get you an apartment overlooking the park. And allow you unlimited time in my special playroom."

He whispered the word *playroom* as if it was a sexual invitation. It wasn't. The playroom was a space where a demon or mage could use their magic without it being detected or traced. Most mages had specific talents. Like brewing potions or using magical items that intensified a spell. Just like the bracelet around her wrist. It absorbed and stored the magical essence of demons, allowing her to convert it into magic. Just like a portable battery.

Her talent was quite simply her amazing power. It came in handy when she was working, but unfortunately created a target that allowed demons and other nasty creatures to pinpoint her location when she was practicing her magic. She preferred to keep her more exotic spells a hidden asset.

She shook her head. "Tempting, but no."

Aston tilted his head, his expression curious. "Is it me specifically that you don't want as an employer?"

Peri stiffened. They both knew why she would never consider Aston's generous offers.

Valen. The local vampire and the ultimate ruler of this particular Gyre.

"I won't bend my knee. Not to anyone. Not again." An icy chill raced over Peri. As if the mere thought of Valen was enough to make her shiver. "Gotta fly."

She was turning away when she felt Aston's hand brush through her hair, destroying the glamour spell to reveal the rich brown strands.

"Be careful out there, Peri," he warned.

"Never," she called over her shoulder.

A wistful smile touched his lips. "No shit."

Dodging her way through the crowd that had thickened until it was hard to breathe in the elegant nightclub, Peri exited through a side door. She paused, sucking in the night air before she plunged into another mass of people. It was midsummer and a horde of tourists clogged the streets around Times Square.

She'd managed to forge a path to Penn Station when she felt another chill brush over her. This time she didn't dismiss it as a product of her imagination. She was being followed.

Resisting the urge to draw on the magic she'd stored in her bracelet, Peri picked up her pace as she entered the large building, congested with hundreds of commuters despite the late hour. She avoided the large, open lobby and instead darted toward the temporary partitions erected around the inevitable construction area. When she'd arrived in the city earlier in the evening, she'd taken the precaution of creating a circle of protection in case things went sideways.

A habit she'd developed after being chased by a gang of young goblins who'd suspected she had sold them a bogus dragon scale. It *had* been bogus, of course. Dragon scales were incredibly rare, but when they were discovered they could be ground up and used by demons as a potent aphrodisiac. It also caused hallucinations and bouts of extreme violence. Which was why they were illegal to sell.

It had been her job to uncover the ringleader who was seeking to find a dragon scale to sell to the local demons. Just one of the many strange tasks she'd been asked to perform for the Benefactor who protected the Witch's Brew.

Stepping through the wards, Peri was suddenly surrounded by a thick, impenetrable wall of silence. She remained on guard, listening to the people as they rushed past. None of them sensed her presence, not even the demons who were mixed among the mortals.

She was on the point of heaving a sigh of relief when the air temperature abruptly dropped and a dark, silken voice spoke directly in her ear.

"Hello, Peri."

Valen.

Peri froze. Even her heart stopped as the icy threat pressed against her. It wasn't exactly fear, she tried to tell herself, just a healthy dose of caution twisting her stomach. Vampires were lethal predators who ruled their territory with an iron fist. Any transgression could lead to instant death. Or banishment from the Gyre. A fate worse than death to most demons.

Sternly reminding herself that she was an independent mage with no ties to Valen or the Vampire Cabal, Peri squared her shoulders and turned to face the male who was standing inches away. She swallowed a low curse as the impact of standing so close to a vampire slammed into her.

No, not just a vampire. *Valen,* a voice whispered in the back of her mind.

He wasn't a large male. He was a whisper over six foot with a slender body that was currently attired in a black Armani suit, a crisp black shirt and a silver tie. The stark, sophisticated style perfectly matched the austere beauty of his chiseled features. His blond hair was cut close to his head and smoothed back from his narrow face, and even in the harsh lighting of Penn Station it shimmered with threads of the purest gold. His eyes, in contrast, were the exact same shade of silver as his tie, although Peri had seen them flash to a steel gray when he was angry. Thankfully, she'd never had that infamous temper directed at her. Probably because she'd done her best over the past nine years to avoid crossing paths with this male.

"What's up?" She forced the question past lips that felt weirdly stiff.

He was silent as his unnerving gaze swept down her elegant gown, lingering on the scar just over her heart. Awareness vibrated through her. If Aston oozed sensual appeal, this male blasted it with the impact of a nuclear weapon.

Not that she was stupid enough to give into temptation, she sternly reminded herself. She might dance close to the flame, but she didn't leap into the fire.

At last his gaze lifted, his expression unreadable. "Are you lost?"

"Just headed home."

"Can I ask what you're doing in my territory?"

"You can ask." The words came out as a taunt. Tension brought out the snark in her. Okay, to be fair, lots of stuff brought out her snark. Mornings. Rain. A bad hair day. However, it was especially high when she was standing inches from Valen. "But that doesn't mean I have to answer."

"Yes." The word was soft, but the silver eyes were suddenly as hard as steel. "Yes, it does."

She shrugged. "Fine. I'd heard all sorts of rumors about your new club. I had to check it out for myself."

"And?"

"Really not my scene, but I'm sure it'll make you oodles of money."

"You didn't happen to conduct business while you were here, did you?"

He stared at her, an eerie stillness settling around him. Not the motionlessness of a human. This was absolute. As if he was carved from marble. Most of the time vampires made an effort to appear human. They breathed, they blinked, and she'd heard that they occasionally smiled— although Peri was convinced that was an urban myth—but there was nothing human about them.

She cleared a sudden lump from her throat. She doubted Valen would kill her for being snarky, but business was a different matter altogether. She was in his territory and that meant she needed his approval to earn money.

He was perfectly within his rights to punish her.

She chose her words with care. "Technically the business was conducted at the Witch's Brew," she said, referring to the New Jersey coffee shop/ bookstore/mage-for-hire business she managed with her friends. "The details were negotiated, the contract was signed and the money delivered outside your territory. I just executed the contract here." She did her best to look innocent. It was a stretch. "There's no law against magic, is there?"

"If it's meant to harm a demon." He deliberately paused. "Or me."

"There's no *lasting* harm," she insisted, blocking out the image of Elias's current situation. Now didn't seem the appropriate moment to laugh at the knowledge his balls would soon be expanding to the size of balloons. "Just a couple days of extreme discomfort."

He bent his head, allowing her an up close view of his painful beauty. The narrow length of his nose. The sculpted cheekbones and surprisingly full lips. The smooth perfection of his pale skin. And the hypnotic power smoldering in his silver eyes.

"You play a dangerous game," he whispered.

A warning zinged through her as she began to sway forward. Vampires had the ability to manipulate the minds of both humans and demons. Only mages possessed the ability to resist.

The ability, she reminded herself, but not always the will…

With a jerky motion she stepped back, breaking the spell he was weaving around her.

"Dangerous games are the only games worth playing." She tilted her chin. "It's late and I'm tired. Is there anything else you wanted?"

Peri could have bitten off her tongue as his lips parted, revealing the tips of his lethal fangs.

"I'm currently considering the various possibilities."

The cool words slid over her with a silken promise. Or maybe it was a threat. Hard to tell. Both possibilities sent a tingle of excitement to the pit of her stomach.

Time to make a strategic retreat.

"I'll let you consider them while I head home." She inched away, feeling the protective wards press against her back.

"Run, little witch." The silver eyes darkened to smoke. "You can't hide."

"Annoying bastard," she muttered, even as she turned and did exactly as he commanded.

She ran.

Chapter 2

Peri exited the covered shelter that served as a train station in Linden, New Jersey, grimacing as the night air wrapped around her like a soggy blanket. It wasn't just the humidity, although it was thick enough to cut with a knife. It was the lack of magic. Any area outside a Gyre was called a dead zone for a reason. It was a void between the pools of enchantment.

Thankfully, Peri was a mage, not a demon. She could still use her magic even if it didn't have the same potency. It was the sizzle of electric energy that she missed as she headed down the stairs and across the parking lot to the shadowed street. And perhaps the cool wash of power from a vampire...

No, no, no. She shut down any lingering thought of Valen. She'd done what she was paid to do. Time to move on to the next assignment.

Zigzagging along city blocks lined with auto repair garages, liquor stores and mini marts, she at last could see the neon light in the shape of a witch's hat with a coffee cup in the center.

The Witch's Brew was sandwiched between a tanning salon and a falafel restaurant, with large windows that were currently decorated with unicorns and rainbows, along with the specials of the day: Mocha coffee. Chocolate espresso. Lemon bars. And blueberry scones.

She was halfway down the street when a hunched form detached from the shadows of the tanning salon. The man was wearing a velour tracksuit with a fishing hat pulled low to cover his hair. His face was covered by a bushy beard, making it hard to determine the man's age and ethnicity, but he'd been hanging around the neighborhood for as long as Peri had been there.

"Hey, Joe." Peri had no idea if that was his name, but it's what the neighbors called him. Narrowing her gaze, she watched him shuffle forward. "It's late for you to be out here."

"You smell like you rolled in goblin turds," Joe retorted.

Peri wrinkled her nose. She always looked forward to the man's scathing insults. Some of them were creative enough to win an Emmy. Tonight's was…mundane.

"Hmm. Not your best work."

"I know." Joe lifted a gloved hand to cover his mouth as he coughed. "I think I'm coming down with a cold."

"Come inside and I'll give you something to make you feel better."

"Nah, I gotta move along." Joe cocked his head, as if listening to a voice in his head. "Besides, you're going to be busy."

"Busy?" Peri didn't want to be busy. She was tired and hungry and in dire need of a shower. "Doing what?"

"That," he muttered a second before Skye rushed out the front door of the coffee shop, her golden curls corkscrewing around her heart-shaped face with more bounce than usual. Like a halo on steroids. In contrast, her midnight eyes smoldered with unfathomable depths. Those eyes could see into a person's soul and occasionally catch a glimpse of the future. A rare, sometimes awful power.

"At last." Skye rushed toward her, the gossamer material of her sundress floating around her soft curves. "I was getting worried about you."

Peri glanced back, not surprised to discover that Joe had disappeared into the night. The man was a mystery, but Peri had never tried to probe into where he lived or why he chose their particular street to pass the days.

Everyone was entitled to their secrets.

Even her.

With a smile, she hooked her arm through Skye's and urged her back down the street.

"It took me longer than I expected," she apologized, sensing her friend had truly been concerned. "I had to circle the damned dance floor a dozen times before my mark noticed me," she told Skye, not bothering to reveal she'd also been offered a job by Aston and stalked by Valen. All's well that ended well, right? "Am I losing my touch?"

"Never," Skye assured her with a fierce loyalty.

"Like you would ever tell me the truth."

"The truth is that you're gorgeous. Both inside and out."

Peri snorted. "Now I know you're lying."

They reached the front door, entering the brightly lit coffee shop. It was a narrow space, but the white tiled floor and bright lavender walls made it seem larger. There were small tables set near the window and glass cases at the back. The scent of freshly baked scones lingered in the air, despite the fact the shop was closed.

"Let's have a cup of tea," Skye urged, tugging Peri toward the arched opening that led to the attached bookstore. "I have a tray set up in the office."

"Thanks, sweetie, but it's too late for me." Peri was weary to the bone. "I intend to grab a bagel with a very large schmear of cream cheese, then hop in the shower before I fall face-first into bed."

Skye grasped her arm, her expression apologetic. "Maya needs to talk to you."

"Tonight?" Peri frowned. Had Valen called to complain? That seemed… petty.

"Yes, I'm afraid it has to be tonight." A voice broke into Peri's ridiculous thoughts and she glanced toward the arched opening to discover the owner of the Witch's Brew had stepped into the light.

Maya Rosen was tall and slender with silky-smooth black hair that was bluntly cut at her shoulders. It was impossible to determine her age. Like all mages she stopped aging around thirty, but there was a hint of ancient wisdom in her bright green eyes and a spidery web of scars that ran from her left ear down her jawline. The scars possessed the silvery gleam of a wound caused by a gruesome spell, but they did nothing to detract from her beauty. Just the opposite. They only heightened her regal perfection. Tonight, she was wearing her usual sleeveless sweater and jeans that were dusted with flour.

Maya was magic in the kitchen. Literally. She could not only create a muffin that had customers lined up out the door every morning, but she possessed the ability to conjure potions that could destroy cities.

Thankfully, she avoided the more explosive potions and concentrated on the garden-variety magic. Love potions, disguise spells, alchemy…the sort of stuff demons were willing to pay a fortune to get their hands on even if they knew the magic was temporary.

"Okay." Peri didn't need Skye's clairvoyance to know something was wrong.

Moving forward, she allowed Maya to lead her through the narrow room lined with books. In the center was a wooden table with reading lamps. Between the mouthwatering muffins, freshly ground coffee and free Wi-Fi, Witch's Brew was the go-to location for the local college students.

They at last entered the office at the back of the building. Most people would be surprised to discover how stark it was. There was a desk with a computer, two filing cabinets and three leather chairs. The floor was wooden planks and the walls were paneled, without one picture or piece of art. Overhead there was one bare light bulb.

It looked more like a prison cell than an office, but they dealt with angry customers on a regular basis. Elias, after all, wasn't the first demon who'd been contracted to be cursed. Or blinded by a love spell. And nothing could destroy an office quicker than a pissed-off demon. Plus, it was stripped of any loose objects a mage might use as a weapon.

"Better safe than sorry" wasn't just Peri's motto. All three of them took precautions.

Peri stopped in the middle of the room as Skye moved toward the tray perched on the edge of the desk.

"What are you doing up past the witching hour?" she demanded of Maya, trying to lighten the tension that pulsed in the air.

"Thankfully, I'm not a witch," Maya countered in dry tones.

"No shit." Peri grimaced. A witch was a woman who could use spells and incantations, but they didn't possess wild magic. Which was why they routinely tried to destroy mages. "What happened?"

Maya nodded toward the leather chairs, her scar more pronounced than usual. "Maybe you should sit down."

Peri clenched her hands. She hated surprises. Probably because they usually tried to kill her.

"Maya. Just spit it out."

"Sorry." Maya wrinkled her nose. "There's no easy way to say this. Your mother is dead."

Peri absorbed the news with a small flinch. Her mother was dead. The woman she'd hated with the force of a thousand fiery suns was dead. The bitch who'd condemned her to death on her sixteenth birthday was dead. The leader of a witch's coven who placed her ruthless ambition above the life of her only child was dead.

Dead...

It didn't seem possible.

"When?" The word came out as a hoarse croak.

"Last night," Maya said.

"I..." Peri's words faltered, her brain functioning in weird bursts intersected with blank spaces. "How did you find out?"

Maya touched her temple. "Our Benefactor."

The Benefactor didn't have a name. At least Peri had never heard Maya say it. In fact, all she knew was that the mystery creature spoke to the older woman telepathically and that he offered a cloak of protection to Maya, and indirectly to Skye and Peri. Not a tangible source of security, but a basic understanding that they were allowed to remain independent.

A special gift for mages, who were rare enough to be highly sought after by the Vampire Cabal. And the reason they'd never been forced to become Valen's minions.

In return, he occasionally demanded that they complete random tasks.

"What did he say?" she asked.

"Not much," Maya admitted. "He simply urged me to check out the news connected to Wisdom Ranch."

Peri's breath tangled in her throat. Wisdom Ranch was the name of the isolated compound her mother owned to provide privacy for her coven.

"Let me see."

Maya held her gaze. "It's bad, Peri," she warned.

Peri clenched her teeth, her fingers brushing over the scar in the center of her chest. "When it involves my mother it's always bad."

Maya stepped toward the desk, turning the computer monitor so Peri could see the front page of the Casper newspaper.

Mass suicide at Wisdom Ranch.

Following a tip from an unknown source, law officials made a grisly discovery at the ranch located north of Casper, Wyoming. Twelve women were found dead in a locked barn. Although the sheriff has assured the public that he has ruled out foul play, he refuses to give details, citing an ongoing investigation. More information as it becomes available.

Peri sucked in a sharp breath. "Twelve? That's most of the coven."

"I'm sorry," Maya said.

A strange numbness spread through Peri. Shock. No matter her troubled past with the coven, the thought of twelve women destroyed in one night was horrifying.

"Was there anything else?"

Maya studied Peri with blatant concern. When Peri refused to blink, she conceded defeat with a soft sigh.

"Someone managed to get a picture of the bodies and posted it on the internet." She moved to place her fingers over the keyboard, hesitating as if she regretted revealing that there were photos. "Are you sure you want to see it?"

No…

"I'm sure."

Peri squared her shoulders, her gaze locked on the monitor as Maya touched the keyboard, bringing up a fuzzy image. At first Peri couldn't make out more than a blur of dark objects on a wood-plank floor. She stepped closer and bent down to make sense of what she was seeing. At the same time, she tapped into the magic that flowed through her blood. She couldn't alter the picture, but she could intensify her vision until she could pick out even the smallest detail.

What she noticed first was the strange way the bodies were laid out. They were arranged in a perfect circle with their feet pointed toward the center. Like macabre spokes in a wheel. They were all wearing heavy white robes that fanned around their bodies, concealing any hidden injuries, but there wasn't a speck of blood on the pristine material. Not on any of them. She leaned closer, studying the faces that were pointed at the rafters high above them, their eyes wide open and their gray hair smoothly spreading across the floor.

"Wait." Peri shook her head. "This can't be my mother's coven."

"Why not?" Maya demanded.

"They're way too old."

She studied the deep wrinkles that marred each woman's face. Witches aged like normal humans, but her mother couldn't be more than fifty. The corpses looked like they were all at least a hundred.

Moving her attention from one woman to the next, her breath was abruptly squeezed from her lungs as she caught sight of a distinctive tattoo. Her mother. It had to be. The large raven on the side of her neck was supposed to be a symbol that she was destined for greatness. Returning her attention to the other women, she slowly managed to recognize them despite the dramatic aging.

This was the coven that had raised her from the day she was born until she turned sixteen.

"Oh my God. What happened to them? They look like mummies."

Maya moved to stand next to her, studying the monitor. "I have no idea."

"Someone knows," she suddenly breathed.

Whoever had taken the picture must have been standing at the front entrance. They'd not only captured the image of the dead women, but the stalls that lined the side of the barn.

"Why do you say that?" Maya asked.

"Look." Peri pointed at the eyes peeking through the wooden slats of a stall. "There was a witness."

Maya studied the image. "There's no way to see who it is."

"We might not need to," Peri said. "My mother insisted that there always be thirteen witches in her coven. Specifically thirteen at all times. It was supposedly her lucky number. So one escaped whatever happened."

"Do you know which one?"

"I suppose I could try to guess by process of elimination." Ignoring the sickness that churned in the pit of her stomach, Peri moved her gaze from one face to another. "There are three I don't recognize," she finally concluded. "They must have joined after I left."

"So that means there are four possible witnesses. Assuming the eyes belong to a witch from the coven," Maya murmured. "Who's missing?"

"Irene Webster. But she was close to eighty when I was still at the ranch. It's likely she passed years ago," Peri said, sorting through the names of the women who weren't among the dead. "Pamela Foster."

"She created her own coven in New Mexico," Maya said.

Peri wasn't surprised that Pamela had started her own coven. She'd been blatantly ambitious, often challenging her mother's authority. It also wasn't a surprise that Maya knew she'd created her own coven. The older woman kept a close watch on their enemies.

Peri came to the end of her mental list. "Unless it's a stranger hiding in the stall, then the eyes must belong to Destiny Mason."

Destiny had been four years older than Peri and barely capable of performing the easiest spell. If she hadn't brought a sizable inheritance with her, Peri's mother would never have allowed her to stay at the ranch. It would make sense that she might be excluded from whatever the other witches were doing in the barn.

Peri pressed her hand against her stomach, which continued to rebel at the sight of the mummified women. What the hell had happened? A demon attack? A vampire? Humans?

"Are you okay?" Maya brushed her hand over Peri's hair, her tone concerned.

"Ask me later." Peri wrenched her gaze away from the gruesome picture and focused her attention on the woman standing next to her. "Right now I need to go to Wyoming."

"Yes."

Peri arched a brow. "No argument?"

Maya shrugged. "Is there anything I could say to change your mind?"

"No."

"Then what's the point?"

Peri wasn't impressed with the woman's logic. "Since when do you need a point to argue? It's your default reaction."

Maya clicked her tongue. "Harsh."

Peri planted her hands on her hips. She'd known this woman for nine years. She was as overprotective as a mother hen. There was no way she would willingly allow Peri to rush into a potentially dangerous situation.

"Maya, what's going on?"

"This needs to be investigated," she said, the scars that marred the side of her face emphasized as she clenched her jaw. "I've been told you are the only one capable of seeing the truth."

Ah. Now Peri understood. The mysterious Benefactor had warned Maya that it was Peri's duty to deal with the death of the witches. And the command to let Peri handle the problem without her was killing Maya.

"But not alone." Skye abruptly burst into the conversation, her curls bouncing as she moved to wrap her arm around Peri's waist. "I'll come with you."

Maya shook her head. "It has to be Peri."

"I don't want her to be by herself," Skye insisted.

Peri brushed a kiss over Skye's curls. "It will be fine, Skye. I'll go to the ranch, figure out what happened and be back before you notice I'm gone."

"I don't like this," Skye insisted.

"I don't either, but I trust that Peri can take care of herself," Maya said.

"Of course she can." Skye tightened her arm around Peri's waist. "That's not why I'm worried. Her mother and the coven who raised her are dead and she needs her family with her."

Family...

Peri's icy shock melted away as Skye's words settled in the center of her heart. Yes. These two women *were* her family. They were the ones she laughed and cried with, who had her back no matter what. The ones she trusted without hesitation.

"Skye, I love your tender heart," she assured her friend. "But if you think I'm grieving for the woman who tried to slaughter me then you don't know me at all."

"You aren't as tough as you pretend, Peri Sanguis." Skye's eyes shimmered with a sudden power. "That's your salvation."

"Skye." Maya's tone was sharp, as if she feared that Skye was about to offer a premonition.

They'd made a pact when the younger woman was invited to join them at the Witch's Brew that she would never reveal the future.

Not to them.

Skye reluctantly stepped back and Maya cleared her throat, taking command of the suddenly tense situation.

"I have you booked on a flight to Casper tomorrow," she told Peri. "A vehicle will be waiting for you at the airport. Stay as long as you need."

Peri jerked her head in a semblance of a nod. She'd sworn she would never return to Wisdom Ranch. It'd been fourteen years since she'd fled the place, but the wounds were still raw. Everything about this trip made her want to vomit.

"I need to pack."

She headed toward the door, her thoughts a tangled mess.

"Peri," Maya called out. "You didn't tell me how things went tonight."

Peri grudgingly halted and glanced over her shoulder. "Just as we planned. You can expect Elias Mitchell bright and early on Monday morning."

Maya arched a brow. "Nothing else?"

With shocking speed the image of Valen's fiercely beautiful face blazed through her brain. And just as swiftly, Peri was squashing the memory of his icy power wrapping around her like a caress.

She had enough problems. She wasn't adding a fascination with the lethal predator to the list.

"Nothing worth discussing."

Maya narrowed her eyes, easily sensing she wasn't being entirely honest, but it was Skye who responded.

"Be careful, Peri."

Peri's lips twisted. "I hear that a lot."

"And you never listen," Maya muttered.

The older woman wasn't wrong, and Peri didn't try to argue. Instead, she turned and headed to her room on the upper floor. There was no way she was going to be able to sleep, but she could at least pace the floor in peace.

Chapter 3

Valen detached his fangs from the delicate wrist that he cradled in his hands and licked the bleeding wounds to ensure they were sealed. The female fairy moaned in pleasure, swaying toward him in blatant invitation. Valen dropped her arm and grasped her shoulder, keeping her at a distance. Not every vampire made the experience pleasant, but he preferred a willing donor.

Stepping back, he touched the light switch to allow a soft glow to chase away the shadows and reveal the elegant details of the room. The décor matched the rest of the lavish penthouse. Sleek furniture in soft grays with charcoal accents. This space, however, was carefully devoid of any personal items. The books on the shelves that consumed one wall had been chosen at random, as had the framed pictures on the wall. Even the marble chessboard arranged on the coffee table had been bought by a servant.

Valen rarely allowed visitors to trespass beyond this formal salon. The less anyone knew of his personal life, the less opportunity they had to discover a weakness. He hadn't lived two thousand years by being careless.

The fairy tossed her reddish curls with a sultry expression. But with impeccable timing, Renee Newark pushed open the door and stepped inside.

His secretary was a diminutive female with short hair that she bleached to a silver-blond and dark gold eyes. Her features were delicate enough to give the impression of fragility, but her aura pulsed a deep green, revealing the power of her ancient fey blood.

It wasn't her fairy magic, however, that made her the perfect servant. It was her discretion, her military-grade skill in organization, and her uncanny ability to sense his needs.

And, of course, her ruthless loyalty.

"Thank you, Lily," Valen said.

"My pleasure." Her lips parted, as if urging him to kiss her. When he simply gazed down at her, she sent him a small pout. "Same time same place next week?"

Valen didn't answer. Lily was a lovely female, but she was unfortunately becoming emotionally invested in the feedings. It was time to find a new donor. As if reading his mind, Renee crossed the room and wrapped her arm around the female's shoulders.

"I'll show you out." With a smooth ease she forced the reluctant fairy from the room. She paused at the door to glance back at Valen. "You have a call. I put it through to your private office."

Valen arched a brow. He was wearing a black silk robe that he used during his feedings. After he finished his meal it was his routine to head to his shower to scrub off the scent of his donor before preparing for the night. Renee would have taken a message if the call wasn't important.

Crossing to the back of the room, Valen placed his hand on the edge of the bookcase. There was a faint click before the shelves slid inward and Valen stepped into his private office.

It was an impressive room, with glass cases displaying rare Ottoman artifacts and daggers from Roman generals. Most of them he'd been given as gifts. A few he'd taken as spoils of war. Another wall was lined with high-tech monitors that displayed images of his various clubs, spread from Boston to Washington, DC. He had managers he trusted—as much as he trusted any demon—but he was very much a hands-on leader. There was nothing that slipped past his notice. No matter how trivial.

He closed the hidden door behind him and headed toward the massive desk. Once seated, he allowed a satisfied smile to curve his lips. From this angle, he had a stunning view of the park through the window that stretched from one end of the office to the other. He smiled. This view was the reason he'd purchased the building. Why create an empire without having the means to survey his territory?

Flipping open the laptop on his desk, Valen pressed a button on the keyboard to connect the video call. A second later an image flickered on the monitor and he was staring into the face of Gabriel Lyon.

The male possessed the ageless perfection of a vampire, but his dark hair was heavily streaked with gray and cut to brush his broad shoulders. His face was square and his features distinguished. To humans he looked like a successful businessman. Perhaps an international banker. And he was both of those things. But a glance into the icy hazel eyes was enough to reveal he wasn't a mere mortal.

"Gabriel," Valen murmured. This male was one of ten vampires who made up the North America Vampire Cabal. His territory included Denver through Salt Lake City. And even by vampire standards he was extraordinarily wealthy. "This is unexpected. Is there a problem?"

The male considered the question. "More a curiosity," he finally said.

"What sort of curiosity?"

"One of your mages arrived in Denver today."

Valen's vague interest was securely snared. *One of your mages...*

They weren't technically, of course. The three women lived inside his territory, but they weren't within the Gyre. And while he could use his power and influence to make their lives a misery until they agreed to submit to his authority, he'd resisted the temptation. It wasn't the knowledge that he could sense a mysterious power keeping guard on the three women. He was an immortal who feared nothing. Eventually he'd figure out who or what was assisting the women.

No. He'd maintained a hands-off approach because he wanted the mages to come to him willingly.

Long ago he'd chosen brutality to enforce his position of power, but the centuries had refined his skills. Oh, he could use violence when necessary. The demons he ruled had to understand that he had zero tolerance for breaking his laws. But he discovered that his fearsome reputation was usually enough to keep order in his territory. Along with a healthy dread of being forced out of the Gyre. No demon wanted to live in a dead zone, where they were unable to feel the ancient magic that pulsed through their veins.

He desired loyalty, not grudging obedience.

"Did you capture their arrival on video?" he asked, knowing that Gabriel would have his territory fully monitored. Both electronically and with his guards.

"Of course." The monitor flickered and Gabriel's face was replaced with a grainy surveillance video. "This is from the Denver airport earlier this afternoon."

Valen placed his palms flat on his desk as he leaned forward, his gaze locked on the dark-haired woman dressed in a pair of cutoff shorts and a T-shirt with a faded Bon Jovi logo. Peri. All mages were rare and special, but Peri...she was gloriously unique. And she'd fascinated him from the moment she'd arrived at the Witch's Brew nine years ago.

A strange sensation clenched his muscles as he watched her weave her way through the mass of travelers. It felt like anger. As if he was disturbed by the knowledge she was so far away from him.

He shook his head, refusing to dwell on the intensity of his reaction. Instead, he focused on the tension detectable in the angle of her shoulders and her grim expression. Whatever had taken her to Denver, it wasn't pleasure.

"Was she alone?" he demanded.

"As far as we could tell." Gabriel was once again visible. "The sensors didn't trigger for any other mages."

"Demons?"

"None that approached her in the terminal."

She was alone? The anger once again flared through him. An icy blast that created a layer of frost over the top of his desk. A lone mage, no matter how powerful, was at risk. They were too valuable not to be the target of a kidnapping attempt by an enterprising demon.

"Is she still in Denver?"

"No. She is currently waiting for a commuter plane to Casper."

"Casper?" Valen was genuinely puzzled. "Why would she go there?"

"Check your email. I sent you a file."

Valen grabbed his phone, which he'd placed on the desk before retiring for the day. Pressing the screen, he swiftly pulled up his private email and clicked on the link that Gabriel had sent him.

"Mass suicide at Wisdom Ranch," he read out loud. "Humans?"

"A coven."

"Do you know what happened?"

"No, but I'd bet my favorite Rolex your mage is here because she knows how they died or to discover what happened."

That wasn't a bet Valen was willing to take. Although mages and witches weren't the same—any more than goblins and fairies were the same—a mage was always born to a mother who was a witch. It was very likely that Peri had a personal connection to the coven.

"Why did you call me?" he abruptly asked.

"The ranch is outside my Gyre, but it's part of my territory. I have every intention of finding out why twelve witches are dead. I can do it or—"

"I will," Valen interrupted.

The hazel eyes darkened with an emotion that might have been amusement. "I thought you might take a personal interest."

"The mages are valuable assets," Valen said in cold tones. "Eventually they'll accept my authority."

"Hmm."

Valen refused to be provoked. It was no surprise that Gabriel was aware of his interest in the mages, and his particular interest in Peri Sanguis.

Even though the Cabal had sworn a peace treaty, they all had spies in each other's territories. A treaty was nothing more than a promise. One that was easily broken.

"Is that all?"

"No. I have a contact in the area."

Valen nodded. Gabriel would be a fool not to keep a close watch on a coven of witches. They didn't have the power of a mage, but they could manipulate magic. That was always trouble.

"And?"

"The coven has always been secretive, but the past few years they've completely isolated themselves."

"Any reason why?"

"My contact said there are rumors that they'd started practicing dark magic."

Valen shrugged. Humans were the only ones gullible enough to believe in dark magic.

"Magic is magic. There's no black or white."

Gabriel's features tightened. "There is, however, evil intent."

"True."

They shared a glance that was filled with ancient pain. They'd both survived the demon uprising that had destroyed several vampires. As immortals, they were resurrected in new hosts, but each rebirth meant that the vampire awakened with no memory of their past and powers that were a small fraction of what they had possessed. It took centuries to regain their strength.

A severe loss, considering there were around fifty vampires in total spread throughout the world, and that they had no means of expanding their numbers. The human myths about a vampire's bite turning them into an immortal were ridiculous. The only things that Hollywood had right were that vampires drank blood and they couldn't go out in the sun.

"For now I have eyes on the property," Gabriel assured him. "Nothing will approach the ranch without me knowing."

"Good. I'll be there as soon as my jet is ready." Valen's mind was already racing with the number of details that needed to be taken care of before he could leave the city.

"I can make a call to delay the commuter flight to Casper," Gabriel offered.

"I would appreciate that. I would also appreciate if you'd spread the word that I'm not invading your territory," Valen said. "I don't want any messy misunderstandings."

Gabriel nodded. "In return I want a full report on what you discover."

"Fair enough."

Valen was preparing to end the call when Gabriel abruptly smiled, revealing his massive fangs.

"Valen."

"Yes?"

"You have excellent taste."

* * * *

The darkness was absolute as Valen exited the helicopter that had been waiting for him at the private airport outside of Casper. The ranch was too far from civilization to be engulfed in streetlights and the only glow came from the stars splattered across the sky. Not that he needed light to see the flat, empty landscape that stretched toward the distant mountains. He could easily make out the sagebrush and prairie clover spotted over the hard ground along with the small rodents that scurried to hide in their burrows.

Pausing long enough to make sure there were no hidden dangers, Valen abruptly shivered. There was nothing in the area to threaten him, but the dull lack of magic pressed against him like an invisible weight. Witches sought out dead zones, as if sensing that the natural magic in Gyres would interfere in their spells.

It added to the impression of desolation that shrouded the barren landscape.

With a shake of his head, he crossed toward the patch of buildings that were surrounded by a barbed wire fence. His brows arched as he neared and realized the fence was ten foot tall and darkened from the residue of a powerful spell that was no longer active. A spell that had no doubt ended with the death of the witches.

What the hell had they been trying to hide? You didn't have that level of protection unless you were determined to keep people out. Or…trying to keep people locked in.

Valen circled the fence, glancing up at the wooden sign above the gate.

Wisdom Ranch

Trespassers will be shot on sight

Blunt. At least by human standards. And yet another indication that the witches were harboring a secret.

Entering the compound through the open gate, he headed toward the red, four-wheel-drive truck parked in the center of the narrow pathway. As he passed by the front of the vehicle, he could feel the lingering warmth of the engine. It hadn't been parked there for more than a few minutes. Gabriel had kept his word and delayed Peri's flight long enough for Valen to get his jet prepared and in the air.

He moved forward, spotting the mage standing in front of one of the long wooden buildings. She was still wearing the shorts and T-shirt she'd been wearing in the airport, with her lush brown hair flowing freely down her back. The casual style emphasized her youth. Or perhaps it emphasized his extreme age, he wryly concluded.

He was still several feet away when she stiffened, the jade bracelet glowing around her wrist as she prepared to launch a magical attack.

"Easy, Peri," he murmured.

She jerked around, her face pale and her eyes suspiciously red. Had she been crying? Interesting.

"Valen." Her hands clenched at her sides, the bracelet still throbbing with unused power. She held her spell, as if debating whether to punish him for intruding into her private thoughts. At last discretion overrode her desire to lash out and the magic faded. Wise choice. "What are you doing here?"

"The same as you, I imagine."

"Doubtful." Her eyes narrowed. "It was your helicopter I heard."

"Yes."

"Did you follow me?"

Valen arched a brow. "You assume I spend my time keeping a constant eye on you?"

She flushed, but with her typical rash courage, she refused to back down. "This is my land now. You have no authority here."

The temperature dropped until Peri shivered and wrapped her arms around her waist, but it wasn't her defiance that caught his attention.

This is my land now...

"You knew the witches who died here."

Another shiver. "My mother and her coven."

Valen studied her tense features and the lack of emotion in her stunning eyes. He didn't need his superior senses to realize she was in shock.

"I'm sorry."

"Don't be." Her hand pressed against her chest. "They stuck a dagger in my heart when they realized I possessed true magic."

Ah. That explained the scar just over her heart and the chip on her shoulder. He'd always wondered.

"How old were you?"

"Sixteen."

Valen was caught off guard. Not because her coven had tried to kill her. There were some witches who feared that the wild magic flowing through the veins of a mage would expose them to the witch hunts that killed so many in the past. At least that was their excuse to hunt down and execute mages. Valen suspected it was a combination of jealousy and fear that drove them to murder. They would never be able to possess or control true magic. So they sought to destroy it.

"You were young to come into your powers," he said.

"I didn't stay young for long."

Valen glanced around, once again aware of the emptiness that surrounded the ranch. "How did you escape?"

She held out her hands, revealing the silvery marks in the center of each palm.

"The wild magic burst out of me, driving them away long enough for me to disappear into the mountains."

Valen didn't press for details. At any moment the shock was going to wear off and she would once again be the Peri Sanguis he'd known since her arrival in New Jersey. A prickly, secretive woman who used mockery as a weapon.

"Did they realize you survived?"

"I'm not sure." Her jaw tightened, a sudden emotion flaring in the depths of her blue eyes. "As you can imagine, the whole trying-to-kill-me thing put a strain on our relationship. I never spoke with any of them again."

"I assume that means you don't know why they are dead?"

"Not a clue."

"Could it have been suicide?"

She laughed. A sharp, brittle sound. "No."

"You sound very certain."

"My mother was cunning, ruthless, and consumed with her lust for power. She would kill without mercy if she thought it might give her some sort of advantage." Her lips twisted into a bitter smile. "But take her own life? Never."

Valen accepted her words without question. "Then who—or what—had the skill to murder an entire coven?"

With a shudder, Peri glanced toward the barn at the far side of the compound. She was silent for a long moment, as if considering the various possibilities. Valen did the same.

It didn't take long. He didn't have enough evidence to develop a logical deduction and he wasn't foolish enough to leap to conclusions. At last, Peri seemed to come to the same deduction. She shook her head, as if trying to clear her mind, then slowly turned back.

She stared at him, then without warning her eyes narrowed. He didn't have to read her mind to know that she'd just remembered he was the enemy.

"The more immediate question is why you're here," she said in sharp tones. "This has nothing to do with the Cabal."

He hid a smile. Peri was once again the defiant, pain-in-the-ass mage that had captured his interest. Although she would stab him in the heart if he ever called her a pain in the ass. And oddly, he was fiercely relieved to have her back.

"Twelve witches die under mysterious circumstances. No obvious wounds, no sign of struggle, no indication of an intruder," he smoothly replied. "Do you think a human could accomplish such a thing?"

She studied him, as if not entirely reassured by his explanation. "You think it was a demon?"

"I'm here to discover the truth."

"Why you?" she pressed. "This area isn't even close to your territory."

"Gabriel asked for my assistance and I agreed."

"Why?"

"I have a unique talent," he informed her.

"A talent for showing up where you're not wanted?"

He allowed an icy silence to settle between them. He gave her more leeway than any other creature. But he had limits.

"Take care, mage," he whispered softly.

Peri flushed, smart enough not to provoke the annoyed vampire. "What sort of talent?"

"For tracing the scent of a demon. Or mage. If one was here I'll be able to follow his trail."

She blinked, as if caught off guard by his words. Then, abruptly, she turned to walk briskly toward the barn.

"Follow me."

Chapter 4

Be careful…

Skye's soft plea before Peri left New Jersey whispered through the back of her mind. Was wandering through a crime scene with a pissed-off vampire at her back being careful? Doubtful. Of course, he wasn't the only one pissed off, she wryly acknowledged.

Valen's surprise arrival had happened while she was still unbalanced by her return to the ranch. She'd given away too much personal information. And worse, she'd allowed him to see she remained vulnerable to wounds that hadn't entirely healed.

Nearing the large barn, Peri grimaced in resignation. From the moment she'd driven onto the ranch, her emotions had been scrubbed raw. It looked the same as the night she'd fled. The long wooden bunkhouses with the rusting tin roofs. The main L-shaped lodge that doubled as the kitchen and dining hall. The stone sheds that held grain for the livestock. The corrals and pigsties and chickens pecking at the hard ground. And the center firepit with a huge caldron used to create spells and potions.

All the same, except that it was eerily silent now.

Only the ghosts remained.

She couldn't pretend indifference, but she could use Valen's unwelcome arrival to her advantage.

Stepping over the police tape that acted as a flimsy barrier, Peri pressed open the door to the barn and stepped into the shadowed interior. Then, moving toward the exterior wall, she fumbled for the light switch. She could see better than a human in the dark, but not as well as a vampire. The dull glow from the bare light bulbs hanging from the rafters provided a faux sense of security.

She glanced around, absently noticing the signs of decay. It wasn't the recent deaths that had caused the warped floorboards or the rotting stables at the back of the open space. It was years of neglect.

The coven had never kept horses, so it was understandable that the stables would be in disrepair, but the barn was used to store the precious herbs and spices that were necessary for their potions. It was also where they cast their most powerful spells.

What had happened?

Reaching the center of the space, Peri studied the ground where the witches had been stretched out like pagan sacrifices. She could see a charred spot on the floorboards. A fire? A weapon from a demon?

Peri lifted her head, discovering Valen inspecting the stables. Her breath stuck in her throat as her gaze swept over his lean form, impossibly elegant in his soft black sweater that clung to his chest and the silky black slacks. His hair shimmered with golden strands in the dull light and his profile was chiseled perfection.

Everything about him is perfection, a voice whispered in the back of her mind.

Peri clenched her hands, battling back her fierce attraction. This male was nothing but trouble. On an epic scale.

"Did you see the picture of the corpses?" She forced the words past her stiff lips.

Valen smoothly turned and crossed directly in front of her. "I did."

"They looked like they had been drained. Could it have been a vampire?"

He arched a brow at the blunt question. Vampires considered themselves above the law. And certainly they didn't tolerate accusations of murder from lowly mages.

Surprisingly, however, he merely shrugged. "It's possible. A vampire could have drained them and left them posed to send a message to Gabriel."

"That's why you're here," she breathed before she could halt the words. "To make sure there isn't a rogue vampire causing havoc."

His exquisite features might have been carved from marble. "As I said, I want the truth."

Her harsh laugh echoed through the barn. "Wisdom Ranch is a place of lies and deceit. There's no truth to be found here."

"Gabriel mentioned that the coven had been secretive over the past few years."

Peri didn't press for more information about his reason for being in Wyoming. Valen would tell her what he wanted her to know. Nothing more.

"They were always secretive," she instead said, returning her attention to the reason she'd spent the entire day and half the evening traveling to Wyoming.

"Why?"

"My mother was paranoid that someone might arrive and challenge her place as leader." Peri recalled the image of her mom, Brenda Sanguis. She grimaced at the memory of a reed-thin woman with thick black hair and cold blue eyes. Peri had done her best over the years to scrub the woman from her mind, but the details of her features were still crystal clear. Including the gnawing hunger in her eyes. As if the older woman was desperate for something just out of reach. "And she was willing to use forbidden objects of power to maintain her position."

"Risky."

"Yes."

Valen studied her in silence. Did he sense she was hiding the depths of her mother's evil? Probably.

"It would have made more sense to keep you alive," he finally said. "No witch would dare to challenge her authority so long as you stood at her side."

"My mother was under no illusion she could control me."

The silver eyes flickered with an emotion she couldn't read. "She's not the only one," he said dryly.

"Good, I—"

"Stand back," he commanded, moving so fast he was a blur before he was abruptly moving in front of her.

Peri shivered as an icy blast of power spread through the air. "What's wrong?"

"There's someone here." He tilted back his head. "A human."

Peri abruptly recalled the eyes she'd spotted in the picture of the dead witches. It had to be the witness she'd come here to find.

"Let me."

Peri moved so he was no longer blocking her view of the hayloft. Ignoring Valen's glare of annoyance, she tapped into the magic she'd stored before leaving New Jersey. Her bracelet glowed as she released the spell, the sizzle of power filling her with a heady sense of pleasure.

It was better than sex.

Well, it was better than what she could remember about sex. It'd been a while, and never with a male like Valen—

"Stop!" a female voice cried out, thankfully interrupting Peri's treacherous thoughts.

"Come down," Peri ordered, maintaining the magic that she'd wrapped around the hidden woman's throat. It would feel like a noose, tightening with every beat of her heart.

There was a shuffling sound as the person crawled to the edge of the loft, swiveled at the edge and used the ladder to climb down. As she reached the bottom, she slowly turned to face them with a terrified expression.

"Please don't hurt me." She lifted her hands to her throat, tears in her pale blue eyes.

Peri studied the round face streaked with dust and the messy cloud of blond hair. She was several inches shorter than Peri, with soft curves that she displayed in a tube top and tight jeans. It'd been fourteen years, but Peri easily recognized her.

For a tense moment, Peri battled against the urge to keep squeezing. This witch deserved to suffer. Not only for helping Peri's mother try to kill her, but for the years of petty insults and jealous backstabbing. She'd done her best to make Peri's life in the coven a living hell.

"Destiny." She forced a humorless smile to her lips as she released her spell. She was there for information, not revenge. "I thought you must be the skulker in the background when I saw the pictures."

"Who are you?" The woman flicked her gaze between Peri and Valen, her fear pungent in the air. "What are you doing here?"

"You don't remember me?"

"Should I?"

"Peri."

"Peri." The pale eyes widened. "I thought…" Her hand remained pressed against her throat, as if suddenly realizing what had made her feel as if she was choking.

"You thought I was dead?" Peri finished for her.

Destiny nodded. "Brenda told us that she'd killed you and disposed of your body while we were unconscious. Where have you been?"

Of course her mother had lied to the others. She wouldn't want them realizing just how badly she'd botched her attempt to kill Peri. Besides, the older woman had probably assumed that Peri crawled off and conveniently died. She'd been gravely wounded and losing blood at an alarming rate. Brenda couldn't have realized the level of power pumping through her daughter, or how swiftly she would heal.

"I've been trying to avoid the women who wanted me dead," Peri said dryly.

Destiny shuddered, her gaze lowering to the floor where the bodies had been discovered.

"They're gone. They're all gone."

"What happened?" Peri demanded.

"I don't know," Destiny muttered. "I...I wasn't here."

"She's lying." Valen's cold voice sliced through the air.

Destiny jerked her head up, but before she could respond, Peri smoothly turned Destiny's attention back to her. The witch was already trembling with fear. She didn't want her shutting down completely.

"What happened, Destiny?"

The witch hesitated, obviously reluctant to admit what she'd seen. At last she heaved a harsh sigh of resignation.

"It started shortly after you were..." She faltered. The woman hadn't hesitated to join in the attempted murder of Peri, but she found it hard to say the word. "After you left."

"What happened?"

"Brenda was even worse."

Peri arched a brow. That covered a lot of territory. "Worse in what way?"

"She was constantly leaving the ranch in search of powerful artifacts at auction houses and cheesy magic shops. She claimed that she wanted to protect us, but she was never around. The place started falling apart. But that wasn't the worst."

Peri shot a quick glance toward the stables. That explained the creeping rot. "What was worse?"

"I don't think she was entirely stable."

"Mentally or physically?"

"Mentally." Destiny sniffed back her tears. "We all thought it must be the grief at being forced to kill her own daughter."

Peri made a strangled sound. "Are you serious? My mother wouldn't recognize grief if it smacked her in the face. She was like a reptile. Nothing but basic survival instinct."

"A lesson learned too late," Destiny whispered.

Valen stepped forward. "Why did you believe she was suffering from grief?"

Destiny glanced toward Valen, only to have her gaze slide away. Few people could actually look a vampire in the eye.

"She had a bizarre certainty that there were demons in the world."

Peri jerked in surprise. "Demons?"

"Crazy, right?"

It wasn't crazy, but it was certainly unexpected. Few humans realized that they weren't at the top of the food chain.

"What made her believe in them?"

Destiny hunched her shoulders. "She was deciphering some old text she'd found in a spell book. She claimed it revealed that there was demon blood in the world. And that it infected people to make them super strong and even gave them immortality."

"She must have misinterpreted the text," Peri hedged.

"That's what we all said." Destiny shook her head in disgust. "Brenda refused to listen, insisting that there was some sort of magic in the ground that could give us the same power as the demons."

Peri shared a startled glance with Valen. It was one thing to believe in demons. Many human religions included them in their tenets. But humans should be oblivious to the fact that they lived side by side with them. And that the demons were capable of tapping into the magic of the Gyres.

"Where is this strange text?" Valen demanded.

"In here."

Destiny moved to the side of the barn, sweeping away a layer of straw to reveal the hatch carved into the floorboards. She bent down to tug it open, but even as she was reaching into the opening, Valen had moved to stand next to her.

"No. I'll get it."

"Okay." Destiny stumbled back, landing on her butt before she was instinctively scrambling to put space between her and Valen.

She didn't know that Valen was a vampire, but she could easily sense he was a dangerous predator. It pulsed in the air around him.

"You said my mother was searching for some magical object." Peri once again claimed the witch's attention as Valen reached into the hole to pull out an ornately carved wooden box.

Peri recognized it. Her mother kept rare spell books and objects of power in the ancient case. Usually protected by a potent curse. Valen glanced in her direction and she gave a small shake of her head. The curse would have ended with the death of her mother, but there was the possibility that she'd placed other layers of protection around the box.

They wouldn't hurt a vampire, but they might destroy the contents inside.

"Brenda tried to tap into the supposed magic in the ground, but nothing worked," Destiny answered Peri's question. "Not until last week."

Peri turned toward the witch, who'd moved until she was on the opposite side of the barn from Valen, her arms wrapped protectively around her waist.

"What happened last week?"

"She returned from her latest trip with a small marble statue in the shape of a white owl. Brenda was certain it was special because an owl represented wisdom." Destiny's lips twisted. "I assumed it was going to be yet another failure."

"It wasn't?"

"Brenda told us that it was working. First, she used it to light the fire in the main lodge. It looked spectacular, but even I can light candles. None of us were that impressed." Destiny shrugged. "Next she claimed she used it to create a simple glamour spell that not only gave the illusion she was blond, but genuinely bleached her hair of color. It was supposedly proof that she'd tapped into the wild magic that mages used."

"Was her hair blond?"

"Yes, but she could easily have bleached it herself to fool us," Destiny said.

Peri snorted. That was the sort of talk that could get a witch tossed out of the coven. Or worse.

"Did you mention your suspicion?"

A dark flush replaced Destiny's pallor. "Not to Brenda, but someone must have told her what I said."

"Why do you think that?"

"Last night she called for the coven to gather in here so they could combine their magic." Destiny tilted her chin, her expression defensive. "I wasn't invited."

Peri nodded. If the witches were melding their magic into one spell, that would explain why they were standing in a circle. They would have been holding hands as they chanted the words, with the object of power in the middle of the floor.

"My mother wanted them to combine their magic to do what?"

"I don't know." Destiny lowered her head, as if studying the tips of her shoes. "I told you, I wasn't invited. I didn't see anything."

"She was here." A rush of cold air swept over Peri as Valen suddenly appeared next to her. He was pointing toward the stables at the back of the barn. "She stood there."

"How did he know that?" Destiny licked her lips, still refusing to glance in Valen's direction. Smart witch. "Who is he?"

Peri ignored the questions. She had no words to explain Valen.

"What was the spell?"

"A simple spell to draw the energy from the earth and store it in the owl. We had been practicing it since Brenda first started to believe in demons." The witch sucked in a harsh breath that sounded like a sob. "I never expected it to work."

"But it did?"

"I sincerely don't know what happened."

"Tell me what you saw," Peri commanded.

Destiny pressed her hand to her stomach, as if she suddenly felt sick. "They finished the spell and the owl started to glow."

"With magic?"

"It wasn't any magic that I'd seen before," she muttered. "It was red, as if there was lava inside the statue. Your mother was ecstatic. She was laughing and telling everyone she'd captured the demon power. She looked...wild."

Red like lava? Peri was as baffled as Destiny. Witches couldn't see magic in a physical form. Not unless it was an illusion or a glamour. So why was the statue glowing?

"What happened to the statue?" she asked.

"It shattered when the lava exploded out of it."

Peri glanced down at the floor. The explosion must have caused the charred stain on the wooden planks. She frowned as she caught sight of a white shard wedged between two boards. Bending down, she carefully pulled it out before she straightened and showed it to Destiny.

"Is this a part of it?"

Destiny shrugged. "I think so."

Peri tucked it in the front pocket of her shorts. It just felt like a piece of marble. Was whatever magic that had once clung to it gone? Something she intended to find out.

"What happened to the lava?" she asked, feeling ridiculous asking the question.

What kind of spell created lava? And how had a bunch of witches managed to trigger it?

"It kept spreading and spreading." Destiny's voice shook as the memories threatened to overwhelm her. "The others wanted to run."

"Why didn't they?"

"Brenda ordered them to stay." Her laugh came out as a sob. "She promised they would have the true magic of a mage. Just like you." There was an edge in her voice that warned Peri that the witch considered it her fault that Brenda had been crazed by her lust for power. Or maybe she blamed Peri for being a mage. Whatever. "She even promised immortality."

"So they stayed."

Destiny nodded. "Even when the magic crawled over them, coating them in a glowing red. Your mother's laughter turned into screams. It was awful." Destiny shuddered. "I can still hear those screams."

"What did you do?"

Destiny flicked a quick glance toward Valen. Was she considering a lie? Probably. Just as quickly, however, she returned her attention to Peri.

"I wanted to run, but I was afraid it would follow me," she grudgingly confessed. "I just hid in the shadows until the screaming stopped. When I managed to get enough nerve to look again, they were all dead. Like they'd been sucked dry."

"And the lava?"

"It was gone." Destiny lifted her hands in a helpless motion. "I think it must have sunk back into the earth."

Peri nodded, but she knew damned well the magic didn't just disappear. Not when it had absorbed the power of twelve witches. But it was obvious that Destiny didn't know what had happened to it, and she didn't want to reveal her concern in front of Valen.

This was mage business. The last thing she wanted was more interference from the vampires.

"Did you call the police?" she instead asked.

Destiny's lips parted, but it took her a few seconds to settle on her answer. "I placed an anonymous tip that something bad had happened at Wisdom Ranch."

Peri studied the witch with raised brows. "The cops don't know you were a witness?"

Destiny was instantly on the defense as she started backing toward the open door.

"Look, I just want to get out of here and forget everything about this place. I was packing the last of my things when I heard you drive in."

"Why hide in the loft?"

Destiny continued to back away, her movements awkward, as if she was close to total collapse. And she probably was. It was doubtful that she'd managed to sleep since she witnessed her family murdered in front of her.

"I assumed you were cops. Or reporters. I didn't want to answer awkward questions. They'd already searched the barn so I didn't think they'd look in here again." She paused as she reached the door, her expression one of genuine regret. "I'm sorry about your mom and I'm sorry for what happened to you in the past. This has all been a terrible mistake."

There was a harsh sincerity in her voice as she turned to leave.

Peri frowned. "Where are you going?"

"Home. I should never have left."

With a muffled sob, the woman fled the barn. Peri took a step forward, but before she could follow, Valen was already moving.

"I need to wipe her memory of us," he said, fading into the darkness until he was no more than a shadow. "Wait here."

His cool power brushed over her and Peri shivered as he passed by to disappear into the night. She was on the point of following—she didn't take orders from a leech—when she realized that he'd left her mother's treasure box in the middle of the floor.

With a sigh, she moved to scoop it into her arms.

Chapter 5

Valen silently followed the witch as she entered the bunkhouse and moved toward the stack of suitcases on a long, wooden bench. She hadn't lied about her desire to pack up and leave the ranch, but that didn't mean Valen trusted anything else that she'd told them.

Closing the door behind him, Valen whispered her name. "Destiny."

"Who's there?"

The woman whipped around, her eyes wide with fear. Valen moved with a speed impossible for her to detect, pressing his fingers against her forehead. Instantly her muscles relaxed and her expression eased as he gained command of her mind.

Swiftly, he managed to remove the memories of the past hour, and at the same time searched for clues about Peri's mother and the death of the coven. It wasn't a simple matter of plucking out the information he desired. Memories weren't like a movie that played in one smooth direction. They were disjointed and fuzzy and biased by the person's ability or inability to accept the truth, even when it was in front of them.

At last concluding that she'd revealed everything she knew about the strange magic that had killed the other witches, he led her to a nearby bunk and urged her to lie down before putting her to sleep. She would wake in a couple of hours with no lasting effects.

Leaving the bunkhouse, he made a thorough search of the rest of the compound to make sure he hadn't overlooked any stray intruders or surveillance equipment. Cameras couldn't detect his presence, but they would capture Peri's image.

At last satisfied he'd erased any indication of their presence at the ranch, he headed back to the barn. He was passing the large firepit when he was suddenly certain that there was something lurking just out of sight.

He halted, searching for the source of his unease.

There was nothing. No movement, no scent, no prickle of heat.

Unable to determine what was stirring his instincts, Valen continued into the barn. The sooner he removed Peri from the cursed place the better.

He discovered her standing where he'd left her, gazing at the floor where her mother had died while her fingers traced the intricate design carved into the wooden box.

There was no need to read her mind, even if he could. She was deeply troubled by the strange magic that had destroyed the coven.

"Will you stay in Wyoming?" he asked, attempting to distract her dark thoughts.

"No." Sucking in an unsteady breath, she lifted her head to meet his searching gaze. "Technically I suppose I'm my mother's heir since it's highly doubtful she bothered with a will, but I don't want anything. I'll make a call to have the livestock taken in by another rancher, but the rest of it can rot as far as I'm concerned."

"I'm returning to New York. You can join me if you wish." Valen kept his tone casual despite the fact he had no intention of leaving her behind.

Peri glanced toward the open door. "I rented the truck at the airport."

"Gabriel will send someone to deal with it," he smoothly insisted. "I have a helicopter waiting to take me back to the jet. You can be home before daybreak."

Her jaw tightened, as if willing herself to say no. Thankfully, her obvious weariness overrode her preference to avoid his company.

"Yeah. Okay."

Smart enough to hide his satisfaction, Valen led her out of the barn and through the gate that protected the ranch. They remained silent as they crossed the empty prairie to reach his waiting helicopter, Peri lost in her thoughts and Valen keeping a watchful eye for any hidden dangers.

Less than an hour later they were comfortably seated in his jet as they winged their way back to New York. Waving a hand toward the copper-haired fairy who waited at the front of the cabin, Valen waited for the servant to leave and close the door behind her before he swiveled his chair to study his companion.

Peri had her eyes closed as she relaxed into the soft leather seat, the box clutched tightly in her hands. If she was trying to pretend to be asleep, she was doing a terrible job. He could feel the anxiety vibrating around her.

"You're worried." He stated the obvious.

"Stay out of my mind," she muttered.

Valen's lips twisted. They both knew that he couldn't force his way into a mage's mind.

"I have no need to enter your thoughts, they're leaking beyond your barriers."

As he'd hoped, her eyes snapped open to glare at him in outrage. "Did you just say I'm leaking?"

He shrugged. "Seeping?"

"That's worse."

"Tell me why you're frightened."

Her annoyance faded at the abrupt question, her gaze lowering to the box in her arms.

"I'm not frightened, I'm furious."

Valen was confused. "Furious your mother is dead?"

"Furious that she took her coven to hell with her," she clarified. "I could have stopped her."

"How?" he asked. "It's obvious from your conversation with Destiny that you didn't have any contact with the coven."

"I knew," she insisted.

"You weren't aware of what she was doing."

"No, but I had proof she was willing to sacrifice everything, including her own daughter, to gain power."

Valen tapped his finger on the arm of his chair. It was a habit he'd developed to make himself appear more human. Peri was hiding something. The question was whether it was a private secret or one that might be a threat to Gabriel's territory.

"It's common for witches to fear true mages, and even to condemn them to death," he pointed out. "Your mother wasn't unique in her willingness to try to kill what she thought was a threat."

She hesitated before releasing a humorless laugh. "My mom didn't try to murder me out of fear, she was trying to steal my magic."

Valen's confusion deepened. "How could she steal your magic?"

"She suspected I was a mage months before I realized what was happening to me. And my mother being my mother, she saw it as an opportunity to take what she felt should have been hers."

Valen had never heard of a witch attempting to steal the powers of a mage. Usually they sacrificed them before they could attract the attention of mortals and stir up a hunt for magic users.

"What did she do to you?" he demanded.

"At first she tried various spells, using the objects of power she'd collected over the years." Peri shook her head, her expression hard with disgust. "She told me they were rituals all young witches went through to become a part of a coven."

"Did you believe her?"

"It felt sketchy, but I was too isolated to call her a liar."

Valen didn't have trouble believing her. The ranch was miles from the nearest town and at one time it'd been heavily protected by magic. No one would have been allowed in or out without the coven's permission. It would be easy to keep Peri isolated from the outside world.

"I assume she eventually accepted that the magic would never belong to her?"

Peri stared at him in blatant disbelief. "Clearly you never met the woman. Nothing was going to stop her. When she realized she couldn't siphon the magic from me while I was alive, she decided to steal it as I died."

Valen's slender fingers abruptly curled around the arms of his chair, the polished wood cracking beneath the pressure. If Brenda Sanguis wasn't already dead, he would have hunted her down and destroyed her.

It took more effort than it should have to keep his voice steady. "That makes no sense."

"It did in my mother's twisted brain." Peri couldn't disguise the lingering pain at her mother's betrayal. "She infused a dagger with a spell that was supposed to absorb my magic, then she called together the coven and revealed I was a mage. They happily held me down as she shoved the blade into my chest."

"Including Destiny?"

"She was smiling as the knife slid in."

The wood beneath his fingers cracked again. He was going to have to replace the seat after they landed.

"Do you want her dead?"

She sent him a warning glare. "If I did, I'd kill her myself."

Valen put aside thoughts of the nasty little witch. For now. He would deal with her later. "Continue."

"The blade was inches above my heart and the spell was cast, but it didn't do what my mother expected." Peri turned her hands over to reveal the silvery scars in the middle of her palms.

"It ignited your wild magic," Valen easily concluded.

"Yes."

A mage could use an object or spell to cast their magic. It not only provided a focus, but the object or spell could hold extra power so the mage was never fully drained. It was only when the wild magic first appeared to mark them as a mage that the power burst out in lethal bolts. Valen had only seen it once in his two thousand years and he'd never forgotten the devastation the mage had caused.

The coven was fortunate Peri had been so young when her magic had ignited. If her powers had had time to mature, they would never have survived the storm.

"That must have been a shock," he said.

"It knocked them unconscious and I ran from the ranch." Her fingers tightened on the box until her knuckles turned white. It was the only indication that the memories still caused her pain. "I never looked back."

He slid his gaze over her bold features. The wide brow, the vivid blue eyes and the lush curve of her mouth. He wasn't admiring her beauty. Her image had been engraved in his mind from the first moment he'd seen her.

It was her strength that caught his attention. "You didn't consider returning to punish them?"

Peri shrugged. "I could move forward or I could dwell in the past. I couldn't do both."

"Very wise."

"Maybe, but it was also selfish."

"Why do you call it selfish?"

"If I'd stayed and revealed that my mother hadn't tried to kill me because she feared my wild magic, but because she was trying to steal it, the coven might have walked away from her," she confessed, her teeth clenched so tight she could barely spit out the words. "They would be alive."

Valen wasn't as generous to her coven mates. "They lived together as a family for years. They knew exactly who your mother was and they stayed. It was their choice and they got exactly what they deserved." He stretched his lips into a humorless smile. "Except for Destiny. No doubt fate will eventually catch up with her."

Peri sent him a warning glare. "As long as fate doesn't go by the name Valen."

"We'll see."

Her lips parted, but the only thing that came out was a weary sigh. "I'm too tired to argue."

"Then sleep."

She settled back in her seat and closed her eyes. She wasn't obeying his command. She would battle him to the death before she submitted. But her weariness was genuine.

Valen swiveled his chair back to gaze out the window while his thoughts remained centered on the woman next to him.

He believed Peri's story about her mother's attempt to steal her magic. It'd obviously been painful to dredge up the memories and even more painful to share them with him. But he also suspected that she'd shared a glimpse into her violent past in an effort to distract him.

She might be furious at the knowledge her mother had destroyed the coven in her lust for power, but she was also afraid.

Deep to the soul afraid.

So what was she hiding?

And was it a threat to the Cabal?

* * * *

It was midmorning the next day when Peri managed to drag herself out of bed and into the shower. And almost noon before she headed downstairs to grab a cup of coffee and a blueberry scone.

Her late start, however, did have its benefits, she discovered. Not only was she rested after her deep, thankfully dreamless sleep, but she was still walking down the stairs when Elias Mitchell slammed out of the building after paying to have his curse removed.

Today, she wasn't in the mood to enjoy the male's petulant anger. She had far more important matters on her mind.

Heading straight for the back office, she placed her mother's box on the desk and shared what she'd discovered with Maya, who'd been impatiently waiting for her report.

Once Peri finished her story, Maya stared at her in disbelief. This morning the older woman had made a concession to the summer heat by choosing a sleeveless silk shirt and yellow capris. Peri was wearing her usual cutoff shorts and T-shirt. This one had Thor on the front. She had a massive crush on the God of Thunder. Or rather Chris Hemsworth.

"How could your mother have realized that there were demons and that the source of her magic came from the ground?" Maya asked, as she tried to process what Peri had discovered.

It was a question that gnawed at Peri. It was one thing for her mother to believe she could steal magic from a mage. Most witches were aware that true-magic users existed. But she should never have known about demons, or the Gyres that allowed them to tap into their ancient powers.

"Destiny said she was translating an old text. I'm hoping it was in one of her spell books." Peri ran her hand over the top of the box, seeking the hidden lever that would trigger the lock.

"No, Peri." Maya abruptly reached out to grasp Peri's hand, tugging it away from the box.

Peri instinctively took a step away from the desk. "What's wrong?"

Maya shook her head, her worried gaze focused on the wooden box. "I'm not sure, but I sense a power."

"Magic?"

"Ancient magic."

Ancient meant that the magic was connected to demons. Or the Cabal. So how did a witch get ahold of it?

"Is it evil?" she asked.

"I can't be sure, and until I am, I think we should keep the books in our ward safe."

Peri nodded. There weren't many things that frightened her. A fact that was a constant source of annoyance for Maya.

"Can you deal with them?" she asked the older woman. "I need to make a trip into the city."

Maya settled on the corner of the desk, studying Peri with a curious gaze. "Does this have anything to do with Valen?"

Peri flinched at the unexpected question. She was trying to put the aggravating vampire out of her mind. Okay. It was a futile task. Even her dreams had been plagued with the image of his fiercely beautiful face and the icy brush of his power. But her pride demanded that she pretend to be impervious to the outrageously compelling male.

"Nothing I do has any connection to the leech." She tossed her hair, which she'd left loose to tumble down her back. "In fact, I plan to go to great lengths to avoid crossing paths with him again."

Maya pursed her lips. "I wonder if he feels the same?"

A treacherous tingle inched down her spine. Was that excitement? Peri sternly squashed the sensation.

"Vampires consider us food or slaves," she said, as much to herself as to her companion. "They don't have feelings for us lowly creatures."

Maya straightened from the desk, her expression suddenly hard as she reached up to touch the scars that marred the side of her face. "Don't dismiss his interest, Peri. There was a reason he was in Wyoming, and I don't believe it was just to discover why the witches were dead. He would be a lethal opponent."

Maya was right. Valen had a reason for being in Wyoming. It could have been that he feared the deaths were related to a rogue vampire. But that didn't mean there wasn't more to his arrival. Only a fool would underestimate one of the Cabal.

"He's not an opponent, he's a nuisance," she insisted. "One I intend to avoid."

Maya looked as if she wanted to press the issue, then, sensing Peri's discomfort with the subject of Valen, she heaved a sigh.

"Why are you going into the city?"

Peri reached into the front pocket of her shorts to pull out the shard she'd discovered in the barn.

"I think this is a fragment from the statue my mother used as a focus for her spell. I want to know what the hell it is, where it came from, and if it caused the death of my coven."

Maya was shaking her head before Peri stopped speaking. "It's too dangerous. We have no idea how it will react to your magic."

"That's why I want to take it to the playroom," Peri said, referring to the protected space owned by the fairy Aston. "Once I have it properly warded, then I can examine it without worrying about outside magic triggering the shard. Or anyone sensing that I'm investigating it."

Maya wasn't appeased. "Even with protections it's still dangerous."

"I'll be careful, I promise." Peri tucked the shard back into her pocket with a grimace. "I haven't forgotten what happened to those women."

Chapter 6

Leaving Penn Station, Peri used the subway to head to the Upper East Side. The neighborhood was quiet, as most residents retreated from the afternoon heat baking off the acres of cement. It was currently the temperature of a pizza oven. Peri grimaced, feeling her hair sticking to her nape as the humidity pressed against her.

Ah. Nothing like New York City in the summer.

Strolling through the maze of streets, Peri halted in front of a large, three-story brown house that spread the entire block.

The Warehouse was another property owned by Valen and managed by Aston Wellman. Unlike Neverland, however, it offered hush-hush entertainment. Peri had no idea what happened in the basement, or the other select areas of the club. They were specifically designed for the fetishes of various demons. Her interest was in the small room at the back of the building.

Climbing the steps, Peri pressed the button next to the heavy wooden door. Seconds later a voice drifted through the intercom.

"We're not open."

The male sounded bored, as if she'd interrupted his nap. And maybe she had. The Warehouse didn't officially open for several hours. She'd heard rumors, however, that Aston lived on the upper floor. She wanted to catch him before he headed to one of the other nightclubs he managed.

She pressed the buzzer. "I need to see Aston Wellman."

"Are you deaf? We're not open." The voice wasn't so sleepy this time. It was downright rude. "So fuck off."

She tilted back her head, glaring at the security camera above her. "Tell him it's Peri Sanguis."

"Look, you—" The angry words were abruptly cut off. Was the intercom broken?

Before she could press the button for the third time, there was a loud beep and then a click as the door was unlocked. Peri waited, preparing herself for the annoyed receptionist to appear and punish her for being a pest.

Instead, the ridiculously handsome fairy suddenly appeared, his copper hair spilling down his back and his muscular body in glorious view. Only the loose dogi pants hanging low on his hips obstructed the view.

A shame.

She tried not to stare at the broad chest that tapered to a narrow waist or the bulging muscles of his arms.

"Hello, Aston."

"What a lovely surprise." He flashed a charming smile, waving her forward. "Come in."

Entering the building, Peri breathed a sigh of relief as the AC washed over her sweaty skin.

"Sorry, I know it's early."

"No problem."

Aston escorted her across the marble foyer that was split by two separate staircases. One headed down to the basement and the other angled up to the upper floor. They moved upward, entering a large lobby complete with marble columns, a crimson carpet, and a massive chandelier hanging low over their heads. It looked like a place where she should be singing opera, not meeting with a half-naked fairy.

Passing by the reception area, her attention was captured by a young male fairy who was kneeling next to an ornate desk with his head bent so low his face nearly touched the carpet.

"Good help is so hard to find," Aston mused as Peri sent him a questioning glance.

She grimaced. She was assuming this was the rude receptionist. What had Aston done to him? Probably best not to ask.

"Yeah, I've heard," she muttered.

Aston waved his hand toward another flight of stairs. "Let's go into my office."

Peri shook her head. "Actually, I was hoping to use the playroom."

Aston turned to face her, his expression impossible to read. "An expensive request."

"I have money," Peri assured him. Since joining Maya at the Witch's Brew, she'd acquired an impressive bank account.

"So do I. Lots of it."

Peri stilled, studying the fairy with a sudden wariness. She'd been prepared for Aston to demand an outrageous sum. The room was perfect for a mage to test new spells without causing damage. Or to defuse dangerous magical artifacts before they could harm anyone. Or best of all, a place where a mage could come and play with forbidden spells without getting caught. There were some mages who were willing to pay top dollar for the pleasure.

She hadn't expected to have to barter for the privilege.

"What do you want?"

Smoldering magic prickled in the air as Aston slid his gaze down the length of her bare legs.

"An interesting question filled with all sorts of possibilities."

Any other day Peri would have enjoyed the flirtation. Aston was a master at making a woman—or man—feel beautiful. And just imagining what he could do with that powerful body was enough to bring a smile to her face. Today, however, she had too much on her mind to play.

"My body is off the table."

He stepped closer, his eyes darkening with a sensual promise. "What about under the table? Or hanging from the chandelier?"

Peri tilted her head to gaze at the exquisite light fixture that shimmered with a thousand crystals.

"Have you really?"

His soft chuckle brushed over her like a caress. "Someday you'll find out."

"We all live in hope." She took a deliberate step back. "Tell me what you want."

Aston stilled, studying her with a searching gaze. As if she was a puzzle he was determined to solve. At last, the lazy charmer was replaced with the male who ran multimillion-dollar businesses.

"I need a potion."

Peri arched her brows. When a man wanted a potion it was usually for one thing. "Oh. I'm sorry. No chandelier for you."

Aston's lips twisted into a wry smile. "Not that kind of potion."

"Then what?"

Aston touched her arm, discreetly leading her away from the receptionist, who continued to kneel next to the desk.

"There's someone stealing money from the petty cash at Neverland," he said in a low tone.

Peri made a strangled sound of disbelief. Steal from a vampire?

"Are they suicidal?"

"Suicidally stupid," he ground out.

"What sort of potion do you want?"

"A truth potion."

Peri was confused. "Valen doesn't need magic to get the truth."

"I'm hoping to avoid bothering His Excellency. The amounts taken have been relatively small."

"And?" Peri prompted. There had to be more to his desire to avoid including Valen. Stealing was stealing, no matter what the amount. And if they'd take money, what else would they be willing to do?

"And all three potential suspects are my nephews," Aston grudgingly confessed.

"Yikes."

"No shit." Aston shook his head in disgust. "As much as I currently want to hand them over to Valen and watch them squirm, I'm afraid my sisters would make my life a living hell."

"What will you do with the culprit?" Peri asked. The fey could be just as brutal as any other demon when it came to justice.

"My plans are still fluid, but whichever one has sticky fingers will deeply regret breaking my trust," he admitted in harsh tones. "He will, however, survive so he can work to regain the honor he's lost."

"Okay. Once I return to the shop I'll brew your potion and have it delivered."

"Deal."

With a formal nod to complete the contract, Aston headed toward an opening at the far end of the lobby. They entered a narrow hall that led to the back of the building. As they walked, the marble and crimson disappeared to be replaced with barren walls and a wood plank floor. Peri assumed this area had been stripped down to prevent any magical accidents.

At the end of the corridor they stopped in front of an iron door set in a metal frame.

Aston glanced at her with a surprisingly somber expression. "The door automatically locks from the inside. Once you reach the center of the room, the wards will be activated." He reached to push the door open. "Don't do anything stupid, Peri. I can't get to you once you're locked inside."

"Have you been talking to Maya?" Peri demanded, stepping into the small space that was painted white from floor to ceiling. There were no windows, no furniture, no smells, or sense of magic.

It was like being smothered in a white box. Or a coffin.

"No, but I'm not going to be the one who has to tell Valen you're dead," Aston answered her question in dry tones. "Unlike my nephews I don't have suicidal tendencies."

Peri twisted around to glare at the fairy. "Why would you tell—" The door slammed in her face. "That stupid vampire?"

With a muttered curse, Peri shoved all thoughts of Valen from her mind. Maya could be overprotective, but she was right when she warned that testing the shard would be dangerous. Peri needed her full attention on what she was about to do.

Walking to the center of the empty room, Peri pulled the shard from her pocket and bent down to place it on the smooth floor. Then, wiping her suddenly damp palms on her shorts, she stepped back and touched the magic that raced through her blood.

She was accustomed to using magical objects to amplify her powers, but she'd rarely tried to manipulate them to perform other tasks. Right now, she wanted to determine if the statue had been responsible for the death of the coven. And if so, she wanted to make sure any lingering magic was destroyed.

Releasing her power in a thin thread, Peri directed it at the shard. It connected with a loud sizzle, warning Peri that there were still residues of the spell clinging to the statue. She widened the thread to encompass the entire shard, puzzled by the reddish glow that was beginning to bloom just above it.

It was a power she didn't recognize. Usually a spell or portions of one tingled with an electric energy. As if they were alive. This one was just the opposite. It felt as if it was sucking the air from the room.

Peri frowned, recalling Destiny's claim that her mother was attempting to draw the magic from the earth. Was that what it was doing? Trying to find magic to absorb?

She continued to watch the shard even as the thought of Destiny brought back memories of her mom and the coven. They were dead now, but obviously their evil legacy lived on. Not only in this strange artifact, but in the wounds she carried.

Years of being judged and found unworthy by her mother. Endless days and nights, cooking and cleaning for the coven as if she was a slave, not a member of the family. And then the ugly jealousy as Brenda realized her daughter possessed what she so desperately wanted.

The red glow started to pulse, growing larger and larger as her anger at the thought of her mother sent a swell of fury through her. Why hadn't she gone back to the ranch and exposed Brenda Sanguis as a narcissistic bitch who would eventually destroy her coven? *Not that they deserved my concern,* a voice whispered in the back of her mind. They'd been eager to get rid of her once they discovered she was a mage. Maybe they deserved exactly what they got…

A bitter pleasure at the image of the coven lying lifeless on the ground was still passing through her mind when the red glow struck out, slamming into her with the force of a hurricane. At the same time, she felt a painful tug in the center of her being.

Stumbling backward, Peri struggled to regain her balance. The pain was debilitating, bending her double as the glow became a tangible mist and wrapped around her. Was she dying? It felt as if the mist was digging into her and hollowing her out. Emptying her of her very soul.

Or was it her magic?

Yes, that was it. It was sucking away her magic.

She was being drained. Just like her mother and the other members of her coven.

It was sheer instinct that had her cutting off the magic connected to the shard. That, and the words from a poster Skye had hanging in the bookshop: *When you're in a hole, stop digging.*

There was an audible snap as the red glow recoiled back into the shard. Like a door being slammed by an angry neighbor. A second later a hauntingly human screech shattered the silence of the room.

With a wince, Peri forced herself to her feet. The pain was gone, along with the sense of her magic being drained. But an acute fear remained firmly lodged in her heart.

She didn't know what was clinging to the shard, but she knew it was bad. Really, really bad. And she had to get the thing locked behind an indestructible ward before it could escape.

Grimly moving to snatch the shard off the floor, Peri hurried to the door and jerked it open. Her breath tangled in her throat when she discovered Aston standing a few inches away.

Had he heard the scream? Something had alerted him that things had gone sideways. His elegant features were set in worried lines.

"Peri, are you okay?"

"I'm " Belatedly realizing that she must look a mess, Peri reached up to run her fingers through her tangled hair. "Yes, I'm fine." She moved forward, trying to inch her way past his muscular form. "Thanks. I'll have your potion sent to you tonight."

"Let one of my staff drive you home."

"No."

The word came out sharper than she intended, but she wasn't going to risk anyone getting their hands on the shard. And while she enjoyed flirting with the handsome fairy, she didn't trust him any farther than she could throw him. Especially not with a powerful artifact that would be worth millions on the black market.

"Are you sure?" he demanded, continuing to regard her with blatant concern.

"Positive." She forced a stiff smile to her lips. "I'll see you later."

Peri scurried down the hall and across the lobby. She caught a brief glimpse of the male receptionist, who regarded her with a resentful frown, and she sent him a finger wave as she hurried past him, but didn't pause to enjoy his annoyance.

The sooner she could get the shard back to the Witch's Brew, the safer everyone would be.

* * * *

Elias breathed a harsh sigh of relief as he caught sight of the dark-haired mage exiting the brownstone and heading down the sidewalk with long strides. He'd been waiting for the bitch to come out for what felt like an eternity. He was hot, sticky, and in the mood to hurt someone.

No, not someone.

Only the mage who'd caused him endless pain and humiliation for the past forty-eight hours was going to sate his thirst for violence.

That was why he'd waited outside the Witch's Brew after paying an outrageous sum to have the curse removed. He'd known she would eventually make an appearance. And why he'd followed her to the city. He couldn't believe his luck. Once they were in the Gyre he'd have his full powers.

Of course, at the time he didn't realize she was headed to the Warehouse. A pain in the ass. He hadn't dared to follow her inside, not when there was the possibility that Aston would be there. Which meant he was stuck waiting in the sweltering heat for her to indulge her fetishes.

Now the sweat dripping from his face as he followed behind her only amped his seething fury. She'd had her fun, now it was time for him to have his.

Waiting until she was passing by an opening between two buildings, Elias rushed forward, slamming her into the narrow alley. She lurched forward, but she didn't fall on her face as he'd hoped. Instead she smoothly turned to face him, a slow smile curving her lips.

"Elias, what a lovely surprise." Her gaze made a slow inventory of the stained gym clothes he'd been wearing for the past two days. Nothing else would fit over his engorged balls. "How's the nether regions? All better?"

His demon blood boiled with a craving for revenge. "You're going to pay for what you did to me."

She blinked, pretending to be confused by his threat. "I've already been paid, remember?"

Elias hissed. "You and your bitch club think you're so clever."

"Bitch club?" The woman abruptly laughed, as if she'd never heard anything so funny. "Oh, Elias, that's not the insult you think it is."

"I think you're nothing more than a witch on steroids." He spit at her feet. "A human."

"Okay."

"I hate humans."

"That's not what your wife said," she taunted.

Elias's gut twisted as her words scraped against his raw wounds. After he'd left Neverland, he'd been prepared for the mortifying pain from the curse. He'd even expected his wife to spend the weekend harping at him until he dreamed about throttling her thick neck.

What he hadn't expected was for her to arrive at their expensive townhouse and immediately pack his bags. In less than an hour he'd been tossed out the door along with his belongings. And there hadn't been a damned thing he could do about it. The house belonged to his wife's family, along with the cottage in the Hamptons and the cabin in Vail. His only property was his Porsche and the tiny apartment he kept for his private entertainments.

The apartment was better than sleeping in the streets. But not much.

"She left me." Elias prowled forward, his hands clenched into fists. "And it's all your fault."

"My fault?" The mage stood her ground.

Elias frowned, his steps slowing. Why wasn't she afraid? Did she think she had enough magic to fight against a demon in the Gyre? Or did she have some sort of nasty curse prepared to throw at him?

"You went to Neverland to trick me," he accused.

"I didn't do anything but show up. The rest was all you."

Elias ground his teeth. That was the same thing his wife had said. As if any male didn't need the excitement of chasing and bagging his prey. Or in his case, bedding his prey. He was doing what he'd been created to do. Spreading his seed far and wide.

"It was a trap."

"It was you being you." She flicked a dismissive gaze down his body. "A cheating, selfish jerk."

His anger surged back, destroying his momentary caution. This bitch had destroyed his life. Now he was going to destroy her.

With reckless abandon, Elias charged forward. He was a full-grown demon with ancient blood pumping through his veins. He wasn't afraid of any damned mage.

The thought had barely managed to form in his fury-fogged brain when the woman lifted her arm and one of the bracelets around her wrist began to glow. She was preparing to cast a spell. Dammit. He needed to rip out her heart and eat it before she could hit him with the stupid thing.

Racing at full speed, he slammed into her slender form, wrapping his arms around her. He was strong enough to break her spine and crush her lungs. It wouldn't kill her, but it would disrupt her spell. Lifting her off her feet, he started to squeeze, but before he could make her pay for cursing him, he felt something strange crawling over his skin.

Distracted by the sensation, he turned his head to glance at his bare arms. A horrified gasp was wrenched from his throat at the sight of hundreds of cockroaches crawling over his skin. He shuddered, telling himself that it was an illusion. It had to be. But what if it wasn't?

He could not only feel the insects as they moved up his arm, but he could also smell them. It was a pungent, musky stench that made him gag. Releasing his hold on the woman, he desperately tried to brush them away. A few fell off and scurried toward the back of the alley; the rest dug their legs into his skin, and as he watched in horror they started to burrow into his flesh.

"No!" Terror blasted through him. This was as bad as having his balls swell to the size of cannonballs. Well, maybe not quite as bad. But it was enough to make him regret ever following the stupid woman. Obviously he needed to hire someone to take care of her. Not as satisfying as killing her with his own hands, but less stressful. "Make it stop," he rasped.

The mage stepped directly in front of him. "Threaten me or my friends again and I'll make sure body parts fall off that you'd rather keep attached. Got it?" she demanded.

Elias continued to claw at his arms, indifferent to the bloody wounds he was causing.

"Yeah, I got it."

He heard her walk away, but he didn't bother to watch. It wasn't until the bugs abruptly disappeared that he lifted his head to glare at the spot where she'd been standing.

"I don't care how much it costs, I'm going to put that bitch in a grave," he muttered, slowly turning to make his way out of the alley.

Consumed with his dreams of a violent, tragic end to the mage, Elias failed to notice the sudden chill in the air. A lethal oversight, he belatedly realized, as the manhole cover abruptly disappeared from beneath his feet and he plummeted through the opening.

Elias managed to avoid landing on his face, but before he could regain his balance, a heavy pulse of power sent him to his knees.

Shit. Shit. Shit.

He had no need to look up to know he was in the presence of Valen. No other creature could create a layer of ice that coated the abandoned steam tunnel. Or create a crushing pressure without even touching him.

"Elias, isn't it?" the deep voice demanded.

Despite the sharp chill in the air, Elias could feel the sweat dripping down his face. He didn't know what he'd done to attract the attention of the Cabal, but it couldn't be good.

"Yes, Your Excellency."

"You attacked a woman on my property."

Elias was confused. Was he talking about the bitch who'd cursed him?

"She's not a woman, she's a witch," he muttered, puzzled by Valen's interest.

"She's a mage," Valen corrected in icy tones. "*My* mage."

"Yours?" Elias jerked his head up, his eyes wide with terror. Why the hell hadn't someone told him? "I didn't know, I swear. They don't live in your Gyre."

"Neither do you."

Elias blinked in confusion, trying to read the male's pale, perfect features. It didn't look like he was teasing. In fact, he looked like he was considering the pleasure of draining Elias and leaving him to decay in the dank tunnel.

"I..." Elias licked his lips. "What?"

"Pack your bags and be out of the Gyre before nightfall."

"For how long?"

Valen folded his arms over his chest. "Eternity."

"Banishment?" Elias shook his head, barely capable of accepting that this was his life. Just days ago he'd been a wealthy, highly respected male who indulged his desires with reckless abandon. Now he'd been stripped of his fortune, humiliated, and banished. "Where will I go?" he rasped.

Valen's power pressed against Elias until he cried out in pain. "I suggest somewhere far away," the vampire warned. "If I see you again I'll kill you."

Chapter 7

It was just past five that evening when Peri joined Maya and Skye in the office at the Witch's Brew. The shard had been safely stored in a warded safe with her mother's spell books, and she'd spent an hour in the shower scrubbing off the stench of Elias Mitchell.

The shower hadn't gotten rid of the bruises the furious demon had left on her arms, but Peri had more important matters on her mind. She could handle the petulant Elias. She wasn't so confident about the spell that had attacked her in the playroom.

Maya paced from one end of the office to the other, her Louboutin stilettos clicking on the floor as she considered what Peri had revealed. At last she spun around, her green eyes shadowed with concern. The same concern was written on Skye's face as she leaned against the desk, her summer dress floating in the breeze from the AC.

Peri was the only one seated. She'd expended a lot of magic. First in the playroom, then again battling the demon. It would be a few hours before she was fully recovered.

"Was the red glow created by the shard?" Maya abruptly asked.

"I don't think so. It felt as if it was a..." Peri shivered as she forced herself to dredge through the memory of the nasty mist that had attacked her. "A residue left behind by my mother's spell. Or maybe it was a residue of whatever was inside the statue."

"And it was draining your magic?"

"Yes." That was the one thing Peri knew beyond a doubt. "If I didn't have the power of a mage it would have sucked me dry. Just like it did to the coven."

Maya clicked her tongue in frustration. "I've never heard of a spell that consumes magic."

It was Skye who answered the question hanging in the air. "Miasma," she breathed.

Peri glanced toward the younger woman. "What?"

"It's a miasma." Skye wrinkled her nose as Maya and Peri stared at her in confusion. "I read about it when I was...young."

Peri leaned forward. Skye rarely talked about her childhood. Or what she'd suffered. All they knew was that she'd been held captive by demons until she'd managed to escape and find her way to the Witch's Brew.

"Tell us," Maya commanded.

"In the earliest days of the Gyres, the magic was a lot stronger," Skye answered. "Sometimes too strong."

Peri blinked. She'd been born long after the Gyres had lost power, but she'd heard the complaints from demons at the loss of the ancient magic.

"How could magic be too strong?"

"It would react to its surroundings. Usually that meant creating lush swamps or arid deserts." Skye shuddered. "But during wars or times of plague it could turn toxic."

"It poisoned the earth?"

"Yes. And worse." Skye reached up to shove her fingers through her thick curls. Was she disturbed by the thought of the miasma? Or the fact that she was forced to remember her early life? Hard to say. "It was manipulated by demons to use as a weapon."

"How could they use it as a weapon?" Peri asked.

"They would lure a mage into the quagmire of miasma until they were drained. It would be easy to kill them after that."

Maya slowly nodded. "I've never seen one, but I've heard rumors that they once existed. In the Dark Ages it was called mage's bane."

Peri frowned, trying not to imagine poor women being caught in such a nasty bog.

"How did my mother summon an ancient power? Even with the addition of her coven they didn't have the magic necessary to create more than a rudimentary spell."

"I don't think she did," Skye said. "From what I read, the mages began searching out the miasmas and trapping them in vessels that were eventually destroyed. Or at least, most of them were destroyed. It's possible that a few survived."

"Oh." Peri was struck with a sudden realization. "The owl statue must have been one of the vessels that survived. That would explain how the shard attacked me. There must have been a part of the magic left on the piece."

Maya nodded even as her expression remained troubled. "Even so, how could she have broken through the spells to release it?"

"The wards might have weakened over time or…" Peri's words trailed away as she recalled the horrifying moment the red mist had slammed into her.

Skye moved to brush her hand down Peri's arm. "Peri? What's wrong?"

Peri pressed a hand against her stomach, still sore from the blow. "It was her anger."

"Her anger?" Maya moved to stand directly in front of her. "Why do you say that?"

"When the miasma was trying to drain my magic, it was feeding on my emotions." Her voice was oddly hoarse. "My anger at my mother and my guilt that I didn't try to stop her before she destroyed her coven." She shook her head, forced to wet her dry lips. "It all blasted through me as if the miasma was deliberately goading me to increase its power."

"It makes sense," Skye said. "If it was created in a time of chaos it would need those emotions to help fuel it."

Peri's sharp laugh echoed through the small room. "My mother had enough bitterness in her soul to fuel the magic for an eternity."

Maya's brows drew together as she considered the implications of what had happened at the ranch.

"The question now is where did she find the statue," she at last said.

"No, the question is how to stop the miasma," Skye corrected her.

Both Maya and Peri stared at the younger woman in horror.

"What do you mean?" Peri demanded.

Skye's eyes were suddenly distant, as if she was seeing beyond the walls. "I feel it."

Magic snapped in the air as Maya drew in her power, prepared to launch an attack.

"Here?"

Skye shook her head. "No. It's moving through the world."

Maya remained ready for battle. "Where?"

Skye held up her hands in a helpless motion and Peri shoved herself to her feet, a sudden dread lodged in the pit of her stomach. The mere thought of that…thing out in the world was enough to give her nightmares.

"Damn. I was worried it hadn't ended with the death of the coven. How did it escape?"

"If it's earth magic, I suppose it could be traveling through the soil," Maya said, although her voice didn't sound as if she believed that explanation.

Peri didn't have a better suggestion. Instead, she concentrated on how to stop the evil that was spreading.

"Where is it going?"

"Perhaps we can find out."

Maya moved to take a seat at the desk, typing on the keyboard of the laptop. Peri followed to glance over her shoulder.

"What are you looking for?"

"Unusual deaths." Maya scrolled through the various headlines that popped up. At last she pressed on a link that took her to a breaking news story. "Here. Bar fight leaves four dead."

"Not that unusual these days," Peri retorted, quickly skimming through the story. "And they died of gunshot wounds."

"Three of the victims were shot, but look." Maya pointed at the bottom of the screen. "The female bartender was discovered in the alley. The cause of death has yet to be determined, but the police fear involvement of a satanic cult."

"It could be a coincidence." Peri stated the obvious.

"The Jackalope Station is in Wyoming." Maya pulled up a map to check the location. "Less than a hundred miles from your mother's ranch. More than just a coincidence."

Peri straightened, pulling her phone out of the pocket of her jeans. Maya was right. There was a possibility it was connected.

"Do they give the bartender's name?"

It took Maya a minute to find the woman's identity. "Cherry Gladstone," she finally revealed.

Peri looked up the name on social media, easily finding a profile for the young, bleached blonde. She was twenty-four with several stylized tattoos on her arms and across her chest. She was in a complicated relationship and she was going to junior college to become a CNA.

So young and full of promise. Peri shook her head, but her regret was forgotten as she came to the last line in Cherry's bio.

"Wiccan." She lifted her head to meet Maya's steady gaze. "I need to check this out."

Maya slowly nodded. "Yeah, you need to check it out. I'll make the reservations—" Her words were cut off as her cell phone on the desk began to buzz. "Hold on." Grabbing the phone, Maya glanced at the screen. Her brows arched in surprise. "It's Valen."

Peri instinctively stepped back. As if the vampire was about to make an unwelcome appearance.

"What does he want?" she muttered.

"Let's find out." With a wicked smile Maya lifted the phone to her ear rather than putting Valen on speaker. Annoying woman. "Witch's Brew. Yes, she's here." Maya glanced pointedly at Peri's flushed face. "Can I take a message?" There was a lengthy pause before Maya was speaking again. "I'll let her know."

Peri waited until Maya had cut off the connection and replaced the phone on the desk. She didn't want Valen to know that she was in any way curious about his call.

"Let me know what?" she demanded.

"Valen has information he believes you'll be interested in."

"What information?"

"He said it's connected to Wisdom Ranch." Maya deliberately paused. "And that he's sending a car to fetch you in an hour."

Peri's mouth dropped open. "Fetch me? Like a dog?"

Maya held up a hand. "Those are my words, not his. He simply said that he'd send a car to pick you up."

Peri remained outraged. Or at least she told herself that it was outrage causing the knots in her stomach and her sweaty palms. Otherwise she'd have to admit she was sizzling with anticipation to see Valen again.

Unacceptable.

"Why didn't you tell him to shove his invitation up his—"

"Because the next time he calls it won't be an invitation." Maya rose to her feet, her smile replaced by a stern expression. This was the Maya who was not only in charge of the coffee shop, but the mage who kept both her and Skye safe. A gloriously powerful woman with connections to a secret guardian who only added to her air of mystery. "And because we need all the help we can get if a miasma really did kill your mother's coven. It has to be stopped before it does even more damage."

Peri flinched. "Stop it," she growled.

Maya scowled. "Stop what?"

"Making sense." Peri marched toward the door. "It's annoying when I'm trying to be a petulant child."

Skye reached out to touch her shoulder as she passed by. "Where are you going?"

"To replenish my magic." Peri held up her arm, revealing that the jade bracelet had lost its glow. "I'm not going to deal with that infuriating leech without having a backup supply."

Chapter 8

Valen's penthouse was shrouded in darkness even though the sun hadn't fully disappeared below the horizon. The entire building had steel shutters that remained in place until night had fallen. He wasn't a vampire who took unnecessary risks.

A wry smile twisted his lips as he sipped the expensive brandy he had imported from France. Actually, he did occasionally take unnecessary risks. Like when Aston called him in the middle of the day to tell him that Peri Sanguis had fled from the Warehouse as if the hounds of hell were on her heels. He hadn't hesitated for a second to leave his bed and travel through the tunnel system to make sure she wasn't in danger.

He didn't question why it was so urgent to reach her, or why his anger had exploded when he realized she was being attacked by a demon. It didn't even matter that Peri had clearly been capable of dealing with the idiot.

He'd made sure she would never be troubled in his territory again.

Not when word got out that you would be banished from the Gyre if you threatened the young mage.

His thoughts were interrupted by a soft tap on the door to his office. Setting aside the brandy, Valen smoothed his hands down the tailored jacket of his silver Gucci suit that he'd paired with a white shirt and light blue tie.

"Enter," he said, turning to watch Renee walk into the room.

As always, the female was professionally attired, in a black pencil skirt and yellow silk blouse. Her silver-blond hair was smoothed away from her pretty face. A face that was currently set in lines of disapproval.

"She's here."

"Good. I want you to personally escort her to the office." Valen arched a brow as Renee remained standing in the doorway. "Is there a problem?"

"I don't trust her."

The brow inched higher. "You have information you want to share?"

Renee pinched her lips. "The mages have no respect for you or your authority. They should have been forced to pledge their allegiance years ago."

Valen was aware that there were more than a few demons who agreed with his secretary. None, however, were foolish enough to challenge his decision.

"You think it would be better to have a group of resentful mages plotting behind my back?"

His voice was silky soft, but Renee instinctively pressed herself against the doorjamb.

"They should be trained to obey," she stubbornly insisted.

"Obey?" Valen shook his head. "You clearly haven't met Peri Sanguis."

The gold eyes flared with a hungry desire to punish the woman who'd captured Valen's attention.

"I could—"

"You'll escort her to my office." Shards of ice suddenly floated in the air as Valen released a tendril of his enormous power. "Nothing else. Is that clear?"

Renee was bold, but she wasn't stupid. She offered a deep bow as she backed away. "Crystal."

Renee disappeared down the hallway and Valen moved to perch on the corner of his desk. Less than ten minutes later, Peri strolled through the open door. Unlike his secretary, Peri wasn't immaculately groomed. Her lush curls spilled down her back and she was wearing a pair of faded jeans and a green crop top. She looked like she was headed to the park for a picnic, not meeting with the most powerful male in New York City. Perhaps the most powerful male in the world.

Not that it mattered. She was still the most stunning woman he'd ever seen.

Tilting her chin at his steady gaze, Peri strolled forward. "Your Renfield doesn't look happy that I'm here."

Valen waited until she'd reached the center of the room to answer. "Her name is Renee. And she believes you should be forced to bend the knee to me."

"Bend my knee? Is she brain damaged?"

Valen narrowed his gaze. "She's a loyal member of my staff who I greatly value."

Peri turned to study the office, not willing to admit she'd stepped over the line, but smart enough not to press her luck.

"Can I ask why I was summoned?"

"Please have a seat."

Valen watched her stiffen, as if she was longing to insist on standing. Then, surprisingly, she moved to gracefully sink onto the leather chair directly facing the desk. He was betting that she'd been reminded he could offer her access to his extensive network of contacts throughout America to assist in discovering what happened to her mother. Or on the flip side, he could make it all but impossible for her to gain information.

"Would you like a drink?" He nodded toward the built-in bar across the room. "I have a particularly fine Cabernet Sauvignon."

"I'm fine, thanks."

Valen folded his arms over his chest. "Before I reveal the information I received, can I ask what you were doing at the Warehouse this afternoon?"

Once again Peri surprised him. He'd expected her to dig in her heels and refuse to answer his question. Not because she had anything to hide, but simply to piss him off. It gave her inordinate pleasure to poke the bear. Or in this case, the lethal vampire.

"I took the shard I found in the barn to the playroom," she said without hesitation.

Valen had forgotten that Peri had pocketed a small piece of the statue her mother had used to cast her spell.

"Did you discover what it is?"

"We have a theory."

"Yes?"

"We believe my mother found a statue that contained a miasma."

"Mage's bane." Valen straightened as he considered her unexpected words.

"You've heard of it?" Peri demanded.

Valen nodded. It'd been centuries since he'd last witnessed a miasma. That one had been created in a cesspool on the fringes of London during the Great Plague. The seething magic had looked like a crimson tar pit when he'd seen it, and the Cabal had commanded a protective temple to be built around the spreading abomination. Valen had heard rumors, however, that demons had been using the poisonous magic to destroy the local mages.

"I'm certainly no expert in magic, but from what I've seen in the past, the miasma is a corrosive power that destroys everything in its path. We didn't see that sort of utter ruin in the barn."

"It wasn't created at the ranch," she corrected him. "According to our books, the mages would trap the magic in warded vessels to contain it."

Valen considered her words. It made much more sense that the miasma had escaped rather than being created in the barn.

"If your mother accidentally released the toxic magic, it would explain how the witches died. They wouldn't have any protection against it."

Her features tightened at the memory of her dead coven. "It's a theory."

"It makes sense."

Peri cleared her throat. She wasn't as indifferent to the tragedy as she wanted him to believe.

"Why am I here?"

Valen leaned to the side, tapping a key on his laptop. There was a soft buzzing sound as a wall panel slid open to reveal a large monitor. A second later, a grainy, black-and-white image filled the screen.

"Gabriel sent me a security video I think you'll be interested in," he told his companion.

Peri swiveled her seat and leaned forward. She frowned at the sight of the shabby space that looked like someone's garage. It had a cement floor, corkboard on the walls, and an open beam ceiling. Only the tables arranged in a haphazard pattern and the long counter near the back revealed that it was used for something other than storing lawn equipment.

"A security video from where?" she asked.

"It comes from Garland, a small town a few hours from your mother's ranch."

She sucked in an audible breath, her eyes widening. "Is this the local bar?"

"Yes, the Jackalope Station." Valen studied her exquisite profile. She wasn't puzzled as to why he would be showing her this particular video. She was anxious to discover what it was going to reveal. "You know about the incident?"

"Only what we could find on the internet. Does the video show what happened?"

"You can judge for yourself."

Valen pressed another button and the video flickered to life. On the screen the handful of customers jerked into motion, ambling around the tables or leaning against the bar.

Peri made a sound of annoyance as the video zoomed in and out of focus. "Is it a law that security tapes have to be crappy?"

"More of a precedent than an actual law."

"Hmm."

Her lips twitched but she refused to smile. Or even glance in his direction. Instead she continued to study the video, tension vibrating around her slender body. Did she sense what was about to happen?

On cue, she jumped to her feet. "Wait." Valen reached to pause the video as Peri walked toward the monitor to point at a smudge near the doorway. "Why is this blurred? A technical glitch?"

"Gabriel studied the original tape. There's nothing wrong with the video," he assured her.

"Magic," she breathed.

"This bar is outside the Gyre so it can't be a demon."

"A mage?"

"Possibly. Watch."

He pressed the Play key and the video stuttered back into motion, revealing the smudge moving forward. A customer glanced around and nodded toward the blurred object. Obviously it appeared normal to the crowd, which meant that it was deliberately obscuring the security camera. They watched in silence as the smudge angled toward a nearby table surrounded by a group of six guys all dressed alike in jeans, flannel shirts and cowboy hats. The men glanced up, and without warning the beer bottles in front of them toppled over. They jumped to their feet, and even without sound it was clear they were shouting abuse at each other, blaming the man next to them for the beer carnage. The blurred object hovered next to them, and a strange shadow seemed to flow from man to man. Like a ribbon of evil tying them together.

Nothing happened for a full minute, just the men glaring at each other. Then, as if there'd been some hidden switch flipped, the men reached for the guns they had strapped to various parts of their bodies and started shooting.

Peri hissed in shock as the smoke from the weapons filled the air and the men began to drop like flies. The carnage was swift and ugly, sending the rest of the customers fleeing in a stampede of terror.

The shadowed form avoided the escaping crowd and headed toward the back of the room where the bartender was holding a shotgun. The frightened woman pressed the trigger and jerked backward from the recoil. The blurry object never slowed, and with a last-ditch effort to save herself, the bartender tossed the shotgun at the advancing form and sprinted toward a nearby exit. The smudge followed, and within seconds the bar was empty except for the wounded and dying left lying on the cement.

Valen stopped the tape and Peri slowly turned to face him, her expression troubled.

"It's the miasma. It has to be."

Valen frowned. He had limited experience with the toxic magic, but he'd never heard of it traveling from one place to another.

"Can it take human form?"

She grimaced. "Honestly, I have no idea. Once the magic was forced inside the vessel it might have evolved over the centuries into something completely new. Like Darwin's theory on steroids."

Valen slowly straightened. "There's only one way to find out."

"How?"

"We talk to the witnesses."

She stared at him in confusion. "In Garland?"

"Do you have a better suggestion?"

Her lips parted, but no words came out. Valen hid a smile. He was betting he was one of the few to ever render this woman speechless. A victory.

Finally she cleared the lump from her throat. "I don't have a better suggestion, but I'm not sure why you say 'we.'"

Valen strolled toward her, savoring her warm scent. The light aroma of lilies with an undertone of rich spices. She'd been mixing potions before she'd come to see him, and the pulse of her power stroked against him like a caress.

"I can get you to the location in a fraction of the time it will take for you to fly commercial," he pointed out in reasonable tones.

She scowled. "And your interest being?"

He nodded toward the monitor. "This chaos can't be allowed to spread. It has already attracted the attention of human authorities. And once it reaches the power of a Gyre we can't predict what form the destruction might take."

She slowly nodded, unable to argue against his logic. "When do we leave?"

The question was harsh, as if she had to force the words past her stiff lips. Valen felt a fleeting pang of annoyance. Had there ever been a woman so reluctant to spend time in his company? In truth, he couldn't think of one.

Not until Peri.

"As soon as the sun sets."

She squared her shoulders, no doubt stiffening her spine at the knowledge that she had no choice but to accept his help.

"I'll need to pack a bag."

"My driver will return you to your home and wait to take you directly to my private airport."

She snorted as he took command of their upcoming adventure. "It's nice to be the king."

"Yes. Yes, it is." He stepped close enough that he could see the shards of ebony deep in the vivid blue of her eyes. Exquisite, and yet there was a guarded wariness that refused to let him fully see into her heart. His attention shifted to the marks that were visible on the tanned skin of her upper arms. He lightly brushed his fingers over the bruises. "You're wounded."

"It's nothing." Her voice was thick with the awareness that pulsed in the air.

Valen took another step forward, their bodies a mere breath apart. "You need to take better care of yourself."

"I'm doing fine."

His fingers slid down to press his thumb against her inner wrist. Her pulse raced.

"Nothing will be allowed to harm you while you're in my protection," he swore in low tones.

Without warning, Peri jerked her arm out of his grasp, and with a toss of her curls was heading toward the door.

"I don't need protecting, Valen. Save your heroics for someone who appreciates them."

A wry smile tugged at Valen's lips as she walked away. It'd been centuries since anyone had tried to put him in his place. At least anyone who'd survived such a perilous encounter.

"Why you, Peri Sanguis?" he whispered.

Chapter 9

Destiny huddled in the empty bathtub of the cheap motel, fully dressed, with the hexed dagger Brenda had used to try to kill Peri clutched in her hand. She was supposed to be well out of Wyoming by now. At least as far as Denver to catch a flight to her parents' Florida beach house.

Instead she'd barely driven away from the ranch in Brenda's beat-up van before she sensed she was being followed. At first she had no idea who could possibly be interested in her flight from the ranch. Everyone she'd known in Wyoming was dead. Then, a vague memory of Peri Sanguis returning from the dead floated up from the deepest corners of her mind.

Had the mage's arrival at Wisdom Ranch been a dream? Or rather a nightmare?

No. She'd been real, Destiny slowly forced herself to accept. Peri had appeared from the darkness, asking questions as if she had any right to answers. Then she'd obviously done some evil sort of magic to try and make Destiny forget that she'd been snooping around like a scavenger picking over the bones of her long-forgotten family.

Typical.

Destiny had always hated the bitch. It hadn't been fair that the younger girl had managed to master spells and enchantments that eluded Destiny no matter how often she practiced. And the entire coven had oohed and aahed over the potions she'd brewed. Destiny had been delighted when they realized that Peri was a mage. It not only excused Destiny's inability to magically compete with a mere child, but it meant she had the pleasure of watching her die.

Of course, the bitch had to ruin that. Like she ruined everything. Brenda had barely managed to stab her in the heart when a blast of magic had knocked Destiny senseless. By the time she'd finally managed to clear the fuzz from her brain, Peri was gone.

At the time, she'd accepted Brenda's claim that Peri was dead and her body hidden somewhere on the range. It was good riddance as far as she was concerned.

She should have known she couldn't be that lucky. It was inevitable that Peri would stroll back to the ranch looking liked she owned the place while Destiny was cowering in a pile of hay. She even had a sinfully gorgeous man with her who made Destiny tingle in all the right places.

It also seemed predictable to Destiny that Peri would follow her when she fled the ranch. It was obvious she suspected that Destiny had something to do with the death of the coven.

That's when she'd been struck with the bright idea to try to lose her tail.

She'd pulled off the highway and zigzagged her way through the empty prairie. It didn't occur to her until too late that she was lost.

Annoyed with Brenda for refusing to allow any cell phones on the ranch and with herself for being paranoid, she'd followed lights to a nearby town. It was late enough that the only place open was a shitty bar stuffed with the two things she hated as much as she hated Peri Sanguis. Drunk cowboys and cigarette smoke.

Perfect.

Determined to get in and out as quickly as possible, Destiny had barely walked through the door when she'd been hit by a powerful wave of magic. It had seemingly come out of nowhere. One minute she was waving away the cloud of cigarette smoke and the next her mind had faded to black. After that, she had no idea what happened. Not until she regained consciousness some time later to discover she was hiding behind a dumpster in the alley. That was bad enough, but true terror had slammed into her when she caught sight of the dead woman lying on the dusty ground.

Destiny didn't recognize her, but she looked exactly like the witches after they'd been drained of their magic. Abruptly she understood the truth.

The lethal spell hadn't vanished after killing the coven. It'd remained hidden, and when she left the ranch it followed her.

Why?

Because she'd witnessed its power? Because she knew the secret of where Brenda had gotten the statue that started this nightmare? Because it couldn't bear for one of the coven to survive?

It didn't matter. The only thing Destiny cared about was finding a way to keep the stupid thing from following her.

Creeping around the weirdly silent bar, Destiny had hopped into the van and squealed her way out of town. She hadn't stopped until she'd spotted the remote motel.

Nothing could find her here. But just in case, she'd barricaded herself in the bathroom and wrapped the bathtub in the strongest wards she could cast.

Would she live to see the dawn? The odds didn't feel in her favor.

* * * *

The remote town in the corner of Wyoming had once been a booming location. It'd attracted the local miners as well as the overly opportunistic gold hunters and even a few tourists. There'd been a dozen bars, a large hotel, and a smattering of churches spread among the neighborhoods. Eventually the mines had run dry and the gold hunters had moved on. Even the tourists preferred the lure of Yellowstone. Now Garland was rotting from the inside out, leaving the town center a dead zone, as if it'd been sucked dry by the surrounding scrubland.

Or at least that's what Gabriel had told Valen when Valen had called to warn the vampire that he was returning to his territory.

Strolling past the empty stores and crumbling streets, Valen halted in front of the Jackalope Station. It wasn't much of an improvement from the abandoned taverns they'd passed. If you weren't a local, there would be no way to guess it was still in business if it wasn't for the police tape haphazardly tied in front of the open door.

"This is the place?" Peri wrinkled her nose as she studied the narrow building with its peeling paint and rusty tin roof. There was a large window with the words *Jackalope Station* painted in the center along with some sort of logo that was lost beneath the layers of dirt. "Why would the miasma be attracted to this place?"

It was one of a thousand questions that nagged at Valen. "Could there be a coven nearby that would draw the magic in this direction?"

"Not an official one. My mother wouldn't tolerate competition so close to her ranch." Peri peered through the window, her brow furrowed. "But the bartender was a practicing Wiccan according to her social media."

"She was the target?"

Peri shrugged. "She might have some connection to Wisdom Ranch. Or the statue."

"That feels like a long shot. Unless the magic that destroyed the coven was aimlessly roaming through the prairie and stumbled across this bar."

She nodded. "Probably a case of being in the wrong place at the wrong time. If the attack was caused by the miasma, it might have sensed the bartender and drained her magic."

"Let's interview one of the witnesses." Valen stepped back. "He might be able to tell us about the woman. Or at least share what the miasma looked like and why they decided to start shooting each other."

Peri glanced at him in surprise. "At this hour?"

It was late. So late that this small town had not only been tucked in their beds for hours, but there were probably a few on the verge of waking to begin their day.

"One of them had minor injuries and is currently the guest of the sheriff's department. I'm sure I can convince the deputy to give us access to his prisoner."

"Lead the way."

Valen glanced down the empty street. The air was laced with the usual human scents, but he ignored the rotting trash from a nearby dumpster and the musky scent of the stray dogs who'd scurried away in fear. When he was sure there were no threats, he walked toward the brick building at the end of the block. It was the only business around that had light spilling from the windows.

Peri remained silent as she walked next to him, her expression distracted. Valen could taste her worry as if it were a flavor. Sharp and bitter. She carried the burden of locating the power that murdered her mother's coven and personally making sure it was destroyed.

It pulsed around her with a tangible force.

He didn't bother to reassure her. She didn't need his sympathy. She needed someone at her back who could kick ass when necessary. Fortunately for her, Valen excelled at kicking ass.

Among other things...

Reaching the glass door, Valen pressed the button on the intercom, hearing a low buzz echo through the building. A second later a sleepy voice drifted through the speaker.

"Unless this is an emergency, come back in the morning."

"Open the door," Valen commanded.

"Is this an emergency?"

Valen tilted back his head, gazing directly into the security camera. "Open the door."

"Christ, are you deaf?" There was a pop and crackle as the unseen man shouted into the speaker. "I told you to come back in the morning."

"Humans." Valen grabbed the knob and with a flick of his wrist busted the lock.

An alarm blared, but Valen released a burst of power that jolted through the electric grid, shutting down the annoying sound. At the same time, he stepped into the building and followed the scent of humans down a narrow hallway that opened into a cramped office stuffed with two desks, an old-fashioned filing cabinet, and a plastic plant coated in a thick layer of dust. This was a police department with a budget that hovered near nonexistent.

On cue, a middle-aged man in a tan uniform appeared from what Valen assumed was a break room. He was a head shorter than Valen and three times his width, with a round face pinched with fury as he pointed a handgun in their direction.

"Stop right there." The man licked his lips. "I'm Deputy Anderson of the Garland Sheriff's Department and I'm authorized to shoot you."

"Put down the gun." Valen halted in the middle of the room, motioning the man to lower his arm.

There was a brief silence as the deputy tried to battle against the mental compulsion. A wasted effort. A bead of sweat rolled down the side of his flushed face, but he obediently returned his weapon to the holster at his side.

"Who are you?" the deputy demanded, his voice harsh. "And what are you doing here?"

"You were expecting us, Deputy Anderson," Valen assured him.

There was a long pause. "I was?"

"Yes. We're from the FBI."

"FBI."

"We're here to investigate the shooting."

"Oh. Right, right. The FBI. Gotcha." The suspicion slowly melted away to be replaced with poorly suppressed excitement. "I'm not gonna lie, it's big news here in town. Never had anything like this happen before. We don't have them gangs and hoodlums causing trouble like they do in the city." The deputy hitched up his pants, his chest puffed out. "Not that we don't have plenty of crime, mind you. This office is busy twenty-four seven with one call after another and now the chief suspects we're dealing with one of them Satan cults—"

"You were offering to take us to speak with the prisoner," Valen interrupted.

The deputy coughed, looking embarrassed. "Of course. Sorry about that. It's been a long night interviewing the witnesses and inspecting the crime scene. The sheriff's still in Laramie keeping an eye on a couple of locals who are at the hospital. We still don't know if they're victims or perps. Makes our jobs a lot tougher I can tell you. Well, I guess you already know that, being with the FBI. I bet you have some crazy-ass cases to investigate."

"The prisoner?"

"Oh. Yeah." The deputy moved to unlock a door at the back of the office. "Follow me."

Valen ignored Peri's wry glance as they headed out of the office. He could seal the man's lips shut, but he needed information.

"What can you tell us about the incident at the bar?"

"Not much." The deputy shrugged. "We got a call saying that shots had been fired at the Jackalope Station. Not the first time. That bar is always filled with a bunch of drunks carrying guns. But usually they shoot out a window or take a potshot at beer bottles. They don't kill each other. This time we got there..." The words trailed away as a visible shudder shook the deputy. "We found the place covered in blood and bodies piled on the floor."

Valen maintained a distance from the man as they walked down the short hallway to the steep flight of metal stairs. He didn't fear him. Even without the magic of the Gyre he was impervious to human threats. But he wasn't going to blindly stumble into a trap. Not when it would put Peri in danger.

"You said that you spoke with the witnesses?" He prompted the man to continue his story as they headed up the stairs.

"Yep." The deputy's heavy boots clanged loudly on the metal steps. Valen and Peri moved in silence. "All of them."

"And?"

"They claim that they have no memory of what happened."

Valen frowned. "No memory of the shooting?"

"No memory of anything after a crew from the local stockyard came in and started drinking. It was as if they were in one of those sci-fi movies where aliens come down and scrub away people's memories." The man glanced over his shoulder. "You ain't here because the government thinks this was aliens, are you? Honestly, I hope you are. To me aliens makes more sense than some weird cult."

Valen ignored the question. Let the man believe aliens had visited. He'd sleep better.

"You're saying that not one witness remembers what happened during the shooting?"

"Not a single one." They reached the top of the stairs and the deputy pulled out a key card to open the heavy metal door. "It's a case of mass amnesia."

Valen glared impatiently at the man's back. "That's not rational. There's no such thing as mass amnesia."

"Rational or not, no one is willing to admit what happened at the bar. And I mean *no one.*"

The door swung open to reveal a large room divided by two cells with a narrow pathway between them. At first glance they both appeared empty, but turning to his left, the deputy grabbed the bars of the door and gave it a shake. There was a loud metallic rattle that grated against Valen's nerves. Super hearing wasn't always a blessing.

"Hey, Jerry. Wake up."

A shadowed form lying on a cot at the back of the cell slowly rolled over, the blanket pulled over the prisoner's head.

"Fuck off, Anderson," Jerry called back.

The deputy clenched the bars, clearly intending to give them another shake. Valen reached out to touch his shoulder.

"We can take it from here," he said, the words filled with command. "You return to your office."

The man's beefy features smoothed into a blank expression as he obediently turned and retraced his steps. Like a wooden soldier marching off stage.

There was a stir inside the cell. Had the prisoner finally sensed the danger that prickled in the air? Slowly the blanket was pulled down to reveal Jerry. He was a human male in his early twenties with tangled black hair and a thin face that was pale in the glow from the fluorescent lights.

"What the hell?" Jerry glowered at them as he shoved himself to his feet. He was wearing a sleeveless T-shirt that revealed a dozen tattoos on his arms and worn jeans that hung loosely on his gaunt frame. "It's bad enough to be locked up when I'm a wounded victim." He lifted a hand to touch the gauze taped over the side of his neck. "At least I should be allowed a decent night's sleep."

Valen stepped toward the bars. "Stop talking."

The man took an instinctive step back even as he tried to pretend he wasn't terrified of Valen.

"Who the fu—" Jerry's mouth snapped shut as Valen released a burst of power.

"That must come in handy," Peri mused, moving until she was standing at Valen's side.

Valen sent her a wry glance. "You have no idea." He returned his attention to the cowering prisoner. "Tell me what happened at the bar."

Jerry wrapped his arms around his waist. "You mean the shooting?"

"Start from when you entered the bar." Valen had zero interest in listening to the human ramble, but he needed to nudge the man's thoughts in the right direction as he peered into his mind.

"It was just another night. As usual there was nothing to do in this shithole town so me and a crew from the local stockyard met up at the bar." Jerry's mind was suddenly filled with the image of walking through the door of the Jackalope Station and heading toward a center table where five other men were already several beers deep into the evening. "We drank and pissed away a few hours. Like I said, just another night."

"Clearly not just another night," Valen corrected. "Unless you always end the evening by shooting your companions?"

"Course not."

"Then tell me what happened."

"We were drinking and joking around. I think Martinez passed around a joint..." The words died on Jerry's lips.

"Go on," Valen commanded, startled when the man's memories began to fade. As if they were being obscured by a reddish mist.

Jerry's hands clenched and the veins in his neck protruded as he struggled to dredge up the events of the night.

"I can't," he at last conceded. "Everything went black, and when I woke up the EMTs were there loading people into the ambulance and I was tossed into the back of the sheriff's car." He shook his head, something that might have been genuine regret darkening his eyes. "They said I shot my friends, but that's bullshit. I might punch them in the face, but I'd never kill them. Even if they deserved it."

"Think about the moment right before you passed out." Valen mentally probed against the darkness in Jerry's mind. It wasn't a gaping hole caused by sleep or unconsciousness. It was as if the reddish mist had shrouded the memories, obscuring them from view. Valen had never encountered anything like it. "What was happening?"

"Nothing."

The bars iced over as Valen struggled to contain his impatience. "No one came into the bar?"

Jerry shrugged. "Lots of people."

"A stranger?"

"Here? You gotta be shitting me. Why would a stranger come to this town?"

"You're sure?" Valen pressed.

"I'd remember," Jerry insisted, his thin face flushing. "It was the same stupid crowd of losers. Christ."

Without warning the memories shattered as a tidal wave of emotions crashed over the human. Spinning toward the back of the cell, Jerry hunched his shoulders and covered his face as he burst into loud, gut-wrenching sobs.

Valen broke his connection to the man's mind. Jerry was too busy wallowing in self-pity to think coherently.

"I doubt there's any point in continuing this conversation." He turned toward Peri, who watched Jerry with a frown. "Something's tampered with his memories," he told her. "Could it be magical?"

She considered the question before answering. "There are spells and potions that can cause a human to forget certain events, but none that would erase the memories of so many people at one time." She arched a brow. "Only a vampire has the ability to manipulate human minds."

Valen glanced back at the sobbing man. "I would have seen in his mind where the memories had been erased. These memories were coated in some sort of magic."

He didn't add that a vampire capable of wiping the mind of so many would have been sensed by Gabriel this close to his Gyre. And that the attack would have been an open declaration of war.

Vampire politics were Cabal business. No one else's.

"What if a vampire was infected with the miasma?" Peri demanded, her eyes shimmering the precise shade of turquoise in the harsh lighting. "It might disguise his presence."

It was doubtful. Vampires were immune to most spells and potions. Only one of many reasons they'd earned the right to control the Gyres. Then again, the miasma wasn't normal magic, Valen reluctantly acknowledged. It would be foolish to dismiss a potential threat out of sheer arrogance.

"Do you think it's possible?" he asked.

"Anything is possible."

That was painfully true. "Let's hope that theory stays nothing more than a wild guess. A rogue vampire would be bad enough. A vampire with toxic magic?" Valen's fangs lengthened. He'd been in his current body for several centuries, but his inner demon was ancient. It'd gone through the age of dragons, and later the demon wars that had created a wasteland across the world. He couldn't dredge up the precise memories—they were erased when a vampire was destroyed and reincarnated in a new body—but he retained a stark desire to avoid the bloodbaths that had nearly destroyed his people. "Armageddon."

As if sensing his reluctance to discuss the horror of a crazed vampire on steroids, Peri glanced toward the prisoner.

"Should we ask him about the bartender?"

"I don't think we're going to get anything else out of him tonight." Valen abruptly headed toward the door. He wanted to be away from the human who reeked of stale alcohol and a fear so pungent it soured the air. "According to Gabriel the woman had a small apartment above the bar. We can check there for more information."

Chapter 10

Peri allowed Valen to take the lead as they headed out of the sheriff's office and down the street to the bar. Not because she needed a man in charge. The day that happened, she'd hang up her mage card and retire to a vineyard in France. But she wanted to concentrate on what they'd discovered from the eyewitness.

Unfortunately, there wasn't much to concentrate on. Just that some sort of magic had entered the bar and presumably wiped the memories of over a dozen humans. And that during the magical blackout they'd been infected with a lethal urge to commit violence.

They still didn't know how the magic was moving from place to place. Or why it would be in such a remote location.

Honestly, they didn't even know if it *was* magic. She was assuming that they were chasing the miasma released by her mother, but so far they had no concrete proof. Not unless you counted twelve dead witches and a human massacre…

She shook away the images of corpses that lingered in her mind. Nothing could bring them back. All she could do was try to prevent any future killings.

They reached the bar and Valen halted, his head tilting back as if he was absorbing the sights and smells that surrounded them.

"There's no scent of a vampire. Or a mage. Just humans," he at last pronounced.

Peri frowned. She trusted his assurance that there hadn't been a leech or mage in the area. A vampire's senses were exquisitely precise. It was rumored they could locate every demon in their Gyre by following their scent. Even if they'd disguised themselves with magic. And Valen claimed to have uber senses.

So, if there hadn't been a vampire or mage in the area, who or what else could have attracted the attention of the miasma? There was only one way to find out.

"Let's go inside," she said, brushing aside the police tape to step through the open door. Valen was swiftly at her side, his arm lifting as if he intended to press the switch on the wall. She didn't have his ability to see in the dark, but she didn't need light for her spell. "No." Peri touched his hand. "Leave the lights off."

He stilled, as if caught off guard by her touch. A burst of his raw power spilled over her, sparking shivers of excitement. Peri jerked her fingers away from the cool satin of his skin, forcing herself to cross to the center of the bar.

Valen was a distraction she didn't want. Her lips twisted into a wry smile. Okay, that wasn't true. She'd have to be dead not to *want* the gorgeous male. And even then she might climb out of her grave if it meant quenching her hunger. But she wasn't stupid enough to give into her desire.

Vampires were trouble.

And Valen was the biggest, baddest vampire around. Trouble with a capital *T.*

Kneeling on the floor, Peri pretended she didn't notice Valen move to stand next to her. Instead, she pressed her hand flat on the cement and closed her eyes. Then, clearing her mind, she touched the magic that flowed through her. She sucked in a deep breath as she felt it pulsing in her blood. It was different for every mage. Some claimed the magic was a whisper in the back of their mind. Others said it was like the flutter of a butterfly wing that gently moved through their body. For Peri, the magic was a bubbling cauldron of power. It flowed and churned, demanding to be released.

The power was a blessing. It gave her the ability to create spells and potions that were beyond the capabilities of most other mages. But it wasn't without cost. The magic could be difficult to leash once she released it.

Whispering soft words that would bind the magic to her will, Peri released a tiny tendril of power. The magic shimmered from her fingers, a spiderweb of glittering strands that would be invisible to anyone but another mage. Once the strands covered the entire floor, Peri spoke another word. This time, the magic sank into the surface to reveal the footprints of a hundred different customers.

The outlines of many feet crisscrossed the room in a confusing tangle that made it impossible to follow any one trail, but Peri wasn't interested in where the customers were going. She was focused on the various colors of the footprints.

The lingering auras would tell her exactly who'd visited the Jackalope Station over the past few days.

"What do you see?" Valen demanded, revealing he'd worked with a mage before.

Peri straightened, her stomach twisting into a knot as she continued to study the floor.

"A witch," she breathed.

"The bartender?"

"I don't think so. I see a paler version there. That's the aura of a Wiccan." Peri pointed toward the back of the room where the bartender would have spent most of the night working. Then she moved her finger toward the table that had been toppled during the gunfight. "There was a full-fledged witch standing there. Recently."

Valen was silent a long moment, his tense expression revealing that he understood exactly what Peri was telling him.

"A witch who's connected to the toxic magic your mother released. That can't be a coincidence. Not in this remote area."

His jaw was clenched with anger, but Peri knew it wasn't directed at her. Valen was angry with himself. They'd both missed the most obvious clue.

"Destiny," Peri muttered, glancing around in hopes that the familiar witch would suddenly appear. She didn't, of course. The building was empty beyond the crickets singing in the shadows. Peri shook her head. "I don't understand. Is she hunting the miasma? Or is the miasma hunting her?"

"Or has it already caught her?"

Peri thought back to their brief encounter with Destiny. The witch had been terrified, but that was understandable considering she'd just witnessed her entire coven being sucked dry by some mysterious power. She'd also been anxious to get away from the ranch. Again, understandable.

But Peri hadn't sensed she was trying to deceive them.

She wrinkled her nose as she glanced toward Valen. "If she'd been infected by the magic, wouldn't we have noticed?"

"It might have the ability to disguise its power," he suggested.

"Maybe." It seemed hard to believe that so much power could have remained hidden from both a mage and vampire. "Or it's possible the magic reappeared after we left," she added. "It might have infected her then."

"And instead of going home as she claimed, she came here. Why?"

"She might have been passing by on her way to somewhere else."

"Yes, but why stop? And why come into the bar?"

Peri considered the question. "She must have been searching for something. Or someone."

Valen glanced down. He wouldn't see the outlines of the footprints created by her magic, but he looked as if he was searching for an unseen clue.

"I should be able to detect her," he abruptly announced.

"Destiny?"

He nodded. "Her scent should be here, but it's been overpowered by the stench of human blood."

Belatedly Peri realized that she'd been doing her best to avoid breathing in the thickening reek that filled the bar. It wasn't just blood that was splattered across the floor. With a shiver, she met Valen's steady gaze. Was he wondering if the miasma had caused the violence between the drunken guests in a deliberate attempt to cover its tracks? The thought was unnerving as hell.

"Let's see if we can find some answers in the upstairs apartment."

Valen abruptly turned to head out of the bar, leading her around the side of the building to the steel steps that led to a door on the second floor. Peri followed in silence, not unhappy to be leaving behind the public area of the bar and its floor stained with violence.

The lingering sense of evil was like a palpable taint in the air.

Valen reached the small landing at the top of the stairs and pushed the door. It slid open without resistance.

"Unlocked, but it's doubtful anyone in town bothers to lock their doors," Valen murmured, peering into the dark space. "It doesn't look like the place was searched."

Peri moved to squeeze past Valen, an electric burst of awareness zinging through her as she brushed against his rock-hard body. She clenched her teeth. Being around the vampire was like standing in the middle of a vicious storm. Thunderous power swirling and eddying with the constant threat of being struck by lightning.

Pretending she wasn't acutely aware of the male eying her with a scorching intensity, Peri entered the cramped space and glanced around. The apartment was composed of one narrow room that had a pullout couch under the window and a dresser that doubled as a TV stand. On the far wall a sink had been built into a cabinet alongside a stove that looked like it'd been brought there by the original pioneers. There was one door that led to a miniscule bathroom.

Peri hoped the bartender didn't have to pay rent on the place. It might be an upgrade from sleeping on the street, but not much.

Halting in the center of the apartment, Peri bent down and touched her fingers to the fur rug. With a soft whisper she released her magic, watching it spread across the floor. It didn't take long for Peri to determine the only recent visitor to the apartment was a Wiccan and a human. Probably the bartender's boyfriend. Or girlfriend.

"Destiny—" Peri bit off her words as she moved to search through the dresser. She was jumping to the conclusion that the witch was her former coven mate. A dangerous assumption that would blind her to other possibilities. "Or whoever entered the bar, wasn't up here."

Once convinced there was nothing but clothes and cheap makeup stuck in the drawers, she wandered toward the small altar that had been erected near the north wall. Lifting her hand, she touched the shallow bowls and carved wood statue before moving to the large candle.

"Harmless earth magic," she concluded, turning back to see Valen standing near the doorway. He appeared as icily composed as ever, but she could see a tension in his shoulders that revealed he was on full alert. He was expecting trouble. "I don't see any obvious connection to my mother or Wisdom Ranch," she told him.

He dipped his head in acknowledgment. "It's getting late. We need to return to Denver. We can spend the day with Gabriel and return tomorrow night to continue our search."

Peri stiffened. She'd been too eager to get to this small town and discover what had happened to think about the coming dawn. Even with a helicopter waiting to take them back to Denver, they would never reach Valen's private jet at the airport before the sun started to rise.

"I think I should stay here," she hedged. Spending time with Valen in the search for the evil magic was one thing. Being trapped in some fancy mansion with him and another absurdly powerful vampire? Nope. No way. That was the stuff of nightmares. "It's possible the witch is hiding in the area."

He made a sound of impatience. "You can't face the miasma alone."

Peri narrowed her eyes. "I can't?"

"If you don't succeed in overpowering the witch, then she'll escape. Along with the magic. Worse, the miasma will know we're hunting it." He kept his tone reasonable, as if he wasn't thinking about tossing her over his shoulder and putting an end to the argument. "Isn't it better to wait until we can combine our powers and bring an end to the threat before it can spread more death?"

"Or I can follow the witch to see if it's Destiny and where she's going." Peri kept her own tone reasonable. Kudos to her. "And you can join me when the sun sets."

"Even assuming the witch and the miasma are connected, and that they are both still in town, how would you follow them?" Valen demanded. "On foot?"

He was right, of course. Even if there was a rental company in this tiny town, which was highly doubtful, it wouldn't be open for at least a couple of hours. It didn't make sense for her to remain here. But Peri wasn't in the mood to be sensible, she decided as she walked past him and out the door. A common theme when she was with Valen.

"I'm sure there's a vehicle in town I can borrow," she insisted, jogging down the steps as if she knew exactly where she was going. Ha. She didn't have a clue.

"You mean steal." Valen closed the door and was swiftly beside her as Peri started down the narrow alley behind the bar.

"Steal implies I intend to keep it." Peri picked up her pace. She felt as if she was drowning in her awareness of Valen. She needed a break to clear her mind. "I promise I'll…"

Her words dried up as she caught a hint of movement out of the corner of her eye. Skidding to a halt, she turned to peer through the filthy window of the bar.

Valen was instantly at her side. "Peri?"

"There's someone in there."

Peri stepped closer to the window, studying the crouched form in the middle of the room. Was it a customer who'd returned to find something they'd lost? Or a law official there to inspect the crime scene? No, she quickly dismissed those theories. They would have turned on the lights if they were there for a legit reason.

So what were they doing?

Her silent question was answered when a tingle rippled through the air and familiar strands of magic shimmered across the floor.

A mage.

Peri sucked in a shocked breath. It wasn't loud enough to be heard by the mage inside, but something must have alerted her that she was no longer alone. Surging upright, she turned toward the back of the building. It was dark inside, but the streetlight leaking through the open door bathed the woman in a murky glow. Just enough light to reveal her silver-gray hair pulled into a tight bun and a pale, perfect face dominated by dark eyes.

Lifting her hand, Peri pressed it against the windowpane, intending to snare the woman in a web of magic. She was still creating the spell in her mind when she felt an icy blast of power wrap around her. That was her only warning before Valen was slamming into her, driving her into the ground with enough force to bruise her shoulder.

She would have cursed the aggravating leech if she hadn't heard the distinctive buzz of a bullet passing over her head followed by the shattering of the window where she'd been standing less than a second before.

Shards of glass rained down on Valen, who remained protectively on top of her while ice coated the hard ground beneath her. The vampire was in a mood, and someone was about to die.

"Are you injured?" His lips brushed her ear, his raw scent filling her senses.

"I'm fine."

"Good. Stay here."

He was starting to rise when another blast of gunfire exploded. This time the automatic weapon punched holes in the side of the building and annihilated a nearby trash can.

It would have done the same to them if Peri hadn't released the web of magic she'd been creating to trap the mage. It wasn't a true shield, but it managed to deflect most of the bullets. Valen abruptly cursed and Peri grimaced. Obviously a few of the projectiles had managed to penetrate the web and lodge themselves in Valen's back.

The shooting finally stopped, and Valen flowed to his feet at the sound of wheels squealing as a nearby vehicle raced down the street. He was going to chase after the fleeing bad guys, she abruptly realized.

Feeling a pang of something close to panic, Peri scrambled to stand up and grab his arm.

"No, Valen. They might be leading you into an ambush."

Valen's hands clenched, the temperature dropping to a painful subzero as he battled to contain his fury. He wasn't used to anyone being stupid enough to point a gun in his direction. It was going to take him a minute to contain his savage need for revenge.

"Why didn't I sense them?" he at last demanded.

Peri released a silent sigh of relief as the air warmed. She was going to end up with frostbite by the time they figured out what was going on.

"The woman inside was a mage," she told him. "She must have used a spell to cloak their scents."

Valen's brows snapped together. "You claimed that there hadn't been a mage in the bar."

"There wasn't. Not until now."

"What was she doing?"

"I have no idea." Peri lifted a silencing hand. "Can we just get out of here? I'm exhausted, filthy, and starving. And you're leaking. A sure sign it's time to go."

"Leaking?"

Peri pointed toward the dust-packed ground where blood was pooling near his expensive leather shoes.

"You've been shot."

Valen narrowed his gaze. Did he sense that she was hiding something from him? Probably, but with the rapidly approaching dawn and his injuries, he didn't have the luxury of arguing.

With a muttered curse, he pulled his phone from the front pocket of his slacks and pressed in a number.

"We're headed your way. Have the chopper ready to take off."

Chapter 11

Peri hadn't lied when she told Valen that she was exhausted. She hadn't had a moment's peace since discovering her mother's coven had been slaughtered. Add in the magic she'd expended over the past few days and it was no wonder that she'd passed out as soon as the helicopter lifted off the ground.

It was more surprising that she'd barely stirred when Valen had scooped her into his arms to carry her into a massive stone mansion built in the foothills of the Rockies. And that it was noon before she finally managed to wrench open her eyes to discover she was alone in a bedroom that was four times the size of her own.

Sitting up, she stretched her arms over her head as she admired the heavy, handcrafted furniture that matched the glossy paneling and the overhead beams. It had a ski lodge vibe, she decided as she climbed out of the king-size bed that included a canopy.

She reluctantly ignored the lure of the glass sliding doors that opened onto a balcony that offered a stunning view of the nearby mountains. She wasn't a tourist. She had things to do and people to see.

Grabbing her overnight bag, which someone had kindly left next to the door, Peri headed into the attached bathroom. It was obscenely large, with a shower surrounded by rock walls to give the impression of standing in a waterfall. It was beautiful, but Peri was more impressed with the pounding spray that washed away the layers of dust and sweat that coated her skin. The water pressure was shitty at the Witch's Brew. This felt like paradise.

Eventually she forced herself to step out of the shower and pull on running shorts along with a Green Day T-shirt. Then, slipping her feet into her tennis shoes, she twisted her hair into a messy bun on top of her head. She wasn't worried about how she looked. She wanted comfort and the ability to retreat at top speed if things went south. And since she was intending to confront one of the most powerful mages in the world, it was very likely things would go south in a hurry. Last, she grabbed the worn satchel she'd packed in her bag and looped the long strap over her head. It held several emergency potions along with more mundane items, like her driver's license.

As ready as she was ever going to be, Peri left the privacy of her bedroom and made her way through the maze of hallways. She didn't have to wonder where she was. The power that pulsed through the air felt like she was standing on top of a seething volcano. One that was on the verge of eruption.

This had to be Gabriel's private lair. And somewhere beneath her feet two vampires were safely tucked away from the sunlight.

There were also demons in various locations around the house, but none of them appeared as she entered the attached garage. Strolling past the sports cars and motorcycles that were designed to bloat any man's ego, she continued to the end of the long row, at last reaching an old red pickup that was loaded with bags of dirt, shovels and something that smelled unfortunately like fertilizer in the back. Obviously it belonged to the gardener. She didn't care. It had keys dangling in the ignition.

Jackpot.

Climbing in, she started the motor, wincing as it backfired. The sound echoed through the cavernous garage, loud enough to wake the dead. Literally. Peri cursed, silently willing the dead to remain in their beds. Or coffins. Or whatever a leech slept in during the day.

Half expecting the staff to come running to stop her, Peri put the truck in gear and hit the button attached to the sun visor. Instantly the garage door was purring upward, allowing her to pull out of the garage. She followed the curving driveway past the sunken gardens and marble fountains that spurted water toward the cloudless sky. Beyond that was a vast yard framed by a neatly trimmed hedge that hid the ten-foot electric fence that protected the property from unwanted guests. Not that she could imagine anyone stupid enough to trespass on land owned by the Cabal. Even humans would instinctively avoid this place, although they wouldn't understand why.

Reaching the edge of the lawn, Peri breathed a sigh of relief when the ponderous iron gate swung open. There had to be a sensor on the truck to trigger the lock. Or else there was a hidden servant who'd pressed a button to let her out. Either way, she jammed her foot on the gas and rattled her way down the gravel road toward the nearest highway.

* * * *

Valen stood side by side with Gabriel in his office. The long room was lined with rare paintings that any museum would kill to get their hands on, along with a dozen statues that had once stood in Caesar's palace. It was a glorious showroom, but Valen wasn't there to admire the art. They were staring at the computer monitor arranged on a heavy desk next to the glass wall that was currently covered by heavy shutters.

"There." He pointed toward the dark spot blinking on the map that filled the screen. "The tracker is activated."

Valen nodded. Gabriel had interrupted his rest to inform him that Peri was up and entering the garage. His first instinct had been to follow her and keep her from leaving. As long as the sun burned in the sky, she would be beyond his reach once she left the house. The thought was strangely unnerving.

With an effort, he'd managed to control his rash impulse. Peri wasn't one of his servants who was expected to obey his commands. And besides, he wanted to know where she was heading.

Thankfully, Gabriel had quickly assured him that all his vehicles were linked to his tracking system. He'd also promised to send along protection to keep Peri out of danger.

"And your guards?" he demanded.

"They'll keep close enough that they can rescue her if necessary, but far enough so she'll never know they're there," Gabriel assured him.

"Don't be so confident." Valen glanced toward his companion. The vampire was already dressed for the day in a white silk shirt with the cuffs rolled to his elbows and a pair of black silk pants. His silver-streaked hair was pulled into a tail at his nape, revealing the thin lines tattooed on the side of his neck. In contrast, Valen was still in the silk robe he'd pulled on after his shower when he'd first arrived at Gabriel's lair. "Peri Sanguis is unpredictable, with a pathological refusal to use her common sense."

"Then why allow her to escape?"

"She knows more than she's willing to admit."

"Concerning the deaths of the humans?"

Valen shook his head. Peri hadn't been eager to share what information she had, but she hadn't deliberately lied to him while they'd searched the Jackalope Station.

"I didn't sense her deception until the mage arrived," he said.

"The one who shot you in the ass?"

Valen scowled at his friend, who regarded him with a smoothly innocent expression.

"My back," he corrected in sharp tones. He was still annoyed he'd allowed the humans to sneak so close to them. It didn't matter if they'd been hidden by a magical spell or not. It was the principle of the thing. He had a certain image to maintain. "And yes, the gunman was connected to the mage."

"Could they be working together?"

It was a question that should have gnawed at Valen. It was possible that the mages were secretly using the magic to kill their enemies. Or even that they'd set up a clever ambush to destroy him. How his death would benefit them remained a mystery, but he wasn't without enemies who might have paid them. But he hadn't doubted Peri.

"No. She appeared legitimately surprised at the sight of the mage," he insisted. "I don't think she was expecting her."

"Now you're hoping she's driving to meet with the mysterious female?"

"That seems the most likely destination." His attention returned to the dot on the screen that was headed straight for the nearby highway. "If she wanted to go home she would have called for a taxi to take her to the airport. And if she wanted to return to Wyoming and continue her search for the witch she would have bullied your pilot into flying her back to the bar."

"A woman who knows how to get what she wants."

Valen's lips twisted as he recalled Peri's defiant glare and refusal to back down, no matter how easily he could crush her.

"Without a doubt."

There was a short silence before Gabriel asked the question that had clearly been on his mind since they'd arrived at his lair earlier that morning.

"And what about you, Valen? What do you want?"

"For now I want to discover what evil the coven released into the world." Valen smoothly diverted his companion's attention.

Gabriel grimaced. "No shit."

They didn't have to discuss the dangers of allowing the lethal magic to sweep through the world. So far it'd concentrated on witches and humans, but it was more than likely trying to reach the magic of a Gyre. Once that happened, it would begin feasting on demons.

"Have you encountered a miasma in the past?" Valen asked.

"Several centuries ago. I was in Spain during the Inquisition when a pit of the disgusting magic bubbled up and consumed an entire village. The local mages managed to contain the corrosive pool, but not before it spread its toxic evil to the human population." Gabriel shrugged. "There were some who claimed it was responsible for the plague that swept through Europe."

Valen thought back to his own brush with the mage's bane in London. It sounded similar.

"Did you get close enough to sense the magic?"

Gabriel's elegantly chiseled features settled into grim lines. "I'm not entirely sure."

"Not sure?"

Gabriel took a moment to consider his answer. "I sensed fear and anger and a vast hunger, but at the time I assumed it was the emotions of the humans in the area. It was a brutal time for mortals. In hindsight, I suspect that the heavy sense of doom was caused by the magic."

Valen nodded in agreement. "Peri discovered a fragment of the statue that contained the magic. She was convinced the residue of the miasma was deliberately stirring her emotions to feed off them."

"If it's capable of manipulating emotions, that would explain why the supposed friends at the Jackalope Station would suddenly decide to shoot each other."

"Yes." Valen considered what they'd discovered. It was fragmented, and there were still too many gaps in their knowledge, but he could begin to form a basic idea of the magic. "My guess is that it needs emotions to maintain its essence."

"That makes sense," Gabriel agreed. "But why drain the coven?"

"Perhaps it increases its power with their magic."

Gabriel glanced toward the monitor where the dot had reached the highway and headed west.

"I assume it could also feed on the magic of a mage?"

Valen grasped the edge of the desk, watching ice coat the glossy surface as he struggled to contain his burst of fury. Nothing and no one was going to hurt Peri.

"Let's not find out." The words came out as a bleak warning.

Gabriel dipped his head in acknowledgment. Making sure Peri was kept safe was the top priority.

"My people are scouring the area around Garland, but so far they haven't located any clue that would lead them to the magic."

"If it has infected the witch, then she might have a spell to hide her presence." The ice coating the desk thickened. "Or the magic itself might have developed the ability to conceal itself. We have no way of knowing how it changed and adapted during the centuries it was trapped in the statue."

The frustration sizzling between the two powerful vampires was a tangible pulse in the air.

"So we wait until there are more deaths," Gabriel growled.

Valen nodded toward the monitor. "Unless Peri can discover the location of the magic and lead us to it."

"And then?"

"A good question."

They shared a rueful glance. With so few vampires in the world, and a dozen of them barely over a century old, it meant that the older members of the Cabal were expected to manage any threat to the Gyres. And to protect the demons under their care. It wasn't a duty that came lightly. And the penalty of failing that duty wasn't something either of them were eager to face.

"Do you need to feed?" Gabriel abruptly asked.

He did. After being wounded, it was necessary to replenish his strength. But Valen felt a strange reluctance to sink his fangs into an unknown vein. Why? That was easy enough to figure out. The image of Peri's bold features dominated by vivid blue eyes and sensuous lips scorched through his brain. He wanted her blood on his tongue as her lean, muscular body trembled in his arms. He wanted...

The impossible.

At least for now.

"Yes." The word was wrenched from his lips as Valen forced himself to accept that he would need his powers if he was to battle the evil magic and keep the aggravating mage safe.

Easily sensing his reluctance, Gabriel laid a hand on Valen's shoulder before turning to head out of the office.

"Follow me."

Chapter 12

Peri waited until she reached I-70 before she dug her phone out of the satchel. She had a dozen missed calls. Two from Skye and ten from Maya. She didn't bother to listen to her messages. She knew that her friends were anxious to know what was happening.

Hitting Maya's name on her call list, she put it on speaker and settled the phone on the console next to her.

"It's about time you called." Maya's annoyed voice was loud and clear despite the rattle of the ancient engine. "Why the hell didn't you answer your phone?"

Peri rolled her eyes even as warmth flooded through her heart. She was never going to take Maya's concern for granted. Not after a lifetime of being denied affection.

"Love you, too," she teased.

"Just tell me you're okay."

"I'm fine."

"Are you still in Wyoming?"

Peri glanced out the windshield, admiring the dramatic landscape that surrounded her. She'd forgotten how much she loved the majestic thrust of mountains and the rich scent of pine that perfumed the air.

"No, I'm in Colorado."

There was a short pause, as if Peri had caught the older woman off guard. "Did you destroy the miasma?"

"It wasn't there."

"Do you mean it was never there or that it's no longer there?"

"It was there and then gone." Peri returned her attention to the road. There wasn't much traffic, but she didn't have time to deal with an accident. "I think it either infected Destiny Mason or it's chasing her."

"Destiny?" It took a second for Maya to place the name. "Are we talking about the girl from your mother's coven? The one who survived?"

"Yes."

"Are you following her?"

"I wish. The truth is that I have no idea where she is. There was no sign of her or the miasma when we got to the bar, and none of the witnesses could tell us anything that might help."

"So why are you in Colorado?"

Peri cleared her throat. The next few minutes were going to be tricky. Really, really tricky.

"That's the reason I'm calling. I have a quick question."

"What?"

"Tia's home is near Vail, isn't it?"

Maya knew exactly who she was talking about. Tia was like Cher, she just needed one name to be immediately identified. Tia claimed to be the most powerful mage who ever existed, but Maya argued the woman simply had no morals and a good PR department.

It wasn't a stretch to say the two women hated each other with a passion, although Peri had no idea what had happened between them.

"It's a couple miles south of the Vail Pass."

Peri slowed the truck. She wasn't far from the Pass. "What's it called?"

"Emerald Glade. Typical for Tia. A flamboyant name for a parcel of land stuck in the middle of nowhere," Maya muttered. "Why are you asking?"

Peri hesitated. She'd considered lying to her friend. What she didn't know couldn't hurt her, right? But Peri wasn't stupid. Not only would Maya instantly know she wasn't telling the truth, but if she got into trouble, she needed her friends to know where she was. They were the only ones who could battle against the powerful mage to save her.

"I caught sight of her at the Jackalope Station," she reluctantly admitted.

A shocked gasp whispered through the speaker. "Tia was there?"

"Yep."

Peri had recognized the woman the second she'd glimpsed her at the bar, despite the fact she'd only seen her once before. It had happened shortly after she'd been taken in by Maya and before Skye had joined them. Tia had arrived at the Witch's Brew late one night and cornered Peri in the bookshop. Peri had no idea what she wanted, but Maya had suddenly appeared and forced the older woman into her private office. Less than ten minutes later there'd been the sound of raised voices followed by Tia storming out of the building, her hand lifting as she passed through the coffee shop to release a spell that had shattered the mugs and destroyed their very expensive cappuccino machine. The brief encounter had seared itself into Peri's mind.

She didn't add that Tia had brought along a trigger-happy companion to Jackalope Station. Maya was going to be furious enough without adding fuel to the fire.

"Could she be responsible for the miasma?" Maya demanded.

Peri tightened her fingers on the steering wheel, veering off the highway as she reached the Pass. "I'm about to find out."

"How are you about to find out?" Maya ground out a curse as she belatedly realized what Peri intended to do. "No, Peri, I forbid you to go anywhere near..." Maya's words failed her. Which proved just how much she hated Tia.

"Look, I have to find out what she knows, and more importantly, I have to make sure she doesn't have Destiny and the miasma."

"Wait for me. I'll catch the first flight to Denver."

"I can't wait. She knows that she was seen at the bar. I won't risk having her disappear. Or worse, use the magic before I can stop her."

"You don't understand her power, Peri." There was a fierce urgency in Maya's voice. An urgency that Peri had never heard before. "I might hate the ruthless bitch, but I would never deny that she's the strongest mage I ever met."

"I'm not going to fight her," Peri promised. "I just want information."

"Peri—"

"Sorry, I'm losing you." Peri ended the connection and turned the truck onto a narrow track before stopping and pulling up the map on her phone. Typing in the words "Emerald Glade," she waited for the directions to pop up. She blinked in surprise when she realized she was just a few miles away. "Okay. This should be fun."

Ignoring the nerves that were waging war in the pit of her stomach, she shoved the truck back into gear and bumped her way down the dirt pathway.

* * * *

Maya glared at the phone in her hand, as if it was responsible for the fear thundering through her. Dammit. Peri had always been headstrong, but Maya had tried to give the younger woman the space to make her own mistakes. Not only was it the only way she could learn and grow, but

Peri possessed the sort of power that would protect her from most of her impulsive decisions. But now...

Maya clenched her teeth, unaware of the magic pulsing around her tense body until the door to the office was shoved open to reveal a worried Skye.

"What's wrong?" the younger woman demanded.

"Peri."

Skye pressed a hand to her heart. "Is she hurt?"

"No. She's on her way to confront Tia."

"Tia?" Skye furrowed her brow. "Your nemesis?"

"What?" Maya lifted her hand to touch the scar on her face. Skye had never met Tia, which meant the younger woman had been listening to rumors from other mages. "She's not my nemesis."

"Weren't the two of you besties before she stabbed you in the back and you swore vengeance?"

Maya muttered a curse, refusing to allow the painful memories any space in her head. She'd buried the past. That's where it was going to stay.

"Nothing so dramatic. For a brief time we were partners before she proved that she would sacrifice everything for power. Including me." The words came out sharp as daggers. "She's dangerous and Peri is no match for her."

With stiff movements, Maya made her way around the desk and opened the laptop computer. *Calm, cool, and collected*, she silently reminded herself. That was her motto since opening the Witch's Brew and taking in her companions.

Skye made a sound of impatience. "What are you doing?"

"I'm checking for flights to Denver."

"Oh. Good," Skye breathed in relief, headed for the door. "I'll go pack."

"Skye." Maya jerked her head up, watching her friend disappear out of the office. "Wait!"

The younger mage ignored Maya, scurrying through the bookshop. With another curse, Maya sprinted in pursuit of Skye, managing to reach her as she entered the attached coffee shop, heading toward the back stairs that led to the upper apartments. Reaching out, she grasped Skye's elbow and tugged her to a halt.

"Skye, listen to me."

Coming to a reluctant halt, Skye sent Maya an impatient frown. "We need to hurry if Peri is in danger."

"I want you to stay here and take care of business." She glanced around the coffee shop, which was thankfully empty of customers at the moment. Early afternoon was always a slow time.

"No way." Skye shook her head, her curls bouncing around her flushed face. "Don't you watch horror shows?"

"What do horror shows have to do with anything?"

"Seriously?" Skye rolled her eyes. "Peri went off alone and now she's in danger. If you go after her alone something terrible will happen to you. The buddy system is the only way to stay safe."

Maya stubbornly shook her head. "I need you here."

"I..." Skye's eyes widened, her body tensing as she glanced toward the windows of the shop. "Maya, do you feel that?"

She did. It felt like threads of fire were being woven through the air. It was magic, but it wasn't coming from Skye or her. On impulse she crossed to the door, yanking on the handle. It refused to budge.

"Shit," she growled.

Skye crossed to stand next to her. "What's going on?"

Maya barely heard the words. Skye's face blurred as if Maya was suddenly seeing the world through glasses that were out of focus. Maya blinked, trying to clear her vision. It didn't help. In fact, her friend disappeared as a wave of darkness streaked with blood washed over her.

Peri's blood.

"Maya! Maya, can you hear me?"

Maya blinked again and the darkness faded to reveal Skye's pale face and midnight dark eyes.

"The Benefactor," Maya breathed. "Neither of us is going."

"Bullshit."

Skye turned away, clearly intending to head toward the stairs. Maya once again grabbed her arm.

"We can't. Not without putting Peri in more danger."

Skye kept her back to Maya, but a sudden shiver raced through her body and a soft cry was wrenched from her lips. Maya didn't have to ask what was happening. Her friend was lost in a vision.

Wrapping Skye in her arms, she waited as the younger mage trembled, a tear tracing down her cheek.

"Yes," she at last rasped in a harsh voice. "You're right. We have to stay." Pulling out of Maya's arms, Skye walked toward the stairs, her shoulders slumped and her head bent with weariness. "I'm going to lay down for a bit."

"Okay."

Maya waited until Skye's footsteps faded up the stairs before turning to lay her hand against the door handle. It opened easily.

A violent, irrational fury erupted inside Maya. Unlike many mages, she no longer had to bend the knee to the Cabal. Or trade her soul to gain the power to protect those she loved. But her independence came at a price.

The Benefactor. A hidden power that hovered in the background of her life. His requests were usually simple, if odd. This was the first time she'd deeply resented his interference.

To be forced to stay in Jersey twiddling her thumbs while Peri was in danger...

Frustrated power exploded through her, smacking into the front window with shocking force. There was a high-pitched hum as the glass vibrated from the impact, then the window shattered into a thousand pieces. Maya watched the shimmering shards crash onto the tiled floor.

"Impressive." Without warning, a man wearing a velour tracksuit with a fishing hat appeared in the open window frame. He bent forward to peer down at the pieces of glass sparkling in the late afternoon sunlight like a fractured rainbow.

"Temper tantrum over?" he asked.

Maya struggled to control her anger. "Not necessarily," she warned between gritted teeth.

Joe glanced up, his expression unreadable behind the bushy beard. "You could have turned me into sushi, you know."

Maya didn't bother to point out that the glass had been far more likely to turn *her* into sushi considering very few shards had fallen onto the sidewalk. Instead she marched across the room to grab a muffin from one of the glass coolers. Then, whirling on her heel, she marched back to Joe and shoved it in his hand.

"Here."

Joe peered down at the treat. "What's this for?"

"A going-away present."

"Humph." With surprisingly delicate fingers, Joe peeled away the liner before he shoved the entire muffin into his mouth. He chewed and chewed, smacking loudly. At last he swallowed and loudly burped. "Tastes like goat piss."

Maya clicked her tongue. She tried to be patient with the older man. She didn't know his story or why he was a regular on that particular street, and she wasn't going to judge him for his choices. At the moment, however, she wasn't in the mood to deal with anyone. Not even Joe.

"Go away," she demanded.

A strange pressure abruptly spread around Maya, like the g-force of a jet as it screamed toward the heavens. A grunt was wrenched from her throat as the air was shoved from her lungs, her heart struggling to beat. She fell to her knees, her muscles straining against the pulverizing weight.

There was a sense of movement, and suddenly Joe was bending down to stare at her with eyes that glowed with a green fire so deep and ancient she felt as if she was being sucked into a bottomless vortex.

"The world doesn't rest on your shoulders, Maya Rosen. This isn't your battle." Joe's lips didn't move, but the voice pounded through her mind. "Prepare for what is to come."

Profoundly disturbed, Maya tilted back her head, grimly refusing to turn away from the searing green gaze.

"What?"

In the blink of an eye the power had disappeared, as if someone had flipped a switch. A ripple of magic flowed around her. This time soft and infinitely protective. Maya shuddered, staring at Joe, who was again on the sidewalk, peering through the shattered window.

"I said it tastes like goat's piss."

Chapter 13

It took longer than Peri expected to arrive at her destination. The narrow roads that snaked through the jagged foothills would abruptly halt at a dead end, forcing her to double back in search of a new route. To make things even more difficult, the towering pine trees blocked her view. She didn't know what was coming around the next curve, let alone be able to scan the hills for any sign of civilization.

Dinnertime came and went by the time she managed to navigate the spiderweb of roads and at last reach a high stone fence that stretched the length of the road.

This had to be the place, Peri decided, turning her car into the short drive that ended at a massive wooden gate.

Hmm. Now what? She could climb over the wall, but she didn't want to start off the meeting as a trespasser. Sneaking into someone's house tended to give the wrong impression. Plus she might need the truck for a quick getaway. Okay, there was nothing quick about the ancient truck, but it was marginally faster than walking.

She was debating her limited options when there was a whisper of magic and the gate began to topple backward. Peri made a sound of surprise. Not only at the fact this was all happening way too easily, but at the realization it wasn't a gate, It was a drawbridge.

With wide eyes she watched as it thumped against a cobblestone pathway, bridging a narrow moat.

Who had a drawbridge?

Cautiously driving over the wooden planks, Peri soon discovered exactly *why* there was a drawbridge. Nestled in the shallow valley below her was a sprawling castle that might have been plucked from a glade in Ireland and deposited in the foothills of the Rockies.

The main house was constructed in a perfect square with mullioned windows and a slate tiled roof. There were two wings spreading from the central building like a curtain wall, ending with impressive round towers that would make Rapunzel proud.

Tia either expected to fight off an extended siege or she had a queen fetish. Peri was betting on the queen-wannabe theory.

Grimacing as the truck rattled down the cobblestone drive, Peri at last came to a halt in front of the main house. She was switching off the engine when one of the humongous steel doors was pulled open to reveal a large man. He had to be a guard, Peri decided as she grabbed her satchel and exited the truck. He had the shoulders of a linebacker, bulging muscles that threatened to burst through his too-tight T-shirt and a melon head that was shaved until it gleamed in the fading sunlight.

As she neared she could see the faintest red aura flickering around him. Demon blood, but so weak he would have been at the low end of the social ladder in any Gyre. Almost as low as a human.

Was that why he left? Or had he been lured away by Tia's wealth? His demon blood would make him stronger than any run-of-the-mill mortal. He was also a good foot taller than most people, allowing him to loom over Peri as she climbed the steps to stand directly in front of him.

"I'm Peri Sanguis." She flashed her best smile, inwardly wondering if this was the bastard who'd been recklessly spraying bullets in her direction last night. "I'm here to see Tia."

The guard's expression was stoic, but his jaws clenched as he stepped back to give her space to enter the foyer.

"I'll show you to her office."

Unease curdled in Peri's stomach as she stepped over the threshold. It wasn't just the sensation that she was being swallowed by the looming castle, it was the whisper of power that seemed to brush over her. Like an unseen cobweb. And it didn't help that the male hadn't hesitated to allow her into the house.

She would have been less suspicious if he'd pulled a gun and started shooting, she silently acknowledged. To be given unchallenged access to enter the grounds—and now, to be escorted to Tia as if the older woman was a bank loan manager, not one of the most powerful mages in the world—it meant that this was not only a trap, but that they were confident it was a trap Peri couldn't escape.

If she was a person with the smallest amount of sense, she would flee in terror; instead, Peri calmly glanced around the foyer. She caught a glimpse of dark paneling and a sweeping staircase that led to the upper floors along with...oh my God, was that a real suit of armor standing in a shallow alcove? Before she could inspect the shiny metal man, the guard used his bulk to herd her down a long hallway lined with exquisite tapestries that held the musky scent of age. Peri peered closer at the images stitched on the faded fabric. They seemed to portray ancient battles with angels looking down from the heavens. Had the tapestries been imported from an ancient castle? Or stolen from a museum? Either way, the castle was a goth lover's dream.

They at last halted in front of the door at the end of the hallway, and the guard turned to eye her with a grim expression as he stretched out his arm.

"Hand over the satchel."

"Excuse me?"

"The satchel." The guard snapped his thick fingers. "Give it to me."

Peri arched a brow. She might be impulsive, but she wasn't stupid. There was no way in hell she was giving up her potions.

"I don't think so."

"It wasn't a request." The guard lunged forward as if intending to grab the satchel.

Peri slapped the beefy hand away, her jade bracelet suddenly glowing. "Touch me and you'll be very, very sorry," she warned.

The guard jutted out his square chin. "No one sees the Mistress with weapons."

"Mistress?" Peri snorted. "Are you speaking literally or—"

"Give me the damned bag." The guard lunged again, and with a whispered word Peri released a protective spell. Her bracelet flared and the power flowed through her to smack into the male with more force than she'd intended. No doubt the adrenaline pumping through her added an extra oomph. Whatever the reason, the guard slammed against the wall, the expensive tapestry ripping at the force of his impact. "Argh," the male rasped in fury, battling against the invisible bonds.

"I did warn you," Peri reminded the infuriated guard.

"You bitch." Spittle formed at the edge of the male's mouth, the veins in his thick neck bulging to a size that was alarming. "When I get out of this I'll kill you."

There was a soft whisper as the door behind Peri was pulled open. "You can release him." The female voice was low, but with a razor's edge that made the guard flinch in alarm.

Peri wasn't so easily intimidated. She did, however, release the spell before slowly turning to face the older woman.

"Hello, Tia." Peri pasted a meaningless smile to her lips as she allowed her gaze to sweep over the woman, who was wearing a black, floor-length caftan with gold trim. Her silver hair was smoothed back from her face and twisted into a bun at her nape, emphasizing the stark beauty of her face. "Long time no see."

The dark gaze never wavered from Peri's defiant expression. "You can go, Lynch," she told the guard. "I can handle our guest."

Peri sent the male a finger wave. "Bye-bye, Lurch."

The guard snarled something about "bitches" and "teaching her a lesson" as he stormed away, his boots slapping against the floor with the force of a jackhammer. Once he'd disappeared, Peri slowly turned to meet Tia's unnervingly steady gaze.

"Are you always so rude to servants?" the older woman chided, stepping back to allow Peri space to enter her office.

"Only to the ones who try to maul me. Not to mention taking several shots at me last night. It tends to make me cranky."

"Protecting me is Lynch's number one duty. He was just doing his job."

Peri ignored the chastisement, turning in a slow circle. The whole gothic theme carried into this room, with large arched windows framed with velvet curtains. The walls were hidden behind bookshelves loaded with leather-bound volumes and the floor was covered by a handwoven rug. Overhead a purple-tinted chandelier dangled from one of the heavy beams. Venetian glass, Peri silently decided. And worth a fortune.

"Then I should be rude to you?" Peri drawled, pretending she wasn't impressed by her surroundings. Even if she was certain the writing desk with its scrolled legs and delicate drawers was an original from the fourteenth century. "No problem."

"Don't make me regret my good manners."

Her words were once again edged with that ominous tone. It wasn't anger. One glance in the dark eyes assured Peri that Tia was as cold as a snake beneath the perfect façade. But she was a woman who expected unhesitating obedience.

Peri grudgingly swallowed her snarky words. If the woman wanted to play like they were polite strangers, that was fine with her.

She widened her fake smile. "Sorry."

Tia's eyes narrowed, but waving a hand toward the wooden chair set in front of the writing desk, she moved toward the windows.

"Have a seat." Tia reached the sideboard, where several crystal decanters were arranged on a silver tray. "Wine?"

"No, thanks." Peri wasn't about to eat or drink anything in the house of a potential enemy. "I'm driving."

"A shame. It's my own vintage." Tia poured a glass of deep red wine, lifting it to savor the aroma before taking a small sip. "Delicious."

Peri resisted the urge to fidget. The woman was deliberately emphasizing the fact that she was in command of the encounter.

"I have a few questions," Peri said, watching the woman stroll across the carpet to lean her hip against the corner of the writing table.

"We'll get to those," Tia assured her.

"But first?"

"Has Maya ever discussed our time together?"

More games. Peri swallowed a sigh. "Not really."

Tia sipped more wine, her gaze moving to the small ivory statue of a woman shrouded in flowing robes that was set in the corner.

"We met several years ago. I won't say how many. A woman never shares such secrets. Maya had just come into her powers and attracted the attention of Batu."

Against her will, Peri found herself intrigued by Tia's words. Maya rarely discussed her past. And since Peri had no desire to dredge up old memories, she'd never pressed the woman for details.

"Who is Batu?" she demanded.

"The Cabal leader of Cambodia."

"The name isn't familiar," Peri admitted.

Tia drained the wine in one gulp and lifted her empty glass in a mocking toast. "He died under mysterious circumstances. About the same time the Khmer Rouge was overthrown."

Peri stilled. Was the mage implying she had something to do with the vampire's demise?

A dangerous claim. Although any vampire killed would be swiftly resurrected in a new body, the Cabal took a dim view of people randomly offing their leaders.

"I see."

"Doubtful." Tia set the glass on the desk with a sharp click. "You've never been enslaved by a leech who considers you his property. One who uses you as a weapon against his enemies or a toy to entertain him when he's bored."

"No."

Peri had heard the stories, of course. Back in the Dark Ages, most mages and demons were no more than slaves to the Cabal. And even now there were vampires who considered their people lesser beings with no rights.

"When Maya was…invited to join Batu's household staff, she was still an innocent child." The spicy scent of cloves filled the air. As if Tia was more troubled by the memories than she wanted Peri to realize. "I was the one who protected her. The one who taught her to harness the power in her blood. And when Batu unexpectedly perished, I took her with me and kept her safe."

Peri hid her flare of surprise. She had no idea the two women's pasts were so entwined.

"I'm sure she's grateful."

"I didn't want her gratitude." The dark eyes were as hard as obsidian. "I wanted her loyalty."

Peri studied the older woman. She might not know every detail of her friend's past. She certainly hadn't realized she'd been enslaved by a leech, although it went a long way to explain her willingness to bow to the wishes of the mysterious Benefactor. But Peri was certain that Maya would never abandon the mage who had supposedly rescued her from such a grim fate.

"If you're telling the truth, and you truly protected Maya from an abusive vampire then shielded her after you escaped the leech, you must have done something to turn her against you."

"She's a fool," Tia snapped. "A weak fool."

Peri made a strangled sound. "You have to be joking. Maya weak?"

Tia clicked her tongue with impatience at Peri's blatant disbelief. "Not in magic." The older woman touched the center of her chest, directly over her heart. "In here. She refused to make the hard choices to gain what we all desire."

"And what do we all desire?"

"Power."

Peri deliberately glanced around the office loaded with priceless artifacts. Although Maya refused to speak of Tia, there were plenty of mages willing to whisper that this mage possessed a terrifying amount of magic. And that she had acquired a fortune by using her gifts to manipulate both humans and demons.

"Judging from your massive castle, you seem to have plenty of power," Peri said in dry tones.

A hard smile curved Tia's lips. "For a mage."

"What other power would you want?"

"I want what the Cabal has." The dark eyes flared with a craving that stole Peri's breath. This wasn't ambition. This was a vast, roaring need that Peri suspected would destroy the world before it was sated. "I want mages to rule the Gyres."

Peri frowned. Mages didn't need the magic of the Gyre, but if they wanted to rule the demons, they'd have to take control of the enchanted lands.

"You intend to challenge a leech?"

Tia shrugged, her expression giving nothing away. "Let's just say my ambition has never been small. Unlike Maya."

Peri shook her head. It was no use pointing out that the Cabal would destroy her if she was foolish enough to battle for a Gyre. The woman had obviously allowed her hatred for vampires to send her over the edge of reason.

"Why are you telling me this?" she demanded.

Tia pursed her lips, but she allowed Peri to change the direction of the conversation.

"Do you remember when I came to your cute little coffee house?"

"Hard to forget. Your hissy fit cost us a thousand dollars to repair."

She waved a dismissive hand. "I hoped we could have a private conversation, but of course, Maya rudely interrupted us."

"Why would you want a conversation with me?"

Tia leaned forward, stabbing Peri with her dark, ruthless gaze. "Because you're going to give me the power I need to rule the world."

Chapter 14

Destiny wasn't sure what woke her. Maybe the sound of voices outside the window. Or the thump of music from the room next door.

With a groan, she opened her eyes to discover she was still crouched in the bathtub with the dagger clutched in her hand. She groaned again as she crawled out of the tub and forced her cramped muscles to straighten until she was standing upright.

How long had she been asleep? She glanced toward the window where the sun was fading to a soft, peaceful glow. Night was swiftly approaching. It was time for her to go.

But where?

Slowly turning, she studied her reflection in the mirror. Her lips parted in shock. She barely recognized herself. Her golden hair hung in clumps around her pale face and her eyes were circled by dark shadows and sunken into her skull. She looked as bad as her coven. Like a mummy that'd been sucked dry. The only difference was her heart continued to beat.

At least for now, a voice whispered in the back of her mind.

The continued beating depended on avoiding the evil magic that was following her. But how? She'd hoped to return to her parents' vacation home and forget everything about her life at Wisdom Ranch. But she was starting to fear that there was no way she could hide from the spell that Brenda had released into the world. Even assuming that she could reach the beach house before she was consumed.

Destiny shuddered.

What to do?

The question whirled through her brain, creating a headache that pulsed behind her right eye.

She desperately wished that Brenda Sanguis had never brought that stupid statue to the ranch. They'd all warned the arrogant bitch that it was dangerous to screw around with magic they knew nothing about. But the older woman had assured them that she knew what she was doing.

"I did know."

Destiny gasped at the sound of the familiar voice. It sounded just like Brenda. But no. It couldn't be. Could it?

Destiny swallowed the lump in her throat. She wanted to crawl back into the bathtub and pretend she hadn't heard anything. Or better yet, squeeze through the window and make a run for her van. Instead, she forced herself to step out of the bathroom. She was already fleeing from murderous magic. The last thing she needed was to add in the fear that Brenda Sanguis was haunting her.

She had to prove to herself that the voice she'd heard was a figment of her fevered imagination.

Clutching the dagger in a white-knuckled grip, Destiny scanned the cramped space. She expected to find it empty. It *should* have been empty. But like a vision from her worst nightmare, Brenda was standing between the cheap dresser and the steam radiator that had rusted out years ago.

She appeared exactly as she had when Destiny had last seen her, lying dead on the ground, the white robe pooled around her like a shroud.

Her face was gaunt and her skin was a strange shade of ash. Even her hair was stripped of color and floated around her shoulders like a cloud of gray. Only her eyes, which burned with a blue fire, and the black raven tattoo on the side of her neck maintained any color.

"You aren't real," Destiny muttered, wishing she'd eaten something so she could throw it up. Anything would be better than the sour acid that churned in her stomach.

"Don't be stupid, Destiny. I'm very real."

Destiny shook her head. "You're dead. I watched you die."

"I was temporarily incapacitated," Brenda purred, drifting across the room with a rustle of soft satin. She halted directly in front of Destiny. "An unfortunate side effect of the magic. But now I am fully recovered."

Destiny blinked, glancing over Brenda's shoulder as hope surged through her. Was it possible that she hadn't witnessed a mass killing? That it'd been nothing more than a terrible misunderstanding? "What about the others? Are they with you?"

"No, they are very dead."

"But—" Destiny frowned, reaching out to grasp the woman's arm. How could Brenda be alive if the others were dead? It wasn't fair. Destiny squeezed her fingers, her eyes widening in shock as they passed through Brenda's arm. The coven wasn't the only ones who were dead. "You're a ghost," she breathed.

"A spirit," Brenda corrected.

Wondering when she'd turned into Ebenezer Scrooge, visited by unwanted apparitions and threatened by evil magic, Destiny inched away from the ghost.

"Why are you here?"

"You have been chosen."

"Chosen?" Destiny licked her dry lips. "Chosen for what?"

"Greatness, of course."

"I don't want greatness." Destiny's back slammed into the wall. She'd gone as far as she could. "Choose someone else."

A pool of crimson floated across the woman's eyes. Like blood flowing over water.

"That's not how this works."

"Please, I just want to go home." Destiny fell to her knees, her hands pressed over her heart as she pleaded for mercy. "Please."

"Soon, Destiny." Brenda drifted forward, her hair floating around her ashen face. "But first we have something we must do."

"What?"

The ghost bent down, whispering words that sliced through Destiny's brain, destroying any hope she was going to survive. At least not with her sanity intact.

* * * *

Peri leaned back in her chair, her satchel tucked protectively in her lap as Tia's words echoed through her stunned brain.

Because you're going to give me the power I need to rule the world...

She shook her head. She'd never been overly modest. Not when it was obvious she'd been blessed with a powerful magic that could rival the strongest mages. But she didn't have the strength to take on a leech. Even if she was nuts enough to challenge one.

Which she most certainly wasn't.

No matter how often they might aggravate her.

"How many glasses of that wine have you had?" Peri asked, regarding the older woman with a wary gaze.

Tia leaned back, smoothing the silken material of her caftan. "You don't believe me."

"About what? That I have the sort of power that would allow you to rule the world? Or that you would walk away if you really believed it was possible?"

"The answer to both is that I saw you in a vision."

Peri grunted, as if she'd taken a blow. Being seen in a vision was never, ever good. "You're a seer?"

"Not like your friend, Skye Claremont," Tia said, revealing she'd done her research on Peri. "I don't have visions of the future, but I can interpret dreams."

"A dream teller." Peri had never met a mage with that particular gift, but she'd read books on the rare ability. They didn't have the precision of a seer, but they could see their own future. Something denied to seers. "What does that have to do with me?"

"I saw you."

"In a dream?"

"Yes."

Peri sucked in a deep breath. Or at least she tried. It suddenly felt as if there was an unseen heaviness in the air, pressing against her with a smothering force. Was it Tia? Or a subconscious warning?

Maybe both.

"How did you recognize me in your dream?" she eventually managed to rasp.

"I heard rumors that Maya had discovered a young mage with wild magic thundering through her veins. I wanted to discover if it was true," Tia said. "I traveled to New Jersey to monitor your progress."

Peri grimaced. "You were spying on me?"

"Checking out the competition."

"Same thing." Peri wasn't sure if she was more unnerved by the knowledge that this woman had been watching her from the shadows, or that she was claiming that Peri was a part of her vision. "If you were checking me out then it's no wonder I was in your dreams."

"I can tell the difference between a dream and a foreshadow." The hard edge returned to the woman's voice, as if she was offended by Peri's doubt in her vision.

"Fine." Peri hesitated. She didn't want to know her future. After living with Skye, she'd learned that blind ignorance was a very good thing. But Tia obviously wasn't going to be satisfied until she'd revealed how she was going to rule the world. "What did you see?"

Tia's features softened, as if lost in the pleasure of her vision. "I was seated on a throne and you were standing at my side. We were surrounded by a river of magic. More magic than I ever thought possible."

Peri shook her head. She knew she was more powerful than most mages, but she couldn't produce a river of magic.

"Where was this river?"

Tia shrugged. "That hasn't been revealed. All I know for sure is that it's somehow connected to you."

Peri resisted the urge to roll her eyes. Visions were always vague and open to a dozen different interpretations.

"If you're so sure I'm involved, why would you come to New Jersey then leave without even speaking to me?"

Tia pressed her lips together. "It was obvious that Maya was going to be a bitch about my presence. And the dream had the feel of the future. It wasn't worth a confrontation when my dreams would reveal when I needed your presence."

Peri didn't have to be a mind reader to know the woman was lying. Or at least, she wasn't being entirely truthful. Not that it mattered. She hadn't traveled to this estate to talk about dreams. She was there to discover if this woman had any connection to the miasma.

"Why were you at the Jackalope Station?"

Tia's brows arched at the abrupt shift in conversation. "And I should explain my movements to you because...?"

"One of your goons tried to kill me last night."

Something flared in the dark eyes. "An unfortunate misunderstanding," she said, a sudden tension humming around her.

"An even more unfortunate misunderstanding was that he put a bullet into Valen, the Cabal leader of New York," Peri mused, not surprised that the woman was genuinely aggravated by her trigger-happy guard. Whether Tia killed a vampire in the past or not, she wouldn't want to be connected with wounding the powerful leech. "And between you and me, he's not happy. It would be a shame if Valen discovered who was responsible."

Tia regarded her with a searching gaze. "You haven't told him?"

"Not yet. I'm willing to keep my lips sealed if you tell me why you were at the bar last night."

"Blackmail?"

"A barter," Peri smoothly corrected, not bothering to tell the woman that Valen would easily discover where Peri had been regardless of whether she shared the information.

There was a long pause as Tia considered the various pros and cons of confessing her purpose in traveling to Wyoming. At last a slow smile curved her lips. The sort of smile that sent a chill down Peri's spine.

"I suppose there's no harm," she murmured. "I had another dream. This one just a few nights ago. You were in it again, but this time I wasn't seated on a throne. I was standing in the middle of a prairie surrounded by rabbits. I had no idea how to interpret the vision. Not until I happened to see a news story about the shooting at the Jackalope Station. I knew immediately what happened there was important to my future."

Peri shivered, wishing the woman would stop including her in her dreams. It was weird.

"Why go there in the middle of the night?" she asked.

"I was hoping to avoid interruptions."

Peri accepted the explanation. When she'd caught sight of the woman through the window it had appeared she was preparing some sort of spell. It was always easier to do magic without the annoyance of distractions.

"Did you discover anything?"

Tia narrowed her gaze. "That's what you're going to tell me."

Peri frowned in genuine confusion. "How would I know what you found?"

"How did you discover the miasma?" Tia demanded. "The mages who trapped the magic were ordered to destroy the vessels. I'd heard through the grapevine that some of them survived and were hidden away, but I never believed the rumors. Not until last night."

Peri's heart missed a beat. They'd suspected it was the evil magic that had caused the deaths at the bar, but they couldn't be certain.

"How do you know it was the miasma?"

Tia blinked, as if it was a stupid question. "I could feel the vibrations of its passing. Nothing else could have left behind such an intense residue of power. It's..." Words seemed to fail her. Then she squared her shoulders, her features hardening with a sudden determination. "Honestly, I could barely believe what I was sensing. It's been gone from the world for so long I never dared to hope it might return. Where did you find it?"

"What makes you think I found it?" Peri hedged, not certain how much she wanted to reveal.

"You will answer my questions," Tia insisted, allowing a thread of magic to shimmer around her in an unmistakable warning. "One way or another."

Peri grimaced. She wanted to dig in her heels, just to prove she wasn't scared of the older woman, but logically she knew it wasn't worth the pain. Unless Tia was the world's best actress, it was obvious that she hadn't known about the miasma until she'd sensed it at the bar. It was also obvious she knew more about the ancient magic than Peri. She needed to learn as much as possible about the nasty stuff.

"I didn't release it," she told the woman. "My mother did."

"Ah. The massacred coven." A slow comprehension spread over Tia's face. "I should have realized there was a connection. Where did your mother find the magic?"

"I have no idea. Only one of the coven survived, and she said my mother returned to the ranch with a statue in the shape of an owl."

"A survivor? Where is she?"

"We left her at the ranch," Peri said, not about to reveal that they suspected Destiny was connected with the evil magic. "She said something about returning home."

Tia hesitated, easily sensing that Peri wasn't being entirely truthful, but she didn't press for more information. No doubt she had a dozen servants to go in search of the missing witch.

"How did the magic travel from your mother's barn to the Jackalope Station?"

"Another question I can't answer," Peri admitted, turning the questions back on her companion. "Can the magic take a human form?"

Tia's brows snapped tighter. "I never considered the possibility." Her frown deepened. "Are you suggesting it has become sentient?"

When Tia said the words out loud they sounded ridiculous. Magic was an extension of the mage or witch. Like a sculpture creating a work of art out of a lump of clay. It wasn't a living, breathing creature.

Of course, the miasma was created from raw emotion, not an actual spell or potion. No. Peri wrinkled her nose. It still seemed implausible.

"Not really. I'm just thinking outside the box."

"Hmm." Tia shook her head. "It seems...doubtful."

"Can the miasma infect someone?" She asked the second question preying on her mind.

Tia narrowed her eyes. "Why are you asking? Do you think the miasma has invaded the body of someone? Perhaps the missing witch?"

Peri surged to her feet. She shouldn't have revealed her suspicions. Not to a power-hungry mage who acted as if the return of the miasma was something to be celebrated, not treated as an epic disaster.

"I don't know what happened or how it could have gotten to the bar."

"Then why were you there?"

"It destroyed my mother. I'm trying to keep it from harming anyone else."

"Very noble." Tia's tone was mocking. "And Valen?"

"The same."

"Where is the magic now?"

Okay. Enough. She wasn't going to get the answers she'd hoped for, and worse, she'd revealed more than she should have. Definitely a lose-lose encounter.

"I don't know. Not yet. But I intend to find it and send it back to the hell it came from." With stiff movements, Peri crossed the room. "A pleasure to meet you."

"Where do you think you're going?" Tia demanded sharply.

"Anywhere I want."

"I don't think so."

Peri halted, slowly turning to face the older mage. "Excuse me?"

There was a strange glitter in the dark eyes. "The miasma is the magic in my dreams," Tia hissed. "It has to be. There's nothing that can equal such raw power. Not even a leech."

Peri stared at her in disbelief. It was one thing to be in awe of the power of the miasma. It was a whole other thing to think it could offer more than a painful death.

"It can't be controlled."

"Of course it can. Anything can be controlled with the proper restraints."

"You do know that it was called mage's bane, right?" Peri asked. "It was used by demons to murder magic wielders."

Tia sniffed. "I am aware of the dangers."

"No, you're not." Peri's voice was hoarse as a tidal wave of emotions threatened to overcome her. Grief. Anger. Fear. "You didn't see a dozen women who'd been sucked dry of their magic. They looked like zombies. As if their very essence had been stolen. It was awful."

"Witches." Tia waved her hand in a dismissive gesture. "They were helpless to contain the magic. I won't be so foolish."

Peri shook her head. The woman was clearly delusional. No wonder Maya had walked away and never looked back.

"You won't get the chance. I'm going to destroy it."

As if she could read Peri's mind, Tia narrowed her gaze in warning. "Don't make the same mistake as Maya."

"What mistake?"

"Allowing your misplaced sense of grief to overrule your opportunity for greatness."

"What's great about letting an evil tide of magic kill innocent people?" Peri scoffed.

"Once the magic is in my control, I can ensure that no innocents are harmed." Tia held out her hand. "Join me in my quest."

"I don't think so." Peri whirled around and continued toward the door. Did the older mage truly think that Peri was stupid? Anyone willing to try to tame a malevolent power that had destroyed hundreds of mages over the centuries would most certainly sacrifice her the second she no longer needed her. Reaching the door, she grabbed the knob and turned it. Or least she tried to turn it. She muttered a curse as she realized it was locked. Reluctantly, Peri glanced over her shoulder. "Do you mind?"

"I do, as a matter of fact." Tia walked to the center of the room, the silk of her caftan clinging to her lush curves. "My vision included the magic. And you. I don't know where the miasma is currently located, but I do know where you are." The dark gaze bored into Peri. "I have every intention of keeping you close until my dream is fulfilled."

"You're holding me captive?" Peri glared at the older woman, more angered than frightened by the threat.

"You can be a guest. Or a prisoner," Tia countered. "The choice is yours."

Peri made a sound of disgust. "The only thing worse than having that… nightmare crawling through the world randomly killing innocent people is the thought of some egomaniac using it to fuel her delusional dreams of grandeur."

Peri turned back to the door, her fingers wrapped tightly around the knob as she considered the quickest means to bust through the lock.

"So be it," Tia breathed.

Chapter 15

Prickles of magic crawled over Peri. A silent warning that her companion was casting a spell. Accepting she was going to have to fight whether she wanted to or not, Peri shoved her hand into her satchel and pulled out a small vial. Then whirling around, she faced the woman who was sweeping her arm over her head to launch a spell.

There was a loud sizzle as the magic flew toward Peri, the scent of cloves thick in the air. Instinctively she tossed the vial toward the incoming magic. Even at a distance she could sense Tia's impressive power. More power than she'd encountered in a mage before. If it hit her she would be incapacitated for several hours. If not days.

She couldn't let that happen.

Pressing her back against the locked door, Peri braced herself as the vial crashed against the magic. The potion inside the vial wasn't particularly dangerous. It was a simple blinding spell that she kept with her in case she needed a quick escape, but Maya's special talent in brewing the potion along with her own innate strength gave every vial an extra oomph.

The resulting collision of magic was just as shocking as Peri had anticipated. The vial burst into a thousand shards, the tiny projectiles shooting through the room.

Peri felt one slice through the tender flesh of her cheek and another imbed in her upper thigh, but she ignored the pain. Despite the explosion, the potion had done its job, cloaking the room in an inky darkness. This was her opportunity to escape.

Or that was the plan.

She'd taken a half dozen steps when a reddish glow appeared and slowly expanded. Peri shifted her gaze toward Tia, who was standing in the center of the room, surrounded by a halo of magic. The orangish hue pulsed around her with an eerie light, giving the impression the silver-haired woman was standing at the gates of hell, preparing to drag Peri down to the fiery depths.

A melodramatic reaction to a simple spell, Peri acknowledged, but she was happy to indulge her apprehension. Tia was a merciless opponent. The second Peri underestimated her would be the second she found herself locked in the dungeons. And she had no doubt there were dungeons. No castle would be complete without them.

Maintaining the glowing spell, Tia once again lifted her arm, preparing to launch another attack.

Peri dipped her hand back into the satchel, desperately searching through the vials. She'd trained with Maya to defend herself against a magical attack, but Peri knew she was no match for Tia. Not only did the older woman have centuries of experience using her powers, but there was a ruthlessness to her that Peri didn't possess. She might like to think she was a badass, but she wasn't a stone-cold killer.

A head-to-head battle was certain disaster.

So if she couldn't be stronger, she had to be smarter.

At last her fingers wrapped around the one vial that was hot to the touch. Yanking it out of the satchel, Peri boldly stepped toward her companion. Tia's brows arched, as if she was caught off guard by Peri's audacity. Or maybe she couldn't believe anyone would be stupid enough to challenge her.

Peri smiled, inching closer. It wasn't until she could see Tia's fingers twitch as she prepared to release her spell that Peri whirled to the side and hurled the vial against the bookcase. Immediately the potion inside burst into flames.

Tia made a strangled sound as the fire spread over the heavy shelves and began to consume the leather-bound books.

"What's wrong with you?" Tia gasped, for the first time revealing a genuine emotion as she watched the destruction with an expression of horror. "Those are first editions. They're priceless."

Peri kept her mouth shut, not willing to draw attention to herself as Tia rushed toward the shelves and started muttering a hasty spell to squelch the fire.

Silently she backed away, her gaze never leaving Tia as she reached out her hand to fumble for the chair she'd been sitting on minutes earlier. There was no point in trying to force open the door. That left her with one possible exit.

Grabbing the top of the chair, Peri lifted it with a low grunt. She was stronger than any human and even a few demons, but the chair had been built back in the day when craftsmen took pride in producing a sturdy piece of furniture. The thing weighed a ton.

Peri gritted her teeth, hauling the chair toward the nearby windows. Then tightening her muscles, she managed to lift the chair and heave it into the glass.

The large window didn't shatter. It was obviously protected by the runes carved into the wooden frame, but the chair was heavy enough to punch a hole in the lower half of the pane.

Peri didn't hesitate. Dashing forward, she leaped through the small opening, picking up a dozen more cuts as the jagged glass scraped her exposed skin. She landed on her hands, cursing as the impact jolted up her arms. Maybe she should have taken more time to consider her impulsive trip to confront Tia, she conceded, scrambling upright and glancing around to get her bearings. To the left was a pool and fancy pool house that was twice the size of the Witch's Brew. Straight ahead was a sunken garden with trimmed hedges that looked like a maze. And to the right was the long wing with the circular tower. Thankfully, there was an arched opening that led to the front of the castle.

Grimacing at the smoke billowing out of the broken window, Peri hurried toward the passageway. Tia would eventually finish putting out the flames and she wasn't going to be happy. Peri suspected it would be a wise decision to have several miles between them.

She'd managed to make it through the opening and was angling across the manicured lawn toward the driveway when a large form abruptly stepped directly in her path.

Peri grunted, ricocheting off the rock-hard body. Stumbling backward, she managed to regain her balance and glanced up. And then glanced up some more. The guard wasn't the same one who'd greeted her when she'd first arrived at the castle, but he was just as large with the faint aura of red. Another demon.

Great.

"Stop right there," he barked, holding up a large hand.

"Yeah, I don't think so," Peri muttered. "Places to go, people to see. You know the drill."

"What drill?"

Peri stepped closer, acting as if she intended to walk around the hulking guard. As expected, he lunged toward her and Peri danced to the side. She had another potion in her satchel, but she didn't want to use all her ammunition. Not until she was certain she wasn't going to have to face Tia again.

The guard moved to block her path. "Stand still."

"Make me."

His bulldog features flushed as he made another lunge, only to have her easily skip away.

"Don't piss me off," he snapped.

Peri rolled her eyes. "Or what?"

"This."

He lunged again and Peri dodged backward. He followed, his movements awkward, but relentless. She was wasting too much time, she silently acknowledged. Tia was going to come in search of her. Or at least send her guards to stop her from escaping.

It was now or never.

Flashing a mocking smile, Peri spread her arms wide. "Are you an actual guard?" she taunted. "Or does Tia pay you to strut around flexing your muscles?"

"Bitch," he spit out, curling his hands into fists as he took a massive swing at her face.

Peri easily bent backward, avoiding the blow that would have fractured her jaw, and whispered the words to a spell. The magic tingled through her blood, warming her skin and heightening her senses to the edge of pain. It was intoxicating. She never felt so alive as she did when she called on her powers.

Of course, there was a downside, she acknowledged, wrinkling her nose as she caught the stench of sweat coating the guard's face and a blast of garlic from his panting breaths.

Her bracelet glowed, and with the final word of power she sent the magic toward his feet, which were spread wide as he prepared to take another swing at her. The spell flowed through the air, creating a silvery web that laced over his feet and solidly glued his boots to the ground.

The guard was unable to see the spell, but he'd lived with a mage long enough to realize what had happened when he couldn't move.

"You stupid witch," he ground out, obviously aware that "witch" was the worst sort of insult to a mage. "I swear I'll hunt you down and teach you what happens when you screw around with a real man. I'll have you on your knees with my dick stuck so far down your throat—argh."

The piercing scream echoed through the foothills as Peri calmly stepped forward and kicked the dick he was so proud of with enough force to make his eyes cross.

"I was going to walk away, but you threaten a woman again and I'll shrink your balls so small you'll need a microscope to find them."

She didn't bother to wait for his response. Honestly, it was probably going to be an hour or so before he could speak coherently. Instead she strolled toward the ancient pickup that was still parked next to the front steps, where a tall, slender male casually leaned against the front grill.

Peri's heart lodged in her throat, but not from fear. It was raw female appreciation at the purity of the male's flawless features, the shimmer of gold in hair that was as smooth as silk, and the sleek muscles beneath the tailored black slacks and soft cashmere sweater. He looked too perfect to be real. As if he was a fantasy created out of mist and moonlight.

But there was nothing mystical about the power that pounded against her with shattering force.

Peri hissed, refusing to allow her feet to falter as she crossed the driveway to stand directly in front of the vampire.

"Valen."

The silver gaze made a slow inspection of her various scrapes and bruises before slicing toward the guard, who was bent over, throwing up whatever he'd had for dinner.

"Are you done playing?" he drawled.

Chapter 16

Valen watched Peri stride toward him, her chin held high despite the blood that dripped from several nasty wounds. Her hair was tangled and she had a small limp, revealing she'd been in more than one fight since he'd last seen her.

Clenching his fangs, he forced himself to remain leaning against the truck. Just as he'd forced himself to remain outside the castle and wait for Peri to appear. She'd gone to a great deal of effort to make sure that he wasn't involved in her journey to this remote location. He assumed she had a legitimate reason.

At last reaching the vehicle she'd stolen from Gabriel, she sent him a wary glance.

"You could have helped, you know."

Valen arched a brow. "Did you need my assistance?"

Her aggressive expression eased. Whether it was from his acceptance that she could take care of herself, or relief that he hadn't read her the riot act for disappearing, was anyone's guess.

"No." She walked past him, her eyes widening at the sight of the three guards neatly piled near the steps leading to the front door. "Are those yours?"

"Yes."

Valen slid into the passenger seat as Peri climbed behind the steering wheel and switched on the engine. The guards had been prowling the grounds when he'd first arrived. Sensing their demon blood, Valen decided that he didn't want them challenging his right to wait for Peri and incapacitated them before they even realized they were in danger. They would survive, although it would be several hours before they woke.

"Impressive," she murmured.

"Not really." He kept his expression smooth, attempting to pretend he didn't notice the warm surge of pleasure at the soft word. "I can be far more impressive."

"How did you get here?"

"There's a helicopter waiting just a few miles away."

His gaze traced the pure lines of her profile as the dilapidated truck bounced and swayed up the cobblestone driveway before rattling over the lowered drawbridge.

He didn't mind riding in the passenger seat. He was a member of the Cabal. The most lethal predators in the world. He didn't need to oppress others to prove his authority. And if driving gave Peri the illusion of control, then it would make their time together run smoother.

Or maybe he was deluding himself that he was in command, he wryly acknowledged.

Slowing, Peri waited for Valen to point toward the west before she pulled onto the narrow dirt road and pressed the gas pedal.

"Why did you come here?" he demanded.

There was a short silence. Was she deciding how much to reveal?

"I recognized Tia when I caught a glimpse of her in the bar," she finally confessed, her voice terse.

"Tia." Valen had heard of the mage, of course. The Cabal kept a close eye on her. Not just because she was a powerful mage and a collector of rare magical artifacts, but because she made no secret of her hatred for vampires. "That explains the over-the-top castle and demon guards."

Peri released a sharp laugh. "She's a little flamboyant."

"Is she a friend of yours?"

"She's a psychopathic overachiever who intends to use the miasma to rule the world."

Valen stiffened. He'd hoped that Peri had traveled to this location because she recognized the intruder in the bar. And that person could give them information about the evil spreading through the area. What they didn't need was the dangerous magic to be in the control of a powerful woman with a grudge against the Cabal.

"She captured the miasma?"

"No, but she's a dream teller and she had a vision the magic would put her on some mystical throne."

Valen narrowed his eyes. There was obviously no love lost between the two women, but now wasn't the time to pry into their relationship. They needed to concentrate on keeping the magic out of Tia's greedy hands.

"What else did she see?"

"A lot of nonsense." Peri snorted. "But she did see enough to know that the power she's been chasing passed through the Jackalope Station. That's why she was there."

Valen didn't have much faith in dream tellers. The visions they offered were too vague and open to interpretation. He preferred cold logic to mystical imaginings. Still, she might have some insight into what the magic was seeking.

"I don't suppose she saw where it's going next?"

Peri shook her head. "Not that she shared with me." She sent him a warning glance. "We have to destroy it before she can do something to make this shit show even worse than it is."

"First we have to locate it," he reminded her.

She returned her attention to the road. "I've had a few thoughts about that."

"Tell me."

"Since we have no idea where the miasma is or where it's going, maybe we should go back to where it came from."

She couldn't mean the beginning of the miasma. They had no idea where it originated. Or how long ago.

"The ranch?"

She nodded, the moonlight slanting through the windshield shimmering against the dark, glossy curls that had escaped from her braid to spill down her back.

"My mother must have left behind some indication where she found the statue."

Valen considered the possibility. She was right. The statue had to have come from somewhere. It wasn't created by Brenda Sanguis or her coven. Which meant that she had to have talked to someone who told her where to find the statue and then traveled to buy it. Or more likely barter for it.

Somebody knew something.

"Did she have a computer?" he asked.

Peri shook her head. "My mother refused to have any technology beyond a vehicle and a generator. She insisted electronics interfered with her magic."

Annoyance surged through Valen. He wasn't one of those immortals who yearned for the Dark Ages. He fully embraced modern technology and the convenience it offered. Especially when it came to keeping digital surveillance on potential enemies.

"Then what do you hope to find?" he asked.

"I'm not sure. A receipt. Or more statues." She heaved a harsh sigh. "Honestly, it's probably just another wild goose chase."

"It's worth a try." He pointed toward the nearly hidden pathway just ahead. "Turn right. The helicopter is at the bottom of the hill."

She followed his direction, slowing as they swayed over the dips and mounds that threatened to destroy the ancient suspension of the truck.

"How did you find me?" she abruptly asked.

"There are trackers on all of Gabriel's vehicles."

Her lips twisted. "I should have guessed."

Valen studied her profile, his nerves still raw from the hours he'd been forced to pace the floor, waiting for the sun to set.

"Why did you feel the need to slip away when you knew I couldn't follow?"

Her fingers tightened on the steering wheel turning her knuckles white. "Tia is an arrogant bitch, but even she knew she screwed up by allowing one of her guards to shoot a vampire. No one wants to be hauled in front of the Cabal for attempted murder." She shrugged. "I hoped I could use the situation to blackmail her into confessing why she was at the bar."

There was enough truth in her words to convince him that was part of the reason she'd slipped away. But not the full explanation.

Would she ever trust him?

Valen abruptly realized that the answer to that question was more important than he wanted to admit.

"Did your blackmail work?"

She sent him a wry grimace. "Does it look like it worked?"

Valen clenched his hands. He'd done his best not to dwell on the injuries, which continued to leak a small trace of blood. Not only because the intoxicating scent was stirring his most primitive hungers, but the thought that she'd been attacked and injured infuriated him.

"You can park here." He nodded toward a patch of ground that had been cleared of undergrowth. Ahead of them the sleek helicopter was shrouded in darkness. "One of Gabriel's staff will return it to the estate." He watched as she leaned down to shut off the engine and grab her satchel. But before she could push open the door, he leaned across the console and touched her arm. "Wait."

She glanced toward him in surprise. "Is something wrong?"

He held out a slender hand, placing it over the wound on her cheek without touching her.

"Can I?"

She knew what he was asking, and how rare it was for any vampire to offer his healing to anyone. Even those closest to them. At last, she offered a wary nod.

Holding her gaze, Valen lifted his index finger and pressed it against his extended fang, piercing his skin. A drop of blood bloomed and, with care not to hurt her, he rubbed it over the cut. Instantly the flesh pulled together, knitting the cut so smoothly there wasn't a trace of a scar. Peri's sweet, floral scent flooded the air as his hand slowly lowered and he slid his finger beneath the hole sliced in her jeans, pressing against the wound. She winced as the piece of glass still stuck in her flesh was pushed out, but it wasn't pain that darkened her eyes as he sealed the cleaned cut.

Desire in its purest form sparked and flared to life, weaving them together with a compulsive hunger.

Eventually, that hunger would have to be sated.

But not tonight.

His hand moved to a scratch on her upper arm as he studied her wary expression. "I don't suppose you would listen if I asked you to avoid any future solo missions?"

Her brows furrowed at his simple request. "I'm used to solo missions."

"Me too." Vampires were by nature remote, isolated creatures. Valen considered being alone a rare gift, not a punishment. Until Peri. "But for now we have each other. We should take advantage of our partnership."

Her wariness deepened. "Take advantage?"

"You have many special talents. I have a few of my own. Together we make a formidable team."

"I'll...try."

Valen's lips twitched. She'd nearly choked on the word. "That's all I ask."

"We should go." Peri tugged her arm out of his grasp, her defensive shield sliding firmly back into place. "Tia's going to come looking for me."

Valen's gaze moved to the spot on her cheek that he'd recently healed. "You haven't told me why you came out of Tia's castle covered in scrapes and bruises. Or why she would come looking for you."

"She wanted me to stay and I wanted to leave." Peri shrugged. "So I set her library on fire and jumped through the window. Unfortunately, it was closed at the time."

Valen narrowed his eyes. "Why did she want you to stay?"

Peri hesitated, clearly not wanting to share that tidbit of information.

"She glimpsed me in one of her stupid dreams," she grudgingly spit out. "She has a mistaken idea that I might help her achieve her goal of world domination."

The temperature dropped until he could see Peri's breath in a cloud of mist. He wasn't unsettled by Tia's arrogant ambition. They'd always known the mage was desperate for power. He was furious at Tia's belief that Peri's future was in her hands.

"Do you want me to deal with her?"

Peri sent him a startled frown, as if sensing he would return to the castle and destroy the mage without hesitation.

"No. I just want to find the miasma and make sure it doesn't cause any more trouble."

"Then let's go."

For the first time in centuries, Valen gave in to a mindless impulse.

Lowering his head, he pressed his lips against her parted mouth. Valen jerked in shock as her sweet taste hit his tongue with explosive force, pleasure scouring through him. His fangs lengthened in glorious anticipation. It was a kiss. Just a kiss. But it was so much more.

A shiver raced through him. Or maybe the earth shook. Either way, there was a soul-deep certainty inside him that nothing would be the same.

"Valen."

His name left Peri's lips on a shaken sigh. As if she was equally shocked by the intensity of the light caress. But even as his hands moved to cup her face, the sound of the helicopter firing up its engine shattered the moment.

Lifting his head, he peered down at her eyes, which were shadowed with a passion she was struggling to hide.

"All healed," he murmured, refusing to dwell on his fierce compulsion to wrap her in his arms and refuse to let her go. Peri had been an unsettling distraction from the moment she first arrived in his territory.

With movements that felt oddly stiff, Valen opened the door to the truck and slipped out, waiting for Peri to join him before bending low and jogging toward the waiting helicopter. Within minutes they were strapped in and soaring toward the star-spackled sky, headed back to Wyoming.

They were seated side by side, his thigh pressing against the delicious warmth of her body. She ran hotter than a normal human. Even hotter than most demons, he realized with a flare of surprise. As if the magic was a fire burning inside her.

Not entirely sure what that meant, if anything, Valen was distracted when Peri wiggled in an effort to put space between them.

"I suppose I owe Gabriel an apology for borrowing his truck."

Valen settled back in the leather seat, pleased by her wiggles. It meant that she was well aware of the sparks of desire that continued to sizzle between them.

"I'll admit there aren't many who would dare to steal the property of a vampire," he drawled.

She clicked her tongue. "Borrowed."

"Is there a difference?"

"I did intend to return it." She shot him a sideways glance. "Is he angry?"

"Worried."

"About the truck?" She snorted. "Nothing could destroy that thing."

"About you," he corrected. "He knows it would trouble me if you were injured. Or worse."

"I..."

"Speechless?"

She turned her head to gaze out the window as they soared toward the north. A clear indication she didn't want to discuss whatever was growing between them.

"I assumed vampires never cared about anyone but themselves."

"It's a reputation we enjoy promoting."

She released a soft breath, as if she'd been holding it. "The aloof lone wolf?"

"I'd rather not be compared to a dog."

Turning back, she eyed him with an unreadable expression. "The Lone Ranger?"

"Can I at least be Batman?" he demanded. "The mysterious hero tragically forced to protect his people from the shadows."

She stiffened, her eyes widening. "Oh my God. You have a sense of humor."

"Why is that so shocking?"

"You're...Valen." She lifted her hands as if his name explained everything. "Prince of Darkness."

"Just Valen," he corrected.

She continued to stare at him, as if seeing him for the first time. And maybe she was. Not as a powerful member of the Cabal. Not as the ruthless leader of the Gyre. Not as an immortal.

But as a male who wasn't so different from herself.

"Have you always been alone?"

"I've had companions, but during this resurrection I haven't chosen a mate."

She tilted her head to the side, her glossy hair spilling over her shoulder. "Is it rude to ask how old you are?"

"Two thousand years, give or take a few decades."

"That's a long time to be alone."

Suddenly Valen felt the weight of those two millennia pressing against him as a yearning bloomed in the center of his soul.

"A very long time."

Chapter 17

Peri walked onto Wisdom Ranch through the gate that hadn't been locked. There was no sign that the police had been back to investigate the deaths, or even to protect the belongings that had been left behind. Not that there was much to steal, she wryly acknowledged. The witches had lived a simple life with few luxuries. Still, it was annoying to realize that their murders had been dismissed so easily.

Lost in her troubled thoughts, Peri was caught off guard when Valen grasped her arm to pull her to a halt. Lightning streaked through her at his touch, sparking that awareness she could no longer pretend was irritation. She clenched her teeth, reminding herself why they were there.

It was as good as a cold shower.

She sent him a frown. "What's wrong?"

"Let me make sure there are no hidden dangers."

Peri pressed her lips together. Her first instinct was to tell him what he could do with his overprotective he-man crap. She could take care of herself. Then she remembered that the last time they were there, Destiny had been hiding in the loft and the miasma had presumably been lurking in the shadows. It would be stupid not to take proper precautions. And since Valen's hunting senses were far superior to her own, he was the obvious one to check for hidden traps.

"Okay."

He disappeared in a blur of shadows, presumably peering into the various outbuildings before he reappeared directly in front of her.

"It's empty."

"Not empty." She grimaced. This place would always be filled with ghosts. With a shake of her head, she willed her heavy feet to carry her forward, pointing toward the small cabin closest to the center of the ranch. "That's my mother's house." She waved her hand toward the long structure on the other side of the firepit. "The rest of the coven shared the bunkhouses."

Valen fell into step next to her. "Did you stay with her?"

"Until my fifth birthday." She had a vivid memory of waking up on her birthday in the hopes she would have a surprise waiting for her. She did, but not one she'd expected. All of her belongings had been neatly piled next to the door. "Then I was evicted to sleep with the rest of the coven in the bunkhouses."

"Was it a power play, or did your mother have something to hide?"

Peri sucked in a deep breath, grateful for the question that shook her out of her soppy reminiscences.

"I always assumed it was to emphasize her place as leader, but she might have had secrets she didn't want to share with the rest of us."

They reached the door together, but Valen was first to reach out and push it open. "Allow me."

He stepped through the opening, moving to the nearest window to yank open the curtains. Silvery moonlight cascaded into the cramped space, allowing them to catch sight of the worn sofa and chair in the center of the room and the narrow bed pushed against the far wall.

"Another myth destroyed," Peri murmured.

"What myth?"

"That vampires can't enter a home uninvited."

He shrugged. "Of course I don't enter homes uninvited. It's rude."

She snorted, heading toward a large armoire next to the bed. "And you want people to assume they're safe behind their closed doors."

It was certainly convenient to have demons assume that a vampire needed an invitation to step over the threshold. They felt no need to create magical barriers that would make it more difficult for him to enter.

"I want my people to sleep well at night."

She rolled her eyes at his smooth explanation, tugging open the door of the armoire. Instantly she stiffened, as if she'd taken an unseen blow.

"Oh," she breathed.

Valen was instantly at her side. "What's wrong?"

"It still smells like my mother."

He studied her tense expression. Valen had no experience with a family, and what he'd observed from a distance hadn't made him regret the lack of parents and siblings. The relationships appeared far too complicated to be worth the effort.

But he'd been around long enough to accept that no matter how messy the interactions between them, most families remained emotionally anchored to each other. Even if it sunk them to the pits of hell.

"You can wait outside," he offered. "I'll do the search."

She glanced toward the door, as if she desperately wanted to walk out of the cabin. Then, with the courage he was coming to expect from her, she squared her shoulders.

"No, I can't keep running."

"Some memories are too toxic to relive. There's no shame in leaving them buried."

She wrinkled her nose. "I thought you were supposed to dig through them so they could be lanced and drained?"

"Why? You are Peri Sanguis."

"True."

"You don't need advice from the internet on how to deal with your emotions," he insisted. "You are a unique, intelligent, fiercely independent woman who has the sort of magic most mages only dream of." He shrugged. "You get to choose what's right for you."

She released a slow breath. "I need to do this. If only to prove to myself that my mother didn't break me." She tilted back her head, revealing her determined expression. "No matter how ugly her betrayal, I came back stronger than ever."

"Yes." Valen wryly recalled Peri's bold habit of cursing demons and even trespassing into his Gyre. She was far from broken. "You did."

There was a short silence as Peri gathered her composure. "Okay, I'm ready," she announced. "I'll look through her things in here." She nodded toward the armoire. "If you want to check the rest of the cabin."

Valen moved toward the bed that was neatly made with a nightgown tossed over the footboard, as if awaiting Brenda's return. The woman hadn't bothered packing her belongings or preparing to leave the cabin. Presumably she had no immediate plans to use the magic she was so desperate to acquire.

Pulling back the quilt, Valen tossed aside the pillows and lifted the mattress. His brows arched as he caught sight of a familiar item.

"Perhaps your mother wasn't as averse to technology as she claimed," he said, grabbing the computer off the box springs.

Peri stared at the laptop in his hand, her lips parting in genuine shock. "That hypocrite. She slapped my face when I asked for a computer for Christmas."

Valen strolled to stand beside her, using his powers to charge the dead battery. He assumed Brenda had been using the generator just outside the cabin to keep it functioning.

"Let's see what other secrets she was hiding."

He opened the laptop and clicked the folder labeled junk mail. A predictable place to hide secrets. Dozens of pictures popped up, most of them taken outside the Witch's Brew. Peri gasped as she took in the image of herself walking down the street and another one of her standing near the window of the coffee shop.

"She knew I was alive," she rasped.

"It appears she kept a close watch on you. This last picture was taken less than a year ago," Valen murmured, making a mental note to discover who Brenda paid to spy on her daughter. And to make very sure the bastard understood that if he ever got near Peri again, he would be a dead man. "Understandable, I suppose. If I tried to kill you, I might be concerned you would return to seek your revenge."

With jerky motions, Peri turned back toward the open armoire. "I did better. I forgot her."

Valen frowned. It was the ultimate revenge. To scrub her mother from her life. But he sensed that there was more. Not that it mattered. Not now. And one glance at the mage's rigid back assured him that she wasn't in the mood to share secrets.

Valen shrugged and returned his attention to the computer. Clicking on the search history, he scanned the short list.

"It looks as if your mother used the computer to search for magical items. There's nothing on here that specifically mentions the miasma."

"Did the name Masque Salon come up?"

Peri turned back toward him holding a tall, narrow box that would be the perfect size to hold a small statue. The name Masque Salon was printed on the side.

Valen scanned the list. "Yes." He clicked the link and a website popped up with a gaudy smear of green and purple and flashing gold letters. "Masque Salon," he read out loud. "A gathering place for witches."

"A hookup spot for magic users?" Peri wrinkled her nose in confusion. "That doesn't sound like a place where my mom would get her hands on a statue filled with evil magic. Honestly, it doesn't sound like a place my mother would go for any reason."

"It's not a dating club. It's an auction house for potions and unique spells," he corrected her. "Your mother was looking at the auction calendar. There was one held two weeks ago."

She slowly nodded. "I assume that's when she got the fancy box." Tugging off the lid, she peered inside. "There's something…" She reached into the box, pulling out a folded piece of paper. Smoothing it open, she sucked in a sharp breath. "A receipt."

Valen closed the computer and tossed it back on the bed. "Does it say what she bought?"

"No. It just says lot number twelve. And a price of six hundred dollars that she paid in cash." She glanced up at him with a humorless smile. "I suppose it would be too much to hope it would list the purchase of an evil magic."

"I think we should check out the Salon," he said in decisive tones. "Even if she didn't get the statue there she might have mentioned it to one of the customers."

"I agree. It's the only lead we have." Holding the box in one hand, Peri reached out to close the door of the armoire. She heaved an impatient sigh as she noticed that something had dropped on the floor when she'd pulled out the box. Bending down, she plucked it off the wooden planks and straightened, glancing down at the piece of paper. "Oh."

Valen swiftly moved to peer over her shoulder. "What is it?"

"This." Her voice was strained as she held up the paper.

Belatedly Valen realized that it wasn't paper, but a photo of a young man with reddish-gold hair and dark blue eyes. He was smiling directly into the camera as he stood on the edge of a boat with a large lake shimmering behind him. "He has your eyes."

"My father."

Valen studied her rigid profile and the tension in her fingers that clutched the photo. "Do you have contact with him?"

"I've never met him. I don't even know his name. My mother refused to speak about him." Valen felt the shiver that raced through her, as if she were suddenly cold to the bone. "This picture was the only proof that he ever existed."

"Did you ever try to find him?"

"No."

"Why not?"

Peri dropped the photo back onto the floor. As if it bothered her to touch it. "Because I don't want to know."

Valen could sense her intense emotions, but they were too tangled to decipher.

"You don't want to know him in general or as a father?"

"In any way." She closed the door of the armoire with a snap. "My mother was a cold, distant woman who never once said that she loved me. Probably because she didn't."

The more Valen discovered about Brenda Sanguis, the more he wished he'd been the one to drain her. He would have taken pleasure in punishing her for the pain and fear she'd caused her daughter.

"What about the rest of the coven?" he asked.

"They resented my power." Peri shrugged. "Of course, in the beginning we didn't know that I possessed the magic of a mage."

Valen at last understood why Peri had avoided searching out the man who'd given her life.

"And you feared your father would be equally indifferent?"

Peri nodded, turning her head in a futile attempt to hide her vulnerability. "When I was a child I would lay in bed and pretend that my father didn't know I existed. That if he did he would rush to rescue me and make me a part of his family." Her lips twisted. "In my dreams I had a dozen brothers and sisters along with grandparents who doted on me. It was stupid."

"Why is it stupid?" Valen demanded. "Most creatures have a need for the sense of belonging." He could have added that vampires had created the Cabal not only for a power base, but to give them the illusion of a family. "Why didn't you contact him?"

"The fantasy of him gave me courage." She tilted her chin, turning back to meet his searching gaze. "I couldn't bear to have it shattered."

"And now?"

"Now I have a family." Dropping the box and receipt in her satchel, Peri turned toward the door. "I think we're done here."

Valen agreed, following her across the cabin. He would send one of Gabriel's servants to collect the laptop and have it sent to Renee. His secretary could uncover any other secrets that might have been hidden. Even if they'd been erased.

He wanted to know everything there was to know about Brenda Sanguis. And why she'd been spying on her daughter.

* * * *

Peri floated in the space between sleep and consciousness. She was vaguely aware that she was snuggled on a soft mattress in a darkened room that smelled of cedar and...

Raw male power.

The fuzzy fog was blasted away as she wrenched her eyes open and stared at a shadowed form in the corner of the vast room.

"Valen?"

The form rose from the chair and crossed toward the bed with liquid grace. "I'm here," he murmured in soft tones.

Peri pushed herself into a seated position, leaning against the headboard. She should have been terrified to realize she was alone and vulnerable in a room with a member of the Cabal. Instead, she was annoyed by the knowledge that she had to look like a hot mess with her tangled hair and a trace of drool clinging to her chin.

What the hell was wrong with her?

Shoving her curls out of her face, she wiped her chin and glared at the approaching male.

"Were you watching me sleep?" she demanded.

There was a whisper of power and a soft pool of light pushed against the darkness. Of course, he looked perfect. His golden hair lay smoothly against his head and his eyes glowed with a brilliant silver shimmer. Even his clothes fit him with groan-worthy perfection. The charcoal-gray sweater was snug against the broad shoulders and tapered to his slender waist, while the dark slacks clung to the long length of his legs. And then there was his power...

It smashed against her like waves during high tide, wrapping around her and threatening to tug her under. The sensation wasn't frightening. Just the opposite. Each stroke of power was unnervingly erotic.

Dammit. It should be illegal to be so painfully glorious, she grumpily decided.

"Why would I watch you sleep?" he inquired as he halted next to the bed. "That would be—"

"Creepy." She interrupted whatever he was going to say.

With an arched brow, he nodded toward the bedside table where a tray was arranged next to the carved-wood lamp.

"I brought you dinner."

Oh. Peri felt color stain her cheeks, but she didn't apologize for her implication he was some sort of stalker. Not when he was regarding her with a knowing expression. As if he was aware of her seething attraction as well as her reluctance to admit she found him indecently irresistible.

She grabbed the tray and placed it on her lap. Her stomach rumbled in approval as she gazed down at the sandwich piled high with corned beef and Swiss cheese, and the plate of fresh, crisp veggies with a container of hummus. It's exactly what she would have ordered if she'd been at her favorite deli. Could Gabriel read her mind?

With a shrug, she dug into the meal, unashamedly shoving the food into her mouth.

"What time is it?" she asked between bites.

"Almost seven."

Peri reached for the bottle of water, dredging up the memory of returning to Gabriel's private lair. She'd managed to stumble her way to this bedroom and strip off her clothes to pull on her nightgown before tumbling onto the mattress and passing out.

"I can't believe I slept so long," she muttered.

"You were tired."

Peri nodded, polishing off the last of the sandwich. "Tia drained more of my magic than I realized."

He studied her with his smoldering silver gaze, but thankfully didn't point out that it was more likely the emotional toll of returning to her mother's cabin that had exhausted her. Instead, he leaned forward to grab the tray that was now empty except for a few crumbs.

"Allow me."

Peri watched as he set the tray back on the nightstand before he settled on the edge of the bed, his hip pressing against her upper thigh. She jerked as a chill seeped through the covers, sharply reminding her that Valen wasn't just another man. He was a formidable creature who ruled the demon world.

Wariness feathered down her spine, but Peri stubbornly refused to acknowledge the instinctive warning. It was too late to fear what Valen might do to her if she pressed too hard. She'd spent her life flouting authority. She was too old to change now.

"Dinner in bed and served by an esteemed member of the Cabal," she drawled. "I'm honored."

"Doubtful." His eyes darkened to smoke as he braced his hand on the mattress and leaned toward her. "And how do you know I'm esteemed?"

Peri's mouth went dry, her heart lurching and sputtering as if it had forgotten how to beat.

"You wouldn't be in your position if you weren't." Her voice was thankfully steady, although there was no hiding the erratic thump of her pulse. Not from a vampire. "I'm assuming the Cabal has some sort of seniority system to divvy up the world?"

A dark brow arched. "I'm not sure 'divvy up' is the correct term, but you're correct. There is a method to how the leader of each Gyre is decided."

"Cage matches?"

"In the past there were trials to determine the most powerful leader," he conceded. "Now we try to be a little more civilized."

His words reminded Peri of Tia's seething hatred for the Cabal and she eagerly latched onto the welcome distraction.

"Tia suggested that she was enslaved by a not-so-nice vampire by the name of Batu."

The chill in the room deepened. "Batu was an unfortunate example of why we felt the need to modernize the Cabal."

"Was he a friend of yours?"

"Never a friend, although our paths did cross." He hesitated, as if unsure whether he wanted to share top-secret leech business. "He was warned that he would be removed from the Cabal if he continued to terrorize his people."

"Obviously he didn't heed your warning."

Valen shrugged. "Thankfully, the dark days of treating our people like property to be used and abused are in the past. As I said, we've tried to become more civilized."

Peri didn't have to fake her disbelief. Valen might not be as savage as Batu, but there was no doubt he controlled his territory with an iron fist.

She smiled sweetly. "Does that mean you've decided the best policy is to hide your true nature?"

"Don't we all?"

Peri flinched as his words hit a raw nerve. "Not everyone."

"Everyone," he insisted, his silver eyes trapping her gaze. "Including you."

Okay. Time for a distraction.

"Did you already eat?"

The words left her lips before she had the sense to swallow them. Then it was too late as the air suddenly felt too thick to breathe. Valen leaned even closer, his gaze sweeping over her face before moving to settle on the curve of her neck.

"Are you offering?"

Peri made a choked sound. Talk about leaping from the frying pan into the fire.

"I'm sure Gabriel has a ready supply of donors."

"He does, but I'm not interested in nutrition." His power pulsed around her as his hand moved to brush his finger down the length of her jaw. "I'm interested in you. Just you, Peri Sanguis."

"That seems..." Her words faltered as his thumb tracked the curve of her lower lip. "Dangerous."

"When have you ever backed away from a challenge?"

With a deliberately slow motion Valen lowered his head, his hand moving to thread his fingers in her hair as his lips brushed over her mouth. Shock waves jolted through Peri at the soft caress. As if she'd just been struck by lightning.

A groan escaped her parted lips as he tasted her with his mouth, then with the sweep of his tongue. The press of his razor-sharp fangs was oddly erotic, sending a thrill of excitement shooting through her. She'd heard the bite of a vampire was addictive. Now she knew that a leech didn't have to bite his prey. His kiss was enough to enthrall any woman.

Pressing her hands against his chest, she turned her head to the side. Not in rejection. She didn't have the willpower for that. But she wasn't a vampire. She needed to breathe.

"Only a very foolish person would consider you a challenge," she rasped.

"Or a very courageous one." His lips scorched a path of light caresses down the curve of her throat, his tongue sweeping over the pulse hammering just above her collarbone. "I can taste your magic. It perfumes your skin."

She didn't think he was offering her empty flattery. As her body stirred with arousal, she could feel her magic humming through her veins, a layer of power coating her skin in a silvery web.

"I'm a mage."

"Not just a mage." He tugged on her curls, tilting her head to the side to offer him unfettered access to her vulnerable flesh. "Such power. It's unique. *You're* unique."

Peri knew she should put a stop to his lethal seduction. Not only because it was suicidal to put herself in such a vulnerable position; she also couldn't risk allowing anyone to slip beneath her defensive layers. She knew what was possible if she lost control. Sex was one thing. This...

This was something else.

But even as she commanded her hands to push him away, her fingers were curving into the cashmere sweater, as if she wanted to yank him closer.

"I've been told that I'm stubborn, opinionated, and destined for an early grave," she argued. "Never unique."

He kissed the vein that throbbed at the base of her neck. "Weak men feel compelled to make others small. Especially women. And you could never be small."

The tips of his fangs pressed against her tender skin, and Peri curved her spine in silent invitation. She wanted those massive teeth sinking deep into her flesh, she reluctantly acknowledged. And to feel the suck of her blood as he drank deep from her vein. She wanted...Valen.

The terrifying realization was still forming in her mind when she felt a buzzing against her hip. Pulling back, she studied him in confusion. What was happening?

It wasn't until Valen reached into the front pocket of his slacks to pull out a phone that she realized she'd felt the vibration from an incoming text. Saved by the bell. Or in this case, saved by the timely buzzing, she wryly told herself.

"Damn." His exquisite features tightened as he glanced at the screen. "It's Gabriel."

Peri tried to inch away, but she was trapped by the quilt pulled tight over her legs. She swallowed a sigh. It was like fate was doing everything in its power to keep her disturbingly close to Valen.

With an effort, she forced herself to remember why she was in Denver. And the cost of failure.

"Is something wrong?" she inquired.

"He has information he thinks we should see."

"'Information' is kind of vague. I suppose we won't know if it's good news or bad until we talk to him." She sent him a frown. "But first I need to shower."

Cool power swirled over her like a caress. "Alone?"

Did he plant the vision of the two of them entangled in the shower as water cascaded over their naked bodies in her brain? If he didn't, she had a remarkable ability to imagine every solid, perfect inch of him. Including the proud thrust of his erection.

She cleared the lump from her throat. "I don't suppose Gabriel has some clothes I could borrow?"

He leaned back, his expression unreadable as he nodded toward a chair on the other side of the bed where a stack of laundry was neatly folded.

"Yours were cleaned while you slept."

"A full service hotel." She managed a teasing smile. "Nice."

His gaze locked on her lips. "It could be as full service as you desire."

A sharp, unexpected yearning bloomed in the center of her being. She wanted this male. She'd wanted him from the first time she caught sight of him nine years ago. But what she needed was an uncomplicated relationship between a man and woman. The sort you watched on television during the holidays where the ending was always happy.

Unfortunately, there was nothing uncomplicated about Valen. Or her. And they were more likely to end in a fiery collision that would destroy them both than a happily ever after.

"I'm not as courageous as you seem to believe," she whispered.

He stilled, forgetting to look human as he studied her with an unnerving intensity. Did he realize she was hiding something? Probably. Thankfully, he accepted she wasn't yet ready to share. Brushing his fingers lightly down her cheek, he rose to his feet.

"You will be," he murmured with an assurance that bordered on arrogance.

Then, with a wicked smile, he turned to disappear into the shadows of the room. Peri held her breath until she heard the soft click of the door shutting behind his retreating form before she jumped out of bed and headed to the bathroom. Stepping into the shower, she turned on the cold water. Full blast.

She'd obviously lost her mind. Maybe the frigid spray would shock some sense into her.

Half an hour later she was scrubbed clean and dressed as she headed down the long flight of stairs. She wasn't sure she'd managed to erase the smoldering desire or the nagging ache to rip off Valen's expensive clothes and have her wicked way with him, but she'd managed to regain command of her composure. That's all she could ask at this point.

Reaching the ground floor, Peri didn't have to wonder where to find Gabriel. His power radiated through the mansion like the core of a nuclear reactor, pulsing with outrageous force.

With a grimace, Peri headed through a sunken living room and into a large library surrounded by towering bookshelves. Spending so much time with members of the Cabal was a grim reminder of where she stood on the evolutionary ladder. Any one of them could squash her like a bug.

She came to a halt in the center of the massive space, her gaze taking in the slender male who was seated at a heavy desk, concentrating on the computer screen. He had short, reddish-blond hair and eyes the color of minted gold. His green aura pulsed with fey magic, revealing the strength of his ancient blood.

His power, however, couldn't compare to the male who was moving with fluid grace to stand directly in front of her.

Gabriel Lyon. The Cabal leader of the western Gyre. Peri had seen pictures of him, of course. At least the pictures that he'd allowed to be taken. Vampires could avoid being caught on camera if they wanted. Which was most of the time. But these days, the leeches needed the goodwill of the mortals, and while the humans didn't realize Gabriel was a vampire, he was a wealthy entrepreneur who gave big, fat checks to local charities. It made him something of a celebrity.

Add in the fact he was gorgeous. With his long, dark hair threaded with silver framing his square, perfectly chiseled face and his heavily muscled body that filled out his polo shirt and gray slacks with a solid display of male strength, it ensured that he was prized material for the front pages of every newspaper in the country, as well as spotlight stories from national television.

It wasn't until she was up close, however, that Peri could see that the hazel eyes were shadowed, as if he hid a terrible secret.

"Ms. Sanguis." Gabriel offered a slow, dazzling smile that could melt the Arctic. "A pleasure."

Peri might have fainted at the potent charm in that smile if she hadn't spent time with Valen.

"Please, call me Peri."

"Peri," he readily agreed. "I'm Gabriel. I'm afraid Valen is dealing with a business matter. He'll join us in a few minutes."

Peri felt a nervous flutter in her stomach. She had many fine talents, but her repertoire didn't include small talk with a vampire. At last she glanced toward the bookshelves that soared toward the open-beam ceiling.

"You have a beautiful home."

Gabriel nodded, studying her with an unnerving intensity. "It suits my current taste."

Peri turned to pace toward a bronze statue of a bucking bronco with a cowboy arched in an effort to stay in the saddle. Was that a real Frederic Remington?

"I would think it would suit anyone's taste," she muttered.

"You're nervous." The words came out as a soft purr. "Is it me?"

Peri swallowed the panicked laugh. Was he serious? "The Cabal makes most people nervous."

"It was my understanding that you are fearless."

She blinked, wondering if it'd been Valen who'd told him that particular lie. And why.

"I can be reckless," she admitted, "but I try not to be foolish. At least most of the time."

He folded his arms over his chest, a watchful stillness settling around his large form. Gabriel reminded her of a predatory cat. Patiently waiting for his moment to pounce.

All she could do was hope she wasn't the mouse in this scenario.

"Valen was right." He finally broke the awkward silence.

"He usually is. Or at least he assumes he is." The words left her lips before she could consider that they might be an insult to another member of the Cabal. She licked her dry lips. "Right about what?"

"Your magic is exceptional."

"I..." Peri hastily checked her shields. They were firmly in place, so how did he know about her magic?

Gabriel frowned. "Does it bother you?"

"Does what bother me?"

"You hide your truth. What do you fear?"

With an effort, Peri forced herself to meet the curious hazel gaze. Gabriel obviously had a talent for seeing through illusions.

Okay, then.

"Everything," she admitted with a simple honesty. "My mother tried to kill me on my sixteenth birthday. I've pissed off hundreds—perhaps thousands—of demons who all thirst for revenge, and Tia believes I'm a part of her vision for world domination." She held up her hands in a gesture of resignation. "That isn't to mention the mage's bane that's killing witches and humans with reckless abandon. So yeah, I fear lots of stuff."

Gabriel continued to study her and Peri had a flash of insight into what it must feel like to be a bug beneath the microscope.

"Interesting," he whispered.

"Not really."

"Valen has no idea what he has chosen."

There was a blast of power before a low voice sliced through the room. "Are you talking about me behind my back?"

Peri released a shaky sigh. She'd never in her life thought she would be so happy to see Valen stroll into a room.

Chapter 18

Valen felt the tension before he ever reached the library. It hummed in the air like a live wire, threatening to singe the unwary. His first instinct had been to rush to Peri's rescue. He didn't think Gabriel would be a danger to her, not when the vampire knew that Valen had offered her protection. But there was more than one way to injure a woman, and Peri wasn't as tough as she wanted others to believe.

Then logic kicked in, and Valen managed to keep himself from rushing into the room and making a fool of himself.

If anyone needed rescuing it was probably Gabriel, he wryly acknowledged, stepping into the library at the same time he heard his name mentioned.

Gabriel smoothly turned to face him, a mysterious smile playing around his lips. "Nothing that I wouldn't say to your face."

Valen glanced toward Peri, who had moved to stand stiffly next to the windows, which were covered by a steel shutter. The sun was setting, but it would be another hour before the last of the deadly rays were gone. He didn't know what had happened between Gabriel and Peri, but it was obvious she was on edge.

"You said you had something you needed to share with us," he said in an attempt to ease the tension, angling a path toward the wary mage.

"I do." Gabriel waved a hand toward the silent male seated at the desk. "Lars, bring up the video."

The fair-haired demon tapped on a keyboard and the overhead lights dimmed. There was more tapping and an image appeared on the screen covering the window, then one more click and the image rolled into motion, revealing a crowd of humans weaving their way through a double line of tents and concession stands. In the distance the outline of carnival rides was visible.

Valen frowned in confusion. "What is this?"

"It popped up on social media," Gabriel answered. "It's a county fair in Meade, Kansas."

The video continued to capture the small groups of people who clustered around the individual stalls, throwing balls to win cheap stuffed animals or eating fried foods stuck on sticks. Then a low rumble of confused voices started to swell and the camera swung toward a lemonade stand where two men were wrestling on the dusty ground. A second later, several additional men jumped in, one of them holding a knife that he was slashing through the air with reckless abandon. More men and a few women joined in the spreading melee while the onlookers abruptly screamed in fear as they turned to escape the expanding battle.

"Ugly, but the combination of humans and alcohol often leads to violence," Valen murmured. They couldn't jump to the conclusion that every fight that broke out was connected to the magic.

"Keep watching," Gabriel commanded.

The video zoomed away from the fight, sweeping toward the fleeing crowd. They stumbled over the rough ground, ramming into each other until more than a few had been knocked off their feet and were trampled by the stampede. Without warning, Peri waved her hand toward Lars.

"Stop the video." The fairy pressed a key and the image froze on the screen. Peri walked forward, pointing to a familiar woman with blond curls and a round face. "Destiny."

Valen studied the witch's frightened expression as she glanced over her shoulder. She wasn't with the group of fleeing people. Instead, she was running from a side pathway, seemingly oblivious to the crowd that was pushing and pressing each other in an attempt to escape through the gateway to the fairgrounds.

"It looks like she's running from something," he said. "Or someone."

"Can you go back?" Peri asked the fairy.

"Yes."

The video blurred as Lars skimmed back to the point where Destiny first appeared.

"She's leaving this tent." Peri touched the steel screen, her finger planted on a wooden plaque hanging from a pole with colorful scarfs tied at the edges.

"Lars, zoom in on the sign," Gabriel ordered.

The image blurred as it focused on the plaque, but it was still easy to see.

"Madame Ruiz," Peri read the painted letters out loud. "Fortune Teller Extraordinaire."

"Could she be a witch?" Valen asked the obvious question.

"It's possible." Peri shrugged.

A true seer would never stoop to playing games with premonitions. They understood the danger of offering information without context. But many witches made extra money on the side by telling fortunes or selling crystals that offered everything from true love to magical healing.

Gabriel glanced toward his servant. "Lars, can you find any information on Madame Ruiz?"

There was a pause as Lars swiveled toward a separate computer on the desk, typing in the name to pull up several links.

"She has a Facebook page," Lars said, leaning toward the monitor. "Madame Ruiz. The stage name for Georgia Stemp, cashier at Safeway and proud mom of two." He clicked on another link, his eyes widening in surprise.

Gabriel moved toward his servant. "What did you find?"

"There's a news report that Georgia Stemp was discovered dead in her tent after the fairgrounds were evacuated. The death is being ruled suspicious."

"It has to be the miasma," Peri breathed.

Valen didn't argue. It was one thing to have a group of drunken humans wrestling in the middle of the fairgrounds. It was another to have the local fortune teller turn up dead after Destiny visited her tent.

"Perhaps she had some magic," he said.

Gabriel peered over Lars's shoulder at the computer. "Anyone else killed?"

"Several were injured. Six were taken to the hospital, but none in critical condition."

Peri wrapped her arms around her waist, as if she was suddenly cold. "Why would Destiny be at a small-town fair in Kansas?"

"Maybe she's seeking power," Valen offered.

Peri arched a brow. "From a cashier?"

Valen shrugged. "I doubt she has a lot of options."

"Options…" Peri glanced toward the fairy. "You said this was Meade, Kansas, right?"

"Yes."

"Can you bring up the area on a map?"

"Of course."

Peri turned back toward the screen. Curious, Valen moved to stand at her side as a satellite image of the area appeared.

"What are you looking for?"

"I recognize that town. There's a coven there called the Dayan Society. My mom would travel there to exchange magical artifacts when I was young." She pressed the tip of her finger to a spot on the map. "It's less than twenty miles from Meade and located on the main road. Destiny would have driven right past it. If she's fleeing from the miasma, why not go there for protection?"

"Or even if she's been infected, it would make more sense to seek out the coven," Valen agreed, unable to find a logical explanation for why Destiny would have bypassed a large coven to risk exposure at a small human fair. "There were at least a dozen witches there to drain." A coven was usually anywhere from twelve to thirty witches. "Why choose a faux fortune teller?"

"Unless it's moved," Gabriel suggested, strolling to join them.

"Doubtful." Peri shook her head. "It takes years to prepare the ground with layers of spells to enhance their magic as well as provide a circle of protection. And the Dayan Society has been around for nearly a century. It would take a catastrophe for them to relocate."

"Is there something the humans can offer?" Gabriel asked.

It was a good question. Just because mortals didn't possess magic or immortality, it didn't mean they couldn't have value for the miasma. Valen abruptly recalled the screaming crowd as it battled to get out of the fairgrounds.

"Emotions." He spoke his thoughts out loud. "Fear. Hate. Fury. And violence." He grimaced. "Death."

"The miasma could get the same emotions at a coven at the same time they could be drained of their magic. That seems like a win-win," Peri pointed out. "With the bonus of being isolated from their neighbors. The Dayan Society might not be as paranoid as my mother, but they took their privacy seriously."

"Damn." Comprehension hit Valen with shocking force. How had he been so blind?

Peri sent him a confused glance. "What?"

"Publicity," Valen said with absolute certainty. "The miasma wants to be seen. Why else would it bypass a coven filled with witches? Or avoid the dozens of remote farmhouses, if it hungered for human emotions? The miasma could have fed and been long gone by the time anyone discovered the bodies. Certainly no one would have been filming it on their phones and posting it on the internet."

Gabriel studied him as if he'd lost his mind. "You believe the magic has enough self-awareness to select a public location for its feedings?"

Valen didn't flinch. "It has to be self-aware, or it's managed to infect Destiny and she's being manipulated by the evil. How else could it be traveling from one spot to another?"

"But why?" Peri demanded.

"It could be that the evil is trying to spread fear through social media. Eventually the strange bouts of violence will be connected and people will become paranoid." Even as the words left his mouth, Valen knew they didn't feel right.

"It does thrive on chaos," Peri agreed, although she looked equally dubious.

"Why not stay to enjoy the fear it's caused?" Gabriel asked the obvious question. "There's no doubt that the town is still a seething pit of emotions."

Valen arched a brow at his friend's melodramatic description. "Seething pit?"

Gabriel waved a hand toward his vast collection of books. "I like words."

"He's right," Peri retorted. "It could cause more chaos if it'd chosen a theme park or a shopping mall. It didn't look as if there were more than a handful of people at the fair."

"Same thing with the bar," Valen added, accepting that his theory remained frustratingly incomplete. "Why not head straight to Cheyenne or Denver to choose a bar filled with customers?"

"It would certainly make more sense to choose an area dense in population," Peri said.

"Could it be avoiding a Gyre? That's how it appears." Gabriel shook his head, as if irritated by his inability to follow the reasoning of the miasma. "But why? It feeds on magic. The more potent the better, I would imagine."

Yes. That was it.

"Say that again," Valen commanded. Gabriel sent him a wry glance, as if suspecting he was being mocked. "Seriously?" Valen nodded, feeling as if a puzzle piece had just snapped into place.

"It feeds on magic," Gabriel obediently repeated.

Valen deliberately turned toward Peri. "The more potent the better," he said, adding the other words that Gabriel had muttered.

"Yes." Peri hesitantly nodded. "Do you have a point?"

"The miasma is hunting you."

"Me?" Peri recoiled as if she'd been slapped. "That's crazy."

He folded his arms over his chest. "You have twice the magic of an entire coven of witches."

"So why didn't it attack when I was at the ranch?" she reminded him, clearly disturbed by his suggestion. Understandable. Being hunted by the miasma would unnerve the most courageous mage. "It had to be there."

"It was hiding. Otherwise we would have sensed its presence." Valen had no idea how the powerful magic had shielded itself from being detected, but it was reasonable to assume that it had gone into some sort of hibernation to protect itself. "Perhaps it didn't sense your powers until too late."

"Why not follow me?"

"You took off in a helicopter."

"True." Peri wrinkled her nose, as if she was forcing herself to consider the possibility he was right. A second passed, then another before her eyes abruptly widened. "Or..."

"Or what?" Valen asked.

"Destiny was there," she said. "What if the miasma thought she was the power it was sensing?"

Valen slowly nodded. She was right. If the miasma had gone into hiding after it'd destroyed the coven, it might have been capable of sensing the power that had visited the ranch without being able to pinpoint the source.

"It would explain why it followed her," he agreed.

"But surely by now it's realized its mistake?" Gabriel demanded.

"Yes. The miasma might have followed Destiny in the belief she held the power it craved, but once it realized its mistake it would know it was too late to try to trace Peri." Valen paused, considering various explanations for the fact that Destiny and the miasma still appeared to be in the same place at the same time. "Perhaps it hoped the witch would lead it to Peri."

"And that if it created public chaos, that would attract her attention?" Gabriel suggested.

Peri shook her head. "It's not a bad theory to explain why it didn't reveal itself at the ranch, and why it followed Destiny, but why didn't it attack when we were at the Jackalope Station?"

"Maybe it wasn't ready." Valen made a sound of impatience. He sensed he was close to the truth, but too much still remained shrouded in mystery. Then another puzzle piece abruptly snapped into place. Of course. "Or maybe these attacks are designed to lead you somewhere," he said, his voice edged with anger that it'd taken him so long to see the pattern.

Peri studied him as if she thought he might be joking. "Like an evil Pied Piper?"

"The Pied Piper *was* evil," he said dryly.

Dragging in a deep breath, Peri glanced back at the map that was still projected onto the steel screen.

"If you're right, the miasma is making it easy to know where to find it."

"Which is why we won't be anywhere near Kansas."

Valen instantly regretted his words as Peri's brows snapped together, her chin jutting to a stubborn angle. He might as well have waved a red flag in front of her.

"We can't just let it continue to kill."

Ignoring Gabriel's mocking smile, Valen took a moment to frame his words in a way that wouldn't provoke Peri's fierce independence.

"I think we should continue with our original plan," he slowly suggested. "If we can discover where it came from and how it ended up in your mother's possession, we might have a better chance of knowing how to defeat it."

She narrowed her eyes, as if aware he was appeasing her ready temper, then without warning, she nodded.

"I agree."

Valen slowly turned his head to meet Gabriel's amused gaze. "You were wrong, Gabriel."

"About what?" the male inquired.

"Miracles do happen."

Chapter 19

With an ease only a member of the Cabal could have achieved, Valen arranged for a jet to fly them to a private airfield outside of New Orleans and a limo to pick them up. It had, however, taken a considerable length of time to negotiate with the local vampire leader, Micha, to determine the terms of their stay in the area and the boundaries of what they were allowed to do in search of the miasma. Peri hadn't been allowed to listen to the conference call, but Gabriel had revealed that Micha was a recluse who fiercely guarded his territory.

It was just past four o'clock in the morning by the time they were bundled into a limo and headed toward the French Quarter. They had enough time to check out the Masque Salon before they had to travel to the safehouse where Valen had arranged for them to spend the day.

Settling back in the leather seat, which was as soft as butter, Peri heaved a small sigh of pleasure.

"You're lucky," she murmured, savoring the cool whisper of air-conditioning that combatted the thick humidity. It didn't matter that it was still pitch-black outside; summer in Louisiana was its own special hell. "Not everyone can be whisked around the country in such luxury."

Valen sprawled in the corner opposite her, elegantly attired in gray slacks and a soft black sweater. Unlike her, Valen didn't suffer from the smothering heat. In fact, he looked as if he'd stepped off the pages of a fashion magazine, with his golden hair smoothed back from his sculpted face and his eyes shimmering like liquid mercury in the muted glow from the dome light.

He shrugged. His powerful body was relaxed, but nothing could mute the pulse waves of power that pounded through the car. Being in Valen's presence was like standing next to a volcano that could erupt and destroy everything in its path.

"It's more a matter of necessity than luck," he argued.

Peri arched a brow. "It's a necessity to have a stretch limo and a chauffeur to pick you up from a private airport where you just landed in a personal jet?"

"Public transportation is out of the question."

"You don't want to rub elbows with the common folk?"

He studied her with a brooding gaze. "Common folk?"

"You know." She waved her hands. "Humans, witches…mages."

"I don't want to risk being trapped in an airplane or on a train or even in a car when the sun rises," he corrected in soft tones. "A travel delay or traffic jam might be an inconvenience for you. For me it's a potential death sentence." He tapped a slender finger against the tinted window. "All of our vehicles are custom designed with sunproof shutters that can be deployed if we have a mechanical breakdown. Or if one of the jets makes an emergency landing."

"Okay." Peri wrinkled her nose. She couldn't argue with his logic. A deadly allergy to the sun would put a crimp in most travel plans. "I concede the need for private transport, but does it have to be a stretch limo?"

"If you go to the trouble to refit and reinforce a vehicle, you choose one that's worth the expense."

He made it all sound so reasonable, but Peri wasn't fooled. The Cabal had carefully cultivated the image of ruthless leaders who remained aloof from the peasants.

"And you like to make a statement," she said.

"It doesn't hurt." He studied her, as if trying to figure out why she was asking such ridiculous questions. "Are you bothered by my wealth?"

Was she?

Peri hadn't really given it much thought. In some vague part of her mind she realized that Valen possessed an obscene amount of money, but it had never swayed her opinion of him.

"It doesn't bother me, but it adds another layer to the power that makes you a threat to those who have no interest in bending the knee," she said, not being entirely honest about why she kept him at a distance.

"You believe I'm a threat?"

"Are you?"

A dangerous smile hovered at the edges of his mouth. "Define threat."

"That's not particularly reassuring."

"I have no intention of physically harming you," he purred, smoky invitation swirling through his eyes. "I promise my touch will bring you nothing but pleasure."

Excitement buzzed through her, zinging against her raw nerves. Oh... lord. He was already bringing her pleasure. Which was crazy. He hadn't moved a muscle, but a blast of sensual temptation stroked over her like a caress. She shivered, swallowing the sudden lump in her throat.

She had a sudden urge to crawl into his lap and wrap herself around his hard body. After all, there was a tinted glass divider between them and the driver...

Peri gritted her teeth. She needed a distraction. Or a heaping dose of sanity.

"And what about forcing me to bend my knee?" she forced herself to ask, her voice husky.

He hesitated. Was he trying to decide if it was worth defending his habit of demanding a public display of allegiance?

"Bending the knee is a ceremonial act that strengthens the bonds between me and those under my protection," he finally responded.

"Bonds that include obeying your laws with unwavering loyalty."

His gaze narrowed. Her words had touched a nerve. "The loyalty isn't just for my benefit," he said coldly. "It's a visible reminder that these people are depending on me to protect them. And if I neglect my duties, I won't be alone in paying the price for my failure. Each and every demon in my territory is my responsibility. I never want to forget that."

Peri turned her head to gaze out the tinted window. They'd reached the outskirts of New Orleans, but she barely noticed the clusters of apartment buildings and storage sheds that hugged the highway. She was busy battling back the sting of guilt at her eagerness to think the worst of Valen.

"It still seems...feudal," she muttered.

"Why do you dwell on my people's pledge of allegiance to me? I assume you offer Maya your loyalty?" His voice softened, as if sensing the regret she refused to admit.

Peri eagerly latched onto the shift in conversation, turning back to meet his steady gaze. "She earned it."

"How did you end up at the Witch's Brew?"

"After I escaped the ranch I spent several weeks hiding in the mountains," Peri said without hesitation. Valen already knew about her homicidal mother and the coven who'd betrayed her. There was no reason not to offer the details of her journey to the Witch's Brew. At least, the details she was willing to share. "It wasn't until I was fully healed that I headed east."

"Why east?"

"It wasn't really a decision." At the time, Peri had been walking around in a daze. Not only had she just discovered she was a powerful mage, but her mother had stabbed a dagger into her chest and tried to murder her. That was the sort of trauma that took longer to heal than the wound. "I moved from one small town to another, picking up odd jobs to make a little money. I never paid attention to where I was or where I was going."

"You never felt the urge to settle down?"

She shook her head. "Not until Maya."

"Why was she special?"

"I was working as a waitress at a truck stop in Pennsylvania. One night I got off work late and was walking to the trailer I was renting a few blocks away. I didn't sense the danger until a van pulled up next to me and three guys jumped out."

Lost in the dark memory, Peri abruptly shivered as an icy blast coated the windows in a layer of frost.

"Are they dead?"

Peri didn't bother to answer the blunt question. The last thing she wanted was Valen hunting down those creeps. They weren't worth the effort.

"When I finally realized I'd been surrounded, they knocked me out before I could form a spell."

Valen's features remained clenched, but the frost thankfully melted. "What happened?"

"I woke up in my bed with Maya pouring a foul tasting potion down my throat." Peri's lips twisted. Almost nine years later she could still remember the nasty taste. And she was still convinced that Maya added an extra layer of vile to the potion to teach her a lesson. "I tried to fight her, but she wrapped me in magic and told me not to be stupid. Then she spent the next hour scolding me on the dangers of walking around with my head up my ass and not carrying a collection of potions to use in case of an emergency."

Valen arched a brow. "I'm sure that made you happy."

"I was so pissed I would have beat her senseless if I could have broken her spell," she confessed. "Thankfully, I couldn't move a muscle, and by the time she released me I'd calmed down enough to realize she'd not only saved me from a revolting situation, but she'd reminded me that no matter how much power I might have, I'm not immortal. I needed to take better care of myself."

"And that included joining her at the Witch's Brew?"

"Not at first. Maya left her business card and told me to look her up if I was ever in New Jersey. She knew if she tried to pressure me into taking a job at her coffee shop I'd dig in my heels." Peri sent Valen an innocent smile. "It's probably hard to believe, but I used to be a little pigheaded."

Valen made a choking sound, but he didn't bother to point out she was *still* pigheaded. It was one of those things that went without saying.

"What made you decide to look her up?" he asked instead.

"The next morning I read a story in the newspaper about three men found butt naked and tied to a tree in the middle of the local park. All three were covered in a mysterious rash and were babbling about being attacked by flesh-eating butterflies. They were thrown in jail for indecent exposure and the suspicion they were responsible for the opioids flooding the area." Peri chuckled. At first she'd wondered if Maya had someone who'd assisted her in dealing with the men. Although they were humans, they weren't helpless. And the few mages that Peri had encountered since fleeing the coven hadn't possessed more than average magic. Certainly nothing that could have accomplished such a feat. Peri had realized that she'd finally encountered a mage who could teach her to control her magic. "I respected Maya's attention to detail. The illusion of flesh-eating butterflies was a nice touch."

"They should have been destroyed," Valen insisted.

"The last I checked they are back in jail," she assured him, even as she accepted there was a very real possibility that Valen would send someone to track them down. He had a rigid sense of justice. "A few days later I packed my bags and headed to Jersey."

"You've never felt the urge to move on?"

Peri was caught off guard by the question. Probably because she'd known from the second she'd walked through the front door of Maya's coffee shop that she'd found her home. And in nine years, she'd never thought about leaving.

"Maya and Skye are my family," she said with a simple honesty.

"And what about a romantic partner?"

Peri's heart skipped a beat. Logic warned her to tell him that it was none of his damned business. And never would be. Vampires were trouble she didn't need. Her mouth, however, was no longer connected to her brain.

"I have plenty of romance in my life," she bluffed.

With a coiled grace, Valen leaned forward. Like a snake preparing to strike. "Do you?"

Peri's heart continued to skip and skid as her breath lodged in her throat. He was close enough she could see the smooth perfection of his skin and shards of black at the center of his silver eyes. And his power...

It churned and swirled around her, stoking her hunger until she had to clench her hands to keep herself from reaching out and yanking him on top of her.

"I have all the romance I want," she muttered.

Valen dismissed her blatant lie, his gaze focused on her mouth. Was he thinking about kissing her? Would she spontaneously combust if he did? Heady anticipation heated her blood.

"Do you have a personal aversion to relationships or are you waiting for Mr. Right?" he demanded.

Peri licked her dry lips, watching his eyes darken to charcoal. "How do you know it's not Ms. Right?"

"Is it?"

She forced herself to push back into the soft leather seat. Now wasn't the time to have her mind clouded with visions of a naked Valen. She wasn't sure there was *ever* a right time for that, but certainly not when they were in the back of a limo driving into the cramped streets of the French Quarter.

"I'm not interested in being trapped," she told him.

He stiffened, as if startled by her words. Or maybe it was the sincerity in her voice.

"Is that how you see a relationship? As a prison?"

"Not a prison." She shook her head. "At least not exactly."

"Then what?"

Peri considered how to explain her reluctance to commit herself to another. "I'm a mage."

"Yes. A very powerful mage."

"Which means human men are out of the question."

"Naturally." His tone wasn't snobbish, it was just a statement of fact. Demons considered humans to be another species. And while mages were technically human, they were too powerful to remain a part of the normal world.

"And any demon is searching for a bloodline that will increase the power in their children," she continued, stating the obvious.

Valen studied her as if he thought she was joking. "Trust me, any demon would be eager to mate with a mage who has your magic."

She grimaced. "No thanks. I have no ambition to become a broodmare."

"Not all demons are looking to boost their social standing," Valen protested. "There are a few who choose to wed for love."

"That's worse."

Valen slowly sat back, his gaze sweeping over her as if he was trying to pinpoint what was wrong with her.

"Are you truly that cynical?"

"No, I'm a realist." She met his gaze squarely. She didn't know what was happening between them. Probably nothing. Once they'd tracked down the magic and destroyed it, there was every likelihood Valen would return to New York City and forget her name. But just in case this was more than a casual flirtation, it seemed best to be honest. "I've met demons who made my heart flutter. And one who was convinced I was his mate."

His jaw hardened, as if she'd said something that annoyed him. "But?"

"But as soon as the relationship shifts from casual to serious, the male develops an expectation that I will make him the center of my world."

"Isn't that what most people desire?"

"Probably." Peri heaved a sigh. "When I say the words out loud they make me sound like a sour recluse who is too demanding to be satisfied with any male. That isn't true. I've been on several dates where I had a lot of fun. And I would have been happy to continue seeing the guy, as long as it was on a casual basis. I'm just not interested in a serious relationship. They make me feel...smothered. Being in love with a partner you can respect and enjoy spending time with is wonderful. But I'm not a half-of-a-whole sort of woman. I'm whole all by myself."

He tapped the tip of his forefinger on the leather seat, as if he was analyzing her words. Or perhaps he was trying to decide if she was playing hard to get. He wouldn't be the first male to assume her lack of interest was some sort of game.

"You need your independence," he said at last, something that might have been satisfaction in his voice.

"Yes. I want to be with my friends and concentrate on developing my powers." She shrugged. "Or just have some me-time. Other women adore being the entire focus of their lover's attention and that's great. I'm too selfish to be anyone's mate."

"I would suggest you haven't met the right male, but I have a feeling I would wake up with a rash and a fear of butterflies," he murmured.

She narrowed her eyes. "You're not wrong."

"You intrigue me, Peri Sanguis."

"I don't mean to."

A mysterious smile curved his mouth, the tips of his fangs peeking between his lips.

"I know."

Chapter 20

Valen silently studied Peri's defiant expression, wondering if she was attempting to squash his growing obsession with her. If so, she was bound to be disappointed. He wasn't like many of his fellow vampires. He'd never been plagued with a desire to discover a mate who would depend on him for her happiness. Like Peri, he thoroughly enjoyed his independence and preferred a partner who had the strength to stand on their own.

Just like Peri...

Abruptly realizing they'd nearly reached their destination, he rapped on the dividing window. "Stop here," he commanded.

The limo slid to a halt next to the curb and Valen was swiftly out of the vehicle to scan their surroundings.

The quiet cobblestone street was lined with Creole-style townhouses that were shrouded in darkness. It was still too early for humans to be stirring and most demons would be seeking their lairs. A perfect time for a little breaking and entering.

Waiting for Peri to join him, he gestured for the driver to wait for them there and headed around the corner to stand in front of a three-story brick building with a second-floor terrace framed with wrought-iron railings and fluted columns.

"This is the place," he announced.

Peri frowned, studying the heavy green shutters that were closed over the windows and the sturdy padlock on the front door.

"You're sure?"

Valen pulled out his phone and checked the website he'd searched for earlier.

"This is the address listed for the Masque Salon."

"They have it boarded up as if they're expecting a hurricane."

He sent her a wry glance. "Or maybe they feared a mage with anger issues was headed their way."

The air prickled with her ready temper. "Excuse me? If anyone here has anger issues, it's not me."

With a low chuckle, he walked down the sidewalk. "Let's go through the back."

Heading down the narrow alley between the buildings, they entered a small courtyard with a granite fountain in the center of the paved ground. The gentle splash of water was the only sound to disturb the heavy silence. Valen hesitated. The air was oddly oppressive. As if there was a thunderstorm approaching.

Dismissing the foreboding atmosphere, Valen moved to the back door, easily forcing it open. Then, stepping into what appeared to be a storage space, he turned to study the bare shelves. He assumed that's where the auction items were usually kept.

"Nothing," he murmured, leading Peri into the main room at the front of the building. There was a small platform at one end with a podium and a few velvet-covered chairs scattered across the wood plank floor, but there was an unmistakable sense of emptiness. As if the space had been abandoned. He turned to glance at Peri. "Can you sense any magical items?"

"No." She tilted back her head, as if sniffing the stale air. "Which is weird."

"Why weird?"

"If the auction house was here, then there should be some residual magic." She paused, eventually making a sound of frustration. "I suppose it's possible that someone came through with a cleansing spell."

"You sound dubious."

"There's...something." Her brow furrowed, her expression distracted as if she was struggling to pinpoint the source of her unease. "I just can't put my finger on it."

"Magic?"

Valen watched as Peri drifted toward the stairs at the back of the room, her fingers brushing the aged banister.

"The complete *lack* of magic," she murmured.

On the point of joining her, Valen stiffened as he caught the scent of a mortal female.

"A human is approaching the back door," he warned.

"Hey, you guys!" the stranger called out in a loud voice. "I saw you go in there. I have a gun. If you leave now I won't shoot."

"I'll deal with this." Valen retraced his steps to the storage room.

"Not alone," Peri predictably insisted, hurrying to catch up with his long strides.

Valen sent her an annoyed frown. "I'm bulletproof."

With a lift of her brows, Peri deliberately lowered her gaze to where he'd been shot. "Not really."

If it had been anyone else, Valen would have punished them for reminding him he'd recently had a bullet lodged in his backside. But since it was Peri, he didn't mind having her admire his ass.

"Very well, I might not be bulletproof, but I'll heal faster," he insisted. "At least stay behind me."

"Fine," she grudgingly conceded.

Entering the storage room, Valen moved to block the doorway, folding his arms over his chest as a woman in her late twenties came to a sharp halt. She was tall and slender with well-honed muscles beneath the running shorts and T-shirt she'd probably been sleeping in. Her blond hair was pulled into a ponytail to reveal her wide eyes and nervous expression. In one shaky hand, she held a handgun that was currently pointed in Valen's direction.

"We're not here to cause trouble," Valen assured her in low, soothing tones. He'd rather face a trained assassin than an anxious amateur with a gun.

The woman halted in front of him, her eyes widening with shock as she caught sight of his face. She released a tiny gasp and allowed her gaze to skim down his body, at the same time lowering her weapon. He didn't need to use his ability to manipulate her mind to ease her fears. Her attraction toward him blinded her to any danger.

"Who are you?" she asked, her voice breathy.

"Valen." He glanced toward the mage peeking around his arm. "And this is Peri."

"I'm Aline," the woman murmured, her attention never straying from Valen's face. "What are you doing here?"

"We're searching for the Masque Salon," he informed her.

She nodded. "It was here, but it closed down a couple weeks ago."

Valen heard Peri mutter a curse, but he kept his attention locked on the human. She obviously had some connection to this place if she was willing to personally protect it rather than calling the cops when she'd seen them sneaking around.

"Do you know why?"

"Richard didn't say why he was closing." Aline glanced over his shoulder at the empty storage room. "He just packed up and disappeared. Later he left a note on my door asking me to keep an eye on the place until he could get it on the market." She waved a hand toward a building on the opposite side of the courtyard. "I live over there."

Valen ground his fangs together. He felt as if he was running into one roadblock after another, a sensation that was as unusual as it was annoying. He was a member of the Cabal. Nothing and no one put roadblocks in his way.

And worse, he possessed a growing suspicion that the miasma posed a direct danger to Peri. A knowledge that was intolerable.

With effort, he leashed the frustration pulsing through him. He didn't want to frighten off Aline before he could get answers.

"Who is Richard?" he demanded.

"Richard Pascal," Aline readily answered. "He owns this building. And he managed the auction house. Or at least he did." She shook her head, her ponytail bobbing. "I still can't believe he closed it. Masque Salon has been here since I was a little girl. It's hard to imagine it would simply close and disappear overnight."

Valen shared a quick glance with Peri. If the owner had disappeared, it had to have something to do with the miasma. It couldn't be a coincidence that he would abruptly shut down an auction house that had been there forever at the exact same time that Peri's mother had received the statue filled with the evil magic.

"I didn't even talk to him. There was just the note on my door."

"Do you know where we can find him?"

"He lived in the upstairs apartment," Aline said. "I don't know where he's at now."

"Do you have his phone number?"

"Only his business number." She shrugged. "He hasn't been answering."

"Did he have any employees?" Valen pressed, refusing to accept defeat. "Anyone we can contact to find out where he might be?"

"No." Aline abruptly yawned, as if the adrenaline that'd given her the courage to leave her home and confront potential thieves was crashing. "Look, I'm sorry. I really don't know anything else."

Valen could sense the truth in her words. They'd learned all they could from the woman. He stepped close enough to touch the tips of his fingers to her cheek.

"Aline, I want you to relax and listen to me."

A dreamy expression softened her features, her lips parting in an unspoken invitation. "Okay."

"It's time to go home and crawl back into your bed," he softly commanded. "This has all been a bad dream."

Something that might have been disappointment flashed through her eyes. "I'm dreaming?"

Valen ignored the question. "When you wake in the morning you won't remember seeing us."

She yawned again. "I'm so tired."

"Go."

He gave her a mental push, and obediently the woman turned to cross the courtyard, her movements sluggish as if she was fighting to stay awake long enough to reach her bed.

Waiting until he was assured Aline was safely locked in her building, Valen turned to discover Peri staring into space with a wistful expression. She at last heaved a sigh.

"She's so young."

"Aline?" Valen was confused. "She's your age."

Peri shook her head. "She's a lifetime younger in experience."

"Why do you say that?"

"Didn't you notice how she was staring at you?"

Ah. Valen felt a stab of satisfaction. He liked where this conversation was going. "Were you jealous?"

Peri rolled her eyes. "Yes, but not in the way that you assume."

Valen concealed his disappointment. He was genuinely curious what was troubling his beautiful mage.

"Tell me."

"She saw you and reacted like a woman who is attracted to a gorgeous male. It was so..." She seemed to struggle for the word she wanted. "Uncomplicated."

"You think I'm gorgeous?" Valen swept his gaze over her upturned face.

"You *are* gorgeous. And you know it," she said dryly. "But while she was fantasizing about getting you naked, she never once feared that you might crush her mind or stab your fangs into her neck and drain her blood."

Valen stiffened. Suddenly he didn't like the conversation nearly as well.

"You don't fear me." It was a statement, not a question.

She wrinkled her nose. "Probably not as much as I should, but from the moment I fled my mother's ranch I was forced to accept there were demons in the world. And that vampires walked the night."

Valen didn't doubt it had been a shock. Before her wild magic sparked to life, Peri wouldn't have been capable of seeing the auras that surrounded demons, or to sense the power of the Gyres. Being alone and on the run from her homicidal mother would have been bad enough, but to suddenly discover that there were creatures from horror movies walking among the humans must have terrified her.

"Would you have preferred to live in ignorance?" he asked with genuine curiosity.

"Sometimes I wish I could have been normal," she admitted. "It would have been fun to go to college and do a bunch of stupid stuff with the blind belief that nothing bad could happen to me. I might have even found a nice guy and settled down."

Valen scowled. A nice guy to settle down with? Never.

"You could never have been normal," he informed her in clipped tones.

"I suppose that's true." Her magic swirled through the air, as if she was battling back an unwelcome memory. "Even if I hadn't been a mage, my mother would have made sure I never escaped the coven."

Valen reached to cup her face in his hands, feeling her tremble at his light touch. "Your magic makes you a mage, but it's not what makes you special, Peri Sanguis."

"I'm…" Her lips remained parted, but no words came out.

"Speechless?"

With a sharp motion, Peri stepped back, her face reddening as if she was flustered. Valen savored the sight even as he accepted that Peri's rare moment of sharing was at an end.

"Never," she said, her tone unnaturally brisk. "I'm wondering why an auction house that'd been around for years suddenly decided to close its doors without warning or explanation."

"It has to be connected to the statue your mother purchased here." Valen grudgingly returned his attention to why they were standing in the empty building. "But I don't know why that would cause the business to close or the owner to disappear."

"I suppose we should check upstairs before we leave," she said. "Richard Pascal might have left something behind that will give us a clue how to track him down. I have a few questions for him."

Valen hesitated. It was still dark, but he could feel the heavy press of the sunrise.

"We need to be quick. Dawn is rapidly approaching."

Peri glanced through the open door, as if searching for the sun. "I can look around if you want to wait in the car."

"No." Valen moved forward, heading across the storage room. There was no way in hell he was leaving Peri alone in a place where they suspected the miasma had once been stored. Who knew what else might be hidden in the darkness? "We do this together."

Peri hurried to match his long strides. "Stubborn," she muttered under her breath.

Valen sent her an incredulous glance. This woman could give a mule lessons. "Did you call *me* stubborn?"

She waved her hand in an airy motion. "If the shoe fits."

Valen shook his head, but he didn't bother to argue as he entered the main room and crossed directly toward the stairs at the back. The truth was that they were both stubborn. And fiercely independent. And obnoxiously accustomed to doing exactly what they wanted, when they wanted.

It was the sort of relationship that erupted and went down in flames.

But that didn't prevent him from knowing beyond a shadow of a doubt that Peri was destined to stand at his side.

In silence they climbed the wooden steps, reaching the second floor, which proved to be a large office and more empty storage rooms. There was nothing left beyond the furniture and built-in shelves. Not even a stray scrap of paper.

Moving back to the stairs, they climbed to the third floor and entered an open loft with a narrow living room on one side and a kitchenette on the other. It was cramped and stark, but there were several original features, including cornice moldings, a chandelier that hung from an ornate medallion in the center of the ceiling and a wide fireplace that separated the living space from the bedroom. The building itself was no doubt worth a fortune. Which meant the owner would be in contact with someone to sell the place if they didn't intend to return.

Considering whether Renee could dig up the information he needed, Valen strolled forward. He was vaguely aware of the thickness of the atmosphere, as if they were walking through water, but he assumed it was the heavy humidity that clouded the air.

It wasn't until he'd circled the wide fireplace that he abruptly cursed his distraction. There was a dull pop, then the sensation of magic feathering over his skin. As if he was stepping through an unseen barrier. Suddenly the air wasn't thick or heavy, it was ripe with the stench of decaying spores. As if they'd opened a sarcophagus that held an ancient mummy.

"Shit," he muttered.

Peri muttered her own string of curses. "There was a muting spell in the building," she ground out. "That's why I couldn't sense the magic. I should have suspected something like that."

Valen moved to the side, trying to prevent Peri from catching a glimpse of the shrunken male corpse lying with rigid precision on the mattress.

He was wearing a suit that hung on his bony body and his too-thin face was distorted with a soundless scream.

Of course, he was wasting his time. Peri pushed past him to stare at the corpse with a stunned expression.

"Richard Pascal, I presume," she choked out.

"Whoever it is, they've been dead for several days," he said.

"Drained," she shuddered. "Like the others."

"Not exactly." Valen's hands squeezed into fists. "He obviously wasn't a witch."

"Could he have been a demon?" she asked.

Valen started to take a step forward to inspect the body. The blood had dried in the man's veins. He would need to get closer to determine his species. Before he could move, however, Peri's hand shot out to grab his arm in a bruising grip. "No, Valen," she rasped.

He instantly turned to face her. "What do you sense?"

"We triggered something." Her eyes widened with fear. "It's a snare. We need to get out of here."

Valen sent her a shocked glance. A snare spell would trap them in the building until the magic faded. It could last hours—or days—depending on the power level of the mage who created the trap. Grasping Peri's hand, Valen raced toward the door. He could already feel the electric buzz in the air. It wasn't mechanical. It was the warning of an impending explosion.

The spell hit as they left the loft and reached the top of the stairs. The concussion of magic blasted through the building, shaking it to its very foundation.

Valen winced as the painful wave sheered past him. The force of the power was shocking. He'd never felt anything that intense. Next to him, Peri released a sharp scream, grasping her head in her hands as if she was in unbearable agony.

Valen reached out, managing to scoop her in his arms as her eyes rolled into the back of her head and her knees collapsed. The spell had knocked her unconscious.

Holding her tight against his chest, Valen vaulted over the banister to drop to the main floor. He had to get out of there before—

His urgent thoughts were fractured as another blast reverberated through the building. Valen stumbled, abruptly turning away from the windows as the sound of splintering wood echoed through the emptiness. Waiting until the lethal shards had dropped to the ground, Valen turned to discover the shutters had been demolished.

There was also a shimmer in the air that revealed the snare had closed around them.

With a deliberate motion, Valen bent down to lower Peri to the floor. Then, with blinding speed, he ran forward to slam into the invisible wall. He bounced back, a loud crack warning that he'd busted a rib. Grimly, he ignored the pain and plowed forward once again.

It wasn't that he didn't understand the definition of insanity. He knew that repeating the same action in the hopes of a different outcome was a waste of time. Obviously, he couldn't physically force his way through the magic, but the snare was slowly tightening, driving them toward the towering windows that were no longer covered.

As soon as the sun crested the horizon he was going to be fried.

Chapter 21

Destiny crouched in the back of the van, keeping a wary eye on the spirit of Brenda, who was currently lounging in the passenger seat. It'd been several hours since they left the fair and Brenda had forced her to drive south. Finally they'd reached this remote, wooded area where the dead woman had declared they were going to rest for the night.

And that was that. The spirit had tilted back her seat and settled herself in for a nap. Like they were besties at summer camp, not fleeing a murder scene.

She'd always known the leader of the coven was a coldhearted bitch. After all, she'd tried to murder her own daughter, right? But watching her drain that poor fortune teller, and create a massive stampede that had injured dozens of people, without an ounce of remorse was stewing like a noxious poison in the pit of her stomach.

"Did you have to kill her?" she abruptly burst out.

Brenda didn't bother to open her eyes. "Kill who?"

Destiny shuddered at the realization she had to clarify which murder she was discussing.

"That fortune teller."

"Oh. Her." Brenda clicked her tongue. "Of course I did. Human emotion can feed me, but I need to increase my power." Her voice was thick with disgust. "Not that the creature had much magic to offer. She was more a hack than a witch."

Destiny scowled. "So this is what we're doing?"

"Doing?"

"You promised greatness." Destiny's voice was harsh. "Does that mean driving from one backwater to another, terrorizing the yokels?"

Brenda leaned to the side, her head swiveling so she could study Destiny with glowing eyes. Destiny shuddered. It was spooky as hell.

"Do you thirst for more?"

"I..." Destiny was forced to halt and clear the lump of fear from her throat. "I just want to go home."

The strange glow in Brenda's eyes pulsed, as if she was amused by Destiny's unease.

"Liar."

"It's true," Destiny insisted.

"No." There was an arrogant confidence in the spirit's voice. "I see into your heart, Destiny Mason. You joined the coven because you were desperate to gain power."

"I wanted to be a witch," Destiny conceded.

Her parents had been horrified, of course. They couldn't understand how she could walk away from a life of luxury to live in squalor in the middle of Wyoming. They thought she should be pleased to be traded to a suitable man who could add to the family coffers and vault them up the social ladder. It never occurred to them that she might have some worth beyond the ability to breed the next generation.

"You wanted to be *more*," Brenda insisted. "But as Peri began to grow into her powers you realized that she was the one who'd been blessed by the gods."

Destiny flinched. Peri had just been dabbling with her magic when Destiny had arrived at the coven. But by the time the bitch had celebrated her twelfth birthday she could perform spells that most of the coven couldn't manage. Destiny had watched her carefully, certain that she had to be cheating. It had to be a trick, she'd assured herself.

It wasn't possible to have that much magic.

The truth, however, had been far more disturbing than her suspicion that Peri was an underhanded brat.

"She wasn't blessed, she was cursed," Destiny spit out. There was no way she was going to let anyone realize how deeply she envied Peri. Or reveal how willing she would be to gain the magic of a mage.

Brenda chuckled, easily sensing her dark hunger. "So much power in such a young girl. It reminded you that you were nothing more than mediocre, didn't it, Destiny? And warned that you'd never be anything else."

Destiny leaned forward, glaring at her tormentor. "I wasn't the only one to envy Peri's power, was I?"

"No, it called to me with the song of a siren," Brenda readily admitted. "It still calls to me. We are one and the same, Destiny."

Destiny sat back, grimacing at the raw hunger pulsing in the air. It felt weirdly familiar.

"Fine. I'm ambitious," she conceded, not bothering to hide her annoyance with the conversation. "Too ambitious to waste my time in this nasty van while you terrorize humans and suck the life from pathetic women who can barely create a spark of magic."

The glow in Brenda's eyes became a red fire as the air thickened with a force that threatened to crush Destiny.

"Don't think for a second you can lecture me on my decisions." Brenda's voice thundered through the van. "You are alive because I need you. But you can easily be replaced."

Destiny squeezed herself into a ball, struggling to breathe. "At least tell me where we're going."

"We are not going anywhere," the spirit snapped. "We're creating a web."

"Web? What does that mean?"

Brenda made a sudden hissing sound, like a snake's scales rubbing together. Instinctively Destiny braced herself to be punished. Brenda had an unpredictable temper when she was alive, and it didn't seem that her recent death had improved her personality.

But when nothing happened, Destiny glanced up to study the older woman's face. Her expression was distracted, as if she was listening to a sound Destiny couldn't hear.

"Ah." A slow, spine-chilling smile curved Brenda's lips. "Sometimes the prey enters the web you left behind." Lifting her hand, the spirit snapped her fingers. "Get up here and start the van."

Destiny blinked in confusion. "What?"

"You want your reward?" Brenda looked like the cat who'd gotten a fresh saucer of cream. Or a python who'd swallowed a rat. "It's time to claim it."

* * * *

Peri was lying flat on her back, coated in darkness. The sort of darkness that pressed against her with a heavy sense of foreboding.

Had she been buried alive?

That's what it felt like.

Panic gnawed at the fringes of her mind.

What had happened? The last thing she remembered was they'd been in the auction house. Oh...wait. Her heart squeezed with fear. They'd found a mummified body and tripped a snare spell. Then everything had gone black.

Had the building collapsed on top of them? That would explain the darkness. And the choking sense of dread.

The panic stopped gnawing and started consuming large chunks of her. She couldn't breathe.

"Peri."

It was a male voice that whispered her name, hauling her back from the edge.

"Valen," she rasped, a shattering relief battling back her panic as she felt cool fingers skim down her cheek.

"I'm here."

She blindly reached up, her palms landing against his smooth chest as he leaned over her. Was he naked? The realization should have been shocking, or at least baffling; why would he have stripped off his clothes? But as her fear faded, it was replaced with a floating sense of acceptance.

It was quite likely she was dying. From the crushing power of the spell. Or from internal injuries she was too weak to heal. Either way, she abruptly decided that if she was about to leave this earth and this was her mind's way of easing her passage, she was going to take full advantage of the illusion.

Boldly exploring the chiseled muscles of his chest, Peri moaned in satisfaction. How long had she fantasized about touching him? Days? Weeks? Years?

It seemed like an eternity.

Now that she'd given herself full permission, Peri took her time to savor the satin-smooth skin and the power that hummed through his body like a nuclear reactor. Even in a dream he managed to drown her in his raw masculine energy.

It was glorious.

There was a cool rush of air before she felt Valen mold his body against her side. That's when she realized she'd managed to lose her clothes as well.

Convenient.

She rolled over to face Valen, thankful there was no pain beyond a dull ache at the back of her head. She didn't want anything ruining this moment.

As if sensing she'd tossed caution to the wind, Valen stroked his fingers over her face. In the darkness it was impossible to see his expression, but there was a hint of reverence in his touch as he traced each feature. The sweep of her brow. The narrow length of her nose. The curve of her lips.

"Peri," he murmured again.

"No." She pressed a kiss against his mouth, oddly terrified he was going to end her delicious fantasy. "No talking," she commanded. "Just touching."

He jerked as if startled by her fierce urgency, but with a low growl, he returned her kiss with a scorching hunger. Peri shivered, accepting the sharp press of his fangs. The tiny pain amped her pleasure to another level.

It was rumored that demons could become addicted to the bite of a vampire. She'd laughed at the idea any sane creature could enjoy having a couple of massive fangs chomping on their neck, but now...

As if reading her mind, Valen gently tucked her hair behind her ear before skimming his fingers along the arch of her throat. Was he imagining the taste of her blood? The thought sent tingles of excitement through her. If she didn't die quickly, she might give herself the opportunity to fantasize about the pleasure of his bite, but first she had other needs she yearned to have sated.

Lowering her hands, she used the tips of her fingers to trace the rigid six-pack that tensed beneath her touch. He growled in approval, wrapping his arms around her as he devoured her mouth.

Electric anticipation zinged through her, setting off bursts of fireworks. Peri hissed as desire twisted her stomach into a knot. She'd been in lust before. She'd enjoyed sex. But she'd never had honest-to-god fireworks. Slinging her leg over his hip, she allowed her fingers to continue their journey down his body to circle the width of his erection.

Valen muttered something against her lips. The words were in an ancient language that sounded harsh and thick with need. He nuzzled the pulse pounding at the base of her throat. The touch of his lips was cold against her skin, but the heat it produced sent cascades of bliss through her. Of course, it didn't hurt that his hand had moved to cup her breast, his slender fingers teasing her nipple until it tingled with pleasure.

Peri arched against his hard body, her fingers stroking down his cock. Valen made a choked sound, his fangs pressing against her fragile skin.

"I hunger for you," he growled.

"Yes," she whispered in approval, savoring the image of his fangs plunged deep in her neck as his thick erection plunged between her legs. Peri trembled, nearly coming from the mere thought.

"Peri." Valen's tone was oddly insistent as he said her name.

"No," she groused, squeezing her eyes shut as she nibbled kisses over his chest.

This was her death wish. She didn't want it interrupted. Valen, however, refused to allow her to cling to her fantasy.

"Peri, open your eyes," he commanded.

His voice was edged with warning, cutting through the desire that clouded her mind. At the same time, his power shifted from a sensual promise to a pounding urgency.

"Peri, we're out of time." His hands grasped her shoulders, giving her a sharp shake. "Wake up."

It was a rotten end to her brush with paradise, but then again, her certainty that she was on the edge of death was starting to fade as the layer of numbing darkness thinned. Distantly she was aware of the wood planks pressing into her back, and the humid heat that clung to her skin, and a muffled sound of cars rattling over cobblestones.

With a heroic effort, she wrenched open her eyes to discover Valen crouching over her, his eyes glowing with a silver fire.

Maybe she had died, she inanely told herself.

The vampire was certainly beautiful and lethal enough to be an angel of death.

Only one way to find out.

"Am I dead?"

Chapter 22

Valen arched his brows as he gazed down at Peri's pale face. If he hadn't been in a dire situation, he would have taken pleasure in discussing exactly what was happening in her dreams. The rich scent of her desire that spiced the air assured him that it was something he wanted to know more about. Most importantly, was he involved? And how soon could they make her dreams a reality?

But the situation was dire. And becoming more dire with every passing second.

"We are both alive," he assured her. He glanced toward the morning sunlight creeping across the wooden floor. Behind him the magic created an impenetrable barrier that continued to press them toward the front of the building. The very definition of a rock and a hard place. "For the moment," he added in harsh tones.

"For the moment?" The lingering daze evaporated from Peri's eyes as she abruptly sat up to take in the sunshine that was only inches away. "Is the limo still waiting for us?"

"Yes." Valen had called the demons who'd escorted them from the airport as soon as he realized their danger. "They haven't been able to break through the magic that surrounds the building."

"Tell them to get ready." Peri rose to her feet, squaring her shoulders. "I'm going to punch a hole in the spell."

Valen straightened and pulled his phone from his pocket. He didn't question her ability to provide them with an escape. This was a woman who didn't depend on anyone to ride to the rescue. She met danger without flinching. It was only one of many reasons he found her so fascinating.

Contacting the waiting servants, he kept his gaze locked on Peri as she closed her eyes and touched the jade bracelet that encircled her wrist. The sweet scent of lilies filled the air, along with an earthy hint of cumin and raw undertones of power. It all combined to create a heady perfume. He'd spent time with mages, of course. He'd even had a few as servants. But not one of them could create this level of magic. The hum in the air was like standing in the midst of a raging thunderstorm.

Forcing himself to concentrate on the approaching sunlight, Valen pressed the phone to his ear.

"Where are you creating the opening?" he asked Peri.

"The front door." She kept her eyes squeezed closed, her voice harsh with the strain of calling on so much power at one time.

Valen passed along the information to the waiting demons. "Give them a couple minutes to get into position," he murmured. "Do you need anything from me?"

She slowly spread her arms, her hair floating as the air filled with her magic and the glow of the jade bracelet.

"You might want to stand behind me," she suggested. "When two spells meet the reaction can be unpredictable."

Valen stood firmly at her side. If anything happened he wanted to be close enough to protect her.

His phone buzzed as shadows moved outside the front door. "They're ready."

Peri didn't open her eyes. Instead, she slowly lifted her hands over her head, and Valen felt the pressure in the room change. As if she was sucking the magic toward her, like a black hole. The floor planks shuddered beneath their feet and the chandelier swayed overhead. Valen spread his legs as the power battered against him, threatening to drive him to his knees. Next to him, Peri trembled with the effort, a layer of sweat coating her face as her breath came in shallow pants.

Valen remained inhumanly still, knowing that any distraction could create a backlash of magic that would destroy Peri. Maybe both of them.

A full minute ticked past, the sun touching the tips of his shoes before she spoke ancient words that echoed through the room like a melody. There was, however, nothing melodic about the tidal wave of magic that exploded from her.

Valen hissed, feeling as if he was being flayed as the spell blasted past him to slam against the snare. There was a high-pitched squeal as the two magics clashed, like cars slamming together. Or freight trains, he silently amended as the collision yanked the chandelier from the ceiling and sent it flying across the room. It shattered against the invisible magic that held them captive, sending glass shards shooting through the air. Valen used a pulse of power to keep them from injuring Peri as she opened her eyes to focus on the locked door. She spoke another word, releasing a second burst of magic. There was another clash of magic, but this time it was smaller, and focused on a spot directly in front of them.

There was a pulse in the air, as if a live wire was writhing just inches away. Valen grimaced. He sensed that it would be a very bad thing if that pulsing electricity touched them. The sun inched closer, and Valen clenched his fangs as he felt the heat scorch through him. He had mere seconds left...

The thought was still forming when there was an earsplitting shriek as Peri's magic punched through the snare and slammed into the door with enough force to blow it off its hinges.

The demons waiting outside didn't hesitate as they rushed through the opening and headed directly for Valen. He had a brief glimpse of the red auras flickering around the large, sturdy males before they tossed a heavy blanket over his head. Soothing darkness covered him from head to toe as he was hustled out of the building and into the nearby car.

He waited until he was safely tucked in the back of the limo with Peri settled next to him before he pulled off the blanket. The driver weaved through traffic, leaving behind angry honks and a few shouts as if they'd nearly hit a pedestrian. Valen ignored the sounds, as well as the heat that continued to sear through him from his close brush with the sun. His attention was locked on the woman who lay limply against the leather seat, her eyes closed and her face pale. She was obviously exhausted, but he couldn't sense any physical injury.

Remaining silent as they raced through the narrow streets, Valen battled back the thought of how close he'd come to death. Not a true death. He would have been resurrected in a new body, but his memory would have been forever destroyed.

Along with the knowledge that Peri Sanguis was in this world.

And that was more terrifying than being consumed by the sun.

His hands fisted, his gaze skimmed restlessly over Peri's weary face. He'd desired her from the moment he'd caught sight of her. Then he'd learned to admire her as he'd watched her mature from a budding mage into a woman who could terrify most demons. Now...

Now she was burrowed so far into his soul he wasn't sure how he could survive if she wasn't near.

Valen was still trying to process that sudden realization when the limo pulled into a low garage attached to an unassuming brick building.

Thick darkness surrounded them as the door slid shut, blocking any hint of daylight. He heard the demons exiting the front of the car and moving to open his door.

On instant alert, Valen leaned to the side, peering beyond the bulky form of the demon to inspect the narrow space. He trusted Micha, but the vampire was safely tucked away in his mansion on the outskirts of the city. The servants who kept this safehouse might have any number of reasons to want Valen dead. And this was the perfect location to make him disappear.

Once he was certain there were no hidden enemies, he pushed himself out of the limo and turned to help Peri as she crawled out and instantly lost her balance. He wrapped an arm around her waist, pulling her tight against him as he glanced toward the nearest demon. The male was several inches shorter than Valen, but twice as wide with bulging muscles beneath his uniform and a shaved head that revealed several tattoos inked on his scalp.

"We need a computer. And privacy," he commanded, resisting the urge to send Peri directly to bed to rest.

They'd managed to escape the trap that had been set, but it had been too close for comfort. He was done chasing after the miasma. Or whatever the hell it was that Peri's mother had set loose in the world. He was going to end the threat. And the only way to do that was to create a trap of their own. And for that he needed information.

"If you'll follow me."

The demon turned to lead them toward the opening that connected to the main building, while the other one moved to position himself next to the garage door. Valen assumed he would be standing guard to ensure no one had followed them.

Valen applauded their diligence, but he remained cautious as they entered what appeared to be an old warehouse that had the windows bricked over and the cement floors covered with thick carpeting. The furnishings were stark, with a leather couch and a few chairs scattered around the large room. This was a place to go if Micha was in the city and needed a quick place to hide. Or to stash away a demon who needed to go off the grid. It was intended for security, not luxury.

The servant continued across the room before sliding a section of paneling to the side. Valen stepped through the opening, not surprised to discover Micha's office was equipped with state-of-the-art technology that included a wall of monitors showing security video from his various businesses and a sleek computer system on the desk in the center of the room. There were glass shelves that held dozens of disposable phones, electronic trackers, and mini cameras that could be attached to any surface.

Like most vampires, Micha was obsessed with keeping a close eye on his territory and the demons who served him.

Waiting until the servant closed the panel to give them privacy, Valen turned to study the woman who was turning in a slow circle to take in the office. She at last met his gaze with a wry twist of her lips. No doubt she was considering the scope of his own surveillance systems.

They both knew it was equally intrusive.

"Are you okay?" he asked.

"Just tired." She stared at him with an unexpected concern. "What about you?"

Valen froze. In the past two thousand years, he'd had his fellow Cabal members worry whether he could maintain the strength of his Gyre, and his demons eager for him to offer fair and steady leadership, while his lovers were anxious to keep his interest. But he'd never had anyone show concern for him. Not for what he could offer them...but *him*.

It was unnerving. In the best possible way.

With an effort, he kept his expression unreadable. There was every likelihood that Micha was monitoring them from his mansion. He wasn't prepared to reveal his obsession with this woman. Not when he couldn't be certain she was equally obsessed.

He did have his pride, after all.

"Singed, but I'll survive," he assured her.

Her concern transformed to curiosity. "You don't make that sound like a good thing."

"A good thing for me." His fangs lengthened. "A very bad thing for whoever set the snare."

Peri was undisturbed by his blatant threat. As if she was becoming accustomed to being with a vampire.

"It had to have been a mage," she murmured, her brow furrowed. "The spell was beyond what a common witch could create."

He could sense she wasn't satisfied with the mage theory. "But?"

"There was something different about the spell." She shook her head as she struggled to explain what was troubling her. "It felt elastic."

"I'm not sure what that means."

"Once a spell is cast it's static," she said. "The results might change—like if I create a fire, the flames will continue to spread until they are extinguished, but the spell itself would stay the same."

"But the snare changed?"

"Yes." She shivered, her beautiful blue eyes darkening at the memory of her battle with the spell. "When I created an opening I could feel it trying to snap closed. It was like it sensed that it'd been breached and was making an effort to repair itself." She paused, as if she had to gather her composure. "It should never have been aware of what I was doing."

Valen grimaced. It was infuriating to accept that he had no control over the situation. Like all creatures, mages were secretive about their powers. He had a basic understanding of spells and potions, but he was certainly no expert. It put him at a disadvantage.

"The magic was aware of what you were doing, or the spellcaster?"

"The magic."

"Is there a way to track down who cast the spell?"

"Not that I know of." She looked as frustrated as he felt. "Were there any security cameras?"

"Not in the building." He pulled his phone out of his pocket. "But I might have an idea how to get what we need."

"How?"

"Renee."

He pressed the screen to connect with his assistant and turned to pace across the room. Renee picked up on the first ring and with a concise efficiency he explained exactly what he wanted. Cutting the connection, he slid the phone back into his pocket and strolled back to stand in front of Peri.

"It shouldn't take Renee long to locate the information we need."

"The ever efficient secretary," she mocked with a strange smile.

Valen stepped closer. He liked the hint of annoyance he could detect in her voice.

"You wouldn't be jealous, would you?" he asked.

She blinked, as if she hadn't realized she'd spoken the words out loud. Then she shook her head in a decisive gesture.

"No, I'm sorry. That sounded petty. I admire a woman who excels in whatever profession she chooses." There was no doubting the sincerity in her words. "Besides, to be jealous, I would have to covet something she has. I have no desire to be one of your servants."

Valen cupped her face in his hands, peering into the depths of her eyes. "What do you desire?"

The sweet scent of lilies swirled through the air as her lips parted in a blatant invitation. Her expression, however, settled into stubborn lines.

"An end to the miasma," she muttered.

"And?"

"And to return to the Witch's Brew to get on with my life."

His thumb stroked the plush curve of her lower lip. "Nothing more."

She swept her long lashes over her eyes, as if attempting to hide the hunger that smoldered in the blue depths.

"Who doesn't want more?"

He made a sound of impatience. There had been a time when he'd assumed his charm was irresistible. Peri had effectively destroyed that assumption. Along with a portion of his arrogance. Thankfully, he had plenty to spare.

"Is it so difficult to admit you desire me?" he demanded.

"It's..." She paused, licking her lips. "Complicated."

Passion blazed through him. Her skin was so soft. Like silk beneath his fingertips. He wanted her naked. He wanted her wrapped around his body with her luscious scent clouding his mind.

"Why?" The word came out as a harsh rasp.

There was a long pause. Long enough that Valen feared she wasn't going to answer his question, before Peri slowly lifted her lashes to reveal the unease that shimmered in her eyes.

"I'm not sure what you want from me."

She wanted his reassurance. She needed to know that he wouldn't demand more than she was willing to give. Logically, Valen understood. But logic was no match for the pounding need that had his arms whipping around her body to haul her tight against his chest. He wasn't trying to overwhelm her, but he wanted her to understand that he wouldn't be one of those males she could keep at a polite distance.

"Everything," he warned, pressing a kiss against her forehead. "I want everything. This." He smoothed his hands down her back, cupping her ass even as his lips stroked over her cheek. The taste of her was pure magic. *She* was pure magic. He was well and truly bewitched. "And this." He claimed her lips in a kiss that was blatantly possessive. He didn't want to dominate her. Hell, he wasn't sure he could even if he tried. But he did want her to know that there was nothing casual or transitory in his need to have her in his life. He savored her soft sound of pleasure as her lips moved beneath his, returning his kiss with a need she couldn't hide. It was only when she'd melted against him that he turned his head to scrape his aching fangs along the sweep of her neck. "And especially this," he growled.

Her hands rested against his chest, not to push him away, but to keep herself upright. Valen could feel the thick scars that marred her palms from the explosion of magic that had revealed her ancient blood when she was sixteen.

"You want to consume me," she accused.

He lifted his head to study her wary expression with a brooding gaze. "Every glorious inch of you," he admitted without apology.

She trembled as his attention shifted to the vein that pulsed along the side of her neck. She wasn't afraid. Her scent revealed her sharp anticipation.

"Valen," she breathed.

Hunger slammed into him with shocking force. He had no need to feed. His hunger was to taste her sweet blood. To join them together in the most primitive way possible.

With an effort he battled back his urge to sink his fangs in her flesh, although he wasn't going to concede defeat. It didn't matter how long it was going to take. Eventually Peri Sanguis would accept that they were destined to be together.

"You can be consumed without losing who you are," he assured her.

"You're a vampire."

Valen frowned. Where was she going with this?

"True," he slowly agreed.

"A member of the Cabal."

His hands stroked up the curve of her spine, keeping her tightly pressed against him. "Again, true."

"You conquer and move on. It's your nature."

Valen valiantly squashed the urge to laugh at her accusation. She was right. He was a conqueror. He'd battled his way through the Cabal to claim one of the largest, most powerful Gyres in the world. And he continued to battle the demons who challenged his authority. But any hope of walking away from Peri had been destroyed the moment she'd looked him square in the eye and told him that she would never bend her knee.

"I'm not certain I could conquer you even if I wanted to," he admitted in dry tones. "And I have no intention of moving on. I'm comfortably settled in my lair."

She arched a brow. "You call a towering skyscraper in Manhattan a lair?"

He held her gaze, deliberately misunderstanding her teasing. "For now, it's a lair. It won't be a home until I discover someone to share it with me."

Her lips parted, as if her words were lodged in her throat. He lowered his head, savoring the sense that he'd managed to knock her off-balance, but before he could take advantage, there was a loud chirp from his phone.

Muttering a curse, Valen lowered his arms and took a step backward. Regret stabbed through him. His body craved to have her in his arms. In his bed... To have space between them was physically painful.

"Saved by the bell," he murmured, pulling out his phone to glance at the screen.

As expected, it was a text from his assistant. He moved toward the desk to switch on the computer, his movements stiff. His lips twisted into a wry smile. Vampires didn't age, but he was fairly certain Peri Sanguis was shaving years off his life.

"What's going on?" she demanded.

"Renee has the information I requested."

He remained standing as he pressed his finger on the keyboard. The computer would be heavily protected with a variety of passcodes, but his fingerprint should allow him to access his own accounts. A second later he was downloading the file his assistant had sent.

"What did she find?" Peri moved to stand next to him, the heat of her body cloaking him in a scented promise.

With an effort Valen forced himself to concentrate on the screen, which was flickering with a grainy black-and-white image.

"She sent the security video from the gift shop across the street from the Masque Salon."

"Seriously?" She leaned forward, studying the image that revealed the narrow cobblestone road and the edge of the building that housed the Masque Salon. It wasn't a perfect angle, but it did capture the front door. "Does the gift shop know she has it?"

"Micha does." His tone assured her that the approval of the Cabal leader was all that mattered.

Next to him, Peri shook her head. "Vampires."

Valen ignored her exasperation. "This goes back two weeks."

Pressing a key to start the video, they watched in silence as the first day passed with customers entering and leaving the gift shop. It wasn't until that night that the lights across the street were switched on and a man in a suit stepped out to open the shutters on the windows.

"That's the dead man," Peri murmured. "He was a lot larger before he was sucked dry by the magic."

"Yes." Valen watched the man as he stood at the open door, greeting the customers who trickled into the salon. He had a sleazy smile pinned to his lips and a habit of stroking his hands over the women as they passed him. "I'm assuming it's Richard Pascal."

Peri abruptly muttered a curse as a woman with long dark hair threaded with gray appeared from around the corner.

"That's my mother."

Valen studied the woman wearing tailored slacks and a satin shirt that was cut with a wide neckline to reveal the raven tattooed on the side of her throat. She was as beautiful as her daughter with perfectly sculpted features and lush lips, but there was a cold arrogance visible even in the fuzzy video. As she stepped through the door, Richard Pascal reached out as if intending to pat her ass. His hand jerked back before it ever made contact, his body growing rigid with shock. Valen leaned forward, studying the man's face. It looked as if he'd seen a ghost.

"He recognizes her," he murmured.

"He doesn't look happy to see her." Peri's jaw tightened. "Not an uncommon reaction."

Brenda Sanguis disappeared into the building and Richard followed behind her, closing the door. Two hours later the customers streamed back onto the street, including Brenda, who was holding a box identical to the one they'd seen hidden in her cabin. Valen assumed it was the statue that held the essence of the miasma.

The minutes passed until eventually the lights in the Masque Salon were switched off. Valen reached down to press a key to fast-forward it to the next morning. At exactly 8:00 a.m. a large delivery van pulled in front of the building and four men began loading various crates and boxes from inside the auction house into the back. They finished with the larger pieces of furniture.

"Well, we know he wasn't robbed," Peri said as Richard appeared on the sidewalk to talk to the men dressed in blue uniforms. "He arranged to have the business closed down."

Valen nodded, taking in Richard's rumpled clothes and the nervous twitch that hadn't been there the night before.

"He looks scared," he said.

"Yeah, and he's in a hurry to get out of there," Peri added as the man glanced at the watch wrapped around his wrist.

Valen turned his attention to the delivery van that was pulling away. "It's a plain truck and there's no way to read the license plate number. It's going to be impossible to trace."

The video continued to flicker as the man turned back to watch a woman round the edge of the building, as if she'd parked around the corner. She halted on the sidewalk next to him.

"There." Peri pressed her finger against the monitor. "He's handling her a set of keys. He must trust her."

They watched as the woman took the keys and said something to Richard that seemed to annoy him. With a shake of his head, he stepped into the building and slammed shut the door. The woman yelled something before tossing her head and stomping back around the corner.

"He might trust her, but he doesn't want to talk to her," Valen murmured, pressing the fast-forward key.

"Maybe not, but he's still alive at this point. She couldn't have been the one to kill him."

They fell silent as they watched the video roll through the hours. The building remained locked tight for the rest of the day and into the evening. It wasn't until nearly midnight that a shadow appeared at the edge of the building. The form slid forward until it reached the door. Holding out its hand, there was a flash of light as if a firework had exploded. Or a spell.

The glow was muted, but it was enough to reveal a familiar face before the intruder was shoving open the door and disappearing into the building.

"Mother," Peri rasped, fisting her hands at her side as they watched the video for what felt like an eternity.

At last the shadowed form reappeared, closing the door before disappearing into the darkness.

"Oh my God." Peri shook her head, clearly struggling to accept the truth of what they'd just seen. "Why would she break into the Masque Salon in the middle of the night?"

Valen hesitated, reluctant to cause her more pain. "Could she have gone back to kill him?"

She slowly unclenched her hands, as if forcing herself to release the shock clouding her mind.

"My mother is certainly capable of killing Richard Pascal if he stood in the way of what she wanted. Or if she thought he posed a danger. But there's no way she could have set the snare. She was a powerful witch, but only a mage could have...oh."

"You thought of something."

"If she had the statue with her, it might have given her additional power."

"That seems the obvious explanation," Valen agreed, continuing to fast-forward through the video until it reached the moment when they'd arrived last evening.

Turning off the video, he turned to face Peri. He didn't have to point out that no one else had entered the building after her mother had left. Not until they'd arrived to find Richard dead.

Her horrified expression revealed she'd already accepted the knowledge that Brenda Sanguis had been involved in the murder.

"What now?" she muttered, the words harsh as her emotions threatened to overwhelm her.

"Obviously, we can't speak with your mother, but there was the mystery woman who now has Richard's keys," he reminded her. "I want to know who she is and her connection to the Masque Salon."

Closing the security footage, Valen clicked on the second link that Renee had sent. It was the personal information he'd requested.

"Richard Pascal, sole proprietor of Masque Salon," he read out loud. "Born in New Orleans 1968. Unmarried. No children." He skimmed through the various organizations he belonged to and his charitable contributions. "No criminal history. No fines. Pays his taxes on time. No listed employees although he probably has a few that he pays off the books. Nothing here that helps us."

Peri cleared her throat, her expression settling into grim lines. "Any family in the area?"

Valen skimmed through the report. "His parents died several years ago, but he has one sister."

"Where?"

"New Orleans." He typed in her name. "Stella Pascal Hansen."

A picture of a middle-aged woman filled the screen. She had dyed red hair that was smoothed back from her square face and shrewd hazel eyes. Even in the photo she looked like the type of person who didn't take shit from anyone.

Peri moved to study the computer screen, her arm pressing against his. "That's the woman we saw leaving the auction house."

Valen squashed the urge to turn to Peri and continue where they'd left off. As much as he hungered to haul her to the nearest bedroom and forget the world, he understood that keeping her safe was more important than easing his desire.

Once the threat had been eliminated, he would devote his entire existence to exploring their mutual passion.

Scrolling down, he read the bio that was published in the local business register.

"She's a lawyer in town. She's a recent widow. No children listed. Lots of professional affiliations, but nothing that helps us."

"I'm assuming she doesn't know that her brother is dead."

"Let's ask her." Valen turned to cross the room.

"Now?" Peri sounded confused. "You might not have noticed, but it's daylight out there."

"I noticed." He pulled open the door and motioned to the hovering servant. "I plan to have Stella brought to me."

Peri rolled her eyes. "Of course you do."

Chapter 23

Peri was standing in the corner of the room when Stella Pascal Hansen was brought in and tied to a wooden chair. The woman sat stiffly with her chin in the air, her square body stuffed into black pants and matching jacket that was tight enough to reveal her clenched muscles. Peri was guessing she'd tried to struggle when she'd first been captured by the demons, but she'd grimly accepted she couldn't escape from their ruthless grip. Now the woman was no doubt silently plotting her revenge.

"She doesn't look happy," she murmured softly.

Valen's gaze remained locked on the woman, as if seeking to determine if she posed a threat.

"I told the staff I was in a hurry. It's possible they weren't very polite when they collected her from her home."

Peri snorted. "Collected her?"

"It sounds nicer than kidnapping."

"If you say so."

Valen shrugged. "Trust me, she won't remember this happened after we're done with our conversation."

Peri knew he was right. Valen could sweep away any memory of being taken from her home. But it was easier to focus on the dubious morals of kidnapping Stella Pascal Hansen than to let her mind dwell on her suspicion that her mother had returned to the Masque Salon and murdered a man in cold blood. It wasn't like she didn't know Brenda Sanguis was willing to kill to gain power. She had the scar to prove her mother's ruthless ambition. But it was horrifying to see the evidence of her cruelty. She was going to have nightmares of stumbling across Richard's mummified corpse.

"The sooner the better," she muttered.

Valen reached to trail his fingers down the curve of her spine. The cool touch sent sparks of pleasure through her, even as it eased the tension that had her muscles tied in knots. Any other time Peri would have marveled at her reaction. This vampire caused grown men to weep when he frowned in their direction. He entered a room and demons fell to their knees. How could his touch restore her courage?

A question that would have to be answered later. She silently chided herself for her distraction as Valen pressed his hand against her lower back, urging her forward.

"I'll enter her mind. You concentrate on getting her to talk," he murmured softly.

"Okay."

They halted in front of the woman, and Valen gestured at the hovering demons. With a shallow bow they turned to leave the room.

"Ready?" he asked, glancing toward Peri.

"Ready."

Valen reached out, tugged the blindfold off Stella and tossed it aside. The woman blinked, tilting back her head to glare at them.

"What the hell is going on?" Her voice was sharp as a dagger and loaded with authority. A lawyer's voice. "If you think anyone is going to pay one damned dime to have me returned you've lost your blessed mind. I can guarantee that," she continued. "And if you hope to force me into giving you my bank account numbers—"

Valen leaned down. "Hush."

Stella frowned. She had an iron will, but it was no match for a vampire.

"Release me or..." Her words faded as she was captured by Valen's silver gaze.

"There's nothing to fear." His voice was soft, drifting through the room like a lullaby. "You're here with friends."

Stella blinked again. "I know you?"

"Don't you remember? I'm Valen." He waved a hand toward Peri. "And this is my friend Peri."

"It's nice to see you again, Stella," Peri said, her voice equally soft.

"Yes." Stella unclenched her muscles as a tentative smile curved her lips. "I remember now."

Valen nodded toward Peri and she cautiously crouched next to the chair. She wasn't exactly sure how to get the information they needed, but she sensed it would be better to have a friendly chat than to interrogate the woman as if she was a criminal.

"We were hoping to speak with Richard while we were in town. Do you know where he is?"

Stella's bemused expression settled into lines of concern. "No, he wouldn't tell me where he was going. He promised he would contact me when he found someplace to stay, but I haven't heard from him. I'm very worried."

Her worry was genuine. It was obvious she didn't know her brother was dead. Which meant she hadn't been working with Brenda Sanguis.

"He told me he was closing his business," Peri said. "But I didn't understand why."

Stella pinched her lips. "Such a fool. I warned him."

"Warned him about what?"

The woman reached up to touch the pearls that circled her thick neck. "First of all, I warned him not to get involved with magical artifacts. It's not only embarrassing to be connected with that voodoo stuff, but who knows how dangerous they might be?"

Peri ignored the insult to magic. Stella wasn't the only human to be disdainful of witchcraft.

"He wouldn't listen to you?"

"No, he didn't care about our reputation. The family auction house was on the brink of bankruptcy and Richard claimed that magic was all a load of horseshit. He didn't believe the objects were any more dangerous than a lump of granite."

"If he didn't believe in magic, then why would he trade in enchanted artifacts?"

"He was certain that witches were stupid enough to pay any price for what they believed to be items of power." Stella folded her hands in her lap, her spine stiff with disapproval. "Unfortunately, he was right. He's been making a fortune over the past ten years."

Peri silently admitted that there were plenty of humans without magical abilities who would be easily fooled by fake artifacts, but she didn't think for a second that Richard was trying to pass along bogus relics. If so, his name would have been well known among witches as a fraud. Besides, her mother had bought the statue there. That was certainly no worthless piece of junk.

"So why close the doors?"

"He got greedy." She made a tsking sound. "Before last year he was happy to deal with collectors he had personally checked out. They might trade in fake items, but they weren't thieves or black-market dealers."

"What happened this year?"

"Like I said, he got greedy."

"Tell me what that means."

Stella looked annoyed at the question. As if she felt Peri was intruding into private family matters. A cold breeze brushed over her as Valen intensified his hold on Stella's mind. The annoyance faded as Stella settled back in her chair.

"Richard told me that attendance had fallen off at the auctions. He was afraid his customers were becoming bored with the merchandise he was offering. I tried to tell him it was just a lull. It happens in any business."

"But he didn't believe you?" Peri asked.

"When does any man listen to a woman? I've come to accept that there is some genetic default setting that keeps the male gender from believing they can be wrong about anything, even when it's shoved in their face." There was a hint of bitterness in her voice. She was speaking from experience. "Richard was determined to regain his reputation for offering rare and valuable items. He started traveling overseas to deal with collectors who weren't nearly as reputable as the ones he had here. Most of the stuff was stolen from recent archeological digs. No one had any idea what the artifacts were or what they might do." Her irritation with her brother was replaced by a troubled expression. "He swore they weren't real, but…"

"You feared they might be?" Peri suggested, urging the woman to continue with her story.

"He changed. He'd always been devoted to the business. It'd been in the Pascal family for over a hundred years. There was pressure to keep it going for another hundred years. He was terrified of being the one to fail."

"Understandable," Peri murmured.

"That's what I told myself, but then he began ignoring everything but the Masque Salon. He stopped joining me at the country club to share dinner, and even missed his various club meetings. It wasn't like him at all. He understood, as a business owner, the importance of keeping a visible profile in town."

Peri silently acknowledged that running a business without the benefit of magic must be challenging. There was nothing like a compulsion potion to create repeat customers. Then again, he probably didn't have furious demons tracking him down to try to kill him.

"Could he have been distracted by a girlfriend?"

"I don't think so. He was secretive and moody, as if he had something on his mind, but I stopped by the auction house several times without warning and he was always alone."

Peri narrowed her eyes. Was the change in his personality caused by the miasma? If it was in one of the artifacts, it might have been capable of manipulating his emotions.

Of course, there were any number of mundane reasons he might have been moody.

"Was he worried about the business?" she asked Stella.

The woman paused, as if considering the question. Eventually she shook her head. "No, I think he was obsessed with the artifacts he'd bought."

Peri struggled not to react. Valen had lowered the barriers in her mind, which meant she would be open to suggestion. Despite her strong will, she might feel pressured into telling them what she thought they wanted to hear. It was human nature.

"Any item in particular?" Peri asked in casual tones.

"He wouldn't tell me, but he muttered one night he'd found the Holy Grail." Stella lifted her hands. They were as square as the rest of her, with blunt nails that had been painted with a clear polish. This was a woman who preferred functional comfort to glamour. Peri firmly approved her choice. "I laughed at him. After all, every dealer claims to have the Holy Grail." There was regret in Stella's voice. "But day after day, Richard became more distant. He neglected me and even started to neglect himself."

"Neglect himself how?"

"My brother was meticulous. He always thought he was a player with the ladies." Stella smiled fondly even as Peri grimaced. She easily recalled the video of Richard greeting his customers. He'd been more of a perv than a player. "He never left his apartment without showering and shaving. And his clothing was professionally cleaned and pressed," Stella continued. "I used to tease him that he never married because he couldn't find a woman who was suitably obsessed with his looks."

"That changed?"

Stella shivered, as if bothered by the memory. "There were times I would stop by and I would swear he hadn't showered or shaved for days. The only time he bothered with his hygiene was when he was hosting one of his auctions." Her brows snapped together as if she was struck by a sudden thought. "Oh, and there was a strange glow in his eyes."

Peri sensed Valen tense. Becoming a recluse who forgot to shower could be caused by a human illness. Glowing eyes had to be caused by magic.

"Are you sure they were actually glowing?" Peri demanded.

"I know. It sounds ridiculous." Stella glanced down at her hands, which she'd knotted together. "Even more ridiculous, I started to think he'd been possessed by a demon."

"It's not ridiculous," Peri assured her. She didn't want the woman to feel embarrassed. They needed to know what she'd suspected was happening to her brother.

Stella glanced up, her expression hopeful that she wasn't losing her mind.

"It's possible, right? That creepy stuff he got from Greece might have contained an evil spirit that was set loose."

Peri forced a reassuring smile. Inside she was trying to imagine how it was possible to dismiss witchcraft and voodoo as a scam but believe in demon possession. Odd the way the mind could bend facts to fit a person's desired philosophy.

Besides, she was more interested in the collection Richard had received. It was possible the miasma had been buried for centuries and only recently dug up. It would certainly explain why it suddenly appeared.

"Did you see any of the artifacts?"

"I saw a few crystals and some tarnished medallions. The usual hocus-pocus stuff he sold at the auctions," Stella said. "But he had several crates in the back storage room that he never opened when I was around."

"Where are the crates now?"

Stella clenched her hands until the knuckles turned white. "I don't know."

Peri glanced at Valen. He gave a small shake of his head. She was lying, but he hadn't managed to see where the crates had been taken. Peri hesitated. There was no use in pressing her for an answer. It would be like smashing against a brick wall. Better to go around the obstacle and approach it from a different angle.

"It sounds like the auction house was doing a good business. Why shut it down?"

"I have no idea." There was sincere bewilderment etched on Stella's square face. "He called a few days ago and said he was shutting down the Masque Salon and leaving town."

"He didn't give you a reason why?"

"He refused to answer my questions. He simply packed up and handed me the keys so I could give them to the real estate agent. I haven't heard a word from him since that day."

Peri leaned toward the woman. "Where do you think he's gone?"

"I don't know."

Another lie. Hmm. Obviously, she didn't know her brother was dead, so she had to have a place in mind where he might be hiding.

"Is it a secret?"

A muscle twitched in her jaw. "Not a secret, but I'm not supposed to go there."

"Is it his hideout?"

"I..."

"Peri," Valen breathed in warning.

Peri nodded, sensing that he had his own method of getting the information they needed.

"Tell me about Brenda Sanguis," she instead asked.

Stella waited, as if expecting more information. "Who is that?"

"She was a customer at the Masque Salon," Peri told her. "She bought a statue from your brother during his last auction."

Stella shrugged with a hint of impatience. "I wasn't involved in the business. I don't know anything about his customers."

"Richard never spoke her name?"

"No." Stella reached up, touching her face, which was coated in a layer of sweat. "It's very warm in here, isn't it?"

Peri felt a light touch on her shoulder and she glanced up to meet Valen's steady gaze. He tilted his head to the side, indicating he wanted her to move away from the chair. Peri instantly straightened and stepped to the side. A vampire could crush a human mind with a mere thought. But manipulating it took more effort. And the longer they held the connection, the more difficult it was to keep the fragile mind from being destroyed. Stella was obviously reaching the edge of a mental collapse.

Valen took her place, crouching in front of the woman, who started to shake with convulsive shudders.

"Stella, look at me," he commanded.

Unable to resist the power in his voice, Stella met the silver gaze. Slowly the shivers halted and a dreamy expression softened her features.

"You are so beautiful," she breathed, her hand lifting. "Can I touch you?"

Valen neatly avoided her seeking hand. "Later."

"Do you promise?"

"Yes." Valen waited until Stella dropped her hand. "Are you listening to me?"

Stella heaved a deep sigh of pleasure as she drank in Valen's stunning beauty. It wasn't just his compulsion that caused her infatuated smile. Any woman would be captivated to be so close to this male.

"Every word," she promised.

"Good." Valen placed the tips of his fingers against her forehead. "Tonight when the sun goes down, you're going to experience an overwhelming urge to visit your brother at his hideout."

Stella made a strangled sound. "No, I swore never to go there. Not again. He was so angry when he found out that I'd followed him. I told him I was only worried because he'd been acting so strangely, but he didn't speak to me for days after that." Tears formed in her eyes. "How was I supposed to know it was a secret?"

Peri felt a stab of hope. The Pascal siblings were obviously close; the fact that Richard had something he wanted to hide from his sister meant it had to be important to him.

"He's in trouble." Valen trailed his fingers to her cheek. "You need to go to him."

Stella gasped, starting to rise. "In trouble?"

Valen placed his hand on her shoulder to hold her in place. "You can't go to him until nightfall."

"I don't want to wait."

"You won't remember you need to find him until the sun sets." Valen waited for her to stop struggling. "Do you understand?"

She jerked her head in a nod. "Yes."

"Good." Valen patted her shoulder. "You're going to forget you were here—"

"No, please," Stella interrupted in a pleading voice. "I want to remember you. Please."

"Relax," Valen urged. "Clear your mind."

"So pretty."

"Sleep."

Stella gave one last valiant effort to resist Valen's soft command, then with a wide yawn she slumped back in the chair, her eyes closing as her head flopped toward her chest.

Valen straightened and motioned toward the waiting demons. "Take her home and keep a watch on her house."

The larger demon nodded, and with minimum fuss had the snoring woman slung over his shoulder and headed for the door. The second demon followed behind him. The fact that they hadn't hesitated indicated that the local vampire, Micha, had told them to obey Valen without question.

Interesting.

Waiting until they'd left the room and closed the door behind them, Peri turned to study Valen's hard expression.

"You intend to follow her to the hideout?"

"Hopefully."

"Couldn't you just peek into her mind and get the location?"

Valen shook his head, his expression becoming downright grim. "It was odd."

Peri's humorless laugh echoed through the office. "Everything about this is odd, including Stella Pascal Hansen."

A portion of his tension eased. "True."

"What was so odd?"

"I could see clearly into her mind until she thought about her brother's hideout."

"What happened?"

"There was a shroud over it." He glared at Peri as if it was somehow her fault. "As if it's being hidden by magic, even in her mind. Is that possible?"

Peri sympathized with his frustration. He was an ancient, powerful male who assumed he possessed the skill to deal with whatever situation might pop up. He didn't have to worry about the future because he was the uber alpha Cabal leader who bent the world to his rules.

It wasn't easy for him to accept that the threat they were facing was a mysterious magic that was blatantly taunting them with their inability to track it down.

Peri wrinkled her nose, considering the question. "A mage could strip a human's mind, and they can erase certain memories, but it should look like a hole, not as if it'd been shrouded. I've never heard of anyone being able to hide specific thoughts."

"Perhaps the hideaway itself has the magic to prevent it from being located," he suggested.

"There are spells to conceal locations, but they only work for a short period of time. And as far as I know they don't keep people from thinking about them. I can't imagine the power it would take to create such a spell."

"Tonight, we'll discover for ourselves," he said, giving up the futile attempt to figure out the strange shroud as he stepped toward her. "Unless you'd rather wait here."

"Not a chance in hell."

"I assumed you'd say that. You should rest and recover your strength." His hands gently cupped her face, his gaze searing her features with a silver fire. "Unless you had some other plans for spending our day together?"

The memory of her dream scorched through Peri, setting off sparks of anticipation. She wanted this male naked and in her bed. She wanted to straddle that lean body and feel him plunging deep inside her, his fangs buried in her throat as he drank her blood.

She wanted...

Valen.

But they were in a strange safehouse with no guarantee there weren't a dozen cameras watching their every move. Now was not the time or place to fulfill her fantasies.

A damned shame, really.

"Nope, no plans."

Easily reading her mind, Valen lowered his head to sweep a soft kiss over her lips. "I can wait." He straightened to gaze down at her with a possessive expression. "Forever."

Chapter 24

Valen slid out of the Jeep that had been delivered to the safehouse by Micha. Peri quickly joined him, along with the two demon guards who had parked their vehicle behind them.

Together they threaded their way through the towering cypress trees, the ground spongy beneath their feet. The marshy landscape allowed them to move in silence, but it hid thick roots and rotting branches that could trip the unwary. He kept his movements slow as they approached the small opening that had been hacked into the dense foliage.

"This must be the place," he murmured softly.

The Jeep had come complete with heavily tinted windows, allowing them to be stationed outside Stella Pascal Hansen's townhouse when she'd climbed into her car and drove through the narrow streets. Valen had expected her to stop at one of the hotels that had sprouted around the French Quarter and along the streets heading toward the stadium. Instead, she drove out of New Orleans and into the wetlands that surrounded the city.

By the time they'd arrived at this location, Valen had started to wonder if Stella was lost. As far as he could tell she was driving aimlessly from one narrow lane to another, always heading deeper into the bayou. But after an hour of rattling over the rough roads, Stella had left her car parked on the side of the road to walk through the trees.

Peri shook her head as Stella carefully tiptoed up a sinking stone pathway toward a house that had clearly been abandoned decades ago.

"Why would Richard come out here? It looks like it's a sneeze away from collapse."

Valen studied the small house, which was peeling its paint like a snake shedding its skin. It had a rusted tin roof with a chimney that was tilted to a wonky angle. The windows had been busted out and half the porch had collapsed, while the surrounding vegetation was creeping up the sides of the structure as if hungry to consume what remained of the house.

"That might be the point," he replied.

Peri nodded slowly. "True. If Richard wanted to hide something, this would be the perfect location. Who would bother snooping around here?"

Holding up a hand to warn the demons to remain hidden in the trees, Valen led Peri across the soggy front yard to step directly in front of Stella. He didn't want her going inside the house.

As if she'd run into an invisible wall, Stella stopped in her tracks. Valen gently entered her mind, tugging at the threads that had wiped away the memory of him. He didn't want her to remember coming to the safehouse, but he wanted her to feel comfortable in his presence.

On cue she released a small sigh, her lips curving into a pleased smile. "Oh, it's you."

"It's nice to see you again, Stella." He held her gaze. "Do you know why you're here?"

"I'm looking for my brother."

Valen nodded. At least he knew that she hadn't been randomly driving around and decided to get out of the car. She'd followed Richard to this spot. But why?

"What was he doing here?"

She sent him a puzzled glance. "This land belongs to the Pascals. My great-great-grandfather was born in that shack."

Valen glanced at the decrepit building. The Pascal family had certainly gone up in the world.

"It looks abandoned," he said.

"None of us ever come out here. There's nothing left but swamp and bugs." She wrinkled her nose. "I suppose I should say that none of us came out here until Richard returned from Greece. Even then I didn't know what he was doing until I followed him one night."

Valen sensed Peri moving until she was pressed against his back. She obviously wanted to hear the conversation without distracting Stella.

"Why did you follow him?" he asked the woman.

"He'd been acting so strange. I thought something might be wrong."

She was trying to hide something from him. Valen leaned forward, his voice soft, but edged with ruthless command.

"What did you think was wrong, Stella?"

Stella took an instinctive step backward as his icy power cut through the thick, humid air.

"I was afraid he might be addicted to drugs," she ground out, his compulsion overcoming her reluctance to admit her fears. "I was determined to intervene, so I waited in my car one night, and when he drove away from his building I trailed behind him. I never dreamed that we would end up in this place. There's nothing here."

"But he was angry you followed him?"

"So angry." She touched her cheek. Had Richard hit her?

"But he didn't say why?"

"No."

Valen could hear the aching sadness in her voice. She loved her brother, and regardless of their squabbles she was desperate for him to come home. Tomorrow morning, his body would be found and she could start to grieve. It was the best he could give her.

"Stella, look at me."

She obediently peered deep into his eyes. "Yes?"

"It's time to go home and forget you were here."

She reached up to touch his face. "Now?"

"Now."

Valen stepped back as she reluctantly lowered her hand and turned to head back to her car. Once she was through the trees, he gestured toward the waiting demons. They scurried forward and Valen hid a smile. They'd clearly been well trained.

"Follow Stella home," he ordered. "And keep a guard at her house in case anyone has been watching her. It's possible we weren't the only ones interested in her brother and where he stashed his merchandise."

The taller demon, who had a shaved head and stoic expression, nodded. "Do you want backup?"

"No, but inform Micha where we are."

The demons melted into the darkness to retrieve their vehicle and return to town. Standing next to him, Peri heaved a sigh.

"I suppose we should look around."

Valen started to nod when a tingle of awareness brushed over his skin. He stiffened, his fangs lengthening in a lethal warning.

"Peri."

"What's wrong?"

His gaze scanned the darkness. "I feel a presence."

Her hands lifted, as if she was preparing a spell. "Where?"

"Watching us from the trees."

There was no fear on her beautiful features as she squared her shoulders. Like a warrior preparing for battle. "Do you want to…" Her words abruptly faltered, her brow furrowing as she glanced toward the nearby shack. "Oh."

"What do you sense?" he demanded.

She held her hand toward the ramshackle house. "The miasma is inside."

Valen ground his fangs together as Peri moved forward. He didn't know if the greater danger was the lurker in the woods, or whatever was hidden inside the cabin. But he did know that he wasn't going to be separated from Peri. Whatever happened, they would face it together.

Moving to protect her back, he grimaced as they stepped onto the sketchy porch. The warped boards squeaked with the promise of total collapse as they struggled to hold his impressive weight.

"Be careful," he murmured, a strange premonition snaking down his spine as she pushed open the door. "This feels like a trap."

She glanced over her shoulder to send him a wry smile. "A familiar sensation."

The earth shifted as he gazed into her stunning blue eyes. He'd never experienced such a connection to another creature. As if he was being pulled deep into her soul. A place he never wanted to leave.

"Too familiar," he said, his voice oddly gruff. The always smooth and sophisticated Valen had been shattered and reformed by this woman.

For a glorious moment they simply stared at one another, lost in the voracious emotions that bound them together. Then, with a faint shake of her head, Peri stepped through the doorway.

Valen followed close behind her, glancing around the open space. There was nothing left inside beyond a rotting set of cabinets against one wall and several wooden crates stacked in the far corner.

He frowned. He didn't know what Peri was sensing, but there was no visible enemy.

"Those must be the crates from the auction house," Peri murmured, crossing the squeaking floorboards to stand next to the boxes marked FRAGILE.

Valen grabbed her arm as she reached out to open the top one. "Wait, Peri," he commanded. "We don't know what's inside. I'll open them."

She frowned, but she didn't argue as she took a step back. "You're right. We need to be careful." She lifted her hand. "Before you do anything I want to put a protective spell around the crates. We can't risk releasing something worse than what's already out there."

Valen nodded. "Tell me when it's in place."

Peri sucked in a slow, deep breath, her eyes focused on the crates as she moved her lips to speak the words of power. Valen felt prickles fill the air, the crates shuddering as if they were physically attempting to avoid an invisible bubble of magic.

"Now," she commanded.

Valen released a careful burst of power. He didn't want to shatter the crates without knowing what was inside. Peeling away the wooden panels, he held up the items, hidden in a thick layer of packing straw. Then, sweeping away the wooden panels with a flick of his mind, he set them back on the floorboards still wrapped in the straw.

"Nice," Peri teased.

Unable to resist temptation, he brushed his fingers over her cheek and down the line of her jaw.

"I'm more than just a pretty face," he assured her.

She lifted her brows. "Who said you're pretty?"

"Stella."

"Hmm."

Without warning, she grasped the fingers stroking her jaw and pressed them to her lips. Heat erupted at the feel of the soft caress, but before he could react, she was stepping away.

Valen reached out, battered by a sharp urge to keep her away from the strange objects. He couldn't feel the magic, but an unmistakable danger pulsed in the air. There was something nearby that was triggering his primitive instincts. Never a good thing.

Predictably, Peri ignored the potential risks as she knelt on the floor and brushed aside the packing straw. Eventually she revealed a dozen marble statues in various shapes and sizes. A couple were just a few inches high and carved into the shapes of mice and squirrels, while others were a foot tall with spread wings that imitated a bird. The one thing they had in common was a pattern of strange symbols etched into the marble.

"Was your mother's statue a part of this collection?" he asked.

She held her hand near one of the larger statues but was careful not to touch it.

"It's possible the mages who were trying to dispose of the miasma decided to split the magic into several vessels," she said, her expression distracted. "That would diminish its strength."

Valen narrowed his eyes. He'd assumed that the evil magic had been contained in the vessel that Brenda Sanguis had busted open. Now he stared at the remaining statues in revulsion.

"If there was more than one, then it's possible your mother wasn't the only witch to release the magic."

"Yes, it could be anywhere."

"Great."

"It's also possible my mother killed Richard before he could sell anything else," she pointed out.

Valen nodded. That theory made more sense. Or maybe he simply didn't want to consider the idea that the evil magic was being spread by a hundred other witches.

"If she was the first witch to be infected with the miasma, it would explain why she wanted Richard dead and the rest of the statues abandoned in this swamp. She didn't seem like the type of woman willing to share her power."

Peri touched the center of her chest, where her mother had plunged the dagger to steal her magic.

"Never."

Anger jolted through him, but he grimly held on to his temper. Brenda Sanguis was dead. The only way to punish her was to make sure her attempt to release the evil magic was brought to an end.

"We need to destroy these," he growled.

"I can take care of that."

Peri straightened, shoving up the sleeves of her sweater. Like she was preparing to wrestle an alligator, not conjure a spell.

The sight sent a stab of fear through his heart. He knew she was powerful, but if there was miasma in each of those vessels, it seemed an impossible task for any mage to abolish it back to the hell it came from.

"Alone?"

"The magic is muted by the runes etched into the statues." She turned to meet his worried gaze. "I can do this."

Valen battled back his instinctive need to toss her over his shoulder and head out of the cabin. He was a leader who'd spent two thousand years protecting his people. It was shockingly painful to leash his alpha impulses.

"What do you need from me?"

She sent him a searching glance, as if she knew how hard it was for him to accept that she was capable of deciding what risks she was willing to take.

"You might want to go outside. I'm not sure this cabin is sturdy enough to—"

"I'm staying," he interrupted. It was one thing to acknowledge she was the obvious choice to deal with the vessels. But leave her there by herself? No way in hell. He stepped toward her, reaching out to frame her face in his hands. Holding her gaze, he stroked his thumbs along the line of her jaw. "Peri, be careful."

"Well, well. Isn't this touching," an unexpected female voice drawled.

With a hiss, Valen spun around, his fangs fully extended as he prepared to attack. How the hell had anyone managed to creep up on him? It didn't matter that he'd been distracted. He was an apex predator. Nothing snuck past his defenses.

His gaze swept over the woman. She looked like one of the aristocrats he'd known when he lived at the czar's palace in St. Petersburg. Her silver hair was smoothed away from her perfect face, which was set in arrogant lines, and her slender body was shown to advantage in a tight cashmere sweater and black silk slacks.

Valen had never seen her before, but the rich scent of cloves and the fact she'd managed to sneak up on him meant she was a mage. A very powerful mage.

It didn't take a genius to guess her identity.

"Tia," he hissed, his muscles tensed as he prepared to rip out her throat.

The woman lifted her hand, her eyes shimmering with a ruthless power. "Don't be hasty, vampire."

Valen stepped forward. He wasn't afraid of a mage. Not unless her name was Peri Sanguis. But before he could sate his hunger to punish this woman, Peri reached out to grasp his arm.

"Valen, wait."

His brows snapped together. Surely Peri hadn't forgotten this woman had tried to hold her captive? And that she intended to use her for some future power grab? As if reading his mind, Peri lifted her hand to reveal a glowing tattoo that had appeared on the back of it.

"What is that?" he demanded, his gaze locked on the strange symbol burned into Peri's skin. It looked like a snake coiled around a sword.

"A simple tracing spell," Tia answered.

Peri shook her head, glaring at the other mage. "It's more than that."

"Yes." Tia took a cautious step into the cabin, her tone smug. "There is a curse embedded in the mark. A rather nasty one, I'm afraid."

Peri frowned. "When did you…" Her expression hardened as she managed to work out how Tia had cursed her. "When I first entered your gaudy castle."

Tia took another step forward. "I had a dream you might stop by. I made sure I was prepared."

Peri narrowed her eyes. "You also let me escape."

Tia shrugged. "I didn't intend for you to destroy a very expensive window, but I did hope that you would lead me to the miasma."

Valen hissed. This woman was a threat to Peri. One he intended to eliminate. "You will die."

"There's no need for violence," Tia chided. "This is mage business, not Cabal. I'm sure Peri and I can negotiate without your assistance." She waved a dismissive hand toward Valen, but she was abruptly distracted when she caught sight of the statues at the back of the room. "What is that?"

Peri turned toward the vessels that were still nestled in the packing straw and covered by her protective spell.

"Trash that I'm about to dispose of."

Tia held up her hand, a tingle in the air revealing she'd released a burst of magic. The statues briefly glowed before Tia hissed in shock.

"This is the miasma." She sent an accusing glare toward Peri. "I thought your mother released it."

"She released one of them."

Tia walked toward the vessels, her magic still dancing over them. Valen swallowed a growl of frustration. The urgent need to destroy the arrogant mage pounded through him, but he couldn't be certain he could rip out her throat before she could release the curse.

Tia ignored the sharp chill in the air as she bent down to study the statues. "I followed you because I assumed you were hunting the magic. But this…" A visible shiver raced through her body. "So much power. It's making the earth shudder."

"No, don't." Peri rushed to stand next to Tia. "My mother made the mistake of thinking she could control the magic."

Tia made a sound of disgust. "A witch."

"A witch," Peri agreed. "And an egotistical bitch who cared more about her bloated ego than the people who pledged their loyalty to her. Because of her pride, the evil is spreading through the world." Peri squared her shoulders. "I won't let any more be released."

"Don't forget." Tia touched the mark on the back of Peri's hand. "I own you."

Peri slapped Tia's hand away. "Do your worst. I might suffer, but Valen will still kill you and I will destroy the vessels."

Tia blinked, as if she couldn't imagine that Peri would risk crippling pain or maybe even disfigurement to destroy the miasma. Then a cunning smile curved her lips.

"Don't be so hasty, Peri," she said, her tone more imperious than cajoling. She wasn't a woman who would ever beg. "Imagine the possibilities. The two of us could share the magic. Together we would rule the world."

"I don't want to rule the world." Peri turned toward Valen, a slow smile curving her lips. "I just want to enjoy my family in peace."

Valen jerked in shock, once again feeling as if his essence was being molded into someone new. Family. He'd never wanted more than his place in the Cabal and faithful servants. That was enough to satisfy his needs. Or at least, that's what he'd told himself. It wasn't until the pleasure blazed through him that he realized just how desperately he desired to be included in those Peri considered her most intimate circle.

"So stupidly naïve," Tia snarled.

Peri took a deliberate step back. "Take care of her."

"With pleasure."

Valen parted his lips to reveal his massive fangs, not surprised when Tia grimly stood her ground. The mage possessed the sort of ego that would never allow her to back down. Even when she must know that she didn't have a chance of surviving the encounter.

He prowled forward, fully prepared to bring a painful end to the bitch who threatened his chosen woman.

"Stop it!" Peri called out.

Focused solely on Tia, who was moving her lips as she prepared a spell, Valen came to an abrupt halt.

"What's wrong?"

Peri pointed toward the statues, which were suddenly surrounded by a reddish glow. As if they were coated in a layer of evil.

"She's trying to draw on the magic from the vessels."

"It's not me," Tia protested. She stepped away from the statues as the first sign of fear crept over her face. "I swear."

Valen frowned, sending Peri a worried glance. "Is it the miasma?"

She looked momentarily confused. She obviously sensed something she didn't understand. Then, with a horrified gasp she turned to sprint toward the door.

"Get out of here."

Valen didn't need any prompting. A heavy cloud of magic was filling the air, seeping up through the floorboards as if some buried creature had been stirred to life. Even worse, there was a steady pulse at the center of the cloud that warned of a looming explosion.

Reaching out, he wrapped his arm around Peri's waist as they ran toward the door, ignoring Tia, who was several steps behind them.

They were mere inches from the open doorway when the pressure detonated with an audible thud, like a concussion bomb. The blast wave swept through the cramped space with the force of a tidal wave, knocking Valen off his feet and shoving him through the doorway.

He staggered forward, battling to keep his balance even as the force of the blast ripped Peri from his arm. *Shit.* Whirling around, he searched the darkness, expecting to find her lying on the mossy ground.

Tia was there, sprawled face-first just inches away. He didn't know if she was dead or knocked unconscious, and he didn't care. The only thing that mattered was that Peri was nowhere to be seen.

Was she still in the cabin?

Leaping over the motionless Tia, Valen rushed onto the porch. The door was still open, but there was no way to see past the reddish cloud that boiled and churned as if it was struggling to escape the cabin. He was going to have to get inside. Stepping forward, he pressed against the strange mist, shuddering at the oily clamminess that clung to him like a web of evil. He managed to get one foot through the door, when a blast of magic knocked him backward.

Fear scoured through him like acid. Peri was trapped. Jumping to his feet, he raced forward and slammed his fist against the impenetrable magic.

"Peri!"

Chapter 25

Peri hissed in agony as she was surrounded in a cloud of crimson. The magic was biting into her flesh like lethal claws. She wasn't sure if the miasma had come from the statues or if it'd been lurking beneath the cabin, but she recognized its power as it violently ripped her from Valen's grasp.

Flying backward, Peri braced herself to hit the hard floorboards. The red mist made it impossible to see where she was going, but gravity was eventually going to do its thing. The painful thump never happened. Instead she kept flying, as if she had been caught on an air current that was carrying her away from the cabin.

What the hell?

This had to be a spell.

Grimly ignoring the magic that continued to lash against her, Peri concentrated on her body. She started at her feet, envisioning them in the comfortable pair of tennis shoes she'd put on before leaving the safehouse. Next, she formed the image of her long, muscular legs hidden beneath her jeans and then her torso and arms warmly snuggled in a flannel shirt she'd found in the guest bedroom after taking a quick shower. Inch by inch she formed the picture until she could see herself clearly in her mind. Only then did she widen the image to place herself firmly in the center of the cabin.

The sensation of soaring through the air abruptly shattered as she burst through the illusion. Peri cursed when gravity belatedly kicked in and she hit the ground with a heavy thud. With a muttered curse, she dismissed the jolt that compressed her spine. She'd managed to land on her feet. She was taking that as a win.

Holding up her hands, she tapped into her magic and released a burst of power that peeled back the thick red mist. As it cleared, she wasn't surprised to discover she was standing exactly where she expected to be. In the center of the cabin. She also wasn't surprised to realize that both Valen and Tia were gone. They'd no doubt been shoved outside during the initial burst of magic.

But she hadn't expected the woman with a cloud of blond hair and an angelic face who was blinking as if she'd just awakened from a bad dream.

"Destiny." Peri stiffened, running a quick gaze over the woman, still in the same tube top and jeans she'd been wearing at the ranch. Now, however, they were coated in dust and flecks of…was that blood? Peri shuddered. "What are you doing here?" she demanded.

"I don't know." Destiny continued to blink, glancing around in bewilderment. "Where am I?"

"Outside of New Orleans."

"Oh, right." She slowly nodded, as if she'd latched onto a missing memory.

Peri took a cautious step to the side, sweeping her gaze around the room. The magic still thundered in the air, but it had moved to press against the walls of the cabin. She was guessing it was a barrier to keep out Valen. Or maybe it was to keep her trapped. Or probably both. Her gaze landed on the vessels, which continued to glow, although none of them were fractured. She was assuming that was a good thing.

She turned her attention back to Destiny. "How did you get here?"

Destiny wrapped her arms around her waist. "Your mother."

"My mother?"

"Well, I drove the van, but she was the one who directed me where to go," Destiny clarified.

Was this some sort of trick? Was she trying to unnerve her by talking about Brenda Sanguis as if she was still alive? Or had Destiny been driven mad by the magic?

"My mother is dead," she reminded the woman, watching impatience ripple over Destiny's face.

"I know that," she snapped. "It was her spirit."

"My mother's spirit?"

"Yes. She followed me from the ranch."

Peri squashed her flare of anger. Her mother had been a murderous bitch, but she'd been punished for her sins. Wasn't it time to allow her to rest in peace? But then again, what if Destiny wasn't lying? What if she truly believed that she was being haunted by her former coven leader?

"How do you know it was my mother?" Peri demanded.

Destiny frowned in confusion. "I could see her, of course."

"Oh. Okay." Peri didn't press the issue. "What happened?"

"She promised I was finally going to have the power I always craved, but she lied."

Peri narrowed her eyes at the witch's bitter tone. "What have you done, Destiny?"

Destiny cowered back, pressing a hand to her chest. "It wasn't me."

Peri's suspicion that Destiny was involved in the deaths was confirmed by the guilt that shimmered in her eyes.

"You killed that poor bartender at the Jackalope Station, didn't you? And the fortune teller who was just trying to make some extra money for her family."

Destiny tossed her hair in a defiant motion. "I told you it wasn't me, it was your mother."

"Even if my mother did come to you as a spirit, why would she murder those women?"

"She needed the chaos from the humans to feed and the magic from the witches to gain power."

Peri stepped back. The words revealed exactly who was pretending to be her mother. Only the miasma would hunger for chaos. So where was it hiding? And what was it doing with Destiny?

Touching the jade bracelet that encircled her wrist, Peri began weaving a protective spell. It was a damned shame she didn't have the opportunity to brew more potions, but she would work with what she had.

"What happened to the magic that killed my mother?" she asked Destiny.

"I don't know." Destiny held her hands out in a pleading motion, moving toward Peri. "I just want to go home. I mean it this time, Peri. I'm so scared."

Peri hastily snapped the protective spell in place, holding out a hand in warning. "No, stay back."

"What's wrong?" Destiny stared at her in confusion, but she was close enough for Peri to see the shards of crimson shimmering in her eyes.

Acceptance smashed into Peri, destroying any hope that Destiny was an innocent victim. The miasma was inside her, controlling her every move.

"You're not Destiny," she accused.

"Peri—"

"No!" Peri lifted her hand in warning. She didn't know if she could hurt the miasma, but Destiny was human. It was quite possible she could be injured.

She allowed a thread of magic to penetrate her shield, arrowing toward Destiny's cheek to slice a shallow wound. Instantly a trickle of blood wound its way down her face.

Crimson fire consumed Destiny's eyes, her lips parting to release a mocking laugh. "Very good, Peri Sanguis."

Her voice hadn't changed, but it resonated with a power that vibrated against Peri's protective shield. As if it was seeking to snare her with its words.

Peri's mouth went dry. She'd seen what the miasma had done to her mother's coven, and later to Richard Pascal. Not to mention the fact that she'd touched only a small fragment of the magic when she'd been studying it in the playroom and it'd threatened to consume her.

Now she was face to face with it.

The chances of surviving were slim to none.

Stiffening her spine, Peri silently chided her defeatist thoughts. She'd faced death before. At the hands of her own mother. The only certain way to die was to give into her fear.

Forcing herself to meet the smoldering crimson gaze, she concentrated on reinforcing her shield. At the same time, she sought a way to keep the miasma thinking about something other than sucking her dry.

"Is Destiny still alive?" she asked.

"Technically." The magic controlling Destiny lifted her hands over her head as if stretching. "I had need of her body."

"You're the miasma, aren't you?"

The arms spread wide. "There is no name that can capture my splendor. Not since the awakening."

Awakening? Peri continued to weave her magic as she considered the strange word. Was the miasma referring to the moment it became self-aware? That seemed the most logical interpretation.

"How did you...awaken?" Peri forced herself to ask. She genuinely wanted to know how the magic had gone from a puddle of evil to a walking, talking, threatening-the-world sort of evil. But more importantly, she needed to keep the magic from launching an attack before she was ready.

"It was slow. For a long time I only knew that I was buried deep in the earth, and that I was surrounded by magic. It pulsed against me like a heartbeat, piercing the vessel that held me captive." Destiny—or at least the thing controlling her—shuddered in ecstasy at the memory. "Eventually it sparked the understanding that I was more than raw emotion. I could think and reason. And plot for the day I was released from my prison."

Peri cursed. What mage thought it would be a smart idea to imprison the miasma, and then instead of destroying it, bury it deep in one of the most powerful Gyres in the world? Although each Gyre was rumored to be an ancient dragon lair, they possessed their own level of power. The

Gyre that Valen controlled maintained an impressive amount of magic, but nowhere could compare to Greece.

She could only assume they'd buried it so deep they never expected it to be dug up.

But it had been, and it'd been brought to New Orleans, where it'd managed to gain control over the poor fool who had no idea of his danger.

"Richard Pascal released you?" she demanded, sweat beading on her brow. Creating a protection spell was simple enough, but she was attempting to create one layer on top of another. Like building a brick wall. The concentration it demanded was straining her ability to pay more than vague attention to the miasma.

"Only a trickle of my magic was allowed to escape, but it was enough to take control of his mind." Destiny's lips were pulled into a creepy smile. "Humans are so easily manipulated, aren't they? I encouraged him to hide the vessels that contained my essence until I could discover someone with the power to fully liberate me."

"My mother?"

The crimson eyes flared. "I couldn't believe when she passed by me. I hadn't felt that sort of magic since the dragons retreated from this world." She licked her lips, as if trying to taste the memory. "Wild magic."

That explained Richard's strange reaction on the security video when Brenda Sanguis had strolled past him. Still, Peri was confused.

"My mother was a witch, not a mage," she said, pointing out the obvious. "She didn't have wild magic."

"So I discovered after I'd transferred my power to her." A red mist danced around Destiny's body. She was clearly still pissed that she'd been deceived.

"And then you forced my mother to return to the Masque Salon to kill Richard?"

She shrugged. "He'd served his purpose."

"So why go to the ranch?"

Destiny pursed her lips. "I was disappointed to discover that the power I thought would be mine was an illusion. It meant that I needed the combined power of the entire coven to escape my vessel." Her head swiveled toward the statues glowing at the back of the room. "Or at least a portion of me."

"That's when you infected Destiny?"

"I still sensed the wild magic," the miasma confessed, "but now it was connected to the surviving witch."

Peri frowned. Her mother had been a powerful witch who'd honed her skills over several years. Next to her, Destiny was a rank amateur.

"Destiny?"

The woman's features twisted into an expression of self-disgust. "It wasn't until I had chosen her as my host that I could pinpoint the source of the magic." She held up her hand to reveal the dagger she was clutching. "It was this. The blade that she'd taken off your mother's corpse."

Peri gasped. Okay. That was a plot twist that she hadn't been expecting. With an effort, she studied the long knife. Not easy when she remembered what had happened the last time someone waved that dagger around her.

"Because it can absorb magic?" she forced herself to ask. As far as she knew, the knife wasn't any more powerful than any other artifact her mother had collected over the years.

"No, because it has *your* magic."

"My magic? That's impossible." Peri's breath abruptly hissed between her clenched teeth. Maybe it wasn't impossible. After her mother had stabbed her in the chest, she'd managed to drain a large portion of Peri's essence before the wild magic had exploded out of her. She pressed her hand against the scar that suddenly throbbed. "Oh."

"Yes. The runes on this dagger that allowed your mother to absorb your magic kept it stored in the blade. That's what I sensed."

Peri grimaced. The stupid dagger was why the miasma had infected her mother and then Destiny. But that didn't answer why she'd been traveling from small town to small town.

"If that's true, why didn't you capture me while I was at the ranch?" Peri asked the obvious question.

Destiny leaned forward, sniffing the air. Like a dog trying to catch the scent of his prey.

"You have a remarkable ability to keep your magic hidden. I doubt anyone has detected more than a fraction of your talent," she explained. "It wasn't until I searched through Destiny's mind that I realized you were the one I was seeking. By then it was too late. You had disappeared."

Peri leashed the urge to step back. She'd expended a great deal of effort to create her shield; she wasn't going to ruin it because she couldn't control her emotions.

Stiffening her spine, Peri tied off her magic. She'd done what she could. Now she had to hope it was enough.

"Why does Destiny believe she's being controlled by my mother's spirit?"

"I needed her to obey my commands. An illusion was the simplest way to keep her sane."

"There's nothing sane about your killing spree."

Destiny laughed. It was a strange rasping sound. Like snake scales rubbing together.

"Hardly a spree. I needed to feed, and there was the hope you would come in search of Destiny if you thought she was in danger."

"Why would I care what happens to Destiny?"

"She's a member of your coven."

"Not my coven." Peri didn't bother to hide the bitterness in her tone. She'd put what her mother had done to her in the past, but that didn't mean she didn't harbor resentment toward Brenda Sanguis and the women who'd watched her stick a dagger in her daughter's heart. "I walked away a long time ago."

A sneer twisted Destiny's features. "That's your claim, but here you are."

"I didn't come for Destiny." Peri tapped into the magic pulsing in her jade bracelet. "I came to destroy you."

Chapter 26

Valen's hand was aching before he grimly conceded defeat. He couldn't use brute force to battle his way through the seething mist. He needed magic. Luckily, he happened to have a powerful mage at his disposal.

Vaulting off the porch, he crouched next to the unconscious woman and turned her until she was lying flat on her back. Tia's face was pale, but her breathing was even. She was knocked out cold, but there were no life-threatening injuries.

"Wake," he commanded, placing his fingertips against her temple. His compulsion couldn't enter her mind, but he could force her awake. "Tia, hear my voice." Concentrating on the mage, Valen missed the approaching footsteps that were muffled by the spongy ground. Thankfully, he didn't miss the scent of demon that suddenly threaded the breeze. Or the sharp tang of metal.

A weapon.

The thought barely had time to form before he was abruptly rolling to the side. Less than a second later there was the crack of a gun and the sizzle of the bullet as it passed inches above his head. He waited until the second shot buzzed past before he shoved himself to his feet with a furious growl. He'd been shot once this week. It damned well wasn't happening again.

Moving too fast for the demon to track, Valen rushed into the trees. A second later he had his fingers wrapped around the thick neck of a male. Yanking him off the ground, he studied his captive.

The creature was huge with wide shoulders and a shaved head. He'd chosen to wear black jeans and a black motorcycle jacket, the heavy clothing blending in with the night, but they did nothing to hide the dull crimson aura that surrounded him. Valen squeezed his fingers, not bothering to ask the demon questions. There was no doubt he was there with Tia.

Proving his theory, a ring of fire abruptly sprouted around him. The magical flames danced in the thick air, bobbing on the breeze. They wouldn't kill him, but they would cause enough damage to drain his powers. Something he couldn't risk when Peri needed him.

"Stop." Tia appeared through the trees, her steps unsteady as she halted next to the flames. "Lynch was just trying to protect me. Please release him."

Valen shrugged, tossing the demon to the side. As he'd hoped, Tia swiftly doused the fire to prevent her servant from being injured.

Valen pointed toward Lynch, who'd landed on his knees, his hand pressed against his bruised throat.

"Stay down."

"Do as he says," Tia ordered, despite the fact that Lynch didn't look in any mood to continue his battle with Valen. He might be a demon, but he was no match for a vampire. Then she tilted her chin to a proud angle. "Are you going to kill me?"

Valen smiled grimly, grasping her arm, and dragging her back to the cabin before she could regain her balance.

"Not until you break through the barrier keeping me away from Peri," he growled, jerking her onto the porch to face the cloudy mist that blocked the doorway.

Tia's features were clenched hard with fury at being hauled around like a sack of potatoes, but she was smart enough not to protest. And once they were face to face with the boiling mist, her anger was replaced with a shocked fear that tainted the air with the scent of scorched cloves.

She lifted her hand, holding it toward the boiling cloud, but was careful not to touch it.

"This is the miasma?"

"You wanted to gain control of it, didn't you?" Valen demanded. "Now's your chance."

Tia didn't bother to glance in his direction; she was lost in her examination of the magic. Valen gave her a few moments to study the mist, trying to ignore the strange stillness that had fallen over the bayou. It was as if the wildlife had sensed the evil that was brewing inside the cabin and gone into a protective hibernation.

"I had no idea," Tia eventually breathed, shaking her head in disbelief. "It's…"

"What?"

"Hungry." Tia abruptly stepped back and wrapped her arms around her waist in a protective motion. "It's reaching out to drain my powers."

"Destroy it."

She sent him an annoyed glare. "I can't use my magic."

Valen parted his lips, giving her a full view of his razor-sharp fangs. "Do it, or I'll kill you."

She stubbornly shook her head. "If I cast a spell it will only feed the miasma."

"Lies," Valen hissed.

"No, I swear I'm telling the truth."

Valen narrowed his eyes. "The mages used magic to destroy the miasma in the past."

"They joined together to smother it with a dampening spell before it was scooped into containers to be destroyed. No mage has ever battled the miasma when it's like this." The mage shuddered. "My God, it's almost as if it's alive."

Valen wasn't going to waste time explaining that the miasma was not only alive, but they suspected it was capable of infecting people to spread its evil. His patience had been worn to zero. He was getting into the cabin one way or another.

He stepped toward Tia, looming over her as he allowed the temperature to drop until her breath came out in a puff of frost.

"Find a way to get me inside or—"

"How am I supposed to think when you keep threatening me?" Tia snapped.

"Call it motivation."

"Leeches." She started to twist her lips into a sneer only to stiffen when she seemed to be struck by a sudden thought. "Oh."

"What?"

She glanced toward the mist, another shudder racing through her. "It will absorb my magic, but it shouldn't be able to do the same to a potion."

"Why not?"

He expected a sharp response. This mage had an oversize ego and a habit of assuming she was in charge. Instead, she answered his question. Or maybe she was speaking the words out loud in an effort to convince herself it would work.

"A spell is using my magic in real time. It's still attached to me."

Valen accepted her explanation with a nod. "And a potion?"

"The magic is contained within the ingredients I've mixed together. It doesn't need me to fuel it." She grimaced. "In theory it should prevent the miasma from gaining power."

"Do you have potions?"

"Of course." She nodded toward the trees. "In my vehicle."

Valen snapped his fangs. Did she think he was stupid? "Convenient."

"Not really."

"There's no way in hell I'll allow you out of my sight."

She made a sound of impatience. "I'll send my servant."

"Fine."

"Lynch," she called out. "Bring my case."

There was a rustle in the trees as Lynch obediently dashed off, presumably to retrieve the mysterious case. Once he was gone, a thick silence blanketed the swamp, pressing against Valen with a tangible force. It wasn't just the evil that pulsed in the air. Or the thick, humid air that carried the stench of rotting vegetation.

It was the knowledge that every second that passed, Peri was trapped alone with the miasma. The need to battle his way to her blasted through him like acid. A corrosive need that was distorting his ability to think clearly.

Dangerous. The word whispered through the back of his mind.

It wasn't just his strength that made him the most lethal predator in the world. It was the cunning he'd gained over the past two thousand years. Now, when he needed that wisdom more than ever, his mind was clouded by his frantic urge to pound against the barrier until it shattered.

He was no closer to leashing his primitive impulses when Lynch appeared through the trees. On full alert, he watched as the demon inched his way across the clearing.

"No surprises, demon," he warned.

The male was visibly shaken as he crouched low to place a leather case that looked like the old-fashioned satchel human doctors would carry on the porch. Then, bowing his head toward Valen, he backed away, once again disappearing into the trees.

Tia clicked her tongue as she moved to grab the bag off the lower step. "I will be seriously pissed if you've broken him."

Valen dismissed the demon from his mind. "He won't be the only one broken if you fail."

Tia opened the bag and peered inside. "I never fail," she informed him in cold tones, pulling out a slender vial filled with an orangish liquid. "This should create an opening long enough for you to enter."

Valen stepped back, fully prepared to strike if Tia twirled and tossed the potion in his direction. She was a mage who would do anything and betray everyone to achieve what she desired.

"Do it," he commanded.

Thankfully, he had no need to kill the woman. She lifted her hand and tossed the vial toward the center of the doorway. It entered the reddish mist as if it was going to sail through with no impact. But after disappearing into the haze, it must have smashed against the unseen barrier. There was the sound of shattering glass followed by a sizzle of power as the potion reacted with the mist. And then there was nothing...

Not until a deep, thumping vibration could be felt beneath his feet. As if there was an unbearable pressure beginning to build. At the same time, the mist started to pulse in rhythm. The potion was doing something. He just had no idea what that something was.

Next to him, Tia was obviously more prepared. Still clutching her potion bag, she widened her stance as the air thickened until it pressed against them. Valen clenched his fangs as the cabin seemed to hold its breath. Something was about to happen.

The thought had barely managed to form when there was a rumble from inside the mist. It started low, like the sound of an approaching freight train. Then it changed, the rumbling transforming into a high-pitched screech. Was the potion hurting the miasma? Or pissing it off?

Impossible to say.

The screeching was abruptly cut off as the mist swirled and jerked before it reluctantly parted. It was more a crack than an opening, but Tia sent him an impatient glare.

"Go! Now!"

Valen didn't hesitate. Launching himself forward, he reached out as he passed Tia, grasping her arm. Ignoring her struggles, he plunged through the doorway. Until he was sure he was standing next to Peri, he wasn't letting this mage out of his sight.

Together they squeezed through the crack, which thankfully widened to allow them inside. Valen felt the mist brush over him, clinging to his skin like a cobweb. He dismissed the unpleasant sensation as they stumbled through the last of the magical barrier.

At last.

He quickly glanced around, expecting to see the interior of the empty cabin. What he saw instead was an endless landscape of flat, barren sand and overhead a sickly green sky with two moons that circled a black hole. It was as alien as if they'd been transported to a distant planet.

"Where did you take us?" he growled. "Where's Peri?"

"I made the opening you demanded." Tia yanked her arm out of his grasp. "How dare you force me in here?"

Valen sent her a frustrated glare. "You were the one who followed us to take control of the miasma, right? You should be thanking me."

Tia stepped away, but her gaze remained locked on him, as if she was too terrified to actually glance toward the eerie surroundings.

"Gratitude is the last thing I feel," she managed to mutter.

Valen turned away, not daring to move in case there was a hidden trap. "This isn't the cabin." He stated the obvious.

"It has to be."

Valen glanced around. Could the miasma be creating an illusion? That seemed the most logical answer. But then again, they had no idea what sort of power the evil magic possessed. They might have been whisked to another dimension.

Unease prickled over his skin. The foreign landscape hadn't changed, but the fine sand was beginning to stir as a breeze rushed past them. In that breeze was a faint hint of sulfur. Tia grimaced, but Valen stiffened as a fragmented memory stitched together in the back of his mind.

He'd been in this place. Or at least the most primordial part of him had been there. This was where the vampire retreated after his human body had been destroyed. And it remained here waiting for the proper host to summon him. He had no actual memory of being here, but while it'd been two thousand years ago, he would never forget that stench.

"This is the afterworld," he rasped.

Tia clutched the potion case against her chest, as if it might protect her. "Hell?"

"No. The world of spirits trapped between life and death."

Tia paled until her skin looked like ash in the greenish glow, but amazingly, she didn't faint, or crumble into a ball of fear.

"Did the miasma bring us here?"

Did it? Valen considered the question. "It would make sense," he finally conceded, recalling Peri's description of testing the shard in the playroom. And how the residue from the miasma had struck out in an effort to steal her magic. "The miasma absorbs its power by draining mages. Usually to the death."

"Like a vampire," Tia muttered.

That was his thought exactly. And why he was willing to believe that the miasma would have the ability to enter the afterlife. Just like vampires.

Not that he was going to admit as much to Tia. How vampires remained immortal was Cabal business, and not shared with the public.

He shrugged. "There are similarities."

Tia at last forced herself to glance around, her jaw clenched as she caught sight of the black hole swirling above their heads.

"How do we get out of here?"

"We need to find Peri," he stubbornly insisted.

"She's here?"

Valen stepped away, allowing his concentration to focus on the woman who had become more important than life itself. Closing his eyes, he opened himself to his surroundings. The nasty stench of sulfur assaulted his senses, along with the sting of sand as the breeze scooped up the fine grains. In the distance there was a bone-chilling emptiness that revealed the presence of a spirit. There was no rich scent of lilies, which meant that she wasn't in this dimension, but he could feel her presence. Almost as if he could reach out and touch her.

"She's not here, but she's close."

"Then lead us to her," Tia commanded.

"I can't," he admitted, his voice sharp with frustration.

"Why not?"

"The barrier remains." He held out his hand, as if he could touch the unseen wall that separated him from Peri. "I can't get through."

Tia hissed in outrage. "You've trapped me here?"

Valen turned back, his icy power lashing against the mage until she took a step back. He might have matured past the age that he felt the urge to intimidate everyone who challenged his authority, but this woman had held Peri captive, and then placed a curse on her. She was lucky he hadn't followed through on his threat to rip out her throat.

"Unless your servant can summon us?"

Tia wisely lowered her gaze, belatedly realizing that she'd pushed her luck far enough.

"That's not funny."

Valen ignored the muttered chastisement. He was far more interested in the thought that had struck him when he'd mentioned being summoned. What they needed was a tangible connection to pull them through the barrier.

"Perhaps there's a way."

"How?"

"Peri."

Tia frowned. "I don't understand."

Valen folded his arms over his chest. "You marked her, didn't you?"

The woman looked confused. Then her brows arched in surprise. "Are you talking about the tracking spell?"

"And curse," he added in icy tones.

Tia's frown deepened, as if she was mulling over his words. Then, with a sharp nod, she met his gaze.

"You're right," she announced. "I should be able to tap into my spell and use her to lead me out of here."

Valen closed the distance between them with blinding speed, his fingers curling around her upper arm to yank her tight against his side.

"Lead *us* out of here."

Chapter 27

Peri felt the miasma probe the shield she'd built around herself. It wasn't painful—not yet anyway—but it sent chills of horror skittering down her spine. She'd called her mother evil. After all, you had to be wicked to kill your own daughter, right? But as Destiny slowly circled her, sending out small blasts of magic, Peri understood that there were various levels of evil.

The creature that stalked her now was without conscience or morals. It had no thoughts or feelings. Nothing beyond a ravaging hunger for more power.

Destiny came to a halt in front of her, the crimson eyes flaring as if preparing to launch a full-out attack on Peri's defenses. Peri widened her stance, her muscles clenched and her mouth dry with fear. She had no idea what to expect, but she was assuming it was going to be bad.

And painful.

The expected blow, however, was never delivered. Even as Destiny's eyes glowed with power, Peri felt a strange tug on the back of her hand. Bewildered, she glanced down, her heart missing a beat as she realized that the mark made by Tia's curse was suddenly shimmering. Was it reacting to the miasma?

No. That couldn't be right. It would have started shimmering when Destiny had first appeared. And there wouldn't have been a smell of cloves in the air.

Dangerously distracted, Peri lifted her head and struggled to concentrate on Destiny. Tia's curse was at the bottom of her list of things to worry about. But even as she focused on the eyes that glowed with unnerving crimson flames, there was a flicker of movement just over Destiny's shoulder.

At first she thought the stress was messing with her mind. Even obscured by the reddish mist she would have sworn she recognized the broad shoulders and arrogant tilt of the head.

It had to be Valen. But how could he have gotten through the magical barrier that surrounded them? The question was answered when he stepped out of the mist accompanied by a woman with silver-gray hair and smoldering black eyes.

Tia must have had some sort of magic to get them through the mist. Dammit.

"Valen," she breathed, a new fear pulsing through her. "You have to get out of here."

Tia pressed her lips together. "That's what I was just saying to him. The stubborn creature refuses to listen."

Peri choked back a hysterical urge to laugh. She could have told Tia she was wasting her breath to try to convince Valen to do anything he didn't want to do.

Stepping forward, Valen locked his gaze on Peri as if he was intentionally ignoring the other women.

"Are you hurt?"

"No, but you have to leave," she rasped.

"Why do I recognize your scent?" Destiny abruptly broke into the conversation, her nostrils flaring as if she was taking in deep breaths. She moved toward Valen, her feet barely touching the ground, as if the magic was threatening to burst out of the human body. Valen flashed his fangs, but Destiny didn't notice as she laid her hand against his chest. "Ah. Peri's faithful leech," she sneered. "Immense magic, but of no use to me."

Without warning, Destiny used the hand she'd pressed against Valen's chest to send him flying backward. It was done with such ease that Peri gasped, her eyes wide as she watched Valen smash into the invisible barrier. At the same time, the mist swirled and seethed, creating branches to twine around his arms and legs to hold him captive three feet off the ground.

He roared in frustration, but the mist continued to tighten until his face twisted into an expression of unbearable pain.

"Stop it!" Peri called out.

"Hush, I'm busy." Destiny waved a dismissive hand toward Peri as she strolled toward Tia, who was trying to look as if her knees weren't shaking in fear. "A mage," Destiny drawled, sniffing the air. "How nice. I can have a tasty snack before the main course."

Tia arched back, the smell of cloves thick in the air. "I'm not your prey."

"Hmm. What do you think you are?" Destiny halted in front of Tia, her hand lifting to press a finger to the middle of the older woman's forehead. Peri had no idea what the creature was doing until she released a spine-chilling chuckle. "You thought you could come here and control me as if I'm a puppet?"

"Of course not. I hoped we could join forces," Tia smoothly lied. "Together we could bend the world to our will."

"The world will bend, but you're not the chosen one."

Tia licked her lips, her eyes darting toward Peri. She looked as if she was silently blaming Peri for her current danger. As if Tia hadn't been the one to trick Peri, curse her, and then follow behind her like a stalker. Or maybe she was blaming Peri for being the chosen one. Tia was arrogant enough to crave being the superior mage, even if it meant facing her own death.

Reluctantly Tia returned her attention to Destiny, who continued to press a finger to her forehead.

"I'm willing to share."

Destiny shook her head. "If that's true, then why do you imagine yourself with a crown on your head?" There was another laugh. The miasma obviously found Tia's ambitions a source of amusement. "And you're sitting on a throne. How very human. Shall I grant your wish?"

Tia stilled, appearing to be caught between fear and a tentative hope that she might actually achieve her heart's desire.

"What wish?"

"A throne."

Destiny stepped back, waving her hand to direct the hovering mist to coalesce and thicken until it resembled a shadow of a throne, complete with a cushioned seat and high, scrolled backrest. Destiny gave another wave of her hand and Tia was scooped off her feet and dumped on the creepy illusion.

"No!" Tia cried out as the mist wrapped around her waist, trapping her in place. "Release me."

"Why? I'm giving you exactly what you desire." Destiny's lips pulled into something that was supposed to be a smile, although it looked more like a grimace. "And here's your crown."

Destiny slashed her hand through the air and the mist encircled Tia's head, squeezing so tight her back arched in agony.

"Stop," Peri rasped. She had no love for Tia, but she couldn't stand there and watch the mage being tortured.

Destiny turned, drifting back to study Peri with her weird flaming eyes. "Do you want to challenge me?"

Peri stilled, suddenly understanding what the miasma was trying to do. It'd tested the protective shield that Peri had created and obviously decided that she preferred not to waste her power shattering it. Grimly, she forced herself not to move.

Destiny clenched her hands in frustration, as if puzzled by Peri's stubbornness. Then her head swiveled toward Valen, who was glaring at her with grim fury.

"Ah. The wrong leverage," she purred. "Let's try again."

The mist surrounding the vampire thickened, nearly obscuring him from view, but with a bleak determination, he refused to reveal the pain that was obviously slamming through him.

"No," Peri breathed, unable to bear the sight of his body being ruthlessly stretched, as if he was on an old-fashioned rack being pulled in two.

As if sensing she was at her breaking point, Valen twisted his head to send her a fierce glare.

"Peri, don't."

Peri shook her head, glancing toward Destiny, who was smiling as she savored the torment she was inflicting on her two captives.

"Leave him alone," she commanded.

"Only if you give me what I want."

"No, Peri," Valen ground out.

Peri ignored him. She had to do something. And not just because she couldn't endure watching Valen being tortured. Eventually her magic was going to run out. When that happened, she would have no defense to fight against the miasma. If she was going to try to escape, she'd have to go on offense. At least long enough to release Valen and get the hell out of there.

Closing her eyes, she concentrated on the shimmering threads of magic that had hardened into a tangible barrier around her. Then, with meticulous care, she began unweaving the spell, folding the magic back into itself, as if she was wrapping a rope into a neat pile. It was a unique talent that she rarely used. At least not when she was face to face with an enemy. The effort replenished her pool of magic, but it left her vulnerable to attack.

Thankfully, the miasma appeared unaware of her precarious position, and instead of taking advantage, she watched her with a wary expression, clearly uncertain what Peri was doing. It wasn't until Peri's jade bracelet was glowing with renewed power that the miasma realized the shield had been unraveled.

Destiny raised her hand, sending a blast of magic in Peri's direction. Ducking low, Peri felt the heat sizzle past her as she spoke the words of a spell and sent her magic lashing toward her enemy. The shimmering strands wrapped around Destiny's feet, yanking tight to hold her captive. At the same time, she rushed forward, ramming her shoulder into Destiny with every ounce of strength she possessed.

Destiny grunted, caught off guard by the physical attack. Windmilling her arms, she tumbled backward, landing on her ass with a thud. Any other time, Peri would have taken a moment to relish the sight of the woman sprawled on the floor, her puff of blond hair tangled around her startled face. But she was too busy scrambling to her feet.

Realizing her danger, Destiny rolled to the side as Peri swung her foot toward her head, and sent out a blast of magic. The raw power hit Peri square in the face, busting her lip and sending her reeling back. She thought she heard Valen call out over Tia's continued screams of pain, but it was hard to tell. Her ears were ringing.

Shaking her head, Peri wiped away the blood and backed away as she prepared another spell. Destiny didn't have to wait. Her magic was pure energy. There was no need to bind it with an incantation or use a talisman to send it in a specific direction. It simply exploded out of her.

Peri grunted as the mist smashed into her, knocking the air from her lungs and stopping her heart. Panic jolted through her before the organ sluggishly restarted, and she released her spell to briefly blind the woman.

Destiny hissed in frustration as the crimson flames dimmed, and Peri whirled to dash toward Valen. She didn't know how to release him from the magic, but...

She was still working on a plan when she felt two tentacles wrap around her waist. They tightened and jerked her backward, pressing her against Destiny. Glancing down, she could see the reddish mist spreading over her stomach, holding her captive even as she could feel it seeping into her skin.

A shudder of horror raced through Peri. She could feel the evil crawling over her as the miasma pierced deep inside her, tapping into her magic. It was like the creature had created a direct connection to siphon her power.

"At last," Destiny moaned in ecstasy. "You taste divine."

Pain jolted through Peri, but her sheer desperation allowed her to focus on the link the miasma had created between them. She had to break it before she was drained.

But how?

The miasma was simply absorbing her spells, far too fast for Peri to cast a new one. Her only hope seemed to be physically injuring Destiny's body. She couldn't be sure if it would hurt the miasma, but it might slow it down.

"Go to hell," she ground out. Reaching over her shoulder, she grabbed Destiny's hair, yanking it as she turned and used her free hand to punch the bitch square on the jaw.

Destiny was stunned by the unexpected blow and Peri reached out to grab the dagger the witch had stolen from Brenda Sanguis. At the same time, she released the magic from her bracelet, allowing it to flow through her. The extra power gave her the magic necessary to slice through the tether joining her to the miasma.

The sense of being drained abruptly stopped, like a hose being shut off. Thank God. Drawing in a deep breath, Peri resisted the urge to turn and run. The miasma had proved that was a wasted effort. Instead, she lifted her hands as if she was preparing to cast another spell.

Destiny spread her arms, a mocking smile curving her lips. She was goading Peri into offering her more magic.

Peri smiled grimly, as if she was ready to meet the challenge, and instead lunged forward with the dagger clutched in her hand. She was fully prepared to plunge the blade into Destiny's heart. It would be a fitting justice considering the dagger had drawn the attention of the miasma in the first place.

With a sweep of her arm, she managed to slice the blade through the witch's arm, drawing blood before Destiny stumbled back. The mist swirled around her, as if reacting to the miasma's anger.

"Why do you fight?" Destiny demanded.

"You think I'm going to lay down and let you drain me?"

"It's inevitable." Destiny glared at her in frustration. "Why make it more painful than necessary?"

"I never concede defeat."

The mist continued to swirl, thickening around Destiny until she was completely covered by the strange fog. Peri took a cautious step back. She didn't know what was about to happen, but it couldn't be good.

Braced for a blast of magic, Peri frowned when the mist started to fade and the aroma of fennel and ginger bloomed in the stagnant air. It was a peculiar scent she hadn't smelled since she'd left her mother's coven.

Horror crawled over her skin as the last of the mist drifted away to reveal a tall figure wearing a heavy white robe. The face was familiar, although the ashen skin was stretched so tight over her skull it looked like a death mask. And the silvery hair floated on a breeze that Peri couldn't feel. The burning blue eyes and the raven tattoo on the side of her neck were the only things that looked the same.

It was her mother. Brenda Sanguis.

A taunting smile curved the thin lips as she took in Peri's dumbfounded expression. "You always were stubborn."

Peri struggled to swallow the lump lodged in her throat. "Mother."

Emotions churned through Peri, battering her with a blast of agonizing memories. The ruthless years of being trained like she was a hardened soldier, not a child. The cunning plotting when she discovered that Peri's power was far greater than her own. And the ultimate betrayal.

She was drowning when an icy voice pierced the darkness, offering a desperately needed lifeline.

"It's an illusion, Peri." Valen's voice spoke directly in her mind. "Your mother is dead."

Peri blinked. The vision of her mother remained, but she abruptly caught sight of the blood dripping from the tips of her fingers. It had to be coming from the wound she'd given Destiny.

"Dead...yes."

Her mother stepped closer, the robe floating around her gaunt body. "I'll never be dead. You know that. I'll always be haunting you, reminding you that you have no worth beyond your magic."

Peri flinched. This vision might not be Brenda Sanguis, but it possessed the nasty talent of striking Peri where she was most vulnerable. For as long as she could remember she'd been judged on the power that flowed through her veins. Nothing else mattered to her mother, or the women in the coven. Not the fact that she loved to read. Or that she was terrified of the rattlesnakes that would curl in the bottom of the cauldron on cold nights. Or that she hated the smell of the fennel potion that her mother brewed into the candles to extend their life.

It was always her power that attracted people's attention. Without that... she would have been invisible to them.

"That's not true." She forced the denial between stiff lips.

"Who are you without your magic?" the vision of her mother taunted.

Peri shook off the ugly sense of defeat that was creeping through her. No. That was in the past. Her life now didn't depend on constantly proving she was the better witch.

"Who am I?" Peri met the searing blue gaze without fear. "I'm a friend. And a neighbor. And a businesswoman." She slowly turned her head until she could catch sight of Valen's exquisite features and smoldering silver eyes. Even trapped by the evil miasma, he took her breath away. "I'm the partner of Valen, Cabal leader, and his future lover," she announced proudly, returning her gaze to her mother. "I'm Peri Sanguis."

Frustration rippled over the ghastly face. "They desire you because of your magic. They would despise you without it."

Peri shook her head. Before she'd been taken in by Maya or opened her heart to Valen, she might have crumbled at the words slamming into her like bullets. It was, after all, what she'd believed for years.

No longer.

"They don't care about my magic. They love me."

The miasma hissed. "No one loves you."

"I do," Valen said, this time out loud, as if announcing it to the world. "I will love you for all eternity."

Joy exploded in the center of her heart. It was one thing to acknowledge this glorious male desired her. And perhaps even admired her talents. But there was no doubting the stark sincerity that throbbed in his voice.

The earth moved beneath her feet, her soul healed in a way she'd never dreamed possible.

Allowing the joy to spread through her body, Peri glared directly at the vision. Silently she forced herself to recall the image of her mother and the rest of the coven lying dead on the floor of the barn. That was her mother. A woman who'd died too young from her own ambition.

The blue eyes faded and were replaced by the crimson fire, as if the miasma was accepting the deception wasn't going to work. At the same time, there was a high-pitched sound that stabbed into Peri's ears.

With a burst of power, the illusion shattered and Destiny was once again standing in front of her, the blood still dripping down her arm.

"Fine." Destiny stretched out her arms, swirling them through the air in an elaborate pattern. "We could have done this the easy way."

Peri snorted, puzzled by the miasma's strange behavior. "It was never going to be easy."

A low chuckle echoed through the air as Destiny continued to wave her arms. "Then let's do it the hard way."

Peri whispered a spell as she watched the mist begin to gather and grow, pulsing in rhythm to Destiny's spinning arms. The reddish hue darkened until it was the same shade of crimson as Destiny's eyes, and with every pulse it thickened until it formed an impenetrable wall around them. She heard Valen call out her name before the mist threaded together, blocking out everything but the woman standing in front of her.

"Now you're mine," Destiny whispered, lowering her arms as she stepped forward.

The spell tingled through Peri, but as she released it, she didn't aim it at Destiny. The miasma was created to feed on magic; instead, she created a small explosion at the woman's feet. She'd hoped to distract Destiny long enough for her to plunge the dagger in her heart, but even as she leaped forward, Destiny snatched Peri's wrist in a grip that threatened to shatter her bones.

"No." Peri struggled to free herself. Pain shot up her arm like a red-hot poker, but that wasn't what was making her heart thunder in fear.

It was the tendril of mist that was drilling into the center of her chest. Directly through the scar above her heart.

"Stop!" she gasped.

"Give in, Peri." Destiny stepped closer, slamming her hand against Peri's chest as the mist spread over her like a shroud of evil. "Release your magic."

With a strangled cry Peri fell to her knees. The mist was inside her, searching for her magic. Within seconds she would be drained. Just like her mother.

Squeezing shut her eyes, Peri desperately concentrated on blocking the invading evil. She had to fight, but she didn't know how.

Verging on the edge of panic, Peri was distracted by the strange burning sensation in the middle of her palms. It was like something was trying to rip out of her. Something huge…

It felt just like it had when her mother had stuck the dagger into her.

The wild magic that had marked her as a mage was refusing to be taken, she realized with a jolt of shock. And even more shocking, it was no longer nestled so deeply inside her that she couldn't call on it. It sizzled and hissed through her veins like a living thing.

Peri moaned. She felt as if there was a tornado brewing within her, gaining momentum even as the miasma tried to drain it. The wind roared in her ears while the thunder shook her body. She thought she heard Destiny cry out in alarm, but she was no longer concerned with her enemy.

The wild magic was consuming her thoughts. No, it was consuming *her*.

The world disappeared as the tornado raged, the pain so intense it became weirdly pleasurable. As if the magic was transforming her from one being into another.

Or maybe she was becoming who she'd been meant to be from the very beginning.

Opening her eyes, Peri slowly rose to her feet. In front of her Destiny had backed away, her expression one of gnawing hunger, even as she held out her hand as if trying to plead for mercy.

Was she afraid?

She should be. Peri was terrified of the power that reverberated through her. It felt as if it was going to rip her into a thousand pieces. But still it continued to grow and expand, the pressure becoming unbearable. And as it swelled, a strange scent of ozone began to fill the air, as if she were standing in the center of a storm.

"What are you doing?" Destiny rasped, the mist churning around her.

"Becoming...more," Peri managed to bite out.

"No." Destiny made a sharp gesture with her hand, sending the mist toward Peri like a tidal wave. "It's mine."

The crimson mist smashed into Peri, coating her in evil. A shudder of horror raced through Peri, but as if the wild magic had been waiting for this very moment, it stopped expanding and surged through her, aiming for the scars in the center of her palms.

A primal scream was ripped from Peri's throat, her back arching as the tempest blasted out of her with shocking force.

When the wild magic had first manifested all those years ago, it'd exploded with enough strength to knock out her mother and the surrounding witches. The astounding power had lasted less than a minute, but it'd been enough to save her.

This time the magic continued to sizzle through her, bursting from her hands to send jolts of lightning dancing through the air. The dazzling display was blinding as it struck against the mist, scorching and burning the miasma as it writhed in an effort to escape.

Peri watched in amazement as the lightning continued to strike over and over, driving back the evil magic until it was forced to retreat into Destiny. But even then the lightning didn't stop. It slammed into the witch's body, leaving behind charred flesh that filled the air with a horrifying stench.

Hissing in revulsion, Peri tried to halt the magic that ravaged through her. She was almost certain the real Destiny no longer existed. And that the only way to destroy the miasma was to kill the host it was using to move through the world. But she didn't want to be the one to kill the poor woman.

The magic refused to be controlled, however, and it continued to strike against Destiny until she crumpled to the ground with a piercing howl. Her head flopped to the side, the crimson flames in her eyes sputtering before they went completely dark.

Peri stepped back as a sudden breeze rippled past her, the scent of ozone replaced by the stench of sulfur. As if a doorway to hell had just been opened.

And maybe it had, she acknowledged, watching as Destiny's body seemed to shrink, her face becoming mummified and her hair turning from gold to gray. The miasma that had infected her had disappeared, leaving behind the dead shell of the young witch.

Regret washed over Peri, but the magic refused to be contained. It scoured through her, the glow of the lightning revealing she was standing in the center of the cabin. She had a brief glance of Valen and Tia crouched on the floor watching her with wary gazes, but before she could acknowledge the sharp relief that they'd survived, her body was being tugged toward the statues at the back of the room.

The magic was in control and she was nothing more than a puppet. It wasn't until she was standing in front of the pile of statues that remained nestled in the packing straw that she realized why she was there. The magic had appeared to destroy the miasma. It wasn't going to stop until the job was done.

Holding her hands toward the statues, Peri quit trying to fight against the magic and instead released the thunderous power. Lightning smashed into the statues, shattering them one by one.

When there was nothing left but a powdery residue, Peri tilted back her head and laughed.

It was over.

At last.

But still the lightning danced.

* * * *

Maya was lying in her bed, pretending she was trying to sleep. A wasted effort, but it was better than the hours of walking the floor that she'd done the first half of the night.

She didn't know exactly what was troubling her. Well, beyond the obvious fact that Peri was missing. And the Benefactor was being more stubborn than usual. She wasn't the sort of woman who went about her business while her loved ones were facing danger. Even when she was being held captive by the bastard Batu, she'd felt the need to rush to the rescue when someone was in trouble.

Lying in this bed was very close to torture.

She was considering drinking a potion that would force her to sleep when the sound of soft footsteps creeping down the stairs had her shoving aside her covers. Thank God. A distraction.

Grabbing a robe to pull over her silk teddy and shorts, Maya opened her door and followed the footsteps. She didn't bother to turn on the lights as she headed through the silent bookstore. If Skye was sleepwalking she didn't want to wake her. It would be better if she could lead the young mage back to bed without her realizing she'd been wandering around.

Her caution was ruined as Skye entered the bakery and began switching on the overhead lights, as if she was afraid of the dark. Accepting that her efforts at stealth were wasted, Maya moved forward to touch the woman's shoulder.

"Skye," she murmured softly. "Is something wrong?"

Skye twirled to face her, the corkscrew curls bouncing around her pale face. She was wearing an oversize T-shirt with a cartoon character on the front that made her look ridiculously young. At least until she looked into the velvet-night eyes. Those were as ancient as time.

Maya grimaced. Skye was a rare, unique creature who Maya was fiercely protective of, but there was a power inside her that could be terrifying.

"I don't know." Skye wrapped her arms around her waist, her expression troubled. "I feel…"

"Yes?"

"Itchy."

Maya stroked her hand down her friend's arm, feeling the shivers that were racing through her.

"Itchy in a bad way?"

Skye slowly nodded. "In a very bad way."

Maya hesitated. For the first time since Skye had arrived at the Witch's Brew, she regretted her decree that the mage wasn't allowed to share her visions if they had anything to do with Maya or Peri.

"Is it something you can talk about?"

"I think it's Peri."

"You've had a vision?" she cautiously demanded.

"Yes, but it's not the future," Skye clarified, her voice husky as she struggled to contain her fear. "It's now. She's in danger."

Frustration pulsed through Maya like a corrosive acid. She wanted nothing more than to jump on a plane and head out west. Even if she didn't know Peri's precise location, she had full faith in her ability to track her down. But she couldn't risk creating the very disaster she wanted to avoid.

She had to trust that Peri could take care of herself.

"You know we can't help her." She squeezed Skye's arm. "I'm sorry."

Skye's lips parted, as if she was going to insist they do something, but no words came out. Instead she stiffened in shock and her beautiful black eyes were suddenly an incandescent white. As if she'd been lit from a searing fire inside her.

"Peri!" Skye screamed, falling to the floor, her hands reaching for something Maya couldn't see.

Terror drove Maya to her knees, her arms wrapping around her friend, who continued to scream in horror.

"Skye, come back to me."

Skye's head fell back, her eyes flaring with the blinding light. "Stop. Peri, please stop."

"Skye."

Cradling the young mage tightly in her arms, Maya was suddenly hit by a crushing wave of power. Turning her head, she was more resigned than shocked to discover Joe standing in the open doorway to the bakery. She had no idea how he'd gotten past the lock and her expensive security system, and at the moment she didn't care.

"Stay back," she hissed, fully prepared to blast him with a spell. She didn't know his true story, or if he was a friend or an enemy, but with Skye writhing in her arms she wasn't taking any chances.

As if sensing she was on edge, Joe lifted his hands in a gesture of peace. "I'm not here to interfere."

"Then why are you here?"

His eyes shimmered like emeralds as he studied the screaming Skye. "To witness the beginning of a new world." His gaze shifted to Maya, his expression unreadable. "Or the end."

Chapter 28

Valen remained crouched on the ground, his gaze locked on Peri. In the two thousand years of his current life he'd never seen anything so glorious.

Standing in the center of the cabin, Peri spread her arms wide, a dazzling display of lightning dancing through the air. Her hair floated around her face, caught in the sheer power that sizzled around her, her beautiful features set in grim lines. She looked like Astrape, Goddess of Lightning, as she battled the churning red mist. Raw female power at its most primitive.

Stepping forward, she sent shockwaves of magic into the miasma, ruthlessly striking over and over until Destiny was curled on the ground, the flames dying from her eyes.

The smell of sulfur blasted through the air before abruptly fading. As if a doorway had been opened and shut. The retreat of the miasma? That would be his guess.

Slowly rising to his feet, he watched as Peri moved toward the statues at the back of the cabin, the lightning striking them with shattering force. His brows lifted as the marble was disintegrated with unnerving ease, small shards lodging in the wooden walls.

As a vampire, he was one of the most powerful creatures in the world. At least since the dragons had retreated. But watching Peri, he realized that he'd just witnessed a magic that went beyond anything he'd ever seen before. Or ever wanted to see again.

The last of the statues was ground to dust, and Valen waited for Peri to turn off the lightning. It had to be consuming an enormous amount of her magic. The fact that she'd continued for this long was amazing. But a minute passed, and then another while the power continued to dance around her, creating a vortex of chaos.

Was there an unseen enemy that she was battling?

Valen shook his head. No. If there was something in the cabin, he would sense it. It was almost as if she'd become lost in some sort of inner battle.

"Peri."

He stepped forward, the sensation of electricity crawling over his body. He stopped, not daring to go any closer.

"She can't hear you."

The voice came from the shadows and he glanced toward the mage, who had moved to press herself against the door. Tia's silver hair had tumbled to her shoulders and there was a streak of dirt on her cheek. She looked nothing like the proud woman who'd entered the cabin with the arrogant belief she could control the miasma and use it to her advantage.

"What's happening?" he demanded.

Tia stared at Peri with something that might have been awe. "She's released her wild magic."

Valen frowned. He might be a vampire, but he knew that the magic that burned through a human to transform them into a mage was a one-time event. A rebirth, not a steady source of power.

"That's impossible," he growled.

Tia continued to stare at Peri, a naked lust smoldering in her dark eyes. "I've heard stories that long ago, a mage could tap into the ancient magic. But I thought it was a fairy tale. Now this." She shook her head as if she was struggling to find the proper word. "Amazing."

Fear clenched Valen's heart. He didn't care why the magic was flowing through Peri, he just wanted it to stop.

"The miasma has been destroyed. Why is she still releasing the magic?"

"She can't control it."

"What do you mean?"

"Now that she's tapped into the ancient power, there's no way to shut it off," Tia said.

Valen watched as Peri's head tilted back, her mouth opening as if she was releasing a silent scream. *Shit.*

"Will it run out?" he rasped.

"Not until she's dead…"

Tia's words trailed away as she glanced in Valen's direction. As if she could see the merciless determination etched on his face.

Peri wasn't dying. It didn't matter what he had to do, or who he had to kill. She wasn't dying.

"How do we stop her?"

"We can't."

His power snapped in an icy warning, his fangs fully extended. "Tell me."

Tia pressed herself against the door, well aware that Valen was willing to do whatever necessary to protect Peri. Even if it meant sacrificing her to get the information he needed.

"There's no way to get close to her. Not even for a leech." She waved a hand toward the lightning that sizzled and snapped, as if daring anyone to approach. "The magic would destroy you."

Valen pointed toward the case that she clutched close to her chest. "Then use one of your potions to open a passage."

A harsh laugh was wrenched from her lips. "If I had a potion that could match the sort of power that Peri is using, I would never have come here. I would have everything I need."

Her words rang with sincerity. She didn't have any way to allow him to reach Peri. Turning away, he returned his concentration to the woman who had captured his unbeating heart. Her head was tilted back, but her mouth had pressed to a thin line, as if she was struggling against the power that raged through her.

"I have to do something."

He was speaking more to himself than the mage behind him, but Tia answered.

"Do it quickly," she said, an unexpected urgency in her voice. "She's not going to last much longer."

Valen considered his limited options. No, they weren't limited. They were nonexistent. He would have more luck trying to battle against a hurricane than to contain the wild magic.

Accepting that he could stand there and witness Peri's death, or join her, Valen squared his shoulders. The decision was easy. He didn't want to continue in this particular existence if his beautiful mage wasn't at his side.

Walking steadily forward, he didn't allow himself to think about what was going to happen. It didn't matter. Not as long as he was with Peri.

As if sensing his approach, Peri lowered her head, her eyes widening as she caught sight of him. Her features twisted into an expression of horror as she frantically shook her head.

He ignored her terror, each step taking him closer and closer to the lightning that sizzled around her. And with each step he waited for the strike that would bring an end to his current existence. But it never came.

Tightening her jaw, Peri visibly battled to keep the magic from touching him, weaving a tunnel that allowed him to reach her with nothing more than a few scorched spots that would heal.

His relief, however, was tempered by the sight of Peri's ashen face and the deep circles beneath her magnificent eyes. The magic was draining her at an alarming rate. Unless she gained control it would kill her.

Wrapping his arms around her, he pulled her tight against him. "Peri, let go."

She clutched his shoulders, the scent of her panic wrapping around him. "I can't."

"Yes, you can." He buried his face in her hair. "I've got you."

She stubbornly shook her head. "You have to get out of here."

"Release the magic, Peri," he whispered in her ear. "I won't let you fall."

For an agonizing moment, Valen feared that she wouldn't be capable of shutting off the power that was killing her. Then, with a primal scream that came from the depths of her soul, Peri released one last blast of magic before collapsing against him. A blinding light exploded through the cabin and Valen heard Tia cry out in pain, but a second later the light was gone and darkness filled the cabin as Peri fainted in his arms.

* * * *

Peri was floating in a vortex of lightning, the power thundering through her like a hurricane. It was glorious.

This is who you were meant to be…

The strange voice whispered in the back of her mind, and Peri laughed with joy. Yes, she'd always known that there was something different about her. Even after she'd transformed into a mage she'd suspected that there was a magic inside her that was unlike any other. Even Maya.

She didn't know how or why she'd been born with the ability to tap into her wild magic, but it'd always been there. Just waiting for the right moment to reveal itself.

Reveling in the sense of immeasurable power, Peri abruptly realized she was no longer alone. The cool, utterly male scent teased at her before she caught sight of him walking toward her. The joy was replaced with horror as she watched the lightning slam into his body with devastating force.

"No!" she screamed, holding out her hand in warning. But still he came, the flesh melting from his face as he grimly battled to reach her. "Valen."

"I'm here." Gentle fingers brushed over her cheek, the cool touch thankfully penetrating her nightmare.

With a low groan, she wrenched open her eyes, baffled to discover Valen seated on the edge of the bed, leaning over her. He looked as beautiful as ever with his golden hair gleaming in the muted light and his eyes shimmering like liquid mercury. But, oddly, he wasn't wearing one of his expensive tailored suits or a soft cashmere sweater and slacks. He had nothing on but a loose pair of workout shorts that hung low on his waist to reveal the vast expanse of his hard, chiseled chest. It was shocking to see him in such casual clothing.

And more than a little arousing.

Feeling a blush stain her cheeks, she wiggled until she was sitting up with a pillow propped behind her. Then, clearing her throat, she glanced around. The bedroom was as large as most New York apartments, with a glass wall that overlooked the city. The vastness of the space was emphasized by the silver carpeting that matched the walls and ceiling. Even the furniture was painted with a silver luster. The only splash of color was the navy blue comforter that covered the king-size bed.

The stark, elegant style suited Valen.

She glanced back, meeting his watchful gaze. "I assume this is your penthouse?"

He held her gaze. "Our home."

"Our." Her heart zigzagged out of control, trying to lodge in her throat. "That's the hope."

Peri glanced down. She couldn't think when she was lost in those silver eyes. That's when she realized she was wearing an unfamiliar silk robe and nothing else.

"How did I get here?"

"After you collapsed in the cabin, I drove us back to New Orleans, where Micha had a plane waiting for us."

"How long have I been out?"

"Twelve hours."

That explained why she felt so rested. Besides a faint headache that was rapidly fading, the crazy confrontation with the miasma and the explosion of her powers might have been nothing more than a bad dream.

She shook her head. She was going to need time to process what happened in that cabin. Like an eternity.

For now she wanted to focus on the fact that she was alive and back on the East Coast where she belonged.

"I need to call Maya," she murmured, realizing that she wasn't the only one who would be glad she'd managed to survive.

"She knows you're here and that you're currently recovering from your adventures."

Peri's gaze lifted to study Valen's face. His expression was unreadable, but she sensed that his interaction with Maya hadn't been just a pleasant phone call.

"I'm surprised she isn't pounding down the door."

"She tried," Valen admitted in wry tones. "I'll have to replace several windows and most of my security cameras. Plus a very expensive Porsche that was parked in front of the building."

Peri grimaced. She wasn't surprised that Maya would have arrived at Valen's headquarters and demanded to see Peri. She could be as ruthless as a momma bear protecting her cubs. And just as lethal.

"She wasn't hurt, was she?" she demanded.

Peri didn't think for a moment that Valen would personally harm Maya. Not when he knew how much she meant to Peri. But he hired a large, very powerful staff of demons who wouldn't be so understanding if they thought their boss was in danger.

He shook his head. "I convinced her that I was taking proper care of you and that you were free to leave whenever you wanted." He slowly reached to smooth her hair behind her ear. "Which I hope won't be for a very long time."

The cool brush of his fingers over her cheek sent a violent shiver through her body. Peri swallowed her groan, acutely aware of his naked chest, which was inches away. This glorious male was the fulfillment of her deepest fantasies and the urge to lick every inch of that satin skin was overwhelming.

But her fierce hunger couldn't overcome the searing memory of what had happened when the wild magic had flowed through her. She'd come so close to destroying this magnificent male. How could she put him in danger again?

"How did you get through the barrier to enter the cabin?" she abruptly demanded.

An emotion she couldn't read flared through the silver eyes, but Valen didn't push her to admit that she desperately wanted him to stay by her side. Instead, he answered her question.

"Tia."

"Seriously?" Peri was genuinely shocked. Tia hadn't made any secret of her prejudice against the Cabal. "She helped a vampire?"

A cold smile touched his lips. "I didn't give her a choice."

Peri didn't have any trouble believing that. When Valen wanted something, there was nothing that could stand in his way.

Another shiver inched down her spine. "Where is she now?"

He shrugged. "I left her at the cabin. She had her own ride."

Peri wasn't worried about the mage. Tia was a survivor.

"Her dream came true," she murmured, recalling the sight of Tia being abused by the evil magic. "She had a throne and crown. Just not in the way she hoped. I almost feel sorry for her."

Without warning, Valen leaned forward, planting his hands on each side of her hips so she was caged against the headboard. Not that she felt caged. She felt...exhilarated. As if every nerve in her body had been sparked to life by his rich scent and the promise smoldering in his silver eyes.

"I'm not interested in the overly ambitious mage," he informed her, his gaze lowering to the plunging vee of her robe. "As long as she stays in her pretend castle."

"What are you interested in?" The words left her lips before she could halt them.

The temperature dropped, his icy power brushing over her in a promise of pleasure to come.

"You," he murmured softly. "I want nothing but you."

Peri's mouth dried to the texture of sandpaper, her body quivering to give into temptation.

"You don't know me," she forced herself to insist.

He leaned closer. "Not as well as I intend to."

Peri lifted her hands, pressing them against his chest. She'd spent years hiding the suspicion that there was something different about her. It was time for her to take her head out of the sand.

"No. I mean, the truth came out in that cabin," she reminded him, as if he hadn't noticed her lightning storm of carnage. "I can't hide it anymore."

"Good," he said without hesitation. "I've never seen anything more glorious. A goddess at last revealing her powers."

She made a sound of impatience. He was deliberately avoiding the massive elephant in the room.

"I could have fried you. I nearly did," she said bluntly. "It was only sheer luck—"

Her protest was cut short as he pressed a kiss against her parted lips. Desire fizzed through her, like the finest champagne. And just as heady.

"It wasn't luck." He spoke against her mouth, the tips of his fangs pressing into her skin. "It was you. You kept the lightning from striking me."

Peri frowned. The events in the cabin were blurred, as if she'd dreamed the attack from the miasma and the release of her wild magic, but she had a vague memory of desperately weaving the lightning to create an opening for Valen.

Still, she had no idea how she did it or if she could repeat the process.

"I can't control it." She glared into his painfully beautiful face. "I'm dangerous."

"You'll learn."

"How can you be so certain?"

"Because you're Peri Sanguis." He lifted his head to regard her with a somber expression. "You faced down death and an evil magic and called on ancient powers that haven't been seen in this world for endless centuries. There's no obstacle you can't overcome."

There was a fierce certainty in his voice, as if he truly believed that she would learn to control the unpredictable magic.

Peri forced herself to consider his words. Maybe Valen was right. She had survived her mother's attempt to murder her. And she'd battled against an evil that would have destroyed any other mage. She wasn't being vain. It was simple truth. So maybe she could learn to control the magic.

"It doesn't bother you that I could potentially kill you?" she pressed.

He shrugged, turning the tables on her. "Does it bother you that I could potentially kill you?"

Peri considered the question, recalling her defensive determination to keep this male at a distance when she first arrived in the area.

"It did. At first."

"And now?"

Her hands smoothed over the bare skin of his chest, her fear that she might hurt Valen melting beneath the searing heat of her desire.

"Now I trust you."

His expression softened, the silver eyes darkening to a smoky gray. "Just as I trust you."

She wrinkled her nose. "I'm still not sure what's going to happen. The magic might disappear or it might be something that appears whenever I lose my temper. Which is a regular occurrence."

He dismissed her concern with a slow, wicked smile. "We'll figure it out." Using the tip of one fang he traced her lower lip. "Together."

"Together?" Peri slid her hands up his chest and over his shoulders, clasping her fingers together behind his neck. "I like the sound of that."

She felt a shiver race through his body, as if he sensed she'd conceded to the inevitable. "What else do you like?"

From the moment she'd caught sight of Valen he'd fascinated her. She'd known he would be trouble. And that he would demand more than she ever thought she could offer. But for the first time in her life, she was prepared to take a chance and find out where her heart would lead.

"I like this."

Threading her fingers into the short strands of his hair, Peri tugged his head down. Valen didn't hesitate, claiming her mouth in a kiss that sent blasts of pleasure tingling to the tips of her toes.

* * * *

Valen released a low growl of relief.

His nerves had been scraped raw as he waited for Peri to open her eyes. It didn't matter that he could hear the steady beat of her heart. Or that she was resting easily without any hint of pain or discomfort. He'd refused to leave her side until he was certain she had fully recovered.

At last he could allow himself the pleasure of appreciating the sight of Peri in his bed. Or maybe he would do more than just appreciate her. But first he had to be sure she didn't have any lingering repercussions from her battle with the miasma.

Framing her face in his hands, he reluctantly lifted his head to gaze down at her.

"Are you okay?"

She arched her brows, her eyes dark with a passion that was scenting the air with her sweet perfume.

"Don't I feel okay?"

A groan rumbled in his chest. "You feel perfect."

His hands slid down her throat before lightly tracing the deep vee of her robe. He'd sent Renee to purchase the silk garment after he'd returned to New York despite the fact he had a dozen robes in the guest bedroom. Those were for lovers who were passing through on their way to somewhere else. Peri was here to stay. Forever.

"I just want to know that you're fully recovered," he assured her.

A slow smile curved her lips. "I've never been better."

Assured she was healed, Valen lowered his head, unleashing the hunger that pulsed inside him.

"I'm fairly confident you're about to be even better."

"Is that a promise?" she teased, smoothing her hands along the width of his shoulders before she placed her palms flat on his chest. She didn't push him away; instead, she lightly scraped her nails over his bare skin.

Valen shivered in pleasure, holding her gaze as he parted the lapels of her robe to expose her rose-tipped breasts. Her nails dug into his flesh, creating delicious pinpricks of pain. He groaned in approval, his gaze lowering to the soft mounds.

"So much power contained in such a delicate form," he murmured in amazement.

Peri flushed with pleasure even as she clicked her tongue. "There's nothing delicate about me," she protested.

He didn't bother to argue. She enjoyed her image as a ruthless mage who was willing to terrorize the local demons for the right price. And if she felt as fragile as a flower to him, he was willing to keep the thought to himself.

A lifetime together meant compromise. A word that Valen had always considered a weakness. Until Peri.

She'd changed everything.

Trailing kisses down the length of her jaw, Valen exposed his fangs to skim them along the curve of her throat.

Hunger blasted through him. He hadn't fed since returning to New York. The mere thought of taking the vein of anyone but Peri was unthinkable. That intimacy wasn't going to be shared with anyone but the woman in his bed.

But first, there was another hunger that had to be sated.

Nibbling his way downward, Valen savored the taste of Peri's skin. The female spice that marked her as a mage was mixed with her own natural sweetness. A hint of lily that melted something in the center of his soul.

Valen moaned in anticipation, his lips drifting over the curve of her breast before he found the hardened nipple. Peri made a choked sound of excitement, her back arching in encouragement.

"You're right. I am better," she whispered.

Valen chuckled, turning his head to continue his exploration, using Peri's soft sounds of pleasure to direct his seduction.

The brush of his tongue over her tender nipples brought delicious gasps while the graze of his fangs wrenched low moans from her lips.

Pushing aside the comforter, Valen grasped the belt of her robe and tugged it open. Hissing in anticipation, he slid his hands beneath the silky material to peel the garment off her body and tossed it aside.

Like unwrapping a priceless gift, he silently acknowledged, lifting his head to appreciate the beauty he'd just revealed.

"You are a goddess." His admiring gaze slid over the length of her slim, muscular body. "Power and grace." Unable to resist temptation, he wrapped her in his arms to claim her mouth in a kiss of sheer possession. "And magic," he whispered, electric tingles dancing over his skin.

It wasn't just words. He'd felt passion and desire before, but never in his two thousand years had he felt the heady sensation that he was being bewitched.

Impatient to feel her pressed against him, Valen gracefully swiveled until he was stretched on the mattress. Peri smiled as she rolled to face him, lifting her hand to cup his cheek in her palm.

"I feel like I'm dreaming," she whispered.

A strangely tender ache opened in the center of Valen's unbeating heart. He suddenly understood why men had gone to war for the love of a woman. Not that he intended to go to war. He wanted nothing more than peace and solitude. Lots of solitude to give him the opportunity to devote his unwavering attention to this woman.

Valen groaned as the heat of her naked body blanketed him. The magic that thundered inside her created a warmth that seared his skin. It was shockingly hot. Until that moment he would have sworn that the ancient dragons were the only ones who possessed that sort of heat in their human forms.

"If we're dreaming, never wake me," Valen rasped, burying his face in her neck before he urged her to lie flat on her back.

The intoxicating scent of her desire swirled through the air, but he wasn't finished with his explorations. He'd spent years imagining having this woman in his bed. Now he was going to treasure each delectable inch of her.

Rolling until he was pressing against her slender form, Valen braced his hands on the mattress, brushing his lips over the pulse that fluttered at the base of her neck. Then, with slow sweeps of his tongue, he moved to tease the tips of her breasts.

Peri released a shaky sigh, trembling as he continued to move down her body, using the sharp fangs to trace the clenched muscles of her stomach.

His warrior goddess...

Lingering to relish her satin smooth skin, Valen smiled when Peri muttered an impatient curse.

He liked the knowledge that his extraordinary mage was experiencing the same combustible passion that burned inside him.

Kissing a path along the curve of her hip, Valen gently parted her legs so he could settle between them. The lush scent of her desire tormented his senses as he slid his tongue through her soft opening.

Peri cried out, reaching down to tangle her fingers in his hair. Valen continued to pleasure her, his hands stroking up to cup her breasts as he brought her to the cusp of her climax.

"Valen." She tugged at his hair. "I want you in me. Now."

Valen chuckled as he stroked his tongue through her heat one last time before kissing his way back up her body.

"So impatient," he teased, lifting his head to meet her smoldering gaze. "We have an eternity to enjoy each other."

Her eyes narrowed. "An eternity? Perhaps for you, but I'm just a mage. I don't have that long." She wiggled until she was in a seated position, grasping his running shorts and yanking them down to expose his fully erect cock. "Let's see if we can speed this up."

He barely had time to process her challenge when she bent down to wrap her lips around his arousal.

Valen clenched his fangs, his head falling back as a blast of raw bliss ricocheted through him. Peri's mouth felt as hot as a volcano as she drew him deep inside, then slowly pulled up, using her tongue to drive him to the edge of madness.

It was glorious.

Too glorious.

He might be a powerful vampire and ruler of his own empire, but he was no match for Peri's devastating touch.

With a harsh groan, he rolled away from her addictive lips and swiftly pulled off his shorts and tossed them aside.

Peri settled back on the pile of pillows, a smug smile tugging on the edge of her lips. She looked like a siren with her dark hair tousled around her beautiful face and her cheeks flushed with desire.

"I thought we had an eternity," she reminded him.

Holding her gaze, he lowered himself until he was cradled beneath her legs, the tip of his cock perfectly positioned.

"An eternity isn't long enough to sate my desire for you," he confessed, his voice harsh.

Peri wrapped her arms around his neck. "Then let's not waste a second."

Always prepared to go above and beyond to please this woman, Valen pressed slowly into her welcoming body. They groaned in unison as the intense pleasure vibrated through them.

This was the intimacy he'd craved for so long. The knowledge that in this moment they were bound together and she belonged to him heart and mind and body.

He would never diminish her need for independence, but when they were together like this he would cherish the sensation that they were one.

Plunging as deep as possible, Valen buried his face in her neck, his fangs aching.

"I want to taste you," he whispered, prepared for Peri to flinch at the mere thought of having his massive fangs piercing her skin. She wasn't a demon who considered the bite of a vampire the highest honor. It would take time to assure her that he would never hurt her.

But proving she still had the power to blindside him, Peri wrapped her legs around his hips and placed her hand on the back of his head.

"Yes," she breathed. "God, yes."

Valen didn't hesitate, placing his mouth against her throat as he sank his fangs through the tender skin. Valen squeezed his eyes shut as the taste of her blood exploded on his tongue. It was more potent than the finest aphrodisiac. A delicious mix of feminine mystique and primal power.

Feeding from her vein, Valen rocked his hips to stroke in and out of Peri with a slow, ruthless rhythm.

Peri groaned, her hips lifting to meet him thrust for thrust.

"More," she muttered, her voice rough with need.

"Yes."

Withdrawing his fangs, Valen carefully licked closed the puncture wounds as he turned his head to capture her lips in a fierce kiss. His strokes deepened and his pace quickened as the pleasure spiraled toward an impossible peak.

Peri wrapped her arms around him, holding tight as he drove them ever higher.

The temperature plunged as Valen struggled to leash his power. He'd never had to worry about losing control when he was making love, but everything about his relationship with Peri was different.

As if he'd been reborn by her love.

"Let go," she whispered against his lips.

Valen hissed as the pressure built to a critical crescendo. "Peri."

"Let go," she insisted.

Any hope of maintaining control was shattered as his orgasm smashed into him with outrageous force. His body shuddered as the ecstasy exploded and his power blasted through the air.

At the same moment, Peri cried out as her release consumed her and a burst of lightning sizzled against the frigid cloud that surrounded them.

The two magics clashed together, as if battling to gain the upper hand. But as the sparks filled the air, they slowly melded into a searing white aura that pulsed and glowed as bright as the full moon hanging in the sky.

Pure magic.

Chapter 29

Two weeks later

Peri polished off the blueberry scone and licked the sticky goodness from her fingers. She was confident she could travel the world and never find a better scone than the ones that were made at the Witch's Brew. Sipping her hot tea, she met Maya's impatient gaze.

She'd spent time with both Maya and Skye at Valen's penthouse, but this was her first trip to the Witch's Brew, and the first time they could comfortably discuss what had happened to her after she'd taken off for Wyoming.

"You're sure the miasma is gone?" Maya demanded, leaning against the edge of her desk. Skye was in her usual position of tending to the tea tray on the side table while Peri was settled comfortably in the leather chair.

They'd chosen to meet in the privacy of the office to avoid the crowd that was gathering out front. People were leaving work and stopping by to pick up delicious treats for dinner or browsing through the bookstore. Maya had brought in extra help to deal with the customers.

Peri nodded firmly. Her time in the cabin was still fuzzy, but she had a vivid memory of the nasty stench of sulfur as the red mist had disappeared, as if it was being sucked through an unseen opening.

"It's back in hell where it belongs."

Maya's lips thinned. "And Tia?"

"She's hiding in her castle," Peri assured her friend. She'd traveled through the area last week with Valen, spending the night at Gabriel's lair. The vampire had promised to keep a close watch on the overly ambitious mage. "At least for now."

Maya nodded, but there was something in her expression that assured Peri that the older mage hadn't forgotten what Tia had done to her, and that there would eventually be some form of retribution.

For now, she studied Peri with a searching gaze. "And you're okay?"

Peri wrinkled her nose. "I'm getting asked that question a lot."

"It's not every day a mage taps into an ancient magic that has been out of our reach for countless centuries," Maya pointed out.

"I'm fine." Peri hesitated as she caught Maya's steady gaze, at last heaving a sigh. She never could lie to this woman. "Okay. I'm scared," she admitted. "Even now I can feel the magic. It's like lava bubbling inside me, just waiting to explode. I'm terrified I might hurt someone."

"You need to practice controlling it," Maya warned.

Peri nodded, a wry smile curving her lips. She'd spent the first week after returning to New York doing her best to suppress the magic. As if she could somehow stuff it back into the mystical place it'd come from. When that didn't work, she'd accepted that she was going to have to learn to live with it.

"Valen arranged for me to spend time in the playroom. I can practice without worrying that it might spiral out of control," she assured her friend. "I'm already gaining some ability to manipulate it."

"Good." Maya tilted her head to the side, her silky black hair sliding over her shoulder. "And Valen is treating you well?"

"He's..." Peri found it impossible to express her feelings for the vampire.

He was still arrogant and bossy, just as she always imagined he would be, but he was also generous and loving and attentive to her every need. She didn't doubt she was the most spoiled woman in the history of the world.

"What?" Maya asked.

"Everything."

Skye clapped her hands together, her face wreathed in smiles. "I knew it."

Peri sent her friend a startled glance. "A vision?"

Skye touched her chest, directly over her heart. "A feeling."

Maya's expression was more difficult to read. "I suppose you'll be staying with him?" she demanded.

"Yes. But I hope to keep my job here," Peri admitted. "If you'll have me."

Something that might have been relief rippled over Maya's face. "You will always be welcome at the Witch's Brew. You're family."

"Good." Peri glanced around the stark office. It didn't look like much, but Peri loved every inch of this building. It'd been where she'd learned to feel safe and laugh and trust and look toward a future. Her happiest memories had happened here. "I adore Valen, but the Witch's Brew has been my home for a long time."

"It will *always* be your home," Maya assured her. "No matter what."

Peri grimaced as she recalled her first home. A cold, barren place where she'd been a commodity, not a daughter. Thankfully the ranch was now firmly in her past.

"Oh." Peri rose to her feet, grabbing the satchel she'd tossed on the desk when she'd first entered the office. "I just remembered."

Maya arched her brows. "Remembered what?"

"Valen and I traveled to Wyoming to deal with my mother's belongings last week."

Maya reached out to touch her shoulder. "That must have been difficult."

Peri shook her head. "Actually, it felt good to have a small service for Brenda and to spread her ashes." Peri had dreaded entering the morgue to claim her mother's body, but with Valen at her side, she'd managed to make the arrangements without being overwhelmed. And once they'd released the ashes, there'd been an unexpected sense of relief. As if Peri was finally able to purge the bitterness that had infected her for too long. "She's free. Maybe for the first time."

"What about the ranch?" Maya asked.

"I donated it to a charity to use as a campground for the local children to enjoy."

"Generous."

Peri had no idea how much the ranch was worth, and she truly didn't care. Valen was obscenely rich and she had her own nest egg that could support her for the rest of her life.

"A nice end to a place filled with bad memories," she said firmly.

Maya at last smiled. "So it's over."

"Yes, but in my mother's belongings I found these." Peri dug into her satchel. They'd spent a few hours at the ranch clearing out Brenda Sanguis's personal belongings. There hadn't been much. She handed Maya the pictures that showed Peri in front of the Witch's Brew. "Mother was keeping track of me. Or she was paying someone else to keep track of me. Either way, I wanted to warn you in case there was still a lurker creeping around."

Maya studied the photos with a strange intensity. "Can I keep these?"

"Sure. There are copies of them on my mother's computer." Peri closed the satchel and hooked it over her shoulder. "I should get back. Valen and I have a date."

"Are you going anywhere special?" Skye asked, sighing as if imagining a romantic night beneath the stars. Or a midnight cruise along the Seine.

"To Valen's penthouse," Peri said.

Skye wrinkled her nose in disappointment. "Isn't that where you're already staying?"

"Yes, but he's promised no cell phones and no Renee knocking on the door," Peri explained. Since their return, Valen had been dealing with an avalanche of work. And while Peri accepted that his devoted assistant was simply doing her job, Peri had learned to dread her constant interruptions. "Just a bottle of champagne and a few hours of alone time."

"Ah. Okay." Skye winked. "Enjoy."

"Thanks." Peri moved to grab Skye's hand, tugging her toward Maya so they could have a group hug. Warmth flowed through her as they clung to each other. Family. "I love you guys," she murmured, before pulling away and heading toward the door. "See you tomorrow." She flashed a wicked smile. "But not too early."

* * * *

Maya waited until the coffeeshop was closed and Skye had headed up to her rooms before leaving her office and exiting the building through a side door. She didn't want anyone to overhear what she had to say.

Stepping out of the alley, she glanced from side to side, at last spotting her prey leaning against the light pole a few feet away. With firm steps she marched forward, the pictures she'd gotten from Peri clutched in her fingers.

"I thought I smelled fairy farts," Joe called out as she neared.

Maya allowed her gaze to skim over the man who'd managed to hang around her store for years without creating any hint of suspicion. As always, he was dressed in a velour running suit, this one a bright red, with a fishing hat rammed on his head, nearly covering his eyes. His beard was bushier than ever.

"I have something to ask you," she said as she stopped directly in front of the mysterious creature.

Joe shrugged. "It'll cost you."

"Fine."

"You haven't asked how much," Joe chided. "Sloppy."

"Someone was taking pictures." She held out the photos. "I thought you might be interested."

He pressed against the light pole, shaking his head. "Not really."

"You should look." She shoved the pictures in his hand.

Grudgingly, Joe bent his head to study the black-and-white photos, his expression hidden beneath his beard.

"Whoever took this did a terrible job." He jabbed a finger at the image of Peri standing in front of the coffeeshop. "The girl's fat ass is in front of the window sign."

At first glance, Maya had assumed, like Peri, that the pictures had been taken of her. She was in each one of them, after all. But a closer look revealed that Peri was often turned away or at the edge of the picture. There was always one object in center focus.

"The photographer wasn't interested in the Witch's Brew."

"Ah. A stalker," Joe tried to bluff. "You should call the cops."

"If it's a stalker, their only interest was in you," she said in tones that revealed she wasn't going to back down.

There was a long silence and Maya wondered if he was going to continue to deny the truth. Then, without warning, the pictures abruptly went up in flames, as if they'd been lit by an unseen torch. A second later, the ashes were floating on the breeze caused by a crushing power.

"You see too much, Maya Rosen," Joe said, a hint of warning in his soft tone.

Maya tilted her chin, refusing to be intimidated. "I have a feeling my eyes are just starting to open."

Printed in the United States
by Baker & Taylor Publisher Services